THE
DiViNE
SHALLOWS

THE DIVINE SHALLOWS

ALEXANDRA M. TRAN

Copyright © 2024 by Alexandra M. Tran

All rights reserved.

No part of this book may be reproduced in any form or by any electronic or mechanical means, including information storage and retrieval systems, without written permission from the author, except for the use of brief quotations in a book review.

Cover Design: Annguyenart Illustration & Design

Heading Images: LusterLab

CONTENTS

Author's Note	ix
Prologue	1
CHAPTER 1 *Tale of Twin Necklaces*	9
CHAPTER 2 *Myth of the Moon Goddess*	19
CHAPTER 3 *Fang and Fire*	31
CHAPTER 4 *The Fanged King, The Clever Queen, and The Heir of Nothing*	49
CHAPTER 5 *Night Omens*	59
CHAPTER 6 *Whispers of Kingdom Courts*	71
CHAPTER 7 *Timeworn Tradition*	85
CHAPTER 8 *Banquet of the Blessed*	95
CHAPTER 9 *Mirth and Mystery*	105
CHAPTER 10 *Favor of the Seven*	121
CHAPTER 11 *A Fate Set in Stone*	137
CHAPTER 12 *Weight of Worth*	151

CHAPTER 13 *Folded in Fourths*	167
CHAPTER 14 *Lore of Lunaris*	173
CHAPTER 15 *Grimwolf and Hellhound*	183
CHAPTER 16 *Soul of a Stranger*	197
CHAPTER 17 *Eternal Tethering*	207
CHAPTER 18 *Keeper's Aegis*	215
CHAPTER 19 *A Moment of Bliss*	231
CHAPTER 20 *The Willow Spirit*	243
CHAPTER 21 *Offering*	257
CHAPTER 22 *Beginnings of Betrayal*	269
CHAPTER 23 *Vitus*	285
CHAPTER 24 *A Legacy is Born*	311
CHAPTER 25 *Born to Wield*	323
CHAPTER 26 *Remembrance*	333
CHAPTER 27 *The Cherry-Stained Door*	341

CHAPTER 28   349
Crossing of Kin

CHAPTER 29   365
Crossroads of Fate

Thank You   381
Glossary   383
Acknowledgments   387
About the Author   389

AUTHOR'S NOTE

Thank you wholeheartedly for choosing to journey into the enchanted realms of Neramyr. As the concept of this novel began to take shape upon pages, I found myself weaving the tapestry of a fantasy-filled world with spellbinding magic, compelling characters, and mythical legends. I am truly grateful to you for supporting me on this adventure, for it is your readership that is turning my dreams and aspirations into reality.

Note:

The Divine Shallows is an epic fantasy romance novel that contains themes that may not be suitable for some readers. This includes, but is not limited to, profanity, graphic sexual content, depictions and reference to violence and death, themes of discrimination and oppression, distressing family dynamics, and coercion. Readers who may be sensitive to these elements, please take note.

For Austin—my everlasting warmth of sun

PROLOGUE

Where Silence Weeps

BENEATH THE PALE GLOW OF A FULL MOON, THE RULERS OF Neramyr received a summons to gather at the Temple of Caena by order of the High Priestess. Assembled around the Divine Shallows—a sacred underground cistern—stood fourteen formidable kings and queens. In the presence of the fourteen divine fey, the ancient waters pulsed with an otherworldly magic, beckoning to each of them.

The delicately curved edges of the Divine Shallows were hewn from moonstone and marble. These opalescent borders served as the keepers of an ancient, arcane water preserved from the Old Age. Etched upon their stone surfaces were intricate ivory symbols that gleamed softly in the dim light.

Standing barefoot and calf-deep within the center of the Divine Shallows was the High Priestess of the seven realms. She possessed hair of dappled slate-gray, pulled back tightly beneath an ornate headdress. Her floor-length robe was woven from threads of alabaster, the silken material cascading down her lithe frame and billowing around her ankles in the waters beneath her. A long strip of cloth was cinched around her waist as she stood with her time-weathered palms upturned, speaking into the Temple's silence.

Echoing off the hallowed walls, her voice carved through the quiet.

"Tonight, in this sanctuary of Caena, we are gathered to honor the birth of the firstborn princess of Eriden. Tonight, we shall ask the Moon Goddess to grant her divine blessing upon this newborn life."

The High Priestess turned to the white-haired king and queen that stood nearest to her and signaled them to approach.

The queen cradled a newborn wrapped in soft cloth, while the king tenderly placed a hand on her back, guiding them to the edge of the Divine Shallows. With bare feet, they entered the celestial waters, navigating the gentle currents until they reached the awaiting High Priestess.

Gently cooing at the bundle nestled in the queen's arms, the High Priestess remarked, "King Eamon and Queen Eddra, the seven realms of Neramyr celebrate the birth of your firstborn. How fortunate that the Moon Goddess has blessed an heir upon you after a century. What name have you bestowed upon this wonder?"

With a tired smile, the queen softly spoke, "Her name is Elyria."

"A name as beautiful as the child," the High Priestess praised. "Now, as the moonlight draws near, let us begin the sacred rite of the Mark of Caena." Extending her arms, she motioned to receive the infant from the queen. "May I, Your Majesty?"

The High Priestess' arms bore the marks of time, etched with weathered lines that told tales of age and wisdom. Adorning them were intricate ivory patterns, resembling inked descriptions of the eight lunar phases. These markings glinted with luminescence, as if moonlight itself was harnessed and turned to ink, then painted onto her skin.

They were a beautiful thing—the markings.

Iridescent, they shifted between opaline hues at different angles. Starting from the innermost part of the High Priestess' upper arms, the first marking depicted the delicate curve of the new moon. Tracing down her limbs, they portrayed the successive phases of the moon until culminating in the final phase—the waning crescent—resting at the very center of her palms.

"Of course, High Priestess," replied the tired queen as she handed her baby over cautiously. Her own arms were adorned with similarly intricate iridescent markings.

Identical to those of the High Priestess, the palms of the queen's hands bore the same waning crescent. However, the distinction arose in the patterns along the queen's arms. Unlike the High Priestess, her arms bore no lunar phases. Instead, they were enveloped in moonlit strokes shaped in the pattern of dragon scales. These scales extended from her arms, vanishing into the folds of her modest dress. In truth, the intricate scales were inked on every surface of the queen's skin, save for her face and neck.

The queen's husband, the king of Eriden, possessed a similar pattern of opalescent dragon scales on his body, yet his markings were uniquely his own.

The High Priestess cradled the baby in her arms, carefully unwrapping her from the cloth. The infant's skin was lively, still flush with a delicate pink hue. Atop her head lay a crown of hair as pure as freshly fallen snow, while her eyes shimmered with polished silver that rivaled steel. Framing her cherubic face were elegantly pointed ears. She bore the unmistakable traits of her parents and their kin—white hair and silver eyes, distinguishing features of the fey of Eriden.

Yet, her most remarkable trait would reveal itself in time.

In a matter of years, four fangs would emerge from her gums in place of canines. This distinct characteristic was passed down solely to the descendants of the first king of Eriden.

With the infant nestled in her arms, the High Priestess instructed the king and queen to exit the celestial waters and reclaimed her position in the center of the Divine Shallows. The arcane waters lapped at her calves and curled around her legs, radiating with a luminous aura in acknowledgment to her presence.

Then, the High Priestess invoked the words of a divine ritual she had performed countless times before.

"Esteemed kings and queens of Neramyr, we gather on this auspicious day to commemorate a momentous event. After a century's wait, King Eamon and Queen Eddra proudly welcome their heir, Princess Elyria of House Fangwright. Tonight, we partake in a sacred ritual, as old as time itself, witnessed by generations past. We invoke the Moon Goddess to determine the worthiness of this life to bear her Mark. As Elyria enters the sacred waters, we ask the Moon Goddess, Caena, to bestow her blessing upon her. May she welcome another daughter of the moon and grant Elyria her divine magic to wield in our realm."

Following this, the High Priestess cradled Elyria upright in her arms and gradually descended the infant into the celestial waters awaiting below.

In unison, the fourteen kings and queens encircling the celestial shallows upturned their palms and raised them level to their waists. Each of the fourteen pairs of hands bore identical markings to those of the High Priestess—the center of their palms inked with the same crescent moon.

Together, the rulers tapped into the divine magic bestowed upon them by the Goddess, invoking the moon deity to grant her divine Mark upon the newborn heir.

The magic in the Temple surged, filling the air with primordial power and ancient energy. While the otherworldly aura of the chamber intensified, the waters within the Divine Shallows eagerly responded, swirling with anticipation. In the peak of the water's fervor, the High priestess closed her eyes and offered a final prayer as she submerged the infant beneath the arcane waters, releasing Elyria into its embrace.

Curious gazes trailed the infant's descent into the celestial shallows, watching as she disappeared beneath the waters. Gradually, the newborn faded from view until she vanished entirely.

As the seconds stretched into minutes, the surface of the Divine Shallows remained eerily still.

With each passing moment, the queen's tiredness morphed into concern and the king clenched his fists, suppressing his own apprehension.

In the silence, the queen stepped forward, her voice tinged with unease. "High Priestess, what is happening? It has been too long. Where is she?"

The High Priestess reassured her, "Patience, Your Majesty. I sense the tether between our realm and Caena's realm remains firm. The child is still facing judgment through the Moon Goddess. Once a decision has been reached, your daughter will be released, and only then can she return to us."

Minutes drifted by, and once more, the queen's voice pierced the silence, filled with desperation. "High Priestess, too much time has elapsed. You must guide her back to this realm."

The High Priestess shook her head, her gaze meeting the distressed queen's. "We cannot interfere with the ritual, Your Majesty. I'm afraid Elyria is still with the Moon Goddess. Caena is merciful and gracious—your daughter will return to us soon."

Clutching onto her husband, the anxious queen whispered to him, voice laden with fear. "Eamon, we've waited for her for so long. We cannot lose her."

The king held his wife tightly. His heart was pounding with dread, the feeling threatening to consume him.

As tension mounted, the rulers of the seven realms began to break their neutral composure, sensing the shift in the Temple's atmosphere. Unrest began to spread among the other kings and queens of the seven realms—the other six queens cast sympathetic glances towards the monarchs of Eriden, while the remaining kings regarded them with pity.

Panic overwhelmed the snow-haired queen. "Please, High Priestess."

Furrowing her brow, the High Priestess observed the idle surface of the Divine Shallows. In her next breath, she tapped into the divine magic coursing within her. The surface of her eyes began to glaze, coating in a translucent sheen. Her spelled eyes then gazed into the unseen, flickering back and forth as if traversing between realms. Time elapsed, and then, with a blink, the High Priestess' eyes returned to the present.

"My queen, Elyria's aura remains absent in this realm," the High Priestess explained. "As for the divine tether, the powers I possess are finite. I can only perceive what the Goddess allows me to. Once the child's judgment has been declared, only then can I facilitate her passage back to us."

An hour had passed since the infant vanished from the Divine Shallows, and the queen stared vacantly after her child, lost to the unknown.

Breaking his silence at last, the king spoke. "Has this happened before? Why has the Goddess kept my daughter for so long?"

Turning to the king, the High Priestess responded, "Your Majesty, in my centuries of serving the Moon Goddess, I have never encountered such an occurrence. However, you must maintain faith in the Goddess —the same as I do—that she will reunite Elyria with us."

At that moment, shifting shadows appeared beneath the surface of the Divine Shallows.

With ethereal grace, the High Priestess darted forward, plunging her moon-marked arms into the waters. She retrieved the emerging infant, clutching her securely within her arms. A surge of primordial power radiated from the High Priestess' aura as she guided the infant from the otherworldly back to reality.

Once the child had returned to their realm, the High Priestess gently wrapped her once more in the dry cloth.

A shadow fell upon the High Priestess' brow as she stiffened.

Carefully, visible to only her eyes, she unfurled one of the infant's hands, and then the other—both were bare.

The High Priestess cleared her throat, voice weighed with caution. "Your Majesties, the Moon Goddess has returned Elyria to us. She has spoken, and it is time for me to reveal her judgment to you."

Pausing for a moment, the High Priestess turned solemnly to the anxiously waiting king and queen. "This child has not been blessed by the Moon Goddess and will bear no Mark of Caena."

A collective gasp echoed through the hallowed Temple, followed by a heavy silence.

Overcome with grief, the king and queen of Eriden sank to their knees and wept.

1

Tale of Twin Necklaces

Elowyn found herself strolling through the castle corridors she called home, setting off on a quest to find her older sister. The hour was still early as the sun lingered behind a veil of clouds. Soft beams of morning light filtered through the arched windows that lined Elowyn's path, casting a golden glow on the empty hallways. She walked nimbly, careful to not let her footfalls echo off the marble flooring.

Elowyn followed the stone path leading to her sister's chambers and stopped before a cherry-stained door. The wooden door's familiar surface bore intricate carvings that depicted grand mountains, lush evergreen forests, and curves of winding rivers. Each rested beneath a sky of countless stars. And etched at the precipice of the mountains was a large crescent moon, symbolizing their homeland, Eriden.

This door was a testament to their heritage—a wooden portrait of their world. And more importantly, it was a tribute to Caena, the Moon Goddess of the seven feylands.

Gently, Elowyn inclined her head to the wooden door, leaning in to listen carefully. She anticipated, or rather wished, to hear the steady rise and fall of a sleeping chest on the other side of it. Yet, despite her efforts, only silence greeted her ears. She withdrew from the door, deep in thought, and tapped a finger against her chin in contemplation.

Her eyes flickered to the faint energy lining the door and scowled. After a few moments of consideration, Elowyn simply resolved to trying to open it.

She grasped the golden latch and pushed forward, only to be met with an invisible force and jolted back. Her lips pressed into a firm line as she made a second attempt, only to encounter the same problem. Elowyn's older sister had been warding her doors for weeks without offering any explanation—no matter how much she questioned. Frowning, Elowyn ignored the voice in her mind that told her the door would not open regardless of how hard she tried.

Instead, she tried again knowing it would not budge.

It didn't.

Acknowledging her frustration, Elowyn admitted that she *did*, in fact, embody the typical entitlement of a younger sibling. Prior to her older sister's decision to lock her out of her rooms, Elowyn was accustomed to freely entering her sister's chambers as if they were her own.

Exhaling heavily, Elowyn shut her eyes and focused her attention on the energy emanating from the door. It was shrouded in a powerful ward, preventing entry from anyone who tried. The essence of the magic woven into the barrier carried a distinct aroma of lilac and honey—a telltale sign of her sister's enchantments. Any sorceress worth their salt would know to discern the familiarity or unfamiliarity of such abjuration magic. If the magic were unfamiliar, it would raise suspicion and hint towards the possibility of another entity being involved, whether their intentions be either honorable or ill-intended.

Elowyn muttered a string of annoyances under her breath before taking a step back. With a furrowed brow, she tilted her head in concentration, devising how to dismantle the ward. With narrowed eyes,

Elowyn summoned her own magic to inspect the door. She sensed the presence of four distinct connections, four magical bolts or locks guarding the entrance.

Clearly, her sister had no intention of allowing her entry without a challenge.

Elowyn delved into the spell work once again, peeling back layer after layer in search of uncovering more. The links were sound, the magic that created them being cogent and impressive. It was difficult to not take a moment to regard her sister's craftsmanship.

After a fleeting moment of admiration, Elowyn attempted to sever the invisible links guarding the door. She called upon her magic, drawing it forth from the depths of her own reserves. However, as always, it met her with hostility, snarling at her like a caged beast. She tried to rein in the wild of her magic, yet her attempt was hollow and ineffective. The magical force within her was fierce and resisted all attempts at control.

Trying to tame her magic was taxing, strenuous even, like steering a ship through a tumultuous storm with a faulty helm. Despite her best efforts, she failed to command the magic residing within her. The torrents of her power slipped from her grasp, defying her will.

With a sigh of defeat, Elowyn released the hold on her magic.

She chuckled at herself dejectedly, finding the notion of mastering her own powers almost comical. With slumped shoulders and head hung low, she raised a pitiful hand and rapped on the cherry-stained door, muttering shameless greetings.

"Hey, it's me. I'm *certainly* not bothered by the fact that you've magically sealed off your room. But, if you could kindly let me in, I'd appreciate it."

Anticipating an irritated response, Elowyn was instead met with silence.

The absence of an answer indicated that her sister really wasn't in there. Elowyn lingered for a moment, imagining the reasons why her sister lately felt the need to keep her out of her room, or perhaps lock herself in.

With the Trial of Caena looming just days away, Elowyn imagined her older sister was feeling the relentless pull and pressure of anxiety. Despite being incredibly talented, her sister was tormented with insecurities. Elowyn had no doubt that her sister would complete the divine Trial successfully, and better yet—exceptionally.

Elowyn pulled out a smooth, flat, reflective stone from her dress pocket. Holding it within her palm, she drew in a measured breath and tapped into her power. Simple spells like scrying, aided by a scrying stone, were typically feats within her grasp.

A wave of magic pulsed through Elowyn as her silver eyes glazed over, fixating on the reflective surface of the stone.

Gradually, a scene unraveled before her.

Slowly materializing like a misty apparition, a spacious chamber came into view. The room was magnificent and grandiose, with towering bookshelves that lined the halls and enchanted tapestries that hung from the walls—these woven textiles depicted the ancient folklore of her kind. Above, a domed stained-glass ceiling encased an open lounge, showering sunlit rays of striking cobalt, deep scarlet, and lustrous amber down onto the room.

Elowyn's gaze shifted to the corner of the scrying stone, focusing on a table within the vision. The rough-hewn surface was covered with stacks of books, loose parchment, and furled scrolls. Amidst the clutter sat a snow-haired sorceress, her back bent over a tome as she dipped a feathered pen into an inkwell. With careful strokes, she began inscribing something in a journal.

The moment Elowyn's enchanted gaze fixated on the sorceress hunched over, the snow-haired fey stiffened, her back straightening abruptly as she slammed the journal shut. Whirling, the sorceress spun around, rising to her feet, and crossing her arms over her chest. Her expression contorted in irritation as she mouthed something inaudible.

The Divine Shallows

Feeling like a crook who was caught, Elowyn winced as she watched the projected image of the snow-haired sorceress scowl at her through the magical stone. If she had to guess what the sorceress was saying, it would likely involve her older sister reprimanding her behavior.

"Damn it, not again," Elowyn muttered to herself, ceasing the spell. Quickly, she returned the smooth stone back into her dress pocket and hurried down the hall.

In her haste, Elowyn collided with a servant as she rounded a corner, nearly causing the fey to drop the silver tray in her hands. This servant was older and ample, with streaks of gray mingling in the curtain of her short, snowy locks—the only traces of her lost youth.

Elowyn gasped and helped the servant steady her stance. "Oh, moons! Ora, are you all right?"

Ora had been a constant presence in Elowyn and her sister's childhood. She served as their handmaiden and chamber keeper. More accurately, Ora was like a fretting mother-figure to the two of them. Their actual mother, the queen of Eriden, possessed the strength and intellect befitting her station as one of the strongest queens in the seven realms. However, she lacked the gift of nurturing.

"Good morning, Princess Elowyn," Ora responded to her curtly.

Fumbling at the tray in her hands, Ora quickly straightened the items that were strewn about from Elowyn's ill-timed collision into her.

"It would be beholden upon you to mind your steps. A princess should never scurry about in such a manner. Speaking of unflattering behavior, where are you rushing off to at this early hour?"

With a playful grin, Elowyn teased, "Why, good morning to you too, Ora. I'm afraid I'm a bit behind schedule on pestering my dear sister. My regrets to you about my display of undignified manners. I would be absolutely bedeviled if my hallway etiquette did not meet the standards of the monarchy."

That earned Elowyn a good whack atop her head with the cloth napkin tucked away in Ora's apron.

"Ow, I was just joking, Ora! You know me, I wouldn't be careless unless it was absolutely necessary. I only have a few days left with Elyria before the Trial," Elowyn argued, making a case for her innocence.

"Don't play the fool with me girl, Goddess knows you're trouble," Ora snapped back. Then her expression softened as she continued, "Princess Elyria needs you greatly in the days ahead. I worry she is doubting herself. Each time I see her, she seems half-consumed with dread. The divine Trial is challenging for any royal candidate, especially for her, given that she is afflicted with such a... misfortune."

Heaviness filled the air as Ora glumly pushed out the last word.

"I felt she needed some comfort and kindness to start her day." The handmaiden's gaze was downcast, fixed on the tea tray in her hand.

The silver tea tray was elegant, decorated with ornate edges that were slightly raised with handles fashioned on opposite ends. A silver dome covered an oval plate, from which an inviting aroma wafted. Elowyn imagined stacks of freshly baked biscuits drizzled with honey, berry scones with sugary tops, and delectable finger cakes. There was also a darling porcelain teapot, accompanied by two delicate teacups and saucers.

Reminded of the dainty porcelain tea set Elowyn adored in her youth, a memory from when she was eight resurfaced.

IT WAS THE EARLY MORNING OF ELOWYN'S EIGHTH NAMEDAY and she found herself in the front of a large wooden door—a door she knew by heart. Every morning since she could remember, she woke up and made her way to it. Her gaze lingered on the crescent moon carved upon its surface, twin to the ones marked on her palms.

Standing on her tiptoes with her moon-inked palms, Elowyn reached for the door's gold-worn latch.

Quietly as she could, she grabbed for the handle and pushed until there was an opening large enough for her to shimmy her way in. She found her older sister sitting at her desk, hunched over, and pouring herself over a book.

Elowyn smirked to herself, thinking her older sister was caught unawares. She slowly crept behind her sister and planned her calculated ambush. She waited a few more seconds as her sister flipped another page in her book. Close enough now to read the text on the pages herself, Elowyn pounced on her sister's lap.

Feigning shock, her older sister jolted and shrieked. Elowyn cackled with joy, giggling herself into oblivion. Elyria laughed in tandem as she sat Elowyn upright in her lap.

"I got you!" Elowyn bellowed in triumph as settled into her sister's embrace.

Chuckling affectionately, Elyria agreed. "Yes, you did."

"Do you know what day it is Ely?"

"Hmm... It's Tuesday, right?"

"No! Well, yes. But, no! It's my nameday!"

"Oh, so it's Tuesday and it's your nameday?"

"Yes! You said we could have a tea party!" Elowyn griped.

"Of course it's your nameday. I would never forget such a special day. I had Ora bring your favorite tea set and treats."

"This is the best day ever!" Elowyn squealed, elated.

"Here, I also got you a gift," Elyria responded, smiling tenderly.

Elyria retrieved a small wooden box from her desk drawer. She gently handed the box to Elowyn and watched her younger sister untie the scarlet ribbon and lift the lid, her wide silver eyes peering inside. Within it, was a pair of identical necklaces nestled on a cushioned bed. Each necklace was made of a thin silver chain with a solitary gemstone— a breathtaking white opal, skillfully cut into the shape of a teardrop.

Elyria removed one of the necklaces, displaying it to her younger sister. "Remember when you asked me to promise that we'd always be together? Well, I had the royal artificer make us something special. These necklaces are carved from the same stone, fashioned from two halves of a whole. They're charmed with an invisible bond that's inseparable—kind of like sisters."

With curiosity, Elowyn lifted the second necklace from the wooden box and held it in the air. At first, she felt nothing, but then a gentle hum radiated from her necklace, as if it acknowledged the presence of her sister's necklace—a missing piece now complete.

Wonderstruck, Elowyn allowed Elyria to fasten the necklace around her neck, and then watched as her sister donned her own. The necklace felt like a warm pulse, a soothing weight at the base of her neck. Elowyn had never owned any magical objects before. She instantly prized it most above all her other belongings.

"Now we can always feel like we're together?" Tears welled in Elowyn's cherub eyes.

"Yes, exactly. Happy nameday, Elowyn." Elyria laughed, her voice was like a lilting melody.

Her sister then pulled forth a silver tray with a set of porcelain teacups and a plate of shortbread cookies. "Now, now. A princess has no time for tears on her nameday. What do you say, shall we have tea?"

The memory began to fade and Elowyn absentmindedly brushed her fingers over the comforting teardrop chain around her neck as she refocused on Ora.

"Elyria isn't in her room, I already checked. However, she *is* in the royal library. Do you mind if I bring it to her?"

"Bless her heart, that child always has her nose glued to a book. Be mindful of your sister when you see her," Ora cautioned as she placed the tea tray in Elowyn's arms.

"Don't worry, Ora, I promise I'm not as much of a troublemaker as

The Divine Shallows

you make me out to be. Plus, I'm Elyria's favorite person, so I'm sure she'll want to see me," Elowyn said with a wink.

Ora's lips tightened while her eyes narrowed as she watched Elowyn flash another smile and head in the direction of the library.

The gemstone around Elowyn's neck warmed with delight, singing in response to soon being reunited with its other half.

2

Myth of the Moon Goddess

Balancing the tea tray carefully, Elowyn nudged open the towering twin doors of the castle's royal library with her hip, entering carefully so as to not spill a single drop. Stepping inside, Elowyn noticed it was emptier than usual. Normally, scholars of the Seven Spires traveled from all realms of Neramyr to frequent this place, hoping to study the ancient texts it housed, the royal library now seemed eerily quiet.

Eriden's royal library was renowned across the seven realms for its vast collection of knowledge. The fey of Eriden placed great importance on learning, evident by the stacks of written work meticulously documented from the New Age, and even a substantial array of artifacts preserved from the Old Age.

Information about the Old Age was scarce, predating the establishment of the seven realms and the very existence of Neramyr itself. However, there were a select number of artifacts from this ancient era preserved by the first fey. These invaluable texts and scrolls were housed in the cellars beneath the library, safeguarded by extensive wards which prevented unlawful access and ensured nothing ventured out undesired.

Most historians and chroniclers speculate that the feylands of the Old Age were imbued with pure and unclaimed divine magic. It is believed that this boundless magic roamed freely throughout the feylands while vile creatures thrived on it without restraint. Historical depictions portray these beasts as savage and primal, embodying the essence of evil itself.

However, since the dawn of the New Age, such creatures have vanished from Neramyr, unseen for millennia.

As Elowyn traversed the library's wooden labyrinth, she half-expected a scolding to ring out at any moment. She was awaiting to be rebuked for carrying steaming liquid amidst the priceless tomes that lined the shelves, but was surprised to find that no roaming archivist or wandering bookkeeper was there to reprimand her. She simply shrugged her shoulders and let her gaze wander around the library until they were drawn to the tapestries adorning the walls.

The woven textiles depicted a myriad of legends and fables, some of which Elowyn knew well. One tapestry in particular never failed to capture her attention. It belonged to a large series of fabrics that illustrated the lore of divine magic and its connection to the Moon Goddess.

The first time she came across these tapestries, she was five and horror-stricken. Now, at nineteen, she stood before the details of the textile art, admiring the threads that depicted her kind's rich history.

She let her gaze fall to the first tapestry of the series as it began to unfold a primordial tale before her eyes.

The legend began with illustrations of the feral creatures and beasts that roamed the feylands during the Old Age. These savage beings brought chaos, wreaking havoc on the first fey that inhabited the unclaimed territories. Creatures born from nightmares and wrought from hell reigned the lands, plunging the world into a ruinous age of fear and terror.

The Divine Shallows

The desolate skies harbored flying harpies, grisly wyverns, and winged manticores. The depths of the Swyn Sea were swarming with kelpies and wicked water spirits. The shadows of the Elberrin Forest lurked with heinous changelings and fanged tygers. The grassy plains of Highbend were overrun with lindworms, giant cyclops, and nefarious ogres standing taller than three fully matured fey combined. Meanwhile, within the caverns nestled alongside the Eriden and Erimead mountains dwelled hordes of blood-thirsty dhampirs, wretched ghouls, and soul reapers.

The next tapestry that followed this delved into a prelude of a disastrous legend.

During the Old Age, the first fey endured an era marked by brutality and savagery. They rallied against these beasts with their own native magic, but the fey were powerless against the divine magic wielded by the creatures. Their attempts to survive were futile—males, females, and children alike fell victim to the relentless onslaught of these beasts. The first fey lived in a perpetual state of unrest and uncertainty.

For centuries, the fey and these monstrous creatures were entangled in a sordid dance of death and destruction, and resources were depleted until they fragmented to almost nothing. The fey's numbers dwindled as the beasts overwhelmed and vanquished the strongholds of their defenses. Dreadful days befell them, and night terrors became reality. The fey found themselves outnumbered and outmatched at every turn.

As doom loomed near, the fey made a desperate attempt forge their way out of the bloodshed. They sought refuge in a shielded cavern nestled between where the Eriden mountains ended and the Erimead mountains began.

This cavern served as their final sanctuary, a last bastion of hope.

Only seven warlocks and sorceresses remained in their ranks, using the last of their sapped native magic to cast a ward over the cave's entrance.

However, the beasts of night eventually found them. The vile creatures waged another attack, launching a final assault to massacre the last of them standing. That fateful night, the fey prepared themselves for the ruination of their folk. Families and kin gathered, bidding partings and farewells as they awaited their end, dreading when the protective spell guarding them would inevitably falter.

The next tapestry was dyed a maelstrom of grays and browns, depicting the despair and desolation the first fey suffered.

As the night wore on, trepidation and sorrow filled the cavern where they sought refuge. Their vile foes were chipping away at the wards link by link, and the last surviving magic wielders were now weary and exhausted. Knowing that their protective barrier would not last until morning, the seven fey made a final attempt to move their kin further into the depths of the cave, hoping to shield them even mere moments longer. The wards began to crumble, the magical veil shielding the cave entrance trembled and strained, struggling to hold its form. In silent agreement, the seven warlocks and sorceresses stood together at the entrance; a united force, prepared to protect their own to the bitter end.

Elowyn moved onto the next three shimmering tapestries and another spellbinding scene unraveled before her.

As the fate of the fey hung precariously in the balance, the stroke of midnight fell, and the sky was as dark as the shadows in their eyes. Swirling gray clouds churned overhead, parting with a deafening crack of thunder, cleaving a fissure in the heavens. A faint light emerged from the cleft in the clouds and a crescent moon appeared.

Mist began to swirl and coil around the feet of the fey within the cavern. The seven magical fey followed the elusive mist to its origin. It led them to a reservoir of shallow water nestled in the heart of the cavern, its surface tumultuous and turbulent. From within the mist-laden waters, a radiant aura emanated, heralding the arrival of a mysterious figure stepping forth from the ethereal shallows.

The figure flickered in and out of existence, its aura pulsing and glowing with an intensity. The atmosphere in the cave shifted, surging with an arcane power. The figure's form remained elusive, fluctuating from small to tall, slender to robust, while its hair morphed from cascading waves to cropped curls that danced around its face.

With each step taken from the shallows, the figure's hair and robes billowed around in movement, as if gravity ceased to exist in its company. Drawing nearer to the fey, the figure exuded an ethereal feminine presence, though her features remained shrouded in mystery. The seven fey stood transfixed, stunned by the sheer magnitude of the divine power radiating from her.

Advancing past them, the figure centered herself at the entrance of the cave just as the protective wards casted by the fey finally shattered. With a deafening wail, the creatures waiting outside charged in.

The luminous figure raised her arms and unleashed a torrent of moonlight from her outstretched palms. The winged creatures recoiled, their screeches echoing through the cavern as they shielded their eyes from the radiant beams. Another wave of divine energy pulsed from the figure, and she engulfed the beasts in searing moonlight. Their distorted faces contorted in agony as their flesh began to blister and burn, devoured by the divine power.

Amidst their anguished cries, the beasts thrashed violently, their bodies wracked with pain as the moonlight penetrated their very being, consuming them from within. With each agonizing moment, their movements grew weaker until death finally claimed them, leaving only stillness in its wake.

Turning towards the cave's entrance, the otherworldly figure extended her palms once more, moonlight still streaming out from her palms in rivulets. This celestial energy took the form of both gentle rays of light and torrents of flowing energy as it snaked down her arms while she conjured another protective barrier that shrouded the entire cavern, protecting the fey.

Stepping beyond the safety of the cave's confines, the figure left moonlight trickling behind her path. With palms upraised as if in supplication to the heavens, she directed her gaze skyward and drew upon the moon, channeling immense power.

In that moment, the world shattered.

Within the cavern, the fey trembled as the ground shook with each surge of celestial power that raged beyond its walls. Though the figure had vanished from sight, the lingering aura of her magic still saturated the air. For hours on end, the mountain quaked and trembled from the magic that seethed outside.

Eventually, the world quieted, and a calm settled upon the feylands.

Even the air once fuming with celestial power now ebbed into stillness and silence. Dusk was retreating and dawn was nearing as the morning sun creeped through the entrance of the cave.

At last, the figure reappeared in the cave. Her form still flickering with the glow of moonlight as she floated towards them. The seven fey beheld the figure and knelt before her, both in gratitude and reverence. Approaching them, the ethereal figure extended her hands and, one by one, bathed them in divine moonlight. Each of the seven fey were now aglow. As the ethereal beams danced upon their skin, delicate patterns of translucent ivory ink were traced. The patterns etched tales of sacrifice and valor upon their flesh. These markings bespoke the unique journey and devotion each fey possessed, weaving an artwork of courage and resilience across their bodies. Lastly, the shimmering ink drifted down their arms and ebbed at their palms, forming a crescent moon at the heart of each fey's hand.

In that moment, clarity dawned upon the seven warlocks and sorceresses. They accepted that this figure was no mere apparition, but a higher being—a Goddess of Worlds.

With her divine touch, she marked each of the seven fey, entrusting them as the first fey to be able to wield her divine magic. The fey understood that they were chosen as the vanguards of a new era. Under the guidance of the Moon Goddess, they ushered in an age of order and harmony known as the New Age. Establishing seven noble houses across the feylands, they become the first rulers of the kingdoms of Neramyr.

The culmination of the legend ended at this last tapestry.

Since her youth, Elowyn had been mesmerized by these ancient tales. Her fear turned to reverence as she began to understand the origins of how her power came to be. Her father instilled in her the importance of understanding the significance of divine magic. He emphasized how it set her apart from the fey whose abilities were rooted solely in native magic.

Much like Elowyn herself, Elyria displayed an insatiable curiosity of Neramyr's history and origin. She'd even read every book in the royal library thrice. However, Elowyn surmised that her sister was not merely seeking knowledge, but answers to her own story.

Elowyn navigated past the tapestries and through the wooden shelves until she reached a foyer within the library. The room was dim, only lit by the stained-glass windows reflecting colors that painted the furniture and floor tiles. This library held a special place in Elowyn's heart, having spent countless hours here with her sister exploring every corner.

At present, the library seemed deserted, except for one soul.

"Elowyn, how many times must I remind you not to scry on me?" grumbled the snow-haired sorceress that Elowyn glimpsed on her stone earlier.

Even in moments of distress, Elyria looked beautiful. This was a quality that always stirred a hint of envy in Elowyn's heart. While all fey possessed an inherent allure, Elyria surpassed all of them—she was beautiful beyond reckoning. Taller and lither than Elowyn, she moved with an effortless grace while her white hair cascaded down her shoulders and back in gentle waves.

Elyria's eyes were a silver rimmed with ebony, framed with lush lashes that lined their petal shape. A delicate nose was set between high cheekbones and her skin was rich olive. Her lips, a rich warm brown, held a captivating charm, particularly when curved into a smile that revealed her four fangs—a trait no other bloodline in Neramyr possessed.

Elowyn bore a resemblance to Elyria, albeit a slightly less captivating one. She inherited her father's striking features and boisterous demeanor. Meanwhile, Elyria took after their mother, exuding arresting beauty and an almost supernatural grace. Furthermore, Elyria possessed a tremendous amount of wisdom, likely stemming from her seven-year seniority to Elowyn.

"I had to track you down somehow, didn't I? I brought you something because I heard you weren't feeling well. I even brought our favorite treat," Elowyn replied, presenting the tray of tea and biscuits.

"I just needed some space. With the divine Trial approaching, Father has been... overwhelming," Elyria confessed hesitantly.

At the mention of the Trial, Elowyn's cheerfulness shifted to seriousness. "Do you feel prepared?"

"As ready as I'll ever be, I suppose," Elyria responded, her gaze withdrawn.

Elowyn knew her sister well enough to know her eyes were fixated on her palms. The one distinctive feature Elowyn possessed that her sister lacked was the pair of iridescent crescent moons permanently etched onto the skin of her hands.

Setting down the tray of tea and biscuits, Elowyn settled into the chair beside her sister. "You're the strongest candidate across the seven realms." Elowyn lifted her palms, displaying her two crescent moons. "Even with these, I feel rather inept compared to you."

"The Moon Goddess withheld her blessing from me for a reason. And speaking of which, you need to devote more time to your sight scrying. I sensed your spell instantly. Have you been practicing at all?" Elyria scolded.

"Was it really that obvious? I thought I was improving." Elowyn shrugged.

"Watch," Elyria instructed as she lifted one of the cups from the tray and poured tea into it. The liquid was still hot, wisps of steam rising from the porcelain. With a graceful motion of her hand, Elyria dispersed the steam billowing from the tea, cooling the liquid to a lukewarm temperature.

Turning the cup towards herself, Elyria peered into the reflective surface of the tea. Her gaze became distant as she focused, and soon a vision materialized on the liquid's surface. It was slightly blurry, reminiscent of the visions Elowyn had conjured on her stone earlier. On the tea's surface, Elowyn made out the back of her own head and her body suddenly tensed as it detected an unnatural magical presence scrutinizing her from behind.

"Now, observe this," Elyria continued, shifting her gaze once more. The tea's surface now displayed a mirrored image of the current scene in the royal library, viewed from a bird's-eye perspective. With each movement of Elyria's eyes, the image in the cup adjusted accordingly, presenting a clear, vivid depiction of the scene below. Every detail was sharp and unmistakable, from their own figures, down to the motes of dust drifting lazily in the sunlight filtering through the stained-glass ceiling.

This time, as Elowyn observed herself through the tea's reflection, produced by her sister's magic, she felt no sense of danger or foreboding.

"If you aim to scry someone's whereabouts, caution is key. It demands time and dedication, but when executed successfully, your target remains oblivious. Eventually, you'll forego the need for a scrying stone; any reflective surface will serve, much like this tea," her sister lectured.

"Easy for you to say. You've had years of practice over me, not to mention your natural talent. No one your age can scry with such precision without a stone or mirror," Elowyn countered. "And are you ever going to explain why you've started warding your door?"

Elyria chuckled in response. "Because of you and your lack of boundaries. You've been barging in freely for nineteen years, and that's long enough. But if you bothered to learn the basics of warding, you could still enter. I've set up an intermediate spell just to see if you'd attempt it."

Elowyn understood that her sister's remarks stemmed from a place of concern and care. The reality was, Elowyn didn't possess the innate prowess that her sister seemed to effortlessly command in all things.

The magic within Elowyn burned fiercely, but harnessing it was a relentless struggle. Despite the challenges she faced in mastering her native power, Elowyn dedicated herself to it tirelessly, sparing no effort to gain control over the magical energy pulsing within her. Some days, she felt progress, sensing the gap between herself and her native magic narrowing. Yet, on mornings like this one, she felt as though she couldn't be further from achieving it.

"I'm working on it," Elowyn reassured her sister. "Don't worry, my Trial is nearly seven years away. I have plenty of time to earn your pride." Shifting the conversation, she added, "But enough about me. You're the one with the Trial coming up. Look at the bright side—you might even bond with an *animus*. Just imagine the pair you two would make... I can't even begin to fathom it."

Elyria's smile widened at the prospect.

Elowyn knew her sister looked forward to the day she would claim her own *animus*. The Goddess chose only the most deserving to forge this sacred soul-bond during her divine Trial. This permanent attachment must be agreed upon by both parties, and once accepted, it bound them to each other into the afterlife and all the realms beyond. Soul-bonding with an *animus* signified one's tremendous rank as a warlock or sorceress.

"That's true. I wonder what mine will be. Perhaps he or she will be similar in nature as I am," Elyria said wistfully.

"If your *animus* resembles you in any way, I'll be terrified," Elowyn chuckled. "But you know what'll lift your spirits? Let's wander to the mountains and find Bane and Stryx."

Elyria's eyes sparkled with excitement, her fanged smile mirroring Elowyn's own.

3

Fang and Fire

Elowyn and Elyria emerged from the library; their arms intertwined as laughter escaped from their lips. They strolled down the corridors, engrossed in gossip and conversation, deliberately avoiding any mention of the impending divine Trial. Navigating through staircases and corridors, they reached the cherry-stained door of Elyria's chambers. With a flicker of her power, Elyria dispelled the ward cloaking the door, giving Elowyn a playful wink before entering. Elowyn responded with a crude gesture of her own before following her sister inside.

Elowyn entered Elyria's room, greeted by the soothing aroma of lilac and honey that embraced her like a warm hug. The antechamber's walls formed a perfect square, leading her toward a recessed area with marble steps. Elowyn's feet descended the marble steps into the spacious, immaculate room—a reflection of her sister's refined taste.

Sunbeams streamed through a skylight, casting patterns on the marble floor where a table stood, decorated with a glass vase filled with lilacs blooming in bouquets of violet and magenta. Bookshelves lined the walls, overflowing with volumes, novels, and storybooks. A study table bore the weight of numerous spine-bound texts the walls couldn't hold. Nearby, a crimson velvet couch, its cushions sunken, bore the marks of years of reading.

Three arched doorways led to different chambers: Elyria's bedchambers straight ahead, her washroom to the right, and her common lounge to the left. Elowyn followed her sister through the doorway leading to the sleeping quarters.

Elyria's bedchamber was another reflection of refinement. The vaulted ceilings stood fifteen feet tall with a splendid chandelier that centered the room. Stone arches adorned the walls, spaced between elegant pillars. To the left, stood a marble fireplace with the remnants of the morning's fire still crackling with activity. At the center of the room was a cherry-stained four-poster bed, its wooden posts with draping organza.

The plush white mattress looked incredibly inviting and Elowyn debated on launching herself into the luxurious bed. However, she hesitated, knowing her sister's nature would not tolerate even a crumb in her linens.

"I have a surprise to show you. You're going to love it," Elyria hinted.

"A surprise?" Elowyn tilted her head with curiosity.

Moving to another doorway lined with intricate gold trimming, Elyria opened the door to reveal a vast closet. Wardrobes lined the walls, their doors flung open to reveal gowns crafted from swatches of every color under the sun. Elowyn couldn't suppress a gasp as she hurried along the racks, trailing her fingers over silk, chiffon, lace, and satin. Catching Elyria's eye, she received a warning glance, a stern reminder not to soil the pristine garments with her enthusiasm.

The wardrobes supported gold beams from which delicate gowns and dresses hung. Elowyn caught a glimpse of periwinkle blue out of the

The Divine Shallows

corner of her vision and approached the dress, pulling it gently from the wardrobe to admire the craftsmanship.

The floor-length gown featured a small train with a daringly open-backed bodice. The skirt, slightly more relaxed, hugged the body in blending layers of soft blues, light purples, and pastel violets. Patterns of lilacs were embroidered along its skirt, while silver beads cascaded down to the train, resembling a stream of starlight.

Clutching the gown to her chest, Elowyn turned to Elyria, her silver eyes wide as she gestured towards the room filled with the equally enchanting attire.

"When were you going to tell me about *this*?" Elowyn huffed; her tone tinged with annoyance.

"Ora helped the royal seamstress bring them in late last night. Mother apparently ordered enough dresses to clothe all of Eriden," Elyria explained, her lips forming a thin line. "I think she wants me to wear a different gown every second of this week."

"At least you'll be the best dressed for all seven days leading up to the Trial," Elowyn replied with understanding. "Mother's feeling uneasy, isn't she?"

"All I know is that she expects me to look immaculate every night of the Ceremony. Probably so I don't embarrass her in front of the other six kingdoms," Elyria confessed, her gaze fixed on her hands as she turned her thumbs in absent-minded circles.

"You are and always will be the most beautiful fey in all the seven realms—and that's not an exaggeration. Trust me, if you were ugly, I'd be kind enough to let you know," Elowyn teased, placing her palm over her heart mockingly.

"If I mess up or have one hair out of place, father will spurn me for the rest of the Ceremony," Elyria continued.

Elowyn understood the weight behind her sister's words; she knew their father's unforgiving nature all too well. No matter how many triumphs Elyria achieved, a single misstep could overshadow them all.

Raised within the confines of the castle, Elyria faced relentless scrutiny and criticism not only from their father but also from the fey of Eriden. Elowyn herself wasn't immune to King Fangwright's harsh judgment, but she had never felt the same hostility from their folk. Compared to the storms Elyria weathered, Elowyn's own challenges seemed like mere rain showers.

Returning the dress to its place on the golden beam, Elowyn moved to a dresser across the room. She retrieved two white tunics made of lightweight cotton and fetched pairs of leather pants and matching boots from a nearby chest. Silently, she handed a set to Elyria, and both sisters dressed in somber silence, attempting to shake off the lingering memories of their father's cruelty during their childhood.

"All right, enough of the gloomy chatter. Let's have some fun," Elowyn declared, extending her hand for her sister to grasp.

Elyria clasped her younger sister's hand, giving it a gentle squeeze, expressing silent her gratitude.

***

THE TWO SISTERS STROLLED OUT OF THE ROOM, ARMS linked once more, making their way towards the castle grounds near the rock gardens that overlooked the expansive ranges of the Eriden mountains. Elowyn wondered whether her sister's tendencies toward solitude were natural or a learned disposition. Elowyn understood that in the presence of their parents, Elyria did whatever it took to avoid criticism or condemnation. Despite her talent and power, Elyria was treated as an outcast by society simply because she was not moon-blessed after her birth.

Elowyn could sense that her sister was not well. Elyria's laid-back demeanor was merely a facade, an attempt to appear strong for the challenging week ahead. The fey of Neramyr were proud and traditional, but at times, they could also be cynical and disillusioned. The memory of the last Ceremony was still painfully vivid in Elowyn's mind. She had witnessed her sister's radiant spirit dim under the weight of others' cruelty until it was extinguished entirely. The memory of that ordeal still gnawed at Elowyn's core as they wandered further within the familiar walls of their home.

After some time, the two sisters reached an open courtyard settled within the castle grounds. Elowyn inhaled deeply, relishing the fresh air. The sky stretched out in a brilliant blue canvas, adorned with playful clouds that danced across its horizon. They wandered through the gardens, following patterned brick pathways flanked by rose bushes. Every so often, they passed by ornamental trees heavy with berries and blossoms, infusing the air with a sweet fragrance.

In moments like these, Elowyn wished she could spend the rest of her days as an ordinary highborn lady of the court. She imagined leisurely strolls through the castle grounds, indulging in biscuits and tea while gossiping about royal scandals, clad in frilly gowns and carrying lace parasols to shield herself from the sun.

Yet, as the Crown Princess of Eriden, she bore the weight of duties and responsibilities far beyond her personal interests. As they walked, courtiers bowed and curtsied in deference to the two princesses making their way through the courtyard.

Their journey came to a halt as they approached a large cliff that extended from the mountain. Towering above them stood a weathered stone archway, twenty feet tall, with carvings depicting fangs, plumes of flames, and dragon scales etched into the once-smooth surface. A faint, pulsating aura emanated from the archway, growing stronger as Elowyn and Elyria drew nearer.

This stone archway, erected by the first king of Eriden, held sacred significance, and was imbued with divine magic that permitted only members of the royal family to pass beyond its pillars.

Beyond them, lay a vast expanse of rocky terrain ending in a cliff. The landscape, devoid of allure, consisted mostly of an empty stretch save for a watering trough, a handful of cavernous stables, and scant vegetation. In stark contrast to the grandeur of the archway, the cliff failed to captivate the eye.

With Elyria leading the way, the sisters crossed the threshold of the archway. As they did, their surroundings underwent a subtle transformation. Once a mundane dirt cliff, it now revealed a stone pathway leading to a series of snaking stairs ascending the mountainside. Elyria forged ahead, guiding them further up the mountain. As they climbed, the air grew thinner with elevation, yet having been acclimated to the mountains since birth, the sisters showed only a sheen of sweat as a sign of exertion. Step by step, they ascended, bridging the gap between soil and sky.

Eventually, they arrived at another rocky platform that overlooked the mountain's edge. Across from them lay dark, deep caves burrowed into the mountainside. Scanning the area, Elowyn spotted monstrous prints pressed into the dirt beneath them. Both sisters observed the fresh tracks and exchanged a knowing glance.

Breaking the mountain's tranquility with a melodic voice, Elyria called out, "Stryx... Bane... You can stop hiding now."

At her word, a slow rustling sounded from the surrounding evergreens. The trees quivered and shook, then suddenly, two large, winged figures shot into the sky swift as lightning. The two forms arced back down, plummeting hues of charcoal gray and stark chalk. Just before they were about to collide with the rocky platform, their massive leathery wings spread wide, flapping rhythmically in sync.

Despite their imposing size, the two creatures landed with remarkable agility and precision, creating a gust of wind that prompted the sisters to brace themselves, anchoring their feet firmly into the ground.

The slightly smaller of the two creatures, the one with a chalk-colored coat, fixed its eyes on Elyria as it approached her cautiously. Gradually closing the distance, it stopped, extending its scaled snout to sniff her scent. Elyria stood frozen as the creature inspected her, but as it recognized her, a screech of approval escaped its lips, followed by a tender nuzzle.

"I'm glad to see you too, Stryx," Elyria said with a laugh, her voice as sweet as honey. She gently patted the creature's maw, eliciting a purr-like rumble of contentment as it leaned into her touch.

As Elyria continued to stroke Stryx's head, she remarked, "It seems you've missed me as much as I've missed you." In response, Stryx emitted a spirited grunt, demanding more affection, while an ethereal aura radiated from his body.

Elowyn watched her sister joyfully, reveling in her carefree behavior.

Shortly after the warm interaction with Stryx, Bane, the larger companion, began to approach Elyria. His massive form moved with a calculated grace, each step emphasized the power evident in his rippling muscles. As he neared, his towering charcoal-gray silhouette loomed over Stryx, standing an impressive thirteen feet tall.

"Hello, Bane," Elyria greeted softly.

Bane's demeanor was imposing yet measured, his eyes filled with watchful awareness as he sniffed at Elyria's hair. After a moment, he emitted a deep huff, briefly acknowledging Elyria before shifting towards Elowyn, who remained rooted to her spot. Bane approached Elowyn, his eyes locking onto hers with piercing, slit-like pupils. The aura surrounding him felt unsettling as he drew nearer.

Elowyn remained still as Bane scrutinized her, extending her hand in a gesture of trust. Bane sniffed at her moon-inked skin before gently resting his maw in her palm, his gaze never leaving hers. Gradually, the tense atmosphere surrounding Bane dissipated, replaced by a sense of calm and ease. With a grin, Elowyn leaned forward, resting her forehead against Bane's scaled snout in fondness.

Stryx and Bane were firedrakes, commonly known as fire dragons, renowned for their agility, sleek winged forms, and their fearsome ability to breathe fire. These creatures had coexisted with the Fangwrights for generations, first appearing in the New Age during the reign of Eriden's founding king, the first of these dragons being a gift from Caena. Prior to this, their birthplace had been shrouded in mystery. Whether due to their divine origins or their inherent magic, firedrakes varied greatly in size, anatomy, and the extent of their powers.

Bane possessed scales shaped like teardrops, smooth at the base yet razor-sharp at the edges, forming a glimmering, sinister coat of charcoal, smoke, and leaden ash. He was among the largest firedrakes in Fangwright history, exuding a majestic yet bone-chilling presence. His mouth bristled with jagged fangs, while five pointed horns jutted from his skull like a crown of blades.

In contrast, Stryx, also a male fire dragon, hailed from a bloodline known for its litheness and lean physique. His scales, stark white and oval-shaped, adorned his body in overlapping patterns, smooth and uniform in color. Though initially appearing friendly and sociable, Stryx's nature belied the potential for ferocity—only fools would underestimate a firedrake.

Elowyn recalled the moment she witnessed Stryx pin two handlers down as he ripped their limbs one by one from their body. Some found it cruel, but Stryx was not left unprovoked. The handlers attempted to thieve one of his scales and pocket it for their own. In Neramyr, dragon scales were a valuable good, a rarity to come by, as they could be used to concoct powerful potions, manipulated in powerful spells, and sold for large sums of gold. Since that day, her father ceased access to the hallowed dragon's territory unless the individual were of royal blood.

There were only three fire dragons in total that inhabited the ranges of the Eriden mountains: Stryx, Bane, and Nerys. Fire dragons did not roam freely in Neramyr, nor did they dwell spontaneously in the feylands. The first king of Eriden was gifted a firedrake from the Moon Goddess, and all subsequent firedrakes in Eriden were procured in the divine Trial.

Only fey who demonstrate great sacrifice, honor, and integrity during the Trial of Caena were eligible to form a bond with an *animus*.

This mystical connection transcended lifetimes, uniting the magical beast and the fey in service to one another across realms, even beyond death. In accordance with Trial principle, a fey could attempt to soul-bond with an otherworldly creature only once; if rejected, they forfeited the chance to claim an *animus* for the remainder of their life.

Approaching Bane, Elowyn ran her palms along his weathered hide, tracing the rugged terrain of battle scars that marked the surface. She felt the otherworldly aura emanating from him, akin to the one her father possessed.

Bane was her father's *animus*, bound to him by an unbreakable connection. Throughout their lives, Bane had shown favoritism towards Elowyn over her older sister. This allegiance stemmed from the unwavering bond between Bane and their father. Even in their childhood, Bane allowed only Elowyn as a rider, never Elyria.

Stryx was their mother's *animus*, and he was a companionable creature. Elyria delighted in his company, and Elowyn, too, spent countless days soaring the mountainsides with him, finding equal joy in his presence. Unlike Bane, Stryx showed no favoritism between the sisters, living in contentment and doing as he pleased. He was renowned as the fastest of the three firedrakes in Eriden, his deft features fostering great stealth.

While Stryx lacked the brute strength of Bane, he compensated with fierce intelligence, akin to a cardsharp opportunist who both amused desires and preyed on fears. Together, the two firedrakes formed a formidable pairing, much like their parents.

Nerys, a sapphire-blue firedrake, and their uncle's *animus*, was rarely seen in the mountains, as their uncle had resided on the shores of the Elune Isles for the past decade.

Moving to Bane's side, Elowyn patted his hide, prompting him to lower his body closer to the ground. With practiced ease, she hoisted herself onto his back, securing her position by gripping onto the ridged spikes that ran along his spine. Sensing her stability, Bane lifted himself upright once more, ready for their journey.

"Ready for a rematch?" Elyria's taunt echoed behind her.

Turning towards her sister's voice, Elowyn watched as Stryx dashed towards the cliffside, leaping into the sky with Elyria in tow. With a spirited screech, Stryx ascended higher and higher, Elyria's laughter trailing behind her as her ivory hair whipped in the wind. The white firedrake executed graceful loops and sharp arcs with breathtaking precision.

"Showoffs," Elowyn grumbled quietly. Leaning forward, she addressed Bane in a low tone. "Let's show them how it's done."

Bane turned his head towards the sky, emitting a deep rumble from his throat. His massive body began to move forward, each thundering stride shaking the ground beneath them as he gained momentum.

As Bane approached the edge of the cliff, Elowyn gripped the spikes on his back tightly, her knuckles turning white. She knew she had to hold on tightly—for her life depended on it. Ordinarily, only a fully grown male fey could handle riding Bane comfortably, but Elowyn relished the challenge. With an ear-splitting shriek, Bane propelled himself from the ground, cresting the edge of the cliff with powerful hind-legs.

Elowyn's stomach lurched as Bane plunged down the mountainside with his wings tucked close to his body. Descending deeper into the crag, he then spread his wings in a powerful motion, causing Elowyn to recoil at the force, her stomach knotting in her throat as Bane leveled himself in the air. With each colossal flap of his wings, he surged forward, racing towards the other firedrake.

Meanwhile, Stryx and Elyria had already darted away, disappearing into the clouds until they were mere specks in the sky. Undeterred, Bane doubled his efforts, barreling towards them with fierce determination. Elowyn huddled closer to Bane, urging him onward as she felt him gain momentum with each beat of his wings, steadily closing the distance between them and Stryx.

As they neared, Elowyn sensed Stryx beginning to falter, which was uncommon for the swift firedrake. With a smirk, she admired Bane's perseverance, marveling at how he managed to tire his swift opponent. Drawing level with Stryx, Elowyn found herself flying side by side with Elyria. She smirked again as she turned to face her sister, noticing a hint of shock and disbelief in Elyria's expression before it settled into neutrality.

The older sister arched her brows, her voice echoing in Elowyn's mind. *"I'm impressed... Bane's gotten faster. Have you both been holding out on me?"*

"You're probably just losing your touch," Elowyn retorted mentally, shrugging off Elyria's remark.

"Ouch. I would take that to heart, but even I know you don't believe that," Elyria countered, wearing a smug smirk.

"Goddess, your head is bigger than Bane," Elowyn scoffed, rolling her eyes.

"Now that would be a frightening sight," Elyria chuckled. *"Nothing is bigger than Bane."*

Patting the giant beast beneath her, Elowyn conceded, *"You're totally right. Nothing is bigger than Bane."*

"And nothing is faster than Stryx," Elyria added with a wink, her vain words echoing in Elowyn's mind.

As if the earlier exhaustion was a ruse, the white firedrake rocketed forward, vanishing into a curtain of clouds before them.

"Hey, that's not fair!" Elowyn exclaimed aloud this time, uselessly shouting at the empty air where her sister had been seconds before.

Now facing a wall of clouds, Elowyn grumbled as she leaned down. "Come on, Bane. Let's get 'em."

~

ELOWYN KNEW BANE LOATHED THE IDEA OF DEFEAT, SO SHE was confident he'd rise to the challenge. Together, they plunged into the billowing white clouds in pursuit of the other two. Amidst the clouds, their vision blurred by the dense mist, they pressed forward. Despite the obscurity, Elowyn caught sight of Stryx's bristly tail, spurring Bane to accelerate and close the gap. As they drew nearer, Elowyn could distinguish Stryx's form and her sister's silhouette. She had a sense that Bane would emerge victorious today.

Just as Bane was on the verge of overtaking Stryx, the duo veered sharply upwards and vanished from view. Bewildered, Elowyn scanned the sky, her thoughts racing as she speculated her sister's intentions—but she realized her mistake too late.

Emerging from the foggy clouds, Elowyn and Bane were met with a towering mountain ahead, mere seconds away from to crashing into it. Panic gripped her as she scrambled to devise a plan to avert disaster. *Was that always here? How come I've never noticed it before?*

Bane's massive frame made it impossible for him to mimic Stryx's upward arc. With the mountain looming ahead, their only recourse was to descend rapidly. But before Elowyn could react, Bane took matters into his own fate. He folded his wings tightly against his body and dove sharply downward.

The sudden descent threw Elowyn off balance, and despite her desperate attempts to hold on, she began to slip from Bane's back. She clung to his spikes with all her strength, but the force of the drop was unrelenting. Her body gradually lifted away from him until she was left dangling in mid-air, her arms straining to keep her tethered.

Fighting against the pull of gravity, Elowyn struggled to regain her position. As Bane banked left towards a clear patch of sky, she seized the opportunity to swing her legs back around his spine and pull herself back onto his back. With a sigh of relief, she settled back into place as Bane leveled off, narrowly avoiding the mountain.

Cursing under her breath, Elowyn shook off the rush of adrenaline. Elyria's antics bristled her. Scanning her surroundings, Elowyn spotted a streak of white bursting from the narrowly-missed mountain's peak. Stryx emerged into view and Elyria wore a wide grin. As Elowyn

The Divine Shallows

watched, the mountain began to fade away, dissolving into a shimmering mirage.

"You have no shame!" Elowyn jabbed her finger accusingly at Elyria. "Summoning an illusion like that is beyond low, even for you!"

"If you paid attention, you would've noticed something was off. I conjured an entire mountain, for Goddess' sake," Elyria tutted loudly. "Anyway, Stryx and I have a finish line to reach. See you there!" With a chuckle, Elyria flew off.

As her opponents took off, Elowyn crossed her arms and muttered to Bane, "So much for integrity. I guess we'll have to abandon ours, too."

The two of them surged forward. Bane's wings beat thunderously with grit, and he released an ear-splitting cry. Beneath Elowyn's touch, the column of his throat began to rumble and grow warm. The base of his neck began to smolder with the glow of burning coals and Elowyn smiled when she realized what he had planned. Bane reeled his neck back and released a blazing pillar from his throat that shot towards Elyria and Stryx. The inferno scorched the skies, aimed directly at them.

As the fire approached, Elyria yelped and huddled closer to Stryx, who skillfully dodged the flames. Bane huffed victoriously, knowing his tactic would slow his opponents. Though Stryx was immune to fire, Elyria was not. In the chaos of shielding her, Stryx was thrown off course, providing Bane with the opportunity he needed. With a powerful thrust, Bane launched himself towards Stryx, his massive body colliding with the white dragon as he sent his competitors careening, plummeting downwards.

Elowyn cheered triumphantly with a fist thrust into the air and laughed, "Way to go, Bane!"

As Stryx and Elyria struggled to regain control, Elowyn soared past them with Bane, heading towards the Bay of Stags, leaving her sister trailing behind.

"I'll make a deal with you," Elowyn giggled to Bane, patting his hide proudly. "If her eyebrows are singed off, I'll make sure the butcher serves you an extra portion of mutton tonight."

Bane responded with a deep rumble of approval and the two of them sailed onward for a long stretch of sky.

As they soared, Elowyn checked behind her from time to time to see if Elyria and Stryx had caught up to them, but Bane's tactic must have slowed them down significantly because they were nowhere to be found. The corner of Elowyn's lips curved up as she took in the view around her.

There was nothing quite like soaring the mountains of Eriden on a dragon—nothing would ever come close to it.

As they approached their destination, a mountainside covered in foliage came into view. Elowyn recognized the landscape, knowing they were almost there. Elowyn could see hundreds of small sprigs rooted in the soil; their bare branches grew in patterns resembling smooth antlers. This stretch of terrain was aptly named the Bay of Stags.

Bane dipped down, aiming for an area free of branches. With a deliberate beat of his wings, he landed gently on the ground.

Filled with excitement, Elowyn jumped off Bane and rushed to embrace his chest in a hug. Her arms barely wrapped around his torso, but she pressed the side of her face against his rugged breastbone.

"We did it, Bane!" Elowyn exclaimed to the dragon with glee. "Looks like we finally beat them this time."

Suddenly, Elyria emerged from a grove of trees behind Elowyn. "Took you long enough, I was starting to get bored waiting for you both," she remarked flatly.

Elowyn whirled around in disbelief. "No! When did you get here?"

"A while ago," Elyria replied, skipping towards them with an innocent smile. "My eyebrows are intact, by the way. But I think Bane deserves an extra portion of mutton regardless."

Elowyn shook her head in betrayal. "I don't even want to know how you heard that. And you're a real wretch for letting me believe I won."

"I didn't want to ruin your fun," Elyria said sympathetically. "You seemed so happy."

"I was, until now. I guess you win again, you dirty little cheat," Elowyn declared.

"In a week's time, I'll be hauled away for the next seven years. Can't blame me for wanting to show off a bit before then. I had to remind you of who the better dragon rider is while I still can," Elyria teased.

Elowyn groaned in response. "Don't remind me. You're just going to make me even sadder than I already am."

"Trust me, I don't understand it either," Elyria sighed, wandering further into the mountainside. She eventually found a towering pine tree, sitting down beneath it with her back against the trunk, pulling her legs up to her chest and resting her forearms on her knees.

Lost in thought, Elyria plucked a wildflower from the ground and began twirling it between her fingers, which prompted Elowyn to join her.

As the sisters conversed, Stryx emerged from behind a curtain of trees and ambled over to Bane. The two firedrakes lingered near the cliffside and nested comfortably in a patch of grass as they both lounged serenely, sunlight bathing their scales.

Years prior, the sisters had stumbled upon this secluded spot when they were younger. One evening, while riding atop Stryx in search of a sunset-viewing spot, they passed over this area. Elowyn, very young at the time, pointed excitedly at the trees below, mistaking their shadows for antlered stags.

Despite Elyria's attempts to explain that they were just trees, Elowyn insisted on seeing for herself. Elyria, unable to deny her sister, landed, and Elowyn came to realize her mistake. Disappointed, she declared the area their sister headquarters, a secret base camp just for them. The Bay of Stags became a sanctuary away from home, a place they often sought solace.

"We both knew this was coming when my name was called seven years ago," Elyria reminded Elowyn.

"Right…" Elowyn mumbled and then questioned, "Speaking of, have you decided what you're going to do for the *Vitus* on the Sixth Day?"

"I have something planned. You'll just have to wait and see," Elyria replied.

During the Sixth Day of the weeklong Ceremony leading up to the Trial of Caena, the seven Goddess-chosen candidates participate in a ritual known as the *Vitus*. It's a display of power, intelligence, or ability for a chance to be named the *primis* of the current divine season.

Over the centuries, Neramyran nobility had turned the *Vitus* into a competition between candidates and their respective kingdoms. Like all noble courts, news traveled like wildfire. The more impressive the *Vitus* is, historically, the better the chance of becoming *primis* is. This presentation of power set the precedent for the next iteration of divine magic wielders.

"Spare me a clue?" Elowyn pleaded, pinching her thumb and finger together pitifully. "Pretty please?"

"I would, but it's my only upper hand during this season's Trial," Elyria responded grimly.

"I understand," Elowyn said, then added, "The seven realms will be shocked when you become *primis* this season."

Elyria scoffed, "We'll see. Sometimes, I wish my name was never spoken. It would be easier that way."

"Even without being moon-blessed in the Divine Shallows, you are a royal candidate. That counts for something. Every kingdom in Neramyr understands the power behind that title," Elowyn insisted.

"That may be, but I won't hold my breath," Elyria responded, stone-faced.

It troubled Elowyn to see her sister so on edge, but she understood why. The Moon Goddess had dealt Elyria a cruel hand at birth, and this was her only chance to overcome it.

Since the beginning of the New Age, children of royal blood had always been blessed by the Goddess. So, when reports of an unblessed Fangwright plagued Neramyr, the slew of speculations and conjectures concerning the Fangwright bloodline tormented the fey of Eriden. It made Elyria's life a labyrinth of pitfalls without any means to escape. Elowyn knew that Elyria fought each day to break free of the oppressive shackles that weighed her down. With every spell she mastered, with each class of magic she excelled in, and with all the training she labored through, it was all to strip herself of her tainted reputation.

Elowyn hoped that once Elyria emerged from the Bridge Between Worlds, and she earned the ability to wield divine magic, that she would finally be able to find the happiness she deserved. Without the senseless scorn that had followed Elyria from birth, maybe she could finally be seen as more than just her cursed fate.

"I know," Elowyn answered. "This time it's going to be different."

As Elyria leaned further back on the tree trunk, Elowyn moved to rest her head on her sister's shoulder.

"I'm going to miss you, you know. For the past nineteen years, we've spent almost every day together," Elyria whispered.

"It's going to be different around here without you," Elowyn replied glumly.

"It's funny you say that. When you were born moon-blessed, everything changed for me. It was like all of Eriden found hope in you again after I brought the darkest era. Life became endurable, and didn't wake up miserable every day. You became my best friend, and above all, I finally wasn't alone anymore," Elyria confessed.

Elowyn's heart ached at the sincerity of her sister's words, but what Elyria didn't know was that she was petrified to her core. For nineteen years, Elowyn had always faced the world with Elyria's guiding hand,

and now she would have to navigate it all on her own. The simple truth was Elyria already knew what it felt like to be alone, but Elowyn never had, and she certainly was not ready to.

4

The Fanged King, The Clever Queen, and The Heir of Nothing

Having breakfast together was a rare occasion, and the tension in the royal dining hall was intolerable. Elowyn sat beside her sister, with their father and mother seated across from them. Despite the spaciousness of the hall, designed to accommodate sixteen guests, the four occupants seemed oddly outnumbered. Most days, the royal dining hall remained empty, a stark contrast to its lavish decor. Their father was engrossed in ruling their kingdom, while their mother managed affairs in the courts, leaving the sisters largely to their own devices. However, that was not to say they were left without expectations.

The table before them was laden with Eriden's finest delicacies. Plates adorned with sweet berries, dried apricots, and sugared pears mingled with dishes of broiled potatoes, seasoned squash, and sauced turnips. Silver serving trays held an array of meats that tantalized the senses. Despite the opulent spread, Elowyn and her older sister appeared disinterested, appearing as if they would rather be anywhere else at the moment.

Any occasion where the royal Fangwright family gathered never turned out well.

The king of Eriden broke the silence, his voice domineering. "Elyria, you are to begin your Trial in a week's time," he declared, then turned his gaze to Elowyn. "And Elowyn, you are to be named as a divine candidate for the next season's Trial."

He spoke in statements rather than questions and both of the sisters elected not to speak.

The king helped himself to the food, filling his plate with a variety of fruits, vegetables, and meats. He signaled for a servant to pour him wine, then rolled up the tunic of his cream-colored sleeves and began to eat. Meanwhile, the queen, Elyria, and Elowyn sat in silence and the only sounds in the hall were the clinking of silver against porcelain.

"Eriden's reputation has waned since Elyria's birth," King Eamon remarked, seemingly oblivious to Elyria's presence. "The Moon Goddess has granted Elyria another chance to redeem her faults, and furthermore, she has chosen to bless Elowyn with the first Mark." He continued eating. "Among the seven houses of Neramyr, House Fangwright has always stood as a behemoth in comparison to the others. In this lifetime, I will not allow the debasement of the Fangwright name and bloodline."

Taking a sip of his wine and draining the glass, King Eamon continued, "Elowyn, you will one day bear the weight of the Fangwright crown. It is no trivial matter. You were chosen as the next heir of Eriden in your sister's stead—A fate was decided by the Goddess' hand." He wiped his mouth with a cloth. "With the uncertainty surrounding Elyria's completion of the Trial of Caena and return from the Bridge Between Worlds, it is you who must bear the responsibility of ruling this kingdom when I am no longer in this realm."

Elowyn had no idea what possessed her to speak. Her usual inclination was to remain silent when her father spoke, yet she found herself compelled to ask, "What if the Goddess does not choose me on the Seventh Day?"

In Neramyr, as the Seventh Day of the Ceremony of Caena drew to a close, the High Priestess would announce the next seven candidates chosen by Caena to partake in her Trial.

Elowyn understood that her name might not be called on the Seventh Day simply by virtue of her royal blood and first Mark. Elyria served as living proof that the Goddess determined all fates, but if tradition held this season, Elowyn's candidacy was certain.

"You are of royal blood and bear the first Mark—the Moon Goddess *will* select you as a candidate in the upcoming Trial of Caena. This divine alignment will prove as an opportunity for the Fangwright lineage to assert its reputation among the seven realms," King Eamon avowed.

Elowyn acquiesced her father with a stiff nod.

The king's demeanor darkened. "In Neramyr's history, never has a royal child been deemed as unworthy by the Moon Goddess as Elyria. Her unblessed status continues to tarnish the Fangwright name and brings disgrace upon the seven realms. Hence, these upcoming years are crucial for restoring Eriden's eminence."

Turning to Elyria, he continued, "From the moment you emerged unmarked from the Divine Shallows, you have been a disappointment. If it were up to me, I would have ordered your execution as an infant to spare the agony our kingdom has endured at the hands of your existence."

Elyria's gaze fell to the table, her expression empty.

The king opened his mouth to speak once more but was cut off.

"Enough," Queen Eddra intervened. "Elyria is a princess of Eriden, and I will not have her name marred by the mouth of a scorned king."

King Eamon stared at his wife, his tone devoid of emotion. "Eddra, you must have forgotten that it was I who granted you your title as queen. If it were not for me, you would be nothing but another lowborn sorceress. It would be wise to remember your place. It is because of you that our kingdom's reputation is marred. Your cursed womb caused the downfall of Eriden."

With that, the king rose from the table and left the dining hall, his departure marked by the fading echoes of his boots. Three pairs of eyes filled with hatred followed his silhouette until he vanished from sight.

Afterward, Queen Eddra remained silent as she briefly brushed a moon-inked palm against Elyria's hand. Her gaze seemed distant, almost absent, as she rose from the dining table with a dignified step. The queen departed the dining hall, leaving the two sisters alone.

Elowyn cast a worried glance at her sister, trying to discern her emotions. "Are you all right?"

Elyria stayed silent for a while before finally whispering, "No."

Elowyn observed as Elyria quietly stood up, pushing her chair back into place, and without another word, left the dining hall.

∽

LEFT ALONE WITH HER TROUBLING THOUGHTS, ELOWYN SAT in silence, her face buried in her palms, and her stomach tied in knots from the unsettling interaction that had just unfolded.

Once, Elowyn had believed in her parents' love for each other, convinced that they shared a genuine bond. As a feyling, she had been captivated by the story of their romance. Their love was a tale that had been passed down through fables and song for centuries leading up to Elyria's birth. Despite being born to the very heart of these legendary tales, Elowyn never found these retellings to be true.

The stories of the Fanged King and his beloved maiden had been regaled to Elowyn countless times during her childhood. According to legend, the Moon Goddess had chosen a lowborn sorceress, Eddra, over the Fangwright king's own brother, the prince, during the Seventh Day

—the day of divine selection. Eddra had gone on to excel in her Trial, becoming the *primis* of her cohort and earning the final Mark of the Moon Goddess. Her extraordinary magical abilities had captivated King Eamon Fangwright, leading to their union and her eventual ascension to the throne as queen of Eriden.

For centuries, the Fanged King and his maiden, the Clever Queen, lived in bliss, ruling Eriden side by side.

Unbeknownst to the fey of Eriden, an era of humiliation would befall their kingdom as two of the strongest rulers in Eriden's history welcomed their firstborn child. Hours after the folk of Eriden celebrated their heir's birth, the feasting and reveling turned into mourning and mania. Whispers spread like wildfire, claiming that the princess of Eriden had been born without the blessing of the Moon Goddess—the Fanged King and the Clever Queen produced an Heir of Nothing. Throughout the seven realms, speculations ran wild as the fey sought to comprehend the inexplicable absence of the divine blessing. Chaotic theories ran rampant to justify the calamity.

Some blamed the lowborn queen, accusing her of being cursed for outmaneuvering the royal-blooded prince, the brother of the Fanged King, during her season's Seventh Day. Others alleged it was because the lowborn queen became manic with greed and stole the magic from the infant for herself. Elowyn knew that these acts of defamation and libel disparaged her father greatly. Over the years, her father's contempt for the reputation of his kingdom and his first true-born daughter boiled over until he became bitter and rancorous through and through.

Elowyn was born seven years after Elyria. She often pondered the circumstances of her conception, wondering if it had been an act of passionate hatred or merely a duty-bound obligation. To the astonishment of her parents, Elowyn emerged from the ceremonial waters bearing the first Mark, setting her apart from her sister. Consequently, her father always favored her over Elyria.

As a result of Elowyn's birth, her father committed a grave act of betrayal against Elyria. Upon learning that his second true-born daughter bore the first Mark, he stripped Elyria of her title as Crown Heir and declared Elowyn as the rightful heir to the throne of Eriden.

This proclamation by the king of Eriden initially caused uproar across the seven realms, with many viewing it as a betrayal and an affront to his own daughter. However, the Fangwright King skillfully spun a narrative of unwavering devotion to Caena, asserting that the Goddess herself had chosen Elowyn over Elyria. Gradually, allegiance to the Moon Goddess prevailed over traditional notions of royal succession.

The fey of Neramyr ultimately accepted this narrative, reasoning that Caena had blessed Elowyn to rule in Elyria's place. However, Elowyn despised the idea of becoming the next queen of Eriden. Not only was it Elyria's birthright to inherit the Fanged Throne, but Eriden would be better for it.

∼

ELOWYN'S FOOTSTEPS ECHOED DOWN THE MARBLED walkway as she made her way back to her bedchamber. Along the castle halls, she paused to gaze out from one of the elegant stone arched balconies that lined her path. Wandering to the nearest balcony, she leaned against the ledge, her hands resting upon it as she gazed at the scenery before her.

The vista presented a breathtaking skyline, painted with hues of deep blues streaked with wisps of white. The peaks of Eriden's mountains stretched out in jagged lines, framing the landscape with their rugged, asymmetrical contours. Atop these majestic peaks, forests and verdant foliage speckled the sharp summits, while clouds drifted gracefully around them.

Despite having spent her entire life here, Elowyn found herself continuously awestruck by the beauty of her kingdom.

Eriden was truly remarkable.

The Divine Shallows

Elowyn's thoughts mulled over what her father claimed about her fate in the dining hall earlier. Despite never previously dwelling on the implications of the Seventh Day and her supposed divine candidacy, she couldn't shake the feeling that her participation in this season's Trial of Caena was inevitable.

It seemed almost too coincidental that, for the first time in Neramyr's history, each of the seven realms would have a royal offspring eligible to participate in the divine Trial. Elowyn felt the circumstances were too cryptic to be coincidence. Speculations swirled throughout the feylands, suggesting that the upcoming divine season would produce the most formidable wielders of divine magic in Neramyr's history. Elowyn and her fellow royal candidates were now referred to as the 'sacred seven'.

Elowyn couldn't help but furrow her brows in confusion—the mysteries surrounding her destiny and the fate of the seven realms weighed heavily on her mind.

In Neramyr, the number seven held sacred significance. Seven original warlocks and sorceresses, seven kingdoms, and every seven years, seven new divine magic wielders were chosen by the Goddess. *Seven, seven, seven.* Elowyn couldn't comprehend how fate had singled her out to be part of this mystifying septet.

Each divine season, Caena opened the gates to her realm to select seven candidates for her Trial. If successfully completed, they would be granted the ability to wield her divine magic. Crucially, each of the seven candidates hailed from a different kingdom within Neramyr's heptarchy.

Historically, when monarchs of royal houses produced an heir, that heir would be chosen by the Goddess to participate in the subsequent Trial, if of age. However, in cases where a ruler lacked an eligible heir, a highborn individual from the court would be selected by Caena instead. Occasionally, even lowborn fey were chosen by the Goddess to become divine warlocks or sorceresses.

In Neramyran history, there had been only one instance where a non-royal fey was chosen over a full-blooded royal fey for candidacy in the Trial of Caena. This exception was Elowyn's mother, Eddra. Elowyn had heard tales of how this decision had shaken Neramyr to its core. Despite her Uncle Edwyn, the prince of Eriden, being selected for the Trial in the following season, her mother's candidacy had cast a shadow over his reputation as a powerful warlock.

Prince Edwyn Fangwright seldom visited Eriden, preferring to spend his time in the Elune Isles with his firedrake, enjoying the majesty of the Swyn Sea. The mountains of Eriden held little appeal for him. It seemed that all the Fangwrights surrounding Elowyn were powerful and influential. She knew that during her Trial all of Neramyr would be waiting to see if she could live up to her bloodline.

The days were dwindling down until Elowyn would have to begin serious preparations and training for her divine candidacy. It was no secret that Elyria was far more powerful than Elowyn at her age, despite not being moon-blessed. Elyria excelled in every endeavor; her native magic surpassed that of most fey.

Elowyn suspected that this was why her father harbored such resentment towards Elyria. If she had been blessed by the Moon Goddess at birth, her power would have been unmatched. She could have elevated Eriden's status even further, solidifying their position as the foremost among the seven realms. Instead, Elyria remained unmarked, unblessed. Perhaps Caena had deemed it too risky for any single fey to wield such immense power. Elowyn often wondered how strong Elyria would become once she emerged from the Bridge Between Worlds.

In Neramyr, magic was tantamount to power. Since the inception of the New Age, fey born with the gift of magic were hailed as warlocks or sorceresses. For these individuals, magic flowed within them from birth, a native aura that defined their very existence.

This native magic varied in potency and scope, depending on the individual. Some fey could only perform simple spells, like moving objects or conjuring a beam of light. However, others possessed more powerful native magic, capable of weaving intricate spells that could alter perceptions, summon elemental storms, or even enchant other beings to obey their will.

While native magic was impressive, divine magic eclipses it in both potency and rarity. Divine magic not only amplified and enhanced a wielder's native abilities, but also granted them access to a separate, exclusive form of magic bestowed solely by the Moon Goddess. This magic was a tier of power reserved for those handpicked by Caena. Its distinction was even more profound than the divide between nobility and common fey.

One's magical prowess was gauged by the presence of their aura and Elowyn was well-aware that her aura fell short.

Elowyn diverted her gaze from the sky, frowning as she scrutinized her moon-blessed palms. From birth, Caena had chosen to imprint her divine Mark upon her, yet with each passing day, Elowyn found herself questioning the Goddess' judgment a bit more. She was aware that she hadn't been born with an exceptional gift of native magic—the extent of her magical abilities was merely average.

Elowyn's thoughts poured over her struggles with basic summoning spells and defensive wards, feeling the weight of her limitations. Despite her efforts to improve her magic through training, she found herself constantly straining and exerting herself just to achieve minimal progress.

Elyria had always claimed that her native magic felt like an extension of herself, a comfort that came as easily to her as breathing. This fueled Elowyn's frustration and resentment towards the forces that overlooked and disregarded Elyria's skill.

Shock surged through the seven realms when Elyria's name was called out by the High Priestess nearly seven years ago. Many doubted her abilities due to her unblessed status, and some even believed her selection was a waste of a coveted slot in the Trial. Even her own father shared these doubts.

Elowyn's hands tightened on the balcony ledge; her troubling thoughts officially splintered her spirits. She couldn't shake the worry over Elyria's wellbeing after this morning's encounter with their father. The looming reality of Elyria's departure for seven years gnawed at her, leaving her feeling lost.

Elyria had been more than just a sister; she was Elowyn's mentor, protector, and closest confidant. Elowyn admired her sister's strength and wisdom, hoping to become even a fraction of the sorceress her sister was.

With a heavy heart, Elowyn released her grip on the ledge and turned away from the calming vista, determined to seek out her sister. As she made her way through the castle corridors, she couldn't help but feel like she was always following in Elyria's footsteps, chasing after the shadow her sister left behind to follow.

5

Night Omens

On the eve of the Ceremony, under the glow of a full moon, Elowyn found herself ensnared in a fever dream. Her body tossed and turned, trapped in the grip of haunting memories from seven years prior.

In her restless slumber, she relived the moment when the High Priestess had announced Elyria's candidacy on the Seventh Day of last season's Trial.

The dream began with Elowyn fidgeting uncomfortably in the ornate dress her mother had insisted she wear for the evening's event. Throughout the past six days of the Ceremony, she had been confined to similarly restrictive outfits, despite only attending the First and Seventh Day this season. She could still hear her mother's words echoing in her mind, "Dressing well is a form of power and stature, Elowyn. Present yourself as a statement to be remembered."

Standing behind her mother and father near the Divine Shallows, Elowyn was in a winsome gown. The skirts of her dress boasted rich hues of burgundy, maroon, and crimson, cascading down her form like silk petals and pooling around her feet in layers of fabric.

Beside her, stood Elyria, dressed in a gown twin to her own, but the fabric was a shade of dark obsidian. The dress was powerful, haunting even, as it seemed to extinguish the light that surrounded it. Both sisters wore silver circlets on their heads embellished with a singular opal at the crest.

Draped over their shoulders and down their backs were golden cloaks embroidered with dragon scales, known as *aureum* in Neramyr. These cloaks, a customary attire for royalty, served to distinguish them as descendants of the seven founding fey.

At the young age of twelve, Elowyn was witnessing the Ceremony of Caena for the first time. Her mother had explained that today marked the final and most important day of the Ceremony—the day where the chosen candidates would traverse across the Bridge Between Worlds.

Elowyn surveyed the hallowed Temple that surrounded her. It was crowded and filled with noblefolk and distinguished members of the seven courts. Yet, her attention was captivated by the other royal fey that possessed divine markings upon the surface of their skin.

Standing quietly, Elowyn observed the kings and queens that ruled the seven realms of Neramyr.

First among them was a striking sorceress with sharp, angular features and hair as dark as midnight. Her porcelain skin and eyes akin to radiant rubies commanded attention as she moved gracefully. Beside her stood a male of taller stature, sharing her shade of hair, skin, and eyes.

Adorning their heads were intricate crowns embellished with garnets, symbols of their kingdom's wealth from the Iron Hollows. Both monarchs wore *aureum* cloaks decorated with patterns resembling basilisk scales, while the iridescent markings etched onto their skin shared a similar pattern. These two monarchs were King Wilden and Queen Irena of House Bloodweaver.

Shifting her gaze, Elowyn observed the regal figures of King Dren and Queen Maeva of House Mirthwood, rulers of Lochwald. Standing proudly beside them was their son, the prince of Mirthwood.

All three royal fey exuded their own unique beauty. Their umber skin radiated warmth, complemented by eyes of bold and assured charcoal hues. Queen Maeva wore a silver circlet atop her head, her tight curls fell in small ringlets down her back. Beside her, King Dren possessed the robust physique of a seasoned warrior.

House Mirthwood was known for their skill in combat and abjuration magic. The monarchs bore shimmering ivory markings resembling crawling vines and leaves, gracefully patterning their arms in curls. Their son, akin to Elowyn, bore no moonlight ink upon his skin save for his palms. Despite his youth, he carried an air of maturity beyond his years. All three wore golden *aureum* emblazoned with a grimwolf encircled by coiling vines.

Next in line were the rulers of Prymont, from House Skyborn. Elowyn had always harbored a hint of envy toward those born into this house—if lucky enough to inherit it, fey of House Skyborn possessed wings. The wings varied in length, size, and shape, with females typically bearing smaller, more ethereal wings, while males boasted wider, robust ones. Elowyn's gaze fixed upon Queen Emilyn Skyborn, whose honeyed hair fell between her silver wings. Her eyes, a brilliant amethyst, gleamed against her complexion.

Beside her, King Nolas Skyborn possessed a formidable pair of gray wings, nearly touching the ground even in their tucked position. His brown hair was paired with emerald-green eyes, a complement to his markings resembling rippling clouds and streaks of lightning. Standing between the two rulers was their daughter, Princess Syrilla Skyborn.

Elowyn's first encounter with the Skyborn princess occurred during a visit to the kingdom of Prymont as a feyling. The same age as Syrilla, Elowyn cried to her mother and father, longing for wings to soar among the mountain peaks like Bane and Stryx. Though older now, Elowyn still felt a pang of envy for the Skyborn lineage's aerial gift. Clasped from the Skyborn monarch's shoulders, draped golden *aureum* depicting an embroidered sky, their cloaks curving deeply at the small of their back to accommodate their wings.

Continuing her observations, Elowyn spotted the monarchs of Erimead: King Balt and Queen Nyra of House Blackbane. Their kingdom, adjacent to Eriden, shared a similar mountainous terrain, separated only by a vast channel of water. Elowyn was familiar with the tales of their twin sons, Lox and Llyr Blackbane, often glimpsing them riding ophis across the Erimead ranges. These ophis, winged serpents, were smaller than Eriden's firedrakes. They piqued Elowyn's curiosity, fueling her desire to one day ride one. However, her parents remained cautious about her visiting Erimead without a formal invitation.

The Blackbane twins, with their silken onyx hair, bore a striking resemblance to one another save for one distinguishing feature: one set of eyes were a heterochromic sapphire blue and emerald green. Each member of the Blackbane royalty outfitted themselves with golden *aureum* depicting a baleful ophis with outstretched wings.

Then, her gaze fell upon the monarchs of the Elune Isles, King Tydred and Queen Aletta Driftmoor. Their tanned complexion radiated with the glow of their coastal realm. The Driftmoor royals had a single daughter, the princess of Driftmoor, whom Elowyn had yet to acquaint herself with. Stories of the Elune Isles' marvels had reached Elowyn's ears, and perhaps these very stories influenced her uncle's departure from Eriden to the Isles three years ago.

Legend had it that in the Elune Isles, the sun never waned, and the sea stretched endlessly in crystal blue. The king and queen bore ivory markings reminiscent of rolling ocean waves. Elowyn hoped to one day visit their sun-drenched kingdom. The Driftmoor royals wore golden *aureum* depicting the ocean and a surfacing loch hydra—a sinister sea serpent.

Lastly, her attention turned to the monarchs of Orwyn, King Kyrus and Queen Nikoletta of House Darkmaw. The Darkmaw lineage was distinguished by their deep claret-red hair, akin to the Fangwrights' snow-colored locks. Elowyn observed as the king and queen engaged in a quiet, intimate exchange, their skin covered with moonlit strokes resembling wisps of smoke. Their *aureum* were embroidered with the feathers of wicked winged griffons, a symbol of their lineage's power and prowess.

Their son, the prince of Orwyn, was spectating the royalty in the Temple just as Elowyn was. She observed him fidgeting with his hands, and noticed the two crescent moons inked on his palms. Suddenly, as if sensing her gaze, the prince looked up, locking eyes with Elowyn. Startled, she quickly averted her gaze to the floor, feeling a flush of embarrassment wash over her. When she dared to glance up again, she found him still looking at her. With a friendly dimpled smile, the prince waved, prompting Elowyn to timidly return the gesture, her cheeks still tinged with embarrassment.

Her attention shifted as the claret-haired prince turned his focus to the High Priestess. Stepping into the Divine Shallows, the High Priestess waded to the center of the celestial waters, commanding the attention of all those present in the temple.

"Kings and queens, princes and princesses, fey of Neramyr," she began, her voice echoing through the sacred space, "We are gathered here today on this next iteration of the seventh year to witness the Trial of Caena once more. Today marks the Seventh Day, a sacred day upon which Caena opens the gates to her realm to accept seven children of the moon into her Trial.

"These seven candidates are granted the opportunity to traverse the Bridge Between Worlds and seek divine judgment. Should they prove successful in their quest for ascendancy, the Goddess will bestow upon them her sacred Mark and grant them divine magic to wield in Neramyr. May we ask the Goddess for her benevolence to guide them across the Bridge Between Worlds and welcome them safely into her realm."

The High Priestess pivoted towards the audience encircling the Divine Shallows, acknowledging each monarch of the seven realms with a nod. Her gaze returned forward, her eyes turning a translucent white hue, veiled by a mystical force. Motionless, she stood amidst the thrumming energy of the Temple, her ivory markings glowing faintly along her arms.

As the divine waters at her feet stirred, the air within the Temple crackled with energy.

"It's time. We must begin," the High Priestess declared.

In unison, the kings and queens of the seven realms advanced towards the Divine Shallows, their upturned palms radiating with power. Their unique markings upon their skin shimmered with intensity, mirroring the luminosity of the High Priestess' own.

From her vantage point behind them, Elowyn beheld the transformation of her parents' markings as they illuminated. The opalescent dragon scales adorning their skin bloomed with moonlit radiance, enveloping them in a brilliant aura. She watched in awe as a profound sense of belonging washed over her, permeating the air with pure divine energy.

Amidst the chanting of the High Priestess in the ancient tongue of the original fey, the waters beneath her grew turbulent, swirling and rippling around her feet. Within the Temple, anticipation mounted as the assembled fey witnessed the High Priestess and the monarchs of Neramyr channeling their divine magic towards the waters.

Elowyn found herself captivated by the display of magic, her breath catching in her throat as she watched. The High Priestess' incantations ceased with the swirling and seething of the Divine Shallows, signaling the opening of the gates to Caena's realm.

The High Priestess announced, "It is time for the chosen to cross the Bridge Between Worlds! The seven candidates must step forward into the Divine Shallows."

As the High Priestess' words echoed through the temple, Elowyn witnessed seven warlocks and sorceresses, barely older than herself, stepping into the Divine Shallows. Each candidate positioned themselves on a circular tile within the sacred waters, their moon-blessed palms glowing with energy. Forming an outer circle around the High Priestess, they awaited her command.

With the candidates settled into place, the High Priestess addressed them once more. "You seven have been chosen by the Moon Goddess to participate in her divine Trial, and the gates between our realms are now open. The time to cross the Bridge Between Worlds and face Caena's judgment has arrived!"

Elowyn watched as the candidates exchanged tense glances. Suddenly, she noticed one of the warlocks' tiles swelling with water, and before she could blink, he darted forward with a wicked grin. With a swift movement, he disappeared into the shimmering depths of the Divine Shallows, vanishing from sight.

Elowyn could no longer see the warlock's form, but she felt his presence fade from Neramyr.

"Let us celebrate the first candidate to traverse the Bridge Between Worlds! It is with great pride that I announce your *primis*, Prince Thomys Bloodweaver of the Iron Hollows!" The temple echoed with cheers, and Elowyn glimpsed the elation on King Wilden and Queen Irena's faces as their son achieved this feat.

As the remaining candidates awaited their turns, Elowyn observed them vanish one by one into the Divine Shallows, until a single sorceress remained. She watched as panic flickered in the sorceress's eyes, realizing she was the last to cross into Caena's realm. With bated breath, Elowyn witnessed the sorceress lunge forward as the water stirred beneath her, disappearing alongside her companions.

Even after the candidates had vanished, Elowyn's gaze remained fixed on the Divine Shallows.

The High Priestess' palms glowed as she began to speak. Upturning her palms and raising them slightly, moonlight crept along her arms in glowing vines, illuminating the eight phases of the moon etched on her time-worn skin. The stream of moonlight continued to inch up her arms and gently trailed around her throat, encircling it, the light halting right before her lips.

"As the Seventh Day draws to a close, the Moon Goddess has made her choice. It is time for me to reveal her selection for the next seven candidates worthy of partaking in the following Trial of Caena."

Once more, the High Priestess' eyes veiled behind a translucent film, and a soft stream of moonlight fell from her lips. The current flowed down her body and illuminated the waters of the Divine Shallows below.

Though the High Priestess' lips remained still, her voice was joined with another as it echoed within Elowyn's mind. She felt a profound sense of power emanating from it. It spoke in the ancient tongue of Neramyr, in harmony with the High Priestess.

"Since the dawn of the New Age, every seventh year brings forth seven candidates chosen to face Caena's judgment in her divine Trial. The Goddess of the Moon has made her selection, with one candidate hailing from each kingdom."

Eager feet shuffled and tense shoulders awaited the announcement. Elowyn understood the rarity of this opportunity; to wield divine magic set one apart, transforming them from merely mundane to truly exceptional.

Once more, the resonant voice filled Elowyn's mind, announcing, "We shall now reveal the seven candidates chosen for the upcoming Trial of Caena."

Across from Elowyn, she observed a slender figure with soft lavender hair, her eyes widening as her palms began to glow.

The Divine Shallows

The voice continued, "Iva Rosefall, sworn to House Skyborn, step forth into the Divine Shallows and claim your candidacy."

With a trace of surprise, the lavender-haired fey made her way toward the Divine Shallows. Gracefully, she extended one foot over the edge of the stone, dipping it into the shimmering waters. As she advanced toward a circular stone depicting the sigil of House Skyborn, a phoenix, the waters rippled in her wake. Approaching the stone, Iva gazed at the intricate tiled phoenix, inhaling deeply before stepping within its circular border. At her touch, the tile shimmered in acknowledgment.

Cheers erupted from House Skyborn, celebrating their chosen candidate. Beaming with joy, Iva acknowledged her folk and the gathered fey in the Temple. Elowyn couldn't help but share in her happiness, a smile gracing her lips as she witnessed the celebration.

As the cheers began to fade, the next candidate's name echoed through the Temple.

"Galen Wolfspire, sworn to House Darkmaw, step forth into the Divine Shallows and claim your candidacy."

Once more, Elowyn watched as a claret-haired warlock entered the Divine Shallows, standing upon the stone-tile sigil of House Darkmaw. Beneath him, a black and gray gryphon lit up brilliantly, acknowledging his candidacy.

With each announcement, Elowyn observed as the chosen candidates, with their marked palms aglow, stepped forward to claim their candidacy by finding their sworn House's sigil. The candidates named thus far were Iva Rosefall sworn to House Skyborn, Galen Wolfspire sworn to House Darkmaw, Kerrick Graylon sworn to House Driftmoor, Lillia Sagebrook sworn to House Mirthwood, Lynora Lionwind sworn to House Blackbane, and Sylas Fenhart sworn to House Bloodweaver.

As the candidates from six Houses were selected, Elowyn realized that only House Fangwright remained.

Then, the ancient voice echoed once more in her mind.

"Princess Elyria Fangwright of House Fangwright, please step forward into the Divine Shallows and claim your candidacy."

Elowyn's excitement surged as she turned towards Elyria beside her, almost unable to contain herself at the mention of her older sister's name. However, her excitement waned as she noticed Elyria's clenched fists, muted and dark, devoid of the moon's blessing.

With a slow and hesitant stride, Elyria made her way over the ledge and into the Divine Shallows. An air of uncertainty surrounded her as she sought out the sigil of House Fangwright, a firedrake. Stepping onto the tiled dragon, she waited expectantly. However, to her dismay, the stone remained dull and lifeless.

A collective gasp filled the Temple as Elyria stood there in silence, her apprehension palpable.

The primordial voice echoed in Elowyn's mind one last time. "Fey of Neramyr, this marks the conclusion of the Seventh Day, let us welcome the candidates for the next season's Trial of Caena."

∼

THE MEMORY FROM SEVEN YEARS PAST RIPPED AWAY FROM Elowyn's mind, jolting her awake with a gasp, her hand instinctively reaching for her chest. She struggled to catch her breath, a throbbing headache pulsating in her temples. Tossing aside the covers, she swung her legs over the edge of the bed, the cool marble floor offering a momentary relief to her clammy skin. With a series of rapid blinks, she attempted to dispel the lingering fog that obscured her thoughts.

Sitting on the edge of her bed, a knot of unease twisted in Elowyn's stomach. She was not one to often dream, especially not in Neramyr where dreams held weighty implications. The vivid recollection of the memory unsettled her deeply—it was a day she had tried hard to bury in the recesses of her mind. It was the day she realized that while she had

The Divine Shallows

idolized her sister Elyria, the rest of Neramyr held a vastly different opinion.

The memory of that day flooded back, vivid and unwelcome. Elowyn remembered the deafening silence that engulfed the Temple after her sister's candidacy was announced. Whispers, like venomous serpents, slithered through the air, poisoning every corner of the room. The pity once reserved for Elyria morphed into shock and disdain as the fey within the temple turned their scornful gazes towards her.

On that fateful day, Elowyn recalled how her sister stood frozen in the Divine Shallows, the weight of the crowd's judgment bearing down on her. The air crackled with disbelief. In the face of the growing chorus of insults and jeers, Elyria remained silent, her fear apparent amidst the sea of hostility that surrounded her.

The Cursed Princess.

The Heir of Nothing.

The Unmarked Fangwright.

The Unblessed.

Despite the scorn of the seven realms, Elyria maintained a stoic disposition. It was only when their father, the king of Eriden, cast his gaze upon Elyria with disgust that her mask finally crumbled. A solitary tear escaped her eye, then another, until her cheeks were streaked with sorrow. Elyria's head fell to her chest as her aura shattered from the force of an entire realm against her.

Elowyn's heart shattered alongside it as she witnessed her sister's anguish. The cries of injustice caught in her throat. The fey in the temple had no right to judge her sister so harshly. They didn't know Elyria. None of them did. Elyria was Elowyn's sun, her stars, her entire world—her older sister.

Elowyn yearned to rush to Elyria's side, to shield her as Elyria had always done for her. But their father's grip held her back, leaving her powerless as she watched her sister wither under the weight of her kingdom's ire.

That night, back in Eriden, Elowyn climbed into Elyria's bed and held her as she wept. She clung to her sister, wishing she could bear some of her pain. But Elyria's tears seemed endless.

Elowyn could do nothing as she watched her older sister ache and fade into despair.

Sighing wearily, Elowyn felt this dream could only serve as an ill omen on the eve of this season's First Day.

∼

IN THE NIGHT SKY OUTSIDE ELYRIA'S WINDOW, MOONLIGHT cast its gentle glow upon the feylands. She lay in the darkness of her bedchamber, awaiting the embrace of slumber. Her gaze drifted to the silk drapes enveloping the pillars of her four-poster bed, lost in thought.

Tomorrow marked the beginning of the Ceremony of Caena. Her fingers idly traced the opal teardrop pendant adorning her neck, while she focused on the rhythmic rise and fall of her breath. Hours slipped by unnoticed as she waited for sleep to claim her, but it remained elusive.

Unsure if minutes or hours had passed, she finally broke her stoicism. Turning her head towards the window, she noticed the gentle rays of dawn filtering through the curtains.

Releasing a sigh so soft, not even a fey with golden ears could hear, Elyria sat up and swung her legs over the side of her bed and began to dress.

The First Day had begun.

6

Whispers of Kingdom Courts

As the weeklong Ceremony commenced, the kingdom of Eriden held the honor of hosting the First Day festivities. Elowyn wandered through the royal gardens of her home, dressed in a champagne gown. The gown's bodice was fashioned as a corset and the sleeves fell to her wrists while the material wrapped her chest within a curved neckline that bled into the shoulders. Elowyn looked positively radiant for the First Day.

Emphasizing her status as a princess of Neramyr, a golden cloak was clasped at her shoulders. Crafted from the finest silk in the feylands, the cloak was embroidered with a classic pattern of dragon scales, symbolizing her lineage to one of the original founders of Neramyr.

Elowyn had spent the greater part of her morning getting ready with Ora who weaved a portion of her snow-white hair into an updo. Braids intertwined at the base of her temples, forming a half-circlet atop her head, while the rest of her snowy locks cascaded in gentle waves down her back. She opted for a subtle rosy hue on her lips and a chestnut bronze blush to highlight her features. The only adornment she wore was her teardrop necklace, a cherished gift from her older sister she'd worn daily since childhood.

Half an hour had passed since Elowyn's arrival in the royal gardens, where she was patiently awaiting Elyria. However, her sister was late. This prompted Elowyn to walk along the winding paths of the impressively manicured gardens alone. For the past week, the royal castle had been flooded with event stewards, groundskeepers, servants, and cooks. Her mother spared no expense during this time as the most noteworthy members of the seven realms would gather in Eriden to witness the First Day.

Last season, the First Day had been hosted in Erimead by the monarchs of House Blackbane. It was customary for a different kingdom to undertake the responsibility of hosting each day of the weeklong ceremony each season. While the responsibility of hosting a particular day is changed, the sequence of which kingdom it is passed on to remains the same. Last season, though she was seven years younger than she is now, Elowyn still recalled the resplendence and extravagance King Balt and Queen Nyra Blackbane put forth in honor of the Goddess and the First Day. Her mother did the same, if not more, to commence the sacred weeklong ritual.

As Elowyn wandered the paths of the royal gardens, she cast a glance towards the castle entrance, anticipating the arrival of the other six royal families and various courtiers from across the seven realms. Earlier, her father had authorized the castle sentries to temporarily adjust the protective wards safeguarding the castle, accommodating entry for the guests of the First Day.

Naturally, these adjusted wards functioned to allow only invited guests entry; any unauthorized individuals trespassing on the castle grounds risked dire consequences.

During her leisurely stroll, Elowyn paused beside a dewberry tree with petite blossoms. While she appeared to be studying the delicate cream-colored petals intently, beneath the folds of her golden gown, Elowyn nervously tapped her foot. Her mother emphasized the importance of her and Elyria's presence before the arrival of the representatives from the other six kingdoms. Elowyn did not want to find out the repercussions if her sister failed to meet her mother's demands.

Her thoughts were abruptly interrupted as she sensed a looming shadow above her. Gliding gracefully through the open expanse of sky, Elowyn discerned the distinctive form of a sleek sapphire-winged firedrake silhouetted behind a patch of clouds.

Nerys.

It seemed that her Uncle Edwyn was the first to arrive in Eriden.

The sapphire dragon arced down to the royal gardens and landed before Elowyn with broad flaps from its leather-like wings. Elowyn watched her Uncle Edwyn as he swung one leg over Nerys's spine and dismounted, landing firmly on his feet. After his dismount, he patted the massive hide of the sapphire dragon and tenderly stroked her maw. Retrieving a strip of dried meat from a pocket within his cloak, he tossed it towards Nerys. With alarming speed, Nerys snatched the treat from the air and swallowed it whole. Her uncle chuckled, giving Nerys a final pat before turning his attention to Elowyn.

"By the Goddess, is that you Elowyn? Look at how much you've grown," Edwyn smiled at her. "You were just a feyling the last time I saw you."

In truth, Elowyn struggled to recall much about her uncle. She was merely nine years old when he left Eriden to reside on the coast of the Elune Isles, and this marked the first time she had seen him since the previous Ceremony seven years ago. Given Edwyn's absence from Eriden for the past decade, he had become almost a stranger to her. Elowyn was unsure how to feel about his familiarity towards her, so she instead opted for an ordinary greeting.

"Welcome home, Uncle Edwyn. I hope your journey back to Eriden fared well," Elowyn responded, then added, "It's lovely to see Nerys. She's still as beautiful as I remember."

"I managed to bypass your father's wards, so I suppose one could say my journey went smoothly enough," Edwyn chuckled with a hint of resignation. "And it seems Nerys is more thrilled than I am to be back home. She has already reunited with her two brothers."

Edwyn inclined his head in their direction, and Elowyn spotted Nerys nestled between Stryx and Bane. The trio of dragons lounged together on a dais arranged in the gardens. Elowyn suspected that this arrangement was likely organized by her father. Being greeted by three dragons—three divine *animus* no less—made a powerful statement. It was a rare occurrence for fey to encounter a firedrake, and when they did, it often stirred emotions of fear and awe.

Firedrakes were the largest *animus* that a divine fey could soul-bond to, and these sacred dragons were unique to Eriden—a point of pride for her father.

Nevertheless, Elowyn grinned at the three dragons burrowed together like songbirds in a nest. At the sight of the triplet of fire-breathing beasts cuddling, she couldn't help but feel that they were quite the companionable cadre.

"It's as if she never left," Elowyn remarked cheerfully. She suddenly felt bold. "If you don't mind me asking, Uncle Edwyn, what led to your departure for the Elune Isles so many years ago?"

Elowyn found herself quite curious. Her uncle had rarely been mentioned in conversations since his leave from Eriden. Even though he looked the part, she couldn't remember if her Uncle Edwyn were like her father, and as hard as she might, she couldn't place any concrete memories of him.

Elowyn's uncle stood at a similar height to her father, bearing the same angular features, down to the identical silver eyes and matching four-fanged smile. The only noticeable difference between her uncle and her father was their choice of hairstyle. The king of Eriden maintained shoulder-length hair, always neatly tucked behind his ears and beneath his crown, while her uncle sported a cropped style, trimmed shorter on the sides. Unfortunately, Edwyn's striking similarity to Elowyn's father already set her on edge.

When Elowyn inquired about his decade-long absence, Edwyn simply smiled. His lips began to form words but then stopped, as if he had second thoughts about sharing them. It struck Elowyn as odd to see him smile; dressed in the golden regalia of House Fangwright, he bore such a striking resemblance to her father that she had to blink a few times to dispel the illusion. She couldn't help but wonder what her father would look like if he ever allowed himself to smile.

Edwyn's aura shifted as something caught his attention behind Elowyn. It was her mother, every ounce the queen of Eriden, gliding into the royal gardens with an air of poise and dignity. Her arms were folded at her waist, hands draped one over the over. Appearing dignified as always, she approached Elowyn and Edwyn, the echoing clacks of her heels resonating on the stone pathway leading to them.

Queen Eddra wore an exquisite gown the color of rich pine, its skirts were waves of woven crepe. The bodice hugged her waist snugly, accentuated by a square neckline that complemented her elegant figure. Even with her long snow-white hair fell loosely around her, each silken strand falling into perfect place, Elowyn's mother moved with grace. Crowned with a golden diadem and draped in a floor-length *aureum*, she was a picturesque monarch.

The only mar amidst the her mother's perfection was the look of disdain etched upon her face.

Elowyn winced inwardly, knowing her mother was likely seething with anger over Elyria's absence in the royal gardens. Yet, something felt amiss. Glancing at her uncle, she noticed a similar sour expression on his face. In an attempt to avoid drawing any attention to herself, Elowyn stepped back, her anxiety mounting, creating a noticeable gap between the two royals.

"Queen Eddra," her uncle greeted the queen, his tone aloof.

"Prince Edwyn," Eddra responded, her lips tightening into a thin line as she returned his greeting. "Welcome home."

A faint furrow creased Edwyn's brow before smoothing out. Meeting her gaze squarely, he replied, "It's good to be back."

The contempt in the air was palpable as Elowyn glanced between her mother and her uncle, feeling a sense of unease. Had something transpired between them ten years ago? Or was there lingering resentment from centuries past when her mother was chosen by the Goddess over him as a divine candidate? Surely there must be some further explanation as to why the animosity between them was so profound.

Queen Eddra broke her gaze from Edwyn first as she began to depart from the royal gardens. Her only directive to Elowyn was an order, "Find Elyria immediately."

Elowyn nodded in acknowledgment as her mother's silhouette vanished within the castle walls.

Turning to her uncle, she inquired, "What was that about?"

"It's nothing, dear," Edwyn replied with a reassuring smile. Leaving Elowyn to ponder over his cryptic response, Edwyn proceeded to make his way into the castle where he had once grown up and lived.

Elowyn stood there, still processing the exchange between her mother and uncle. It was the first time she had witnessed her mother display such bitterness towards her uncle, and so openly at that. Her mother rarely revealed her emotions, resolute composure being one of her defining traits. Which meant that what happened between her mother and uncle must've been truly dreadful.

However, Elowyn understood the consequences of delving into matters that didn't concern her. The mystery surrounding her uncle's departure wasn't worth the potential fallout of prying into it.

Redirecting her thoughts towards addressing her mother's curt demand, Elowyn wondered about Elyria's whereabouts. Her older sister was never one to be tardy, especially not on the First Day—a time where

The Divine Shallows

punctuality was necessary. Just as Elowyn's concerns began to escalate, Elyria finally emerged from behind a cluster of rose bushes.

"Where have you been?" Elowyn questioned, her tone sharper than intended.

"I'm sorry, I got caught up in something..." Elyria responded, her expression reflecting genuine concern. She added, "Is everything all right?"

"Do you know what happened between mother and Uncle Edwyn?" Elowyn asked.

Elyria tilted her head in confusion. "I'm not sure. Why do you ask?"

Both sisters deemed it to be a matter of lingering grudges and decided to move past it, knowing they had more pressing concerns for the evening.

It was only during their conversation about their mother and uncle's exchange that Elowyn noticed what her older sister was wearing. A wave of déjà vu swept over her as memories of her fever dream from the previous night surged to the forefront of her mind.

Elowyn found herself staring at an older version of Elyria from seven years before.

Her sister was outfitted in a gown identical in color to the one she had worn last season on the Seventh Day—a gown of dark obsidian. Its timeless silhouette hugged her figure, with raven-like sheets of crepe.

It rattled Elowyn how treacherously beautiful her sister was. Elyria's taste seemed unchanged over the years, as evidenced by her choice of attire. Yet, beneath her sister's stunning appearance, Elowyn detected a hint of weariness in her eyes—a hollow stare that weighed heavily upon them. Choosing not to comment on it, Elowyn silently acknowledged that they both were dreading the upcoming week.

"How doom and drama of you to opt for obsidian instead of periwinkle blue from all those gowns in your closet," Elowyn jested, eyeing her sister's ensemble.

In response, Elyria retorted, "And how sneaky and clever of you to borrow one of my gowns without my knowledge, instead of choosing one from your own vast collection."

"Fair point," Elowyn conceded with a grin.

As a surge of magic charged through the air, both sisters recognized the familiar sensation. Turning towards the castle gates with smiles adorning their faces, they presented themselves with the charm befitting of two princesses.

"Ready?" Elyria offered her outstretched hand.

"Ready," Elowyn replied, clasping her hand in hers and giving it a gentle squeeze.

~

Scores of guests from the seven realms had already begun to populate the castle grounds, but the arrival of the newest guests warranted a formal welcome. A portal, known as a moongate in Neramyr, materialized within the royal gardens. The moongate took the form of an arch crafted from twinkling feylight. Stepping out of the moongate were two royal fey: King Wilden and Queen Irena Bloodweaver, rulers of the Iron Hollows.

King Wilden and Queen Irena bore the sacred markings of the divine fey of House Bloodweaver. Their bodies, aside from their faces and necks, were etched with iridescent moon-inked markings resembling reptilian scales arranged in concentric circles. Golden *aureum* embellished with their House sigil, an ophis, trailed down their figures.

Approaching the monarchs, Elowyn and Elyria performed deep curtsies in respect.

Queen Irena smiled warmly, and King Wilden nodded in acknowledgment. "What a pleasure it is to be welcomed by the princesses of Eriden, and how delightful to be within Eriden's borders once more," he began. "It seems it has been years since we last journeyed to the mountains of castle Fangwright. The king and queen of

Eriden have maintained remarkably tight gates around their kingdom as of late."

Clearing her throat, Queen Irena gestured to the manicured gardens. "Indeed, what a display of splendor and beauty. It serves as a generous reminder that House Fangwright extends a warm welcome to its guests."

Elyria responded with poise, "Your Majesties, it is a great privilege to host the Iron King and Queen during the First Day."

The queen offered a pleasant smile before turning to Elowyn. "Princess Elowyn, as you are aware, our youngest son will join you as a royal candidate next season. It would be wonderful if the two of you could become acquainted. It is no mere coincidence that the Goddess has blessed the realms with seven royal offspring awaiting their divine call to candidacy. What an exciting prospect!"

The Bloodweaver queen, much like the entirety of Neramyr, firmly believed that Elowyn and six other princes and princesses from the seven realms would be named as the next cohort of divine candidates. They were the rumored 'sacred seven', destined to become the most gifted and talented divine warlocks and sorceresses the feylands had ever seen.

However, Elowyn regarded these beliefs as mere seraphic speculation and hopeful theorizing, largely due to her current mediocre magical abilities. The notion of her being among the most gifted sorceresses in the feylands seemed far-fetched at present.

"Of course, Your Majesty. It would be my pleasure," Elowyn responded politely.

"How splendid," Queen Irena beamed, clasping her hands together. She then turned to the Iron King. "Now, dearest, shall we greet the Fanged King and the Clever Queen?"

"Let us," King Wilden agreed, offering his arm. With a courteous wave to the two princesses, Queen Irena linked her arm with King Wilden's, and they strolled towards the castle entrance to join the festivities of the First Day.

"That was painless enough," Elowyn muttered to Elyria once the king and queen were out of sight.

Elyria sighed. "Only a few hundred more to go."

∼

As the afternoon wore on, Elyria and Elowyn continued to greet and welcome the guests of the First Day with pleasantries and salutations until their voices threatened to grow hoarse.

Currently, Elowyn found herself ensnared in an endless conversation with a sorceress from Lochwald, despite her attempts to bring it to a close. The discussion had dragged on for nearly fifteen minutes now.

"Yes, the hunt began at dawn for the feast of the Banquet of the Blessed," Elowyn confirmed.

The sorceress gasped, "Outstanding! The elk from the Eriden mountains has always been exquisite. With Eriden's borders being so exclusive as of late, I haven't tasted game of that quality in years." A look of fear crossed her face. "Oh moons, elk will be served tonight, won't it?"

"I assure you that the kingdom of Eriden has prepared a remarkable feast fitting for the First Day," Elowyn reassured her.

"I would hope so! The returning candidates deserve nothing less than a spectacular feast and more!" The sorceress nodded vigorously in agreement before leaning in and adding with a chuckle, "The elk prepared in the Erimead mountains is not nearly as delectable..."

Elowyn responded with a lighthearted, closed-lipped smile that didn't quite reach her eyes. She was well aware that the elk in question by the sorceress was procured from both the Eriden and Erimead mountains. In fact, the two kingdoms shared a contiguous mountain range, separated only by a channel of water, and the same population of elk inhabited both territories. The sorceress's claim was simply nonsensical, and the entire interaction felt absurd.

As Elowyn contemplated feigning lightheadedness to escape the conversation, a moongate began to materialize near the entrance of the royal gardens. With a wave of relief, she bid the Lochwald sorceress farewell and made her way towards the glittering feylight archway, her steps swift as she tried to evade becoming entangled in another mundane exchange. Elyria followed closely behind, eager to escape her own encounters with the guests.

Stopping before the moongate, the sisters felt a surge of magic swirl from the entrance. Two male figures emerged from the portal, stepping into view. The first warlock had a head of rich mahogany waves, warm olive-toned skin, and sandstone-colored freckles lightly dusting the bridge of his nose. His eyes gleamed with a piercing sea-green hue.

The second figure was immediately recognized by the two sisters as the second Bloodweaver prince. Like the king and queen of the Iron Hollows, the prince possessed fair skin and midnight hair. He wore a golden *aureum* embroidered with basilisk scales, draping down one shoulder, and falling just below his waist. As the Bloodweaver prince stepped into the royal gardens, his peculiar, maroon-colored eyes, almost serpentine-like, roamed over the two princesses.

Elyria and Elowyn approached the two warlocks and welcomed their arrival.

The mahogany-haired warlock introduced himself as Sylas Fenhart, the divine candidate for House Bloodweaver. "It's a pleasure to formally meet you, Princess Elyria. I've been curious to meet the Goddess-chosen sorceress for House Fangwright," he said courteously.

Elyria smiled politely and replied, "Likewise. I wish you luck on the Seventh Day."

"Your good fortune is appreciated, Princess Elyria," Sylas responded, his brow furrowing slightly as if contemplating something. His tone turned curious as he continued, "I've yet to see you at the Spires. In fact, I haven't seen you at training once these past seven years... Is there a reason for that?"

The Seven Spires stood as a prominent structure, consisting of seven towers built by the original founders of Neramyr. These towers, joined into one large edifice, served as the primary training grounds for magical fey of the seven realms. Each tower, or spire, was dedicated to one of the seven classes of magic, and only the most gifted warlocks and sorceresses were invited to train there. Among these gifted few were the divine candidates selected to participate in the Trial of Caena.

"No reason of importance. I simply felt better suited to train outside of the Seven Spires," Elyria disclosed, though the truth was her father, the king of Eriden, had forbidden her from training there altogether.

"Oh, I see." Sylas' voice faltered momentarily before quickly regaining composure. "I have no doubt that your abilities are exceptional. I look forward to completing these next seven years with you."

A subtle shift in the Bloodweaver prince's aura prompted the two princesses to pay closer attention to him.

"Moons, I apologize," Sylas cleared his throat. "I got carried away in conversation. I'd like to introduce you both to Theo. Erm, Prince Theoden Bloodweaver of the Iron Hollows."

Both Elyria and Elowyn offered respectful smiles to the prince, though they couldn't ignore the air of arrogance that surrounded him—typical of Bloodweaver royalty. The longstanding rivalry between the Fangwrights and Bloodweavers, the two strongest Houses in Neramyr, was well-known, spanning generations.

Theo spoke impassively, "What a peculiar choice to train outside of the Seven Spires. I haven't heard of a Goddess-chosen candidate declining the teachings there until your decision to abstain from it seven years ago." He raised a single brow. "This divine season has certainly been *unique*."

Elyria met Theo's gaze with an equally impassive expression, making it clear she wouldn't be provoked by his insinuations. He merely smiled back at her before turning to Elowyn.

The Divine Shallows

"Princess Elowyn, I hope you'll prove to be an earnest competitor for next season's Trial," Theo asserted. "The might of House Fangwright has always been admirable; it's rivaled House Bloodweaver since the dawn of the New Age. Though events as of late have proven that history can be capricious."

Sylas' discomfort was evident, and the Fangwright princesses narrowed their eyes at Theo's overt comment.

"Come, Sylas, let us begin the festivities of the First Day," Theo suggested, casting a low whistle as he surveyed the castle. "The walls of Eriden are built so lofty one would suspect that the Fanged King is hiding something." His gaze seemed to hint towards Elyria as he walked towards the castle.

Sylas hurriedly bid farewell to the two princesses and chased after the Bloodweaver prince until he vanished from the gardens and into the castle gates.

Elyria appeared indifferent, though her clenched jaw betrayed her true feelings. Elowyn felt a surge of irritation at the antagonistic remarks directed at her sister by the Bloodweaver prince. It was one thing for such crude comments to be whispered within the circles of your own court, but to be uttered on the soil of Eriden was a brazen act of disrespect.

"It's fine, Elowyn," Elyria reassured her, sensing her sister's aggravated demeanor. "The Bloodweavers have always lacked decorum. We've known this."

Elowyn simply nodded in response, trying to pacify her sister. But inwardly, she vowed that the next time she encountered the Bloodweaver prince, she'd punch him in the face.

7

Timeworn Tradition

In the grandeur of Eriden's Great Hall, courtiers mingled amidst the splendor of Neramyran royalty. The hall's vaulted ceilings, nearly thirty feet tall, played host to thousands of floating feylight spheres, casting a serene twilight glow upon the guests below. Stained-glass windows lined the walls, their colorful canvases adding to the majestic ambiance. At the end of the hall, a raised platform with stone stairs led to two towering thrones.

Crafted millennia ago, from a colossal redwood tree rooted in the Eriden mountains, the twin thrones stood ten feet tall. Charcoal cushions lined the backs and seats, while intricate gold-plated scales embellished their trimmings. Sharp golden fangs were immaculately molded into the structure beneath the palm rests. Above the thrones, a vast stained-glass window depicted the sigil of House Fangwright—a fearsome firedrake.

Seated upon the thrones were King Eamon and Queen Eddra Fangwright, clad in regal finery. King Eamon's crown was a golden diadem of seven peaks and a prominent opal gemstone at its center. Queen Eddra wore a crown made in a similar fashion.

Curled around the base of the thrones were the divine *animus* of the monarchs. Stryx, with his chalky coat and sleek scales, coiled around Queen Eddra's throne, while Bane's massive charcoal body rested beside King Eamon's throne, taking up a sizable portion of the platform, the dragon's torso rising and falling with steady breaths.

Beside the king stood Edwyn Fangwright, the prince of Eriden, with Nerys curled comfortably around his legs. Despite being the smallest of the firedrakes present, Nerys still loomed behind Edwyn, a testament to the formidable reputation of House Fangwright. Throughout history, warlocks and sorceresses from House Fangwright were renowned for their prestigious magic wielding abilities, particularly their distinct psionic powers, often referred to as mind magic.

Throughout the years, the reputation of House Fangwright has wavered from the birth of their firstborn princess, Elyria. It was stated that the kingdom of Eriden was haunted with a cursed fate. This fate was one of being burdened with an unblessed daughter of the moon; a royal child judged to be unworthy of the first Mark. These proclamations festered around the courts of the seven realms, but nonetheless, King Eamon seized the pride and prestige of his bloodline within a vice grip.

There was one unshakable belief that the Fanged King possessed, and it was that he valued his kingdom and its reputation above all else. As King Eamon sat upon his throne, his pensive eyes roamed the dais. He looked to his second-born child, Elowyn, and a pang of reassurance coursed through him. The feeling was akin to preservation rather than pride. Then the king dared to look at his firstborn and the certainty he felt about his kingdom vanished. *Deplorable, plagued child.* As his eyes beheld Elyria, abhorrence overtook his thoughts and threatened to crack his rehearsed self-control.

Deflecting these thoughts, King Eamon shifted his attention to the folk within the Great Hall, observing the courtiers mingling in his halls. He studied the revelers of the seven realms sunk deep into their stemmed glasses as they laughed with merriment. He watched as various noblefolk feasted feverishly and overfilled their gluttonous stomachs, rejoicing in reverence to the Moon Goddess.

However, as the Fanged King observed the scene, a dark expression clouded his face, and he scowled in disgust. The sight before him made him want to retch. King Eamon began to grip the golden armrests of this throne rigidly to tame his revulsion, his aura turning turbulent with emotion.

In the next moment, with a swift and forceful tap of his finger, a loud clang reverberated from his throne.

At the sound, Bane, the smoke-gray firedrake, snapped to attention, his relaxed demeanor replaced by vigilance. He rose upright, muscles rippling as he moved, signaling the attention of Stryx and Nerys. The other two dragons followed suit, rising from their laidback positions, and standing tall.

Only a few guests took notice of the three firedrakes standing in waiting, but many of the revelers continued their conversations with vigor. Amidst the noise, Bane leaned forward, bracing himself with his front limbs and thrusted his head upwards, releasing a guttural screech that pierced through the room. In response to Bane's cry, Stryx and Nerys joined in, adding their own thunderous screeches to the chorus— the three roared, their voices sounding powerful in unison.

The lively atmosphere in the Great Hall quickly fell silent. Some guests staggered back in surprise; audible gasps filled the room. Others watched the firedrakes with a mixture of wonder and fear.

After the dragons finished sounding their call, they lifted their heads upwards once more. Bane's chest swelled as a burnt orange hue bloomed under his neck, gradually spreading upwards. With a mighty thrust, he released a fiery pillar from his throat, illuminating the hall. Beside him, Stryx and Nerys unleashed their own scorching flames, creating a trio of fiery columns that merged at a midway point behind the thrones, emblazoning the stained-glass sigil of House Fangwright above them.

As the flames dissipated into wisps of smoke, King Eamon rose from his throne and adjusted his regal attire. He signaled to a nearby servant, who quickly ascended the steps of the dais and offered him a tray of crystal goblets. King Eamon took a glass and strode to the center of the platform, wearing a simulated smile on his face.

King Eamon raised his glass high and declared, "Fey of Neramyr, it is with pride that the kingdom of Eriden welcomes you to the First Day, the Banquet of the Blessed, during this season's Ceremony of Caena!

"Tonight, we rejoice in the return of the divine candidates who ventured across the Bridge Between Worlds seven years ago. These newly anointed children of the moon will emerge from the Divine Shallows imbued with unparalleled strength and extraordinary abilities—a challenging journey undertaken by only a select few. These remarkable warlocks and sorceresses will continue to uphold the era of peace that has prevailed in the New Age. They will serve the seven realms of Neramyr, protecting our heritage, preserving our legacy, and above all, safeguarding our folk."

King Eamon began to artfully step across the platform.

"Tonight calls for celebration, as many will be reunited with loved ones after seven long years. The hour approaches when we will gather at the Temple of Caena to witness this sacred ritual. Upon the return of the divine candidates, we shall welcome them with the Banquet of the Blessed—a feast befitting the seven realms, as we honor them with the hospitality deserving of their newfound status."

With arms outstretched and a strapping smile, King Eamon addressed the crowd, "It fills my heart with joy to witness such merriment within my realm. Please enjoy the beauty and warmth that Eriden has to offer. The feast and festivities of the First Day will continue until light has long since left. Let the revelry resume!"

The Divine Shallows

The Great Hall erupted in applause as King Eamon emptied his goblet and reclaimed his throne. Conversations resumed with renewed energy, laughter echoing through the hall.

Yet, as the atmosphere shifted back to celebration, King Eamon settled back into his throne, his body tense as he tightly grasped the golden scales of the armrest rigidly once more.

∼

Elowyn had only managed to conjure a moongate successfully twelve times in her life thus far. If this attempt succeeded, it would mark the thirteenth time—a considerable number, to say the least. Normally, it was her sister's expertise that guided them through magical portals, but Elyria had vanished once again after their father's speech. Such disappearances had become increasingly common lately, but Elowyn chose not to inquire further. After all, this was a week fraught with anxiety, especially for a divine candidate.

With determination, Elowyn readied herself to summon a moongate on her own. The act of conjuring portals to transport oneself was a skill rooted in abjuration magic, a specialty of House Mirthwood and the kingdom of Lochwald.

Already struggling with the psionic magic native to House Fangwright, Elowyn found wielding another House's magic particularly challenging. It was a source of frustration, especially considering her sister's effortless mastery of all seven magical disciplines. It would have been aggravating if the two sister's magical abilities were compared, but instead, the fey of Neramyr seemed to disregard Elyria's existence entirely.

Sighing, Elowyn adjusted the skirts of her champagne-colored dress, knowing the First Day would carry on without her if she delayed any longer. With a silent prayer to the Goddess, she tapped into her innate power, urging it to heed her command. To her surprise, her native magic responded, surging through her arm, and manifesting at her fingertips.

Elowyn channeled this power into the space before her, conjuring two shimmering pillars that coiled and intertwined until they formed a glowing archway. As the archway solidified, a feylight portal shimmered beyond it, standing magnificently before her. Elowyn peered at the moongate, scrutinizing her work.

The portal hummed with otherworldly energy, and it beckoned her to step inside. However, she couldn't shake the memory of a childhood mishap when she inadvertently transported herself to a foreign destination. It was long ago, but Elowyn still wasn't sure if she created a portal to this realm. It had taken hours for Elyria to find her, thanks to the link between their charmed necklaces. Without it, locating her would have required a much more advanced location spell.

Elowyn cast one final glance at the magical gateway before taking a deep breath and stepping through the feylight pillars. As she passed through the portal, a gentle breeze caressed her skin, carrying the sensation of thousands of feylight starbursts. In the blink of an eye, she found herself standing on the solid surface of a stone landing, facing the monumental marble stairway leading to the entrance of the Temple of Caena.

With a triumphant smirk, Elowyn silently congratulated herself for *not* accidentally transporting herself to another realm. She was relieved to have arrived on time for the ritual of the First Day, practically ready to skip up the hundred marble stairs awaiting her.

A voice interrupted her thoughts. "What's got you smiling?"

Elowyn turned to see a claret-haired warlock from House Darkmaw standing behind her. Meeting her gaze with his golden irises, a sense of familiarity washed over her, and she vaguely recognized him as the young fey prince who had waved at her during the last Ceremony of Caena. The same prince she had dreamt about in a feverish state that morning.

"Uh, nothing," Elowyn replied, caught off guard.

"Somehow I don't believe that," the Darkmaw prince teased, dimples forming with his smile.

"I remember you from last season's Seventh Day," Elowyn admitted, her words lingered with uncertainty.

"And I remember you," the Darkmaw prince replied confidently, waving at her just as he had done years ago cross from the Divine Shallows.

"Princess Elowyn Fangwright," she introduced herself with a casual dip of her head. "I suppose now that we've formally met, you can call me Elowyn."

The Darkmaw prince returned the gesture with a slight bow. "Nice to officially meet you, Elowyn. I'm Prince Draeden Darkmaw, but you can call me Draeden."

"Ah, a fellow member of the 'sacred seven'," Elowyn joked.

"What's that?" Draeden asked, confused.

Elowyn looked at him incredulously, her attempt at banter falling flat. Before she could respond, Draeden flashed a grin. "Kidding, kidding. So, are you going to tell me why you were smiling earlier, or will I have to begin guessing?"

"Oh, very funny," Elowyn retorted sarcastically. "And no, you'll just have to wonder, I suppose."

"You wound me," Draeden clutched his chest. "Keeping secrets from a stranger you've just met is no fun."

Elowyn's lip twitched upwards. "Fine. I summoned a moongate here."

Draeden tilted his head in anticipation, expecting Elowyn to continue her sentence. However, his expression faltered when he realized that *was* all she had to say.

"You're serious?" he asked, bewildered. "All that fuss over summoning a moongate?"

"You asked," Elowyn replied with a nonchalant shrug. "Repeatedly."

"I only asked twice!" Draeden scoffed. "At least tell me it was an extraordinary moongate."

"Hmm, no. It was quite ordinary," she admitted shamelessly.

Draeden looked incredulous. "Should I expect you to be thrilled when you enter the Heart of the Temple, too?"

"Perhaps. There's just something about portals, don't you think?" Elowyn countered sarcastically.

She had no intention of revealing the truth about her less than exceptional magical abilities. Even now, feylings ten years her junior wouldn't mistakenly portal to another realm like she did in the past.

"The seven feylands could learn a thing or two from you about finding joy in simplicity," Draeden laughed.

"Are you calling me simple?" Elowyn's tone bristled.

Draeden stumbled over his words, "Goddess, no. Of course not! I'm just—"

"I'm just teasing," Elowyn confessed, softening her tone. "Now that we're even... This moongate business stays between us. Promise?" She raised a pinky finger to his eye level.

He let out a brilliant laugh as he complimented her, "You're just as funny as I'd imagined you to be."

Elowyn couldn't explain why she offered him a promise or why she felt so at ease around the Darkmaw prince, but her cheeks flushed deeply as he wrapped his finger around hers, intertwining them.

It was only then that Elowyn truly observed the prince's appearance. Draeden stood several inches taller than her, with claret red hair cropped just above his brow. She noticed the warmth of his bronzed skin where their fingers met, just a shade darker than her own. Her gaze followed the crescent moon marked on her palm, mirroring the one on his. His aura hinted at his age, suggesting he was only a few years older than her.

Draeden's smile remained, his dimples playfully winking at her. Elowyn felt a flutter in her stomach as he continued to gaze at her, his irises resembling two brilliant spheres of liquid gold. Sensing how long she had been holding his finger, she quickly let go and took a step back to create some distance between them.

"The First Day ritual is about to begin. I should get going; I wouldn't want to miss my chance to be captivated by another magical gateway," she chuckled, teasing him about his earlier remark. "Especially one as indulgent as the path to the Heart of the Temple."

"Moons, no. We couldn't have that, could we?" Draeden replied with a smile, taking her palm in his and placing a kiss on the back of her hand. "Until we meet again, Elowyn."

Elowyn couldn't hide her flushed face this time as she felt the warmth of his lips lingering on her hand even after he released it. She gathered the skirts of her dress and hurried up the marble stairs leading to the Temple of Caena, the feelings stirred by Draeden's presence lingering with her every step.

8

Banquet of the Blessed

THE ECHOES OF ELOWYN'S HEELS CLACKED OFF THE polished stone flooring as she stepped into the Temple's grand foyer. Above her, a circular skylight framed the ceiling allowing streams of sunlight into the open space. Though her mind urged her to head straight for the Heart of the Temple, her feet led her to a wall engraved with Neramyr's rich history.

The wall depicted the seven feylands in intricate detail, each blade of grass even scored with precision. It was a tribute to the land of the fey and the Temple's purpose—to honor the Moon Goddess and preserved the very cave where the original seven warlocks and sorceresses sought refuge during the Old Age. Within the Heart of the Temple lay the Divine Shallows, the ancient waters where Caena had emerged to save the first fey from slaughter.

On this hallowed ground, Caena had bestowed her Mark upon the original seven warlocks and sorceresses, granting them an ability to wield divine magic, the very same otherworldly magic that was blessed upon her palms after birth.

As the crowd around her thinned, Elowyn rested her wandering thoughts and headed for the entrance to the Heart of the Temple. Striding to the central spiral staircase, she descended to the lowest level of the Temple. As she hastened her steps, she was mindful not to trip over the skirts of her dress. Soon, she reached the lowermost level, where the walls bore an even more elaborate depiction of the Moon Goddess' origin.

In this empty space stood a magnificent stone archway, a mighty presence. Elowyn approached it, peering beyond the curved stone pillars to observe the magical ward that concealed the entrance to the Heart of the Temple. This sacred entrance was similar to a moongate, but significantly more complex and sophisticated than a mere portal. This divine portal was created millennia ago by the original seven warlocks and sorceresses, their ancient powers sustaining it to this day.

The portal projected an illusion of a midnight skyscape, its dusky azure canvas was a boundless cosmos sprinkled with a sea of stars. Celestial comets streaked across the enchantment, leaving shimmering trails of starlight in their wake. This magical gateway captured the essence of the Heart of the Temple, the most sacred place in all of Neramyr. And within it, Elowyn sensed the primordial aura of the ancient magic that sourced the ward. To say it was breathtaking would only describe a fraction of its beauty.

Artfully engraved onto the marble pillars of the stone archway were the names of the original fey rulers of Neramyr. Elowyn had been taught from an early age that these monikers held more than mere symbolism; they were imbued with the magic of the ancient warlocks and sorceresses they represented. With a gentle touch, she traced the curves of the closest inscription with her fingers: Elmyr Fangwright, the first king of Eriden.

The story of this sacred ward traced back to the dawn of the New

Age itself: the seven founding fey sacrificed a portion of their divine magic bestowed by the Goddess to create this protective barrier around the Divine Shallows. It was a selfless act to ensure the eternal preservation of these sacred waters. This act hailed generations of divine magic wielders who defended Neramyr against the evils of the Old Age, maintaining an era of peace.

Taking a steady breath, Elowyn brought her thumb to her lips and pricked her skin, coaxing a small crimson bead to swell to the surface. She placed her thumb upon King Elmyr's name, pressing the blood into the marble—an offering to her ancestor. The marble marked red, then emitted a pulse of ancient magic. Her blood offering began to shimmer with a pale moonlight glow before vanishing entirely, signifying acceptance by the sacred archway.

Elowyn learned that this ritual served as a gesture of respect to the founding fey and to Neramyr itself. It symbolized a drop of her life offered in tribute to King Elmyr and to honor to all those who had come before her. As a feyling, Elowyn once speculated that these blood offerings sustained the ancient magic protecting the Heart of the Temple. However, she later discovered that every fey who entered the temple performed the same ritual, each honoring their respective House in this tradition.

The archway called to her, and Elowyn heeded its silent summons, crossing into the illusion of the midnight sky. She felt a surge of energy enveloping her, heightening her senses as she awaited entry to the Heart of the Temple.

A fleeting moment passed and she appeared in the Heart of the Temple.

Now amidst a gathering of fey nobility and courtiers, Elowyn surveyed her surroundings. She had ventured into the Heart of the Temple only a few times before, the most significant occasion being her birth when she faced Caena's judgment in the Divine Shallows.

As Elowyn navigated through the crowd, many individuals

graciously made way for her, likely due to the *aureum* draping from her shoulders. Pressing onward, she made her way towards the area designated for House Fangwright during the ritual. Along the journey, she exchanged polite smiles with both strangers and familiar faces until she finally reached her destination. Spotting her parents positioned near the Divine Shallows, she took her rightful place standing behind them.

The ritual of the First Day was about to begin, with the High Priestess already stationed within the Divine Shallows at its center. The scene before Elowyn nearly mirrored the memory she had of it from seven years prior. She recalled that the First Day was one of the most, if not the most, celebrated day of the Ceremony. This day marked the return of candidates from their seven-year Trial, emerging as divine warlocks or sorceresses—the greatest magical status one can achieve in their lifetime.

Sensing a familiar presence beside her, Elowyn turned to see Elyria's reassuring face. With a soft smile, Elowyn greeted her sister, mind-whispering a quiet *"hey"*. Elyria responded in kind, slipping her hand into Elowyn's, offering a gentle squeeze before releasing it. Together, they directed their attention towards the High Priestess standing amidst the ancient waters of the Divine Shallows.

At the center stood the High Priestess, atop a flat circular stone depicting an illustration of a crescent moon. Surrounding her were the seven stone sigils representing the Houses of Neramyr. These sigils encircled the High Priestess, leaving ample space between them, each dedicated to a noble lineage.

The sigil nearest to Elowyn belonged to House Fangwright, marked by a firedrake etched into the flat stone. This would be the very spot where she would eventually stand if chosen by the Goddess on the Seventh Day to claim her divine candidacy. To her right, the next stone bore the sigil of House Bloodweaver—a basilisk coiled on the stone. Following it was the grimwolf of House Mirthwood, then the phoenix of House Skyborn. Next came the gryphon of House Darkmaw, the loch hydra of House Driftmoor, and finally, the winged ophis of House Blackbane.

As the High Priestess shifted from the Divine Shallows, a hush fell over the Temple. Her voice resonated through the chamber as she addressed the assembled fey.

"Fey of Neramyr, I bid you welcome to the Temple of Caena," she began, her gaze sweeping over the attentive crowd. "Today, we gather to witness the First Day of the Ceremony—a sacred day when Caena opens the gates to her realm once more for the return of the candidates who embarked on her Trial seven years ago."

Her words rang louder as she continued, "These candidates were granted the chance to traverse the Bridge Between Worlds and seek divine judgment. Should they prove worthy, the Goddess will bestow her sacred Mark upon them, granting the gift of her divine magic to wield in Neramyr." The markings along her arms glowed, emphasizing her words. "Let us ask the Goddess for her guidance as these candidates return to Neramyr."

Turning to each of the monarchs of the seven realms, the High Priestess nodded once. She raised her palms upward, and the iridescent markings along her weathered arms ignited with moonlight, emanating ethereal energy. Below her, the ancient waters churned and swirled at her calves. Soon, the air in the Temple thrummed with power.

"It's time, we must begin," the High Priestess declared.

Elowyn observed as the fourteen rulers of Neramyr approached the Divine Shallows with upturned palms, summoning their divine magic. The moon-blessed markings on their skin glowed in unison with the High Priestess'. It was always a powerful sight to behold—the strongest wielders of divine magic summoning their power as one.

Amidst this display, the High Priestess began to chant in the ancient language of the fey, and the water beneath her became turbulent, rippling and eddying around her feet. Anticipation filled the Temple as the High Priestess and the monarchs continued to channel their magic into the swirling waters of the Divine Shallows. The magic in the Temple swelled until it reached an apex.

Then, the High Priestess ceased her incantations. "The Moon Goddess has opened the gates to her realm, and we now await the divine candidates as they return from the Bridge Between Worlds! Let us welcome their arrival back to Neramyr!"

A faint glow blossomed from the waters within the Divine Shallows, hovering above the sigil of House Bloodweaver. Elowyn's gaze remained fixed on the shimmering spot, feeling a surge of divine power radiate from the stone. Her breath caught as a figure broke the surface of the ancient waters, rising slowly from the shallows. Encased in divine magic, the figure appeared as though bathed in moonlight. Straining her eyes, Elowyn discerned the figure to be a warlock.

As the warlock fully emerged and stood upon the sigil of House Bloodweaver, the once-rippling waters surrounding his silhouette calmed. Elowyn squinted, attempting to make out the warlock's features amidst the divine aura, when the fey of House Bloodweaver erupted in celebration. Spotting King Wilden and Queen Irena beaming with pride, and even Theo joining in the applause, Elowyn couldn't help but smile.

The divine energy surrounding the warlock gradually faded, and he raised a triumphant arm towards the ceiling. The Temple erupted with cheers, but gasps soon followed as the onlookers noticed the fanged basilisk coiled around the warlock's extended arm—a rare creature procured from the divine Trial. A divine *animus*. Lowering his arm, the warlock turned to face the High Priestess, bending one knee, and bowing his head before her.

Taking the warlock's palms in hers, the High Priestess began to chant once more in the ancient tongue. As her incantations filled the air, the warlock became cloaked in pale moonlight, his entire form glowing with radiant energy as the moonlight embedded itself into his being.

Elowyn was captivated by the divine markings that began to manifest on the warlock's skin. Starting from his legs, the divine energy traced concentric patterns of reptilian scales, winding its way up his torso and neck in delicate strokes of moonlight. The iridescent reptilian markings continued to trace his body, shimmering as they drifted down his arms until they finally coalesced at his palms, framing the central crescent moon. The warlock remained on one knee while the final Mark was bestowed upon him.

As the divine energy surrounding him subsided and the moonlight faded, the High Priestess released his hands and turned to address the crowd. "Caena has marked another child of the moon!" she proclaimed. "And furthermore, he has emerged from the Bridge Between Worlds with a soul-bonded *animus*! It is with great honor that I announce the return of your *primis*, Prince Thomys Bloodweaver!"

Another wave of cheers erupted from the onlookers surrounding the Divine Shallows as Prince Thomys turned to face them, grinning proudly as he lifted the arm coiled with his soul-bonded basilisk once more. Meanwhile, the remaining six candidates emerged one by one from the Divine Shallows, each receiving their final markings.

Amidst the celebration, a sense of unity and belonging washed over Elowyn as she witnessed the ritual of the First Day. Being in the presence of the powerful ancient waters, she felt a deep connection and an unspoken longing stirred within her. It ignited her desire to one day emerge from the Divine Shallows bathed in the shimmering moonlight, to bear the final divine markings herself.

Among the seven candidates emerging from the Divine Shallows, Elowyn could only recognize Prince Thomys Bloodweaver. This cohort comprised a diverse mix of noblefolk and commoners: one royal, five nobles, and a lone commoner. It was rare for a royal to be chosen, given the number of royalty in the feylands, but even rarer was the selection of a commoner over highborn fey. The Fangwright warlock represented this rarity in the divine cohort.

As the newly divine warlock of House Fangwright emerged from the Divine Shallows covered in markings, Elowyn did not recognize him. This was unsurprising, given she was familiar with only those stemming from a small circle of her own court. The warlock approached her father, exchanging nods and handshakes in a display of mutual respect. Elowyn observed with curiosity and a hint of suspicion as her father and the Fangwright warlock greeted each other as old friends, sealing the moment with a one-armed hug.

Though she joined in the celebrations with the fey of Eriden, Elowyn remained cautious, especially upon learning the warlock's name: Finnor Wynward. Any powerful fey who shared a close bond with her father warranted her wariness.

As the newly anointed divine fey returned to Neramyr and the gates to Caena's realm closed once more, leaving the Divine Shallows empty, the High Priestess' commanding voice pierced the air, drawing the attention of all present.

"Fey of Neramyr, we welcome back the seven fey who have successfully completed the Trial of Caena. Upon their return, they are granted the gift of wielding the Goddess' divine magic. With fealty, loyalty, and allegiance, these fey will serve the seven kingdoms in this realm and into all the realms beyond!"

The High Priestess concluded her words with a resounding clap, igniting a wave of enthusiastic applause from the gathered crowd. Extending her arm toward the newly marked fey, she continued, "Let us honor these seven divine warlocks and sorceresses who have braved the judgment of the Moon Goddess and returned to us bearing the final Mark! The First Day's ritual now draws to a close. Let us partake in the Banquet of the Blessed—The festivities will resume in the kingdom of Eriden!"

As the High Priestess finished her address, Elowyn felt a knot tighten in her stomach, the days ahead seeming to shrink in duration. On the Seventh Day, her older sister would embark on her own Trial of

Caena, and Elowyn herself would discover whether she too was to be chosen as a divine candidate.

Elowyn couldn't dispel the foreboding feelings that consumed her aura. It became apparent that everything happening was the way the Goddess intended it to be, but she couldn't help but feel like some part of it was very wrong. Yet, all she could do was steel herself for the night ahead, holding her head high in preparation of what was to come.

9

Mirth and Mystery

THE BANQUET OF THE BLESSED WAS HELD IN ONE OF Eriden's vast banquet halls, which had been lined with dozens of lengthy tables positioned in rows. These tables were adorned with sheer, silk table runners the shade of gold that extended down the centers of each of them, draping off the table's edges. Long garlands of greenery were placed on top of the shimmering runners, adding a touch of foliage to the centerpieces. Ornate iron candlesticks, all varying heights, were arranged artfully alongside the leafy garlands as their flames flickered gently, casting charming shadows on the table's surface.

Hundreds of place settings were made of simple white porcelain, accompanied with silver cutlery and crystal wine goblets. The hour was now dark since the conclusion of the ritual, which left the hall cloaked in amber candlelight and the glow of the floating feylight spheres from above.

Servants greeted guests at the hall's entrance, offering crystal glasses of *vinum*, a honey-hued fey wine. In one corner, a string quartet serenaded attendees with a lilting melody beneath an arched pavilion decorated with florets that fell down its frame in vines and pearl streams. A cleared area in the center of the hall awaited dancers, while enchanting water fountains flowed with soothing songs.

At the head table, the king and queen of Eriden were seated alongside the royal family. As a mark of honor to the newly marked divine fey, they are seated among the monarchs hosting the First Day. Thus, Elowyn found herself seated between Elyria and the newly marked warlock, Finnor Wynward.

Although Finnor did not possess a single drop of royal blood, he looked the part. He was winsome in a simplistic way, his frame was built, strong and rugged. And his skin was bronzed, contrasting the snow-white hair that fell to the nape of his neck. As half of his locks were pulled back, a few strands remained hanging loose that framed his angular jaw. Finnor possessed two brilliant eyes of silver, but more notable were his newfound divine markings. A distinctive pattern of moon-inked dragon scales coated every inch of his body, save for his face. He almost looked like a full-blooded Fangwright; all that was missing was four fangs.

The attention of the banquet hall shifted as King Eamon rose from his seat, raising his crystal goblet for attention. "Fey of Neramyr, joy fills my heart on this sacred day as our seven divine warlocks and sorceresses have returned."

His voice continued in a booming timbre, "The kingdom of Eriden proudly dedicates this season's Banquet of the Blessed to Finnor Wynward, another son of the moon sworn to House Fangwright. Let us raise our glasses to his triumphant return as a divine warlock!"

Beside Elowyn, Finnor stood tall, his smile radiant as applause and cheers filled the hall. Even her father joined in, raising his glass in a gesture of solidarity.

"Before we commence the festivities," King Eamon continued, "I must share news of our recent loss. Mere days ago, we mourned the passing of our comrade, Lord Ewell Highhelm, who faithfully served as Commander of the Feyguard for centuries. Before his service, he stood as a trusted ally, fighting alongside me in countless battles to defend Eriden from the lingering darkness of the Old Age. Lord Ewell's dedication to our realm was unwavering, and his legacy will forever be honored in our kingdom."

A look of morose shaded King Eamon's visage. "His legacy shall not fade into oblivion. In his last moments, Lord Ewell expressed a dutiful wish for his legacy as protector of the realm to endure. Though he lived a long and illustrious life, he bore no heir. It was his desire to pass on his mantle to a successor deserving of this honor. Thus, I hereby bestow upon a worthy warlock the esteemed title of Commander of the Feyguard."

The king's proclamation resounded, "Let us celebrate the ascension of Eriden's new Commander, Finnor Wynward! May he uphold the noble legacy forged by Lord Ewell and ensure the continued peace of our kingdom!"

Applause erupted throughout the banquet hall as Finnor graciously acknowledged the declaration before retaking his seat.

King Eamon raised his glass once more. "Let us revel in the riches we've reaped! Let the festivities of the Banquet of the Blessed unfold!"

With that, the string quartet launched into a lively tune, and the servant doors swung open on both sides of the hall. Kitchen staff emerged, carrying trays gilded with silver domes, which they presented to the seated guests. Gasps of delight filled the air as the domed trays were unveiled, revealing exquisitely plated dishes crafted from the finest ingredients. With the first course served, the guests indulged, and the hall buzzed with animated conversation.

Elowyn toyed with her food, her appetite seemingly vanished. Glancing to her left, she found Elyria and their mother deeply engaged in conversation, or rather, their mother was lecturing Elyria while she was forced to listen. Elowyn wouldn't dare interrupt that.

Turning to her right, she wrinkled her nose as she observed Finnor devouring his meal with the voracity of a feral animal. "You must be famished," she remarked.

Finnor didn't spare her a glance as he replied matter-of-factly, "I haven't had a proper meal in seven years."

Realizing her comment might have sounded callous, Elowyn quickly amended, "Here, you can have mine." She pushed her plate toward him. "Congratulations on your completion of the Trial and new role as Commander of the Feyguard."

As Finnor reached for her plate, his hand halted abruptly. Swallowing his mouthful, he glanced at her briefly, his silver eyes widening in recognition before he swiftly wiped his mouth with a napkin. "No, I couldn't. It wouldn't be appropriate for me to deprive you of your meal, Princess Elowyn. I apologize for my lack of manners; the aftershock of the Trial remains heavily on my mind."

Elowyn offered him a tight-lipped smile. "Please, just call me Elowyn. Besides, I'm not particularly hungry, and I'd hate to see it go to waste." Offering the plate back, she handed it directly to him.

For a moment, uncertainty flickered in Finnor's eyes, but hunger won out. "Thank you, Princess," he murmured, accepting the plate, and transferring its contents onto his own.

Elowyn laced her fingers under her chin and stared at the warlock, now curious. "If you don't mind me asking, since Lord Ewell bore no sons or daughters, how exactly did he select you as his successor?"

A barrage of questions flooded Elowyn's thoughts, but she cautioned herself to tread carefully around the newly marked divine warlock.

"Lord Ewell wasn't bound to me by blood, but he was like to a second father to me," Finnor replied.

"I'm sorry for your loss," Elowyn offered sincerely.

"It's no matter. I was able to make my peace with it seven years ago before I crossed the Bridge Between Words. The last Sixth Day, Lord

Ewell told me of the rare illness that afflicted him. The menders from the Healers Keep could do nothing for it... I knew he would pass during my time in the Trial. He revealed his plan to succeed his legacy to me upon my return as a divine warlock. His memory was the one thing that tethered me to Neramyr during the past seven years."

Elowyn didn't expect the candid response from Finnor. "That's heartbreaking. I wish you could've had more time with him before his passing."

"As do I, but the Moon Goddess determines the timeline of all fates. I often wonder if this hardship was also a part of her Trial for me," Finnor murmured.

"You might be right," Elowyn agreed with a half-hearted chuckle. "Enduring a cruel fate may be among one of her many tests." She thought fleetingly of Elyria, born without the Goddess' Mark, before swiftly changing the topic. "So, accepting the responsibility of being the newly appointed Commander of the Feyguard. That's quite an undertaking."

Finnor was nearly finished with his meal, scraping the last remnants onto his fork. "Yes, it is. I've wanted to serve the realm since I was a feyling."

Elowyn recalled that the Fangwright warlock was of lowborn blood. For Finnor to have ascended into such a highly ranked position, along with becoming a divine fey, was an incredible feat for someone born with a commoner status such as his. His magic must be incredible. She questioned, "And how old are you now?"

"Thirty-four." Finnor answered. In Neramyr, though rarely, the oldest fey could live into their thousandths if fate allowed.

"Really? You must have made quite an impression for my father to entrust you with such leadership at Lord Ewell's behest," Elowyn remarked.

Finnor nodded. "I first met Lord Ewell when my family moved into the inner districts of Eriden. We owned a renowned smithy in the outskirts north of here, supplying weaponry exclusively for the kingdom, and at that time, we corresponded directly with Lord Ewell."

He cleared his throat before continuing, "After some time at the forge, Lord Ewell persuaded me to join the cavalry of the Feyguard. Without his encouragement, I would have remained a simple blacksmith in the countryside. Though that life may have been straightforward, I wouldn't have achieved the feats I have today—I always aspired to be more than just a blacksmith."

Another group of kitchen stewards appeared, clearing their empty plates, and serving the next course. Elowyn extended her plate to Finnor, who accepted it graciously before resuming his narrative.

"After a few years in the cavalry, I was promoted to officer of my own unit. Eventually, Lord Ewell began inviting me to military councils held by the king, where I observed silently for years. Until one day, I spoke up on an issue, and to my surprise, the king was impressed with my suggestion. From that day on, your father acknowledged my potential."

Finnor's voice carried admiration as he spoke further, "King Eamon is a charitable ruler who values his kingdom and his folk above all. His Majesty was filled with pride when I was chosen by the Goddess as a divine candidate. If not for the generosity and opportunities he has offered me, I wouldn't be where I am today."

As Finnor continued speaking about her father, Elowyn's aura became more reserved. If Finnor truly believed what he was saying about her father, he was deeply mistaken. She couldn't help but wonder how many others her father had charmed into his good graces. Despite her reservations, she continued to listen to Finnor's story about his life, offering him portions of her plate as he spoke. This went on for quite some time until the last dish was served.

A servant placed a tray before Elowyn, revealing a porcelain teacup atop a plate piled with scones and teacakes beneath the silver dome. She nearly squealed with delight at the sight.

Glancing at Finnor's plate, she noticed he had been served a berry trifle, just like everyone else in the hall. She turned to her left to ask her sister about it, but Elyria's seat was empty, as was her mother's. Elowyn had been so absorbed in her conversation with Finnor that she hadn't noticed their departure. Her father, meanwhile, was engrossed in an argument with her uncle, his irritation evident on his face as he sipped his *vinum*.

Regardless, Elowyn raised the tea to her lips and savored its fragrance of lilac and honey—clearly a gift from Elyria. She smiled to herself and took a cheerful sip from the porcelain cup.

"Not sharing this time?" Finnor teased.

"Not this time," Elowyn replied with a small chuckle, biting into a teacake. "I'm keeping this one for myself."

"Fair enough," Finnor conceded, crossing his arms, and letting out a tired sigh. "I'm just glad to be home."

"I can only imagine... This morning you were in the midst of the Trial, and now you're back in Neramyr. If I were in your shoes, I'd be shifting between shock and relief," Elowyn remarked sympathetically.

"I'm definitely something close to that," Finnor admitted, clearing his throat uncomfortably. "The Trial is the hardest thing I've ever had to endure. I understand completely now why the Goddess only allows those who survive her Trial to bear the responsibility of wielding divine magic."

Elowyn leaned in closer, intrigued. "What was your Trial like?"

"As you know, it's different each season. My cohort was lucky enough to stick together. The concept of day and night didn't exist where we ended up... at least not like how it is in this realm," Finnor explained, picking at his trifle. "There was dusk and dawn, sun and moon, day and night, but it was all disordered. Sometimes in the thick of nightfall, the sun would blaze. When spring approached, flowers bloomed and flourished as snow blanketed them in powder sheets."

Finnor took a generous drink from his crystal goblet and sighed with exhaustion.

"There were creatures I'd never seen before, colors I'd known my entire life appeared inverted, all my sensibilities were aimless. It was as bewildering as it was baffling. I had to retrain my senses every day for the past seven years in order to survive. The otherworldly beasts that roamed the lands of the Trial were nothing like I'd ever trained for. I lost count of the times I thought I wouldn't make it back here," he confessed, the last sentence falling heavily from his lips.

"Your life was truly at risk?" Elowyn winced. "But everyone that's completed the Trial has returned to Neramyr."

"The Trial is not for the faint-hearted," Finnor responded solemnly. "Those chosen by the Goddess to participate are selected with reason and intent. If your name is called on the Seventh Day, it is because Caena believes you will succeed."

Elowyn's mind swirled with thoughts of her impending candidacy, her stomach twisting in an endless spiral. "Did you really get to face the Moon Goddess?"

"No," Finnor replied frankly. "Nobody can see her, but you can feel her presence all around. Her magic is... it's daunting."

As the weight of her own candidacy settled in, Elowyn slowly replaced the teacake in her hand back onto her plate. In six days' time, her name would be called on the Seventh Day, and she would begin her training at the Seven Spires. Seven years to prepare seemed insufficient, especially considering the poor control she had over her wayward abilities.

Abruptly, Elowyn pushed her seat back and stood up. The occupied seats in the banquet hall were thinning as courtiers took to the dance floor. Ignoring her troubling thoughts, Elowyn extended her hand to Finnor. "Would you care to dance with me?"

Taken aback by her sudden request, Finnor stared at her, momentarily confounded.

"Oh," Elowyn retracted her hand. "That was cavalier. You're probably exhausted, and dancing is the last thing on your mind."

"No, of course. I would love to, Princess," Finnor responded, standing up and offering his hand back to her.

Elowyn smiled, accepting his hand as he led them to the open floor in the banquet hall. She spun on her heels to face him, and Finnor rested his left hand on her waist as he cradled her right hand in his. Elowyn noticed that his hands were calloused and rugged, yet they held her with considerable care. Around them, a few couples had already begun to swirl and twirl. Following suit, Finnor and Elowyn began a graceful waltz at a gentle pace.

As they began their dance, Finnor chuckled beneath his breath. Elowyn tilted her head in response and questioned, "Is something the matter?"

"I just wanted to thank you for making this easier on me," Finnor replied. "It hasn't been the smoothest transition, all this." He tossed his head briskly, his chin pointing to the world around him. "Part of me is unconvinced I'm in Neramyr. My mind is warning me that I'm trapped in another test, and I'll wake up back in the Trial come sunrise."

Elowyn's heart went out to him as she assured, "You're really in Neramyr, Finnor."

"The Trial... It was like one nightmare to the next, but I'm glad it's over. I'm a better warlock for it when it's all said and done," Finnor shrugged.

Elowyn nodded in agreement, her eyes roaming to his hand clasped in hers. The warlock's hands, neck, and body were now covered in pearlescent markings. The moon-inked dragon scales etched onto the surface of his skin were his permanent reminder that he was exceptional —a divine fey.

"Well, your aura is incredibly powerful. From the outside, you look like every bit a divine warlock. If that helps at all," Elowyn said.

Finnor smiled at her comment. "It does help. With everything that—"

Their dance was short-lived as someone tapped Finnor's shoulder. The two stopped their spinning and turned. A bronzed hand was outstretched to Elowyn, the very hand her smallest finger was intertwined with earlier. She recognized the Darkmaw prince's palm before she even looked up to find his claret-red hair and golden irises gazing at her.

"Excuse me, Commander Wynward. May I have a dance with the Fangwright princess?" Draeden addressed him.

A pang of irritation rippled through Finnor's face, but it quickly faded. He reluctantly ceded Elowyn's hand to Draeden's palm. "Take care, Princess Elowyn," he said before stepping away and disappearing into the crowd of fey.

Elowyn turned back to Draeden; he only smiled as he whisked her across the floor, twirling her in place until the skirts of her dress swirled in a champagne spiral. Elowyn giggled at the rush and returned his smile as he artfully placed his hand around her waist, leading her into a dance with spirited steps.

"Hello again, Princess Elowyn." Draeden greeted her mid-step, keeping his lively pace.

Looking into his golden eyes, she said, "Hello again, Prince Draeden." Elowyn's heart began fluttering in her chest.

"Are there any other dreamy portal stories you'd like to share with me?" He teased, playfulness gleaming in his eyes.

"Where do I begin?" She tsked, countering the prince.

He threw back his head and laughed heartily. "Such a clever one you are."

"I'd sure hope so." Elowyn retorted.

He added with a wink, "And ever so enchanting."

Elowyn's face flushed as Draeden continued leading her across the floor in charming steps. Their eyes remained locked on each other as they swayed and swirled in fervent footfalls. Their movements blended as they created a twirling mirage of claret-red and snow-white. Bouts of light laughter escaped from Elowyn and handsome smirks bloomed across the surface of Draeden's face.

The music in the hall guided their graceful steps and as the melody reached its crescendo, Draeden dipped Elowyn by the waist, a grin playing on his lips. They continued their delicate dance that felt like minutes, hours, or days—Elowyn couldn't tell. Time lost its meaning for her in this moment, it let her forget the weight of the world around her. Too soon, their strides began to slow and the song that shepherded their steps ceased. Elowyn was surprised to find herself breathless.

"Can I get you a refreshment?" Draeden offered, wiping a bead of sweat from his brow.

"Yes," Elowyn replied, feeling the need for refreshment. "Please."

He led her through the crowd, weaving them through the waltzing revelers before they stopped at a refreshment table. He filled two goblets with water and offered one to Elowyn. She took it gratefully and drained it entirely as he sipped from his own. He poured her another and it went down quicker than the first. Elowyn rubbed her temple methodically, feeling lightheaded as moved and rested herself on a nearby pillar.

Draeden's expression colored with concern as he placed a hand on her arm. "Are you feeling all right?"

"I'm just feeling a bit faint. I didn't eat much earlier, and the lively atmosphere is a bit overwhelming," Elowyn admitted.

The celebration in the banquet hall was in full swing as nobility and courtiers alike were singing and laughing together in spirited company. Most of the tables were cleared and the dance floor was overflowing. The newest moon marked warlocks and sorceresses, Finnor included, were talking and chatting amongst each other as they sat clustered on one end of a long banquet table. They appeared sapped, but rightfully so.

Finnor sat at the far end of the table, engrossed in conversation with a sorceress possessing mint-colored hair that hinted at her Skyborn lineage, evident from the shimmering aquamarine wings adorning her back. Elowyn observed their interaction, uncertain of what to make of the Fangwright warlock. While their conversation seemed harmless, Finnor's previous remarks about her father left Elowyn wary of placing too much trust in him.

Her attention briefly shifted to her father, who remained deep in discussion with her uncle at the head table. Elowyn felt a wave of relief knowing that their focus wasn't directed towards her or her sister. As the festivities continued to escalate, Elowyn longed for a reprieve from the crowded hall. She couldn't help but wonder where her mother and sister had disappeared to, likely embroiled in yet another argument that only added to Elowyn's mounting anxiety.

Interrupting her thoughts, Draeden's voice drew Elowyn's attention. "Do you have a favorite spot in the castle?"

Elowyn considered the question for a moment before replying, "One of the balconies near the mountainside. Why do you ask?"

"I have a plan," Draeden announced with a mischievous glint in his eyes. "Wait here for me, I'll be right back." With that, the Darkmaw prince disappeared into the crowd, leaving Elowyn leaning against the marble pillar.

Moments later, Draeden returned, balancing a tray of delicacies and a bottle of *vinum* in his hands, his dimpled smile lighting up his face. The tray offered an enticing array of cured meats, fine cheeses, delicate crackers, dried fruits, nuts, and a generous selection of sweets. Elowyn's stomach rumbled at the sight.

"Lead the way," Draeden said simply.

"To where?" Elowyn inquired, intrigued by his sudden plan.

"Where else? To your favorite balcony, of course," Draeden replied, his smirk suggesting an adventure awaited them.

Elowyn hesitated for a moment, feeling a twinge of uncertainty.

However, she recognized Draeden's offer as a chance to escape the bustling chaos of the banquet hall. Whether it was the allure of respite or simply a spur-of-the-moment decision, she grabbed two goblets and nodded in agreement.

She gratefully led the Darkmaw prince to the exit of the banquet hall and the two of them quietly snuck out, slinking carefully through the castle halls.

THE CRISP NIGHT AIR BRUSHED AGAINST ELOWYN'S SKIN, invigorating her as she gazed out at the majestic mountain range. Above, the sky displayed a canvas of midnight gray and indigo blue, sprinkled with stars that gleamed like twinkling gems. A shy moon peeked from behind plush clouds, while the breeze continued to caress her in a gentle current.

Leaning on the balcony ledge, Elowyn breathed in the calm of the night before turning to find an intricately crafted iron-wrought table spread with fare and two goblets filled with fey wine. Draeden lounged in one of the cushioned chairs, gesturing for her to join him. Elowyn accepted it without hesitation as she plucked a dried apricot from the tray and popped it in her mouth, savoring the sweet taste as she settled into her seat.

Draeden admired the skyscape, swirling his goblet thoughtfully before taking a sip. "Do you experience this view every night?" he asked.

"Most nights," Elowyn replied. "Though some are less enchanting than others. I'd like to believe that Eriden holds a beauty that no other place has in Neramyr."

"It certainly is something. My home in Orwyn doesn't hold quite the same charm this place has," Draeden remarked.

"I've never been…This is the first Ceremony where I'll be able to travel to all seven realms," Elowyn admitted. "What's Orwyn like?"

Draeden paused, contemplating his response. "Orwyn lies in the badlands of Neramyr. It's vastly different from Eriden. The air is dry, and the land is mainly rocks and clay soil. We have some grasslands, but they're sparse. Orwyn has its own appeal, though. You'll discover it for yourself soon enough." He chuckled and took another sip of wine, leaving the mystery of Orwyn to unfold in the days to come.

"I'll be sure to report back to you about my thoughts once I've set my eyes on your kingdom myself," Elowyn smiled.

"Please do," Draeden responded with a smirk. "I hear they have a handsome prince."

Elowyn playfully rolled her eyes as she assembled a snack of smoked meat, aged cheese, and salted crackers, pairing it with sips of *vinum*.

"Besides our occasional glances and banter, I realize I don't know much about you," Elowyn mentioned. "Out of curiosity, what prompted this?" She gestured her hand between them, referring to their interactions.

"To be honest, I didn't remember you until I saw you at the Temple of Caena," Draeden admitted. "But once I did, memories of the previous Ceremony flooded back. I was curious about you."

"Interesting. Well, I can assure you I'm not as shy as I used to be," Elowyn chuckled. "How old are you?"

"I'm twenty-two," Draeden answered. "And you?"

"Nineteen," Elowyn replied, taking another bite.

"Our entire divine cohort is young... The infamous 'sacred seven' as Neramyr likes to call it," Draeden mused. "Whatever the Goddess has in store for us, I'm not exactly eager to find out."

"I couldn't agree more," Elowyn confessed. "I'm terrified of the Trial. I spoke with Finnor earlier; he seemed quite shaken. Honestly, all the returning candidates appear to be. Except for the *primis*, of course."

"I've noticed that too. I haven't had a chance to speak with Serafina, yet. But I imagine she feels the same as the Commander," Draeden remarked, referring to the newly divine Darkmaw sorceress sworn to his House.

"Lovely. I can't wait until that's us," Elowyn nervously chuckled.

Amidst the festivities of the Ceremony of Caena, many forget the dangers beyond the Bridge Between Worlds. Those lands harbor beasts and monsters from the Old Age—a dark reminder of the Trial's treacherous nature.

When called to the Trial, a fey must comply; refusal was considered treason against the Goddess. Candidates are expected not only to survive, but to thrive in an environment designed to test their knowledge, strength, and resolve over seven years. There had been candidates who have returned across the Bridge Between Worlds broken and defeated; never living as their former self and wasting away into nothingness. These warlocks and sorceresses were exiled; refusing to wield the divine magic they were given for the benefit of the seven realms.

It was said that to be chosen to receive the final Mark of Caena was as much of a blessing as it was a curse.

"We'll make it through," Draeden vowed, as though he could hear Elowyn's thoughts aloud.

Elowyn's attention turned to him as he as he held out a pinky finger to her in solidarity. After a moment's consideration, she extended her own, intertwining it with his.

Throughout the lulling night, the two heirs delved deeper into conversation, baring their truths and fears, sharing their hopes and dreams, and exchanging quiet laughs and secretive smiles. Their dialogue only ceased when the moon surrendered to slumber, and the sun stirred awake.

As their time drew to a close, Elowyn found herself captivated as she watched the prince disappear through the shimmering pillars of a moongate, leaving her with lingering feelings of mirth and mystery, carrying those emotions to her bed.

10

Favor of the Seven

Elowyn was startled awake as Ora barged into her room unannounced like a wayward windstorm. The headstrong handmaiden began ripping off the covers that enveloped the Fangwright princess and shooed her out of bed.

"Up, up, up! It's well past the hour you should have risen," Ora scolded, nudging Elowyn to get moving.

"Fine, fine. Moons, what a *rude* awakening. I'm getting up…" Elowyn grumbled as she rubbed the sleep from her eyes.

"If I let you sleep any longer, you'll surely be late to the Iron Hollows for the Second Day. You mustn't be late for the Favor of the Seven," Ora lectured. "And don't think I'm oblivious to your spontaneous encounter with the Darkmaw prince last night."

"Oh, come on, admit it. He's rather charming, isn't he?" Elowyn teased, a mischievous grin playing on her lips.

The handmaiden waived away the comment, struggling to conceal the sideways smile on her lips. She hoisted Elowyn out of bed and draped her in a silk robe before seating her at a small table. With a flourish, Ora unveiled a tray containing fruits, sliced meats, and a bowl of warmed oats.

"Due to your tardiness, I've arranged for your breakfast to be brought to your room," Ora said sternly. "Hurry and eat. I'll be back in a few moments to help you get dressed for the Second Day."

With that, Ora bustled off toward the exit of Elowyn's chambers.

Elowyn scooped up a spoonful of brown sugar and dropped it into her oats, followed by a splash of cream. She stirred the mixture as her thoughts drifted to the upcoming Second Day. In the previous Ceremony, she had only participated in the rituals of the First and Seventh Day, confined to the Heart of the Temple. She suspected she had been too young. While her father, mother, and older sister participated in the week-long Ceremony, she remained under Ora's vigilant watch in Eriden.

The Iron Hollows, situated to the southwest of Eriden, was a kingdom she had yet to visit before. Nestled within a cavernous region, their realm was *literally* built beneath a rocky canyon, hundreds of meters below the surface. Their subterranean kingdom resembled a labyrinth, with the royal castle positioned at its core, similar to a hive. King Wilden and Queen Irena Bloodweaver ruled over the Iron Hollows, along with their two sons, Thomys and Theoden Bloodweaver. The mere thought of the second Bloodweaver prince made Elowyn recoil; the image of the dark-haired prince filled her with disgust. She was far from thrilled to spend the entirety of the day in their lightless kingdom.

Finishing breakfast with a frown on her brow, Elowyn rose to refresh herself in her bath chamber. A soft knock on the doorframe interrupted her, and she turned to see not Ora, but Elyria floating into her room. Dressed in a magnificent dress of sage tulle, Elyria's skirts flowed around her like the colors of spring.

Draping around her shoulders, Elyria wore a golden *aureum*, her dress's train flowing behind her as she greeted Elowyn with a warm smile. Today, she wore a silver circlet upon her head, her wavy hair woven into a sleek braid that fell down her back, decorated with miniature wildflowers nestled within the twists. Her attire stood in stark contrast to the obsidian gown she wore the previous day.

"Hey, sleepyhead," Elyria said in a soothing voice.

"Hi, I missed you last night," Elowyn replied with a delighted smile, a sense of comfort enveloping her.

"I stopped by your room late yesterday evening, but it seemed you were elsewhere," Elyria remarked, her gaze probing. "Anything you'd like to share?"

Elowyn blushed sheepishly. "I met someone. He's interesting. We talked for hours, and it was... nice. It was a relief to unwind for a while, despite everything."

Elyria smiled fondly. "Sounds promising, perhaps?"

Elowyn smirked at the question but swiftly changed the subject. "Where did you disappear to last night? What did mother have to say?"

Elyria's expression faltered slightly, but she shook her head. "That's a conversation for another time. Come, let's get you dressed before we're late for the Iron Hollows. I've managed to persuade Ora to let me handle your wardrobe, which was a feat within itself."

Taking Elowyn's hand, Elyria led her to the grand vanity in her bath chamber. Elowyn sat as Elyria picked up an ornate brass hairbrush and began to comb through her sister's snow-white locks. Each stroke was a soothing rhythm, almost lulling Elowyn back to sleep. Soon, Elyria began separating locks of hair in sections, weaving in golden silk ribbons, entwining them to form tight braids.

Once Elyria had fashioned two braids near the temples of Elowyn's head, she brought them together at a central point, weaving them into a crown. The remaining strands fell down Elowyn's back, sleek and smooth like a blanket of snow. Stepping back, Elyria admired her handiwork, pleased with the result.

"I'll just be a moment," Elyria murmured, leaning down to embrace her sister in a fleeting half-hug. Her gaze lingered on the opal teardrop necklace around Elowyn's neck, a soft smile gracing her lips before she vanished into the adjoining room.

While Elyria was off presumably finding a gown, Elowyn reached into the drawer beneath her vanity and retrieved a jewelry box. She began pinning golden flower hairpins into her braids, adding a touch of glint to her hair. Next, she retrieved a compact from the drawer and carefully applied kohl to line her upper eyelids, adding a rosy blush to her cheeks and staining her lips with a floral color to match. Tilting her head, she inspected her reflection just as Elyria returned to the room.

"Surprise!" Elyria announced, presenting the stunning periwinkle gown with silver accents from her own wardrobe that Elowyn adored.

"Wait, seriously?" Elowyn exclaimed, eyes widening in disbelief.

"It's all yours," Elyria confirmed, holding the gown out towards her sister.

Elowyn sprang from her seat, clutching the dress in one arm while enveloping her sister in a tight embrace with the other. "You're the best."

"I know," Elyria shrugged her shoulders, both sisters giggling.

"All right, hurry and get changed before Ora orders for my head to be served on a platter," Elyria chided. "I'll be waiting in the antechamber."

Still marveling at the gown in her arms, Elowyn ran her fingers over the shimmering fabric. Giving Elyria a serious look, she declared, "Just so you know, I'm not giving this back."

Elyria shook her head with a resigned smile. "Oh, I'm well aware."

Once Elyria left, Elowyn wasted no time in shedding her robe and slipping into the periwinkle gown. As she gazed into the mirror, she was nearly taken aback. The dress exceeded all her expectations—it was more beautiful than she ever imagined it could be.

The fabric hugged her figure, the back opening to highlight her curves. Purple-blue organza covered her form in luminous layers, lined with silver pearls arranged in patterns, resembling a stream of starlight. Delicate lilac embroidery decorated the gown, adding to its beauty. She twirled in front of the mirror and the train of her dress whirled with her, gathering in a glimmering spiral at her feet.

Elowyn couldn't tear her eyes away from her reflection, feeling a sense of beauty she rarely experienced—one that rivaled her mother or sister. After a moment of admiration, she reached for her *aureum*, fastening it to each shoulder strap of her gown.

Satisfied with her appearance, Elowyn slipped on her heels and made her way to the antechamber of her bedroom, the periwinkle gown trailing behind her.

"You look amazing," Elyria complimented.

"All thanks to you," Elowyn replied, beaming.

"Always," Elyria murmured, extending her arm with an open palm. "Ready?"

"Ready." Elowyn nodded, taking her sister's hand.

With a surge of Elyria's magic, a shimmering moongate to the Iron Hollows materialized before them. Locking eyes with her sister, Elowyn stepped through the moonlit portal hand-in-hand with Elyria.

THE IRON HOLLOWS APPEARED FAR MORE INVITING THAN Elowyn had initially imagined. She gazed at the inner gates of the kingdom, marveling at the natural crystalline formations protruding from the rock walls. Clusters of rich garnet stones ornamented the surface, casting a warm maroon gleam throughout the cave. Despite being deep below the surface, the kingdom was bathed in a luminous glow from floating feylight spheres suspended high above in the cavern's vaulted ceilings, resembling twinkling stars in a midnight sky.

Elowyn attempted to locate the Bloodweaver castle, but her view was obstructed by iron gates. Glancing around, she found the area deserted. While the situation might have seemed eerie, she found it oddly tranquil.

"Are we running late?" Elowyn inquired, turning to her sister.

Elyria shook her head. "If memory serves, we're not actually at the castle gates. The Bloodweavers don't permit guests to moongate so close to their walls. We'll need an escort."

As if in response to their conversation, the iron gates before them began to move silently, revealing a figure stepping forward. This season's Bloodweaver candidate emerged, offering a respectful bow. His mahogany hair partially obscured his face as he addressed them.

"Welcome to the Iron Hollows," Sylas greeted, his sea-green eyes piercing through the amber glow of the cave.

Both Elowyn and Elyria curtsied in acknowledgment of the Bloodweaver candidate, relieved that Prince Theo wasn't accompanying him this time.

"I apologize if you've been waiting long. The path to the royal castle isn't far, but our larger vessels are currently occupied with other guests. I can only escort one of you for now, but worry not, another escort will arrive shortly," Sylas explained.

"No need for apologies, we've only just arrived," Elyria reassured.

"It would be my honor to accompany you through the Iron Hollows, Princess Elyria," Sylas offered, extending his hand towards her. "May I?"

Elyria glanced at Elowyn, offering a reassuring smile before stepping forward and gently brushing her hand against Elowyn's arm. "See you there," she murmured.

Elowyn nodded, watching as they disappeared behind the iron gates. As the gates slowly closed and locked into place, she found herself alone once more.

Waiting for what felt like an eternity, Elowyn's patience waned as the minutes passed in silence. She wandered to the cavern's jagged walls, running her hands over the crystal and mineral formations that grew along them. Recalling her studies, she remembered the wealth of the Iron Hollows, derived primarily from mining the surrounding caves for export. These resources, including gems, ores, minerals, and natural stones, were sought after throughout Neramyr for various purposes—many being magical in nature.

Absently cradling her necklace, Elowyn wondered if the opal gemstone set in her chain originated from these very mines.

After what felt like a quarter of an hour, the iron gates began to creak open slowly, relieving Elowyn's growing sense of boredom. Emerging from behind the gates, a tall figure sauntered into view. Elowyn sensed his presence before laying eyes on him.

Theo Bloodweaver appeared in a sleek black tunic and trousers, his *aureum* clasped at one shoulder, its golden folds flowing down his right side. A haunting smile played upon his lips as he dipped into a low bow before Elowyn.

"Welcome to the Iron Hollows, Princess Elowyn." His mischievous smile became unnerving. His ruby-colored irises glowed in the darkness. Elowyn couldn't help but compare his affect to a predator gazing at its prey through sunless shadows. "Sylas informed me that the second Fangwright princess awaited an escort at the gates. Considering this such a *notable* task, I came here as swiftly as I could."

Elowyn's irritation simmered. She opened her mouth to strike back, but considered the action carefully and closed it. Meeting the Bloodweaver prince's gaze with a glare, she replied, "Thank you, Prince Theo."

"Now, shall I escort you to the Iron Kingdom?" Theo offered, his gaze equally sinister as he extended a hand towards Elowyn.

"Lead the way," Elowyn grated, striding towards the iron gates and pointedly refusing his hand.

With a nonchalant shrug, the Bloodweaver prince tucked his hands into his pockets and strolled after her.

As Elowyn strode through the now-open gates, she felt a pulse of magic course through her. It was jarring, as she passed the gate, it felt like a tremor rippled through her body when she crossed the threshold. The feeling lingered as she couldn't shake or get rid of it, causing her body to stiffen in discomfort and unease.

Theo noticed her tense disposition. "These outer gates are heavily warded. The magic imbued in these barriers were constructed by the first Bloodweaver queen millennia ago. Their purpose is to safeguard this kingdom and protect its folk from creatures intending harm, wild beast or fey. You never know what lurks in the shadows," he said with a tsk. "Only a faithful member of the royal court can escort an outsider into the innermost walls of the kingdom."

"Do you experience this every time you pass through the outer gates?" Elowyn winced.

"Of course not. I'm not an outsider," the Bloodweaver prince answered, his tone condescending.

Choosing to ignore his attitude, Elowyn pressed on. "And what happens if a not-so-faithful member of the royal court passes through without an escort?" she inquired.

"The protective ward can discern one's essence and character to some extent. If it detects nefarious intentions, the consequences are grave," Theo explained plainly. "The pressure from the surrounding magic would crush them."

"Great," she muttered.

"Isadora Bloodweaver took the welfare of her kingdom seriously," Theo remarked, referencing the first Iron Queen.

"You don't say," Elowyn replied sarcastically, her face a mask of indifference.

Shortly after they began walking, they approached a clearing in the cavern where the ground ebbed into a body of water that was split into two tunneled paths. Theo flicked his wrist and beckoned a beautiful watercraft awaiting in the shallows towards them. It floated gently to them, eager to be put to use. The vessel was modest in size, with cushioned seats large enough for two occupants to sit comfortably.

"Ladies first," Theo drawled, gesturing grandly toward the boat.

Suppressing the urge to roll her eyes, Elowyn shot him a disdainful glance before picking up the skirts of her dress and carefully making her way to the edge of the watercraft. She calculated where she should step on the swaying vessel since she would rather moongate to another realm mistakenly than embarrass herself in front of Theoden Bloodweaver due to a misstep.

A second ticked by and she still hadn't moved. Theo tutted impatiently and extended his hand, offering support. "It seems you're in need of my assistance," he goaded.

Elowyn's irritation flared as she reluctantly accepted his hand. Settling herself onto one of the cushioned seats, she shot him a glare. "Are you always this unpleasant?"

"I'm perfectly pleasant. Although, you seem to be otherwise," Theo remarked as he gracefully stepped onto the watercraft, sinking into a cushioned seat across from Elowyn. With a casual wave of his hand, the vessel began to glide forward at a gentle pace, veering toward the rightmost tunnel.

"What is your problem with me?" Elowyn asked straightforwardly.

"I don't have any problem with you, specifically," Theo droned. "It's more that I find your family a disgrace to all of Neramyr. It's shameful to see the esteemed Fangwright bloodline devolve into something so reprehensible."

Elowyn's grip tightened on the sides of the watercraft, marring the wood with her fingertips.

"Careful now, the primordial Iron Queen's magic is watching you," Theo cautioned.

"You best watch your tongue," Elowyn threatened.

"It's a shame your sister is the way she is. She's stunning, that one," he commented casually. "A damn shame that the blood running through her veins is tainted. So tainted, in fact, that she was stripped of her birthright. The Fanged King made sure of that." Theo frowned pensively. "She's good for nothing now... Not even as a broodmare. However, I suppose she'd make a fine coin in the Iron Hollow's Pleasure District... I'd even be her first patron."

As the last word fell from his mouth, Elowyn snapped. She lunged for Theo so fast that he didn't see the fist that contacted the side of his angled jaw. Elowyn's fist collided into his porcelain chin so violently he recoiled back forcefully enough that he needed to grasp the sides of the vessel to support himself.

Elowyn reeled back her fist again to strike him once more, but before she could throw another punch, she doubled over in shock.

She clutched her throat, feeling it narrow. The magic in the cavern surged around her, crushing her with a relentless force. A thunderous headache blinded her as her skull felt like it was splintering from an unyielding grip. Her heart turned frenzied as it pumped against its own walls being compressed, mustering every effort to remain perfusing her body. Her lungs screamed for oxygen to feed her muscles while she clutched her chest. Elowyn began to panic, and her eyes widened as she realized she couldn't break free of the magical assault.

Muttering something under his breath, Theo wiped his face on his sleeve. Another pulse of magic—Theo's magic—coursed through the air.

At once, the magical onslaught ceased, and Elowyn collapsed on her knees and forearms. She gasped for air in uneven breaths, greedily filling her lungs. On her exterior, not a single hair was out of place, but on the inside, Elowyn felt a fear so heinous it frightened her to the very core. She turned her glowering gaze to the dark-haired prince again.

"You're a hateful beast," she hissed at him.

"Everyone has their vices," he countered as he ran a hand over his jaw, attempting to soothe the bruises that were rapidly blossoming on the left side of his face in angry crimson blotches.

"If you ever utter another word about Elyria again, you'll regret it," Elowyn whispered.

She hardened her eyes and braced herself as she waited for another volley of suffering to strike her, but it never came. With a disgruntled look upon his face, Theo turned his head, leaning over the edge of the watercraft and spat a crimson-colored spittle from his mouth into the clear waters surrounding them. His blood billowed through the deep blue waters, spreading until it faded into the depths.

"We're nearly there," was all Theo said in response.

The two royals sat in silence as the watercraft navigated them through the labyrinth of tunnels ahead of them. The vessel took them in winding paths and bending lanes to their destination, the inner walls of the kingdom. The water lapped the sides of the vessel in a rhythmic tempo as the seconds passed.

Elowyn closed her eyes and used the water's steady cadence to regain her composure before she entered the Bloodweaver castle. Every ounce of her body was filled with detestation for the male sitting across from her. Elowyn knew she had the temperament of an unbroken boar, and it had gotten her in trouble more times than she could count. She breathed in through her nose and exhaled from her mouth, finally opening her eyes once more to find Theo staring at her with an indecipherable expression.

She looked at the prince and examined the aggravated mark on his chin, the maroon blemish already starting to fade and heal.

"I shouldn't have done that." She looked at his bruise, conscience-stricken.

"You didn't take the first shot," he answered apathetically. "Maiming can be done without fists."

She nodded once in acknowledgment as they continued to float down the cavern's tunneled river. For now, both of them seemed to offer neutrality with fluttering white flags. Elowyn had been too preoccupied with annoyance towards him to notice the floating feylight spheres bobbing gently on the water's surface like lanterns, illuminating the tunnel in a soft glow. The feylight reflected off the tiny minerals embedded in the stone walls, twinkling at her with winking flickers, offering a sensation of wanderlust and awe.

Elowyn sat back in her cushioned seat and gazed at the walls, forgetting everything except this moment. There were times like these where she felt so attuned with the feylands of Neramyr—it felt so right, so idyllic, when she took in the world around her, appreciating the sheer marvel that Neramyr was.

She had always felt a strong connection to nature, suspecting it was the reason elemental magic came easier to her than other forms. Closing her eyes again, she focused her senses, drowning out the world. She listened to the rhythmic ripple of the river, inhaled the loamy scent of the natural cavern, and felt the aura of this magical place envelop her in a welcoming embrace. No longer burdened by the unpleasant heaviness of the cave's magic, she found herself in a blissful solitude.

"You're glowing." Theo tilted his head in curiosity.

"What?" Elowyn said, confused.

"Your palms." He pointed his chin towards her palms resting in her lap.

She looked down, and indeed, her palms were faintly glowing. She stared at them, puzzled.

"Isadora has acknowledged your presence," he stated plainly, his eyebrows scrunching unexpectedly.

"Oh," Elowyn said, turning her hands to inspect the illuminated crescent moons, her Mark, on her palms. "So that's what I was feeling?"

"Interesting," was all Theo said as he stared at her incredulously.

Before Elowyn could inquire further, a clearing appeared before them, and the vessel neared the shore's edge, concluding their journey.

Theo skillfully stepped out of the vessel and extended a hand to help Elowyn out. She took his hand with skepticism, attempting to decipher his aura but finding nothing. Giving up quickly, she grabbed the skirt of her dress and stepped onto the clearing. Once steady, Theo promptly dropped her hand and placed his in his pockets. He strode towards an arched entryway, similar to the entrance to the Heart of the Temple. Raising an open palm towards the archway, he extended a drop of his magic, placing his hand on the stone. The archway glowed faintly where his hand made contact, accepting his offering.

"Come," Theo directed to Elowyn as he disappeared through the stone archway, his gold *aureum* floating behind him until he was out of sight.

Elowyn took a deep breath to prepare herself and followed his footsteps to the Iron Kingdom.

For a moment, there was only darkness, then an incredible scene unfolded before her. The Bloodweaver castle loomed ahead, its exterior comprised of soaring columns of mighty stalagmites. It was a breathtaking vision of palatial formations that evoked feelings that Elowyn couldn't quite place. The castle was fortified with a sleek iron skeleton that shaped the palace. Curved archways, doors, and windows were crafted from iron beams, a remarkable tribute to cast-iron architecture. Elowyn couldn't help but feel that the Bloodweaver castle looked every bit as formidable as it was impregnable.

Elowyn spotted Theo marching to the top of the castle's iron stairs without waiting for her. She rolled her eyes this time and made her way up the series of steps. Upon reaching the top, she followed Theo's path through the castle's entrance, guided by the bustling noise of hundreds of courtiers. Stepping into the iron castle, they were greeted by sentries lining both sides of the marbled foyer.

One of the sentries announced their arrival, prompting a few heads to turn, but it was Queen Irena who noticed them first. She approached with graceful poise, wearing a silken smile.

"Welcome, Princess Elowyn. It's a pleasure to host you within our castle walls for the first time." The Iron Queen's voice was smooth as velvet.

"It's an honor, Your Majesty," Elowyn replied with a small curtsy.

"I hope you've had a chance to become acquainted with my son during your journey here," the Bloodweaver queen said, her eyes inquisitive as she glanced at Elowyn.

"Yes, Theo and I had an enlightening conversation," Elowyn said with a smile, turning to Theo. "Wouldn't you agree?"

"Enlightening, indeed," Theo replied, his smile polished as he turned to his mother.

The Iron Queen's posture stiffened, but regained her composure. Her narrowed gaze scrutinized her son's face.

"Darling, you appear to have bruised your chin," Queen Irena remarked, her tone concerned. "Are you all right?"

Elowyn's heart sank as she turned to Theo, searching his face, but found no trace of the earlier blemish. His visage was flawless. She trembled inwardly at the Iron Queen's uncanny ability to uncover what she thought was concealed.

"Ah, I feared we'd be late for the start of the Ceremony. In an attempt to rush here, I slipped as I stepped off the watercraft. A rather memorable experience for Princess Elowyn, I'm sure," Theo explained, dismissing the concern.

"You've always been rather reckless, my love. Please be more careful next time," the queen cautioned, her flawless porcelain hand brushing across his cheek. "For your mother's sake."

"I'm well, mother," Theo assured.

"Good," Queen Irena said tenderly. "I cannot express the pride that overwhelms me at the thought of you soon joining your brother in receiving the final Mark."

Elowyn felt a lingering gaze as the Iron Queen glanced at her before smiling and addressing them both.

"This might be presumptuous, but if I may impart a piece of wisdom: the bonds you form with your peers will determine your success in the Trial of Caena," Queen Irena said, marked with nostalgia. "Even to this day, I cherish and honor the companions who shared the burden of those seven years with me."

Elowyn could only nod in agreement, unsure how to respond.

"Now, I must return to the Iron King before he worries about my absence," the queen said, turning to Elowyn with a chilling gaze. "Once again, welcome to the Iron Kingdom, Princess Elowyn."

With that, Queen Irena gracefully navigated through the crowd, the courtiers parting to allow her passage.

Elowyn released a tensed breath and slackened her shoulders. She turned to speak to Theo, but he had already vanished, leaving her alone in his foreign kingdom.

11

A Fate Set in Stone

As Elowyn stepped into the Great Hall of the Bloodweaver castle, she immediately spotted Elyria's flowing braid amidst the crowd. Her legs instinctively moved toward her sister, but she froze as she witnessed Elyria covering her mouth and sharing a cheerful laugh with Sylas. It was a rare sight to see her sister genuinely happy in the presence of someone else. Elowyn wished she could freeze this moment in time forever, cradling it close to her heart.

Finally noticing Elowyn's arrival, Elyria's smile widened as she waved and beckoned her over. Elowyn navigated through the crowd at her sister's urging, taking a stemmed glass of crimson-red wine from a passing servant's tray, offering a grateful nod.

"You're finally here!" Elyria greeted her with a relieved sigh, pulling her into an embrace. "I was beginning to worry."

"There were a few complications on my way over here," Elowyn replied with a serene smile. "But I made it nonetheless."

Sylas shifted subtly at her words, his expression betraying a hint of understanding. Before he could respond, however, the crowd parted as a figure strode through. All three of their gazes landed on the Iron King.

With a few powerful strides, King Wilden made his way to the dais of the Great Hall. Upon the raised platform, melded to it, sat two formidable iron thrones. To the throne on the left sat Queen Irena Bloodweaver. A sleek emerald basilisk coiled around the armrest. It was a wicked, beautiful creature. The serpent was gleaming, its emerald reptilian scales like overlapping jewels. The upper half of the serpent was entwined around the right arm of the queen with its sheeny head resting near the nape of her neck and its tail dangled from the armrest.

Elowyn observed the queen's basilisk with a hint of skepticism. For a divine *animus*, it didn't appear all that intimidating to her. She had seen harmless garden adders larger than it back in the castle grounds of Eriden.

Her thoughts were quickly abandoned as King Wilden claimed his iron throne. She sucked in a breath when she first noticed the creature. From behind the dais, a monstrous russet colored basilisk began slithering towards the king, its massive form stretching at least three meters in length and nearly the circumference of her thigh at its widest point. The face of the basilisk was more draconic than reptilian, horns sprouted from its head in vicious rods and whetted fangs protruded from its closed jaw. With smooth, twisting motions, the colossal basilisk coiled around the throne of the Iron King, its imposing head resting at the base.

"Welcome to the Iron Hollows," King Wilden's voice echoed through the Great Hall. "On this Second Day, we prepare to witness a sacred rite, the Favor of the Seven." He remained seated, his gaze sweeping over the assembled crowd. "In this hallowed ritual, we ask the Moon Goddess to bestow her divine favor upon the next candidates who will face judgment in her Trial. This long-standing custom has infallibly curried grace from the Goddess and sanctioned the safe passage of our candidates to her realm.

The Divine Shallows

"Following tradition, our newly divine fey will seek the favor of the Goddess for the candidates of this season," the Iron King announced with a smile. "It has been many moons since the duty of the Second Day has fallen upon the shoulders of our kingdom. We invite you to assemble in the Den of *Lunaris* at sunset to witness this sacred rite."

King Wilden's gaze shifted to his right, where his two sons stood upon the dais. Thomys and Theo Bloodweaver resembled near-perfect mirror images of each other. Both clad in onyx-shaded finery, their *aureum* clasped on their shoulders, hanging in golden layers. With hair as dark as obsidian, skin fair as porcelain, and eyes resembling opulent rubies, the brothers were mesmerizing. The only notable contrast between them was the faint, concentric, reptilian moon-inked scales that adorned Thomys' skin, along with the sleek basilisk draped across his shoulders, coiling at his arm. Standing proudly before their father and king, the brothers presented a dangerously captivating sight.

"It is a blessing from Caena herself that Queen Irena and I were graced with two children," King Wilden's powerful hand tenderly grazed Queen Irena's forearm. "It brings me great joy that my firstborn son, Thomys Bloodweaver, will seek divine favor for our Bloodweaver candidate this season, Sylas Fenhart. Undoubtedly, Sylas will prove indispensable in this season's Trial of Caena."

The Iron King gestured towards Sylas in the crowd, drawing the attention of hundreds of eyes. Elowyn shrank under the scrutiny and as she dared to glance up, she found Theo's odious maroon eyes boring into her own. Attempting to meet his gaze with her own hardened silver eyes, she was abruptly pulled away by the voice of the king.

"And it is my hope that in seven years, Sylas will seek the divine favor of the Moon Goddess for my second born son, Theoden Bloodweaver, in his Trial of Caena. Although his name has not yet been spoken for candidacy by the High Priestess, I shall await her verdict with bated breath."

King Wilden rose from his seat and approached the front of the dais with a smile. "Fey of Neramyr, welcome to the Kingdom of the Iron Hollows! Let the Second Day of the Ceremony commence!"

The Great Hall erupted into applause at King Wilden's declaration, with Elowyn and Elyria joining in along with the courtiers. Conversations resumed and music filled the air in a symphony of strings.

Elowyn and Elyria exchanged a weary glance, both releasing heavy sighs.

"Here we go again," Elyria muttered to her sister.

They shared a knowing look, bracing themselves for the remainder of the night.

∼

Sylas had taken it upon himself to chaperone the two Fangwright sisters for the Second Day. While it bothered Elowyn, Elyria seemed unfazed by his presence. Throughout their time in the Bloodweaver castle, Sylas followed their every step, which Elowyn found inconvenient. However, if he was offering himself for their disposal, she decided to seize the opportunity to ask him some lingering questions.

"So, Sylas, did you grow up in the inner walls?" Elowyn prodded.

"Yes, I come from a noble family entrusted with overseeing many essential trade affairs of the Iron Hollows. They serve the Bloodweaver family as high treasurers of sorts," Sylas replied willingly.

"I see," Elowyn nodded. "So, you've known the Bloodweavers your entire life?"

"I grew up alongside Thomys and Theo. They're almost like brothers to me—our dynamic certainly feels that way. Thomys, the eldest, is wise and sensible. I'm in the middle, often overlooked and excluded," he chuckled. "And then there's Theo, indulged and rebellious."

Elyria's eyes widened at the remark about the second born prince, but Elowyn simply joined in with a snicker.

The Divine Shallows

"Now that's a classic trope," Elowyn retorted loudly, tapping her finger against her chin. "Theo certainly *is* indulgent and rebellious, all right."

Sylas' expression turned serious. "I would take caution when saying that aloud, princess. While I tease, our relationship borders on that of brothers... and even that is tenuous. He has only ever tolerated such comments from Lyra, but that's a thing of the past. Since their separation, it's changed him."

"Who's Lyra?" Elowyn asked, her curiosity stirred.

"She's my younger sister... Years ago, Lyra became enamored with Theo despite all my objections. They were inseparable for a while. He charmed his way into her bed and her heart, but he never reciprocated the feelings." Sylas' voice was slightly bitter.

"I remember one day Lyra came home in tears. When I asked what happened, she told me that Theo suddenly flew into a rage for no apparent reason. He just snapped. He spewed hateful slurs at her and declared he wanted nothing to do with her again. He even threatened to have her exiled from the Iron Hollows." Sylas rubbed his temples as if trying to ease a headache. "Despite everything, Lyra still loves him. She loved him with all her heart. Even after what he did, she hasn't stopped trying to win him back, and it breaks my heart."

"Goddess, and he couldn't even offer a reason? Rather juvenile," Elowyn scoffed, her disbelief evident.

Elyria glanced around uncomfortably, her eyes scanning for any eavesdropping courtiers. Speaking openly about royalty could lead to trouble. She swiftly changed the subject with a delicate question, "Sylas, how many *animus* reside in the Iron Hollows?"

Turning to Elyria, Sylas' brow furrows softened, and he offered her a warm smile. "There are three: King Wilden's, Queen Irena's, and now, Prince Thomys'."

"Hopefully, soon to be four," Elyria remarked gently. "Once you claim one in the Trial this season."

Sylas' cheeks flushed crimson, and Elowyn couldn't blame him. She would have been blushing too if someone as captivating as Elyria had subtly complimented her.

"I couldn't help but notice that Queen Irena's and Prince Thomys' *animus* are, well, more moderately sized," Elowyn stumbled, trying to phrase it delicately. "Is there a reason for that?"

"Well, Queen Irena's basilisk may appear willowy, but I fear it a thousand times more than King Wilden's. Even a drop of its venom could prove fatal to a fey a hundred times over... And its temperament is simply atrocious," Sylas grimaced. "On the other hand, King Wilden's basilisk can constrict and compress a creature with lethal force. It would be a reality borne of nightmares to be strangled into smithereens by that russet serpent." Sylas shuddered at the thought. "As for Thomys, I haven't had the chance to speak with him since his return, so I'm not entirely familiar with his *animus'* capabilities."

"I have," a lively voice bloomed from behind them.

Elowyn turned to see who it was, locking eyes with an angelic fey. She had rich mahogany curls that flowed down her back in rivulets. Her skin was deeply tan, while freckles dotted her nose and the apples of her cheeks. Lastly, her eyes were a piercing sea-green that seemed almost otherworldly.

"His *animus* is quite fascinating. Apparently, his basilisk can transiently duplicate herself. Although, she needs to lay a clutch of eggs and hatch them, Thomys claims he can control the clones with just his thoughts. He can see what they see, hear what they hear, taste what they taste," her enchanting voice elaborated.

Turning to her, Sylas inclined his head. "Hello, Lyra. Allow me to introduce you to the princesses of Eriden, Princess Elyria and Princess Elowyn Fangwright." He gestured towards the silver-eyed sisters.

Lyra curtsied and nodded to them. "I'm Sylas' sister, Lyra Fenhart. It's lovely to meet both of you."

"Your dress is stunning," Elyria complimented with a soft smile.

Lyra returned the gesture, her eyes lingering briefly on Elyria's palms before refocusing her attention to the three of them again.

"It seems like you know more about the Iron Kingdom than Sylas does. Maybe we should have you give us a tour instead," Elowyn suggested.

"I know many things about the Iron Kingdom, but sometimes the things I want to know most about evade me." Lyra chucked with morose as her sea-green eyes flickered to somewhere else in the room.

Elowyn sensed a longing emanating from Lyra's aura, nearly tangible in its intensity. She almost felt sorry for her, but quickly reminded herself that any affection directed towards Theo didn't quite warrant her sympathy.

Turning to Lyra, Elowyn asked, "Would you mind showing me around? I feel like the candidates already have important matters to attend to besides a castle tour, especially with the preparations for the Favor of the Seven."

Elyria shot her sister a curious glance, silently questioning her decision. Elowyn responded with a reassuring look, conveying her certainty. They had perfected the art of communicating through glances and raised eyebrows long ago.

In truth, Elowyn had no desire to spend the evening in Sylas' company; he'd likely bore her to tears. Elyria, on the other hand, seemed to enjoy his presence. Why not leave them to it?

"Of course. It would be my pleasure," Lyra agreed.

"Wonderful!" Elowyn beamed, linking her arm with Lyra's, and whisked her away.

∽

Elowyn and Lyra wandered through the halls of the Bloodweaver castle, wine glasses in hand, losing themselves in the amber-lit passages teeming with captivating artwork. They peered at abstract statues and studied the freeform sculptures that decorated the hallways while having to stifle giggles at some more progressive pieces. Lyra narrated certain fables and tales of particular sculptures that Elowyn pointed out in curiosity. An hour passed in this manner, the wine blurring their senses.

"What's down there?" Elowyn gestured vaguely towards a hallway; her voice slightly slurred from the wine.

"That leads to the royal atrium," Lyra responded, her words sluggish.

Elowyn sniggered. "An atrium in a cavern? What good would an atrium do underground?"

"Just wait and see. Beauty can be found underground, too," Lyra replied, grabbing Elowyn's hand clumsily and leading her towards the hallway.

The two of them meandered forward, as uncoordinated as newborn fawns, while they awkwardly made their way to the looming iron doors that towered before them.

"This is one of my favorite places in the castle for a thousand reasons," Lyra mumbled with a thick tongue. "And here's the first one."

Lyra conjured a shimmering bead of magic in her palm and pressed it to the door. The aura of the door responded to her touch, swinging open slowly to reveal the atrium beyond, welcoming them with a gentle breeze from within. Lyra wandered through the entrance and beckoned Elowyn to trace her footsteps.

Elowyn didn't expect what she saw next.

The atrium unfolded before her, and her breath hitched at the sight. The atrium was enormous, and much to her chagrin, it wasn't made of glass. It was a deep underground sanctuary opened to the night sky above. She tilted her head back to stare at the heavens as millions stars twinkled. A natural stone path snaked between endless landscapes of rock formations ranging in various heights, lengths, and textures. If she desired, Elowyn could ascend to higher levels of the atrium to where the path led. Brilliant crystal growths sprouted from the rocks and glistened in hues of aquamarine, emerald, and violet.

But what made Elowyn want to fall to her knees with wonder was what she found in the center of the atrium. There was a feylight waterfall that streamed from the sky and flowed into a large lake below, forming billowing gentle waves that lapped the shore surrounding it. It was one of the most beautiful things she'd ever seen. She closed her eyes and breathed in deeply as she felt another pull towards the ethereal cave around her. She had no idea how there was the open air several meters below the soil's surface or why there was a feylight fountain pouring from the sky.

She knew it shouldn't be possible, but somehow, this felt logical; it felt sound.

"How?" Elowyn whispered, unable to tear her gaze away.

"The divine Goddess of course... And the fifty-third Iron King, King Furno Bloodweaver. He created this atrium," Lyra mumbled, taking a seat on a nearby bench and patting the space beside her. "The fey of House Bloodweaver are masters of alteration magic, silly. Come, sit."

Elowyn settled onto the bench next to Lyra, who miraculously produced a bottle of wine from beneath her skirts. Elowyn raised an impressed eyebrow as the brunette fey took a swig before passing it to her.

"I can understand why you're able to find a thousand reasons to adore this place," Elowyn remarked, taking a generous sip from the bottle.

Lyra leaned back, releasing a sigh. "Of all the reasons, the one that stands above all is because I fell in love here."

Elowyn struggled to control her expression, feeling awkward with this type of conversation. She wasn't accustomed to offering comfort or discussing matters of the heart, except with her sister. Growing up, her father had kept her isolated, allowing her to interact only with those he approved of. Any budding friendships were swiftly extinguished by his disapproval. This left Elowyn feeling lonely, but Elyria was always there to fill the void.

"Sylas told us about Theo," Elowyn confessed, handing the bottle back to Lyra. "He's a twat."

Lyra looked back at her, surprised.

A moment of silence passed between them before they both erupted into laughter. Tears welled in their eyes as they laughed, the tension dissipating. But then Elowyn noticed the change in Lyra's demeanor. Her aura darkened, and her expression turned somber.

"He's not though," Lyra said, her voice heavy with emotion. "Theo is wonderful. He's kind and clever. He's unlike anyone I've ever known. He makes me laugh like no one else."

Elowyn struggled to hide her disdain, her expression betraying her despite the alcohol clouding her judgment. She couldn't fathom how Lyra could see Theo in such a positive light after their earlier encounter. Unable to find the right words, she remained silent.

"I know, I know," Lyra admitted, her voice beginning to wobble. "But I've seen a side of him that nobody else has. He's just not what he shows to the world. We spent endless nights here, talking until we fell asleep in each other's arms. We laughed until our bellies hurt, made love under the stars, danced in the moonlight. We were truly, deeply in love."

As Lyra poured her heart out, Elowyn couldn't help but think of Draeden. Just last night, they had stayed up until dawn, sharing their deepest thoughts and feelings. Elowyn remembered the thrill of excitement that surged through her veins in Draeden's presence, the anticipation of the unknown. Despite her initial reluctance, Elowyn found herself sympathizing with Lyra's pain. She reached out, placing a comforting hand on Lyra's arm.

"Sylas mentioned something about him getting upset, but no one seems to know why," Elowyn said, her tone gentle yet probing.

Lyra's expression turned pale at the question. "I don't know what happened. I told him I loved him... and he snapped. He became hysterical, said terrible things to me. He hasn't spoken to me since. He won't even look at me," she whispered, tears streaming down her face. "I wish I could take it all back."

Elowyn's heart went out to her. "You have nothing to feel guilty about. You deserve to be loved for who you are, completely and unconditionally." She articulated the words slower than she intended.

"But I can't help it. I still love him, even now. I'd do anything for him, but he would never do the same," Lyra said, her voice hollow with despair. "It's cruel."

As Lyra finished the wine, lost in her own thoughts, Elowyn felt helpless. She had never experienced a love so intense, so consuming, before. Unable to offer any more comfort, Elowyn squeezed Lyra's hand gently before rising from her seat.

Well, it was more like Elowyn *stumbled* to her feet.

Extending a hand toward Lyra, Elowyn declared, "No more tears. Today, we're celebrating Sylas and Elyria. I'm setting one rule: we're here to have fun. No moping or sulking allowed."

Lyra looked at her through watery eyes and pitifully raised her hand in agreement.

"Okay, we might be off to a terrible start, but we can turn this around. Come on, let's get you some water," Elowyn said, gently tugging at Lyra's limp arm and helping her stand.

Lyra lurched upright at the pull, sniffing pitifully. "Your dress is really pretty."

"Thank you, it's a gift from my sister—It's the most beautiful dress I've ever owned," Elowyn replied, grateful for the distraction.

Lyra ran her hand along the periwinkle organza and tilted her head as she brushed the golden *aureum* draping from Elowyn's shoulders. She examined the pattern of dragon scales embellishing the golden silk, acknowledging what it symbolized.

"What's it like being a princess of Neramyr?" Lyra murmured, still admiring the golden cloak that skimmed between her fingers.

"Well, I'm not sure," Elowyn stumbled over her words. "I guess it's all right..."

Elowyn could have said so much more, but she was unsure of what was appropriate. Being born into a position of power and respect, she hadn't felt like she earned any of it. She had grown up with a negative view of royalty, especially given her family's circumstances.

Every day she felt the weight of her responsibility and her duty to the realm. As a princess, she would never be able to escape it. Her life was set in stone the moment she was born into it, shackled to a fate that she didn't choose. But she knew there were worse fates out there. She lived in splendor and opulence, never knowing what hunger was or the burden of a laborious livelihood. She felt guilty about feeling resentful about things; she knew she should be grateful for the hand she was dealt.

"You're lucky, you know. One day you'll marry a prince and live happily ever after. Maybe if I had been born a princess, things would be different... Theo would still love me," Lyra said defeatedly, slumping back onto the bench.

"Oh, no. We are *not* doing this. Firstly, being a princess of Neramyr isn't all that glamorous. Secondly, you've broken my rule twice now, and we're not going to have you break it a third time," Elowyn lectured her, hauling her upright again.

Hooking an arm around Lyra's waist, Elowyn supported her as they began walking down the natural stone that led back to the exit. Elowyn's mind became less foggy as they ambled through the path, though she was certainly still tipsy. Lyra's aura remained thoroughly morose, dismal at best. As for her mind, Lyra was definitely plastered.

"This sky fountain was one of my favorite things growing up as a feyling. And now I can barely look at it without my heart aching," Lyra murmured as she grieved. "I fear I'll never feel happiness in this place again."

Elowyn sighed in exasperation. She opened her mouth as a curt response danced at the tip of her tongue, but chose to close it, keeping her frustration at bay. Peering at Lyra's desolate aura again, she saw the weeping wounds. Huffing, Elowyn steered their path to a stone clearing and planted Lyra in the middle of it.

Slightly confused, Lyra stood there silently, her legs now steady enough to balance herself for the time being.

Elowyn stepped a few paces back and released a breath. "It's just elemental magic," Elowyn said to herself as she rallied her confidence.

She lifted her moon-inked palm and called to her magic, summoning it from the well of her reserves. From the lake behind them, two streams of feylight floated towards their direction, drifting through the air in a delicate dance. With a twist of Elowyn's wrist, the streams twirled and whirled, effortlessly weaving around Lyra in a playful pattern.

Lyra reached out and brushed her fingers along the feylight streams as they began to curl around her, ascending upwards until they crested at a peak above her head, collecting into a sphere. Tilting her head back, Lyra gazed up at the feylight orb in awe.

Elowyn shifted her palm and unfurled her fingers purposefully. Responding to her command, the feylight orb above Lyra shattered, fracturing into a starburst of thousands of feylight droplets. The shimmering droplets showered around Lyra, painting a rainfall canvas of brilliant emerald, amethyst, and aquamarine as the crystals in the atrium reflected off it. Lyra audibly gasped, clasping her hand over her mouth as her eyes widened in wonder. Reaching out again, she grazed the feylight canopy surrounding her, a shadow of a smile danced upon her lips while her eyes glittered with delight.

With her other hand, Elowyn called to the wind, beckoning it under her command. She willed it into a gentle breeze that flowed towards

Lyra, brushing her cheeks, and swaying through her hair like a morning dove taking flight. A tiny laugh escaped Lyra's lips as Elowyn urged the breeze to warm, wrapping Lyra in a balmy, breathy blanket. Shifting her palm again, Elowyn directed the feylight droplets to morph into crystalline snowflakes. Thousands of ice crystals drifted around Lyra, each with its own unique lattice artwork. Lyra caught them by the cupful, spinning underneath the frozen crystals.

Watching a tiny sliver of Lyra's morose aura glow faintly amidst a sea of black, Elowyn sensed a glimmer of light fighting to stay afloat—a beacon of resolve, an unyielding gateway to healing.

As the last of the feylight faded in a halo around her, Lyra steadied her feet. "Thank you," she murmured softly to Elowyn.

"Your happiness is your own, Lyra. Share it with those who want to nurture it; shield it from those who threaten to take it away. Trust me, your life will be better for it," Elowyn spoke with candidness, her sympathy apparent as she took Lyra's hand once more. "Now that you're smiling again, let's make it back before the Favor of the Seven begins."

But Lyra didn't budge as Elowyn moved to usher them forward. Her eyes clear and sober, a mountain of appreciation behind them that words could never convey.

"I'd like it if we could become friends," Lyra said, looking to Elowyn.

Taken aback by the sudden invitation, Elowyn hesitated. Anxiety bubbled within her, but she reminded herself that her father wasn't here to know. For tonight, she allowed herself to believe it would be okay.

A moment later, Elowyn smiled. "Yes, I'd like that very much."

12

Weight of Worth

The Den of *Lunaris* exceeded even the royal atrium in beauty, if such a thing were possible. Nearly four times larger, it boasted a network of channeled rivers and feylight waterfalls. Like the atrium, the cavern's ceiling displayed a star-filled night sky. The gentle glow of moonlight illuminated the spacious, multi-leveled expanse. The natural stone flooring was covered with richly pigmented green moss, while flowing rivers and trickling waterfalls created a soothing chorus. This sacred place was nothing short of breathtaking, imbued with an undeniable sense of divinity.

On each level of the den, hundreds of fey gathered to witness the Favor of the Seven. Lesser nobility occupied the higher tiers, while the seven royal families were positioned on the main level, closest to the central point of the cavern. At the heart of the den, upon a raised stone platform, stood the fourteen warlocks and sorceresses who would soon participate in the rite of the Favor of the Seven. They were arranged in two parallel lines, their rank distinguished—one line comprised of the newly moon-marked fey, and the other of the current candidates. Their placement followed the established order of the royal houses: House Fangwright, House Blackbane, House Driftmoor, House Darkmaw, House Skyborn, House Mirthwood, and finally, House Bloodweaver.

Surrounding them, the royal families stood in their designated order, remaining close to the fey sworn to their court. Elowyn strained to catch a glimpse of her sister, Elyria, amidst the crowd. Though she could only see Elyria's back and Finnor standing before her, Elowyn sought any hint of her sister's expression. But Elyria's aura remained calm and serene, impervious to the tension that gripped the other candidates. Elyria's constitution was honed into a steel fortress in the face of the seven realms—she would never break in front of them again.

Elowyn was flooded with a sense of pride and comfort at the sight.

From the corner of her eye, Elowyn noticed the High Priestess emerge from the crowd, striding purposefully towards the center of the den where the fourteen fey stood. As the room fell silent, she weaved through the room. She was dressed in her usual flowing white robes, but for this ritual, she wore an ornate headdress that veiled her entire face. It was boxy, nearly six inches tall with seven points. The front of the headdress was made of sheer ivory organza that fell to her waist in a sheet. The back of the headdress was made of extensive lengths of layered ivory silk that draped across the stone floor with each of her strides. Around her waist were two alabaster cables of corded rope tied around her in a knot. In her hands, she held seven ancient relics from the Old Age.

The gravity of the moment hung in the air.

In the High Priestess' weathered hands lay a stack of delicate thin sheets of cloth, *tela*, but they were no mere swatches of fabric. The power emanating from the textile collection was staggering. As the eight phases of the moon along the High Priestess' worn arms glowed brightly, Elowyn felt chills trickle down her spine. She felt the pure,

12

Weight of Worth

THE DEN OF *LUNARIS* EXCEEDED EVEN THE ROYAL ATRIUM IN beauty, if such a thing were possible. Nearly four times larger, it boasted a network of channeled rivers and feylight waterfalls. Like the atrium, the cavern's ceiling displayed a star-filled night sky. The gentle glow of moonlight illuminated the spacious, multi-leveled expanse. The natural stone flooring was covered with richly pigmented green moss, while flowing rivers and trickling waterfalls created a soothing chorus. This sacred place was nothing short of breathtaking, imbued with an undeniable sense of divinity.

On each level of the den, hundreds of fey gathered to witness the Favor of the Seven. Lesser nobility occupied the higher tiers, while the seven royal families were positioned on the main level, closest to the central point of the cavern. At the heart of the den, upon a raised stone platform, stood the fourteen warlocks and sorceresses who would soon participate in the rite of the Favor of the Seven. They were arranged in two parallel lines, their rank distinguished—one line comprised of the newly moon-marked fey, and the other of the current candidates. Their placement followed the established order of the royal houses: House Fangwright, House Blackbane, House Driftmoor, House Darkmaw, House Skyborn, House Mirthwood, and finally, House Bloodweaver.

Surrounding them, the royal families stood in their designated order, remaining close to the fey sworn to their court. Elowyn strained to catch a glimpse of her sister, Elyria, amidst the crowd. Though she could only see Elyria's back and Finnor standing before her, Elowyn sought any hint of her sister's expression. But Elyria's aura remained calm and serene, impervious to the tension that gripped the other candidates. Elyria's constitution was honed into a steel fortress in the face of the seven realms—she would never break in front of them again.

Elowyn was flooded with a sense of pride and comfort at the sight.

From the corner of her eye, Elowyn noticed the High Priestess emerge from the crowd, striding purposefully towards the center of the den where the fourteen fey stood. As the room fell silent, she weaved through the room. She was dressed in her usual flowing white robes, but for this ritual, she wore an ornate headdress that veiled her entire face. It was boxy, nearly six inches tall with seven points. The front of the headdress was made of sheer ivory organza that fell to her waist in a sheet. The back of the headdress was made of extensive lengths of layered ivory silk that draped across the stone floor with each of her strides. Around her waist were two alabaster cables of corded rope tied around her in a knot. In her hands, she held seven ancient relics from the Old Age.

The gravity of the moment hung in the air.

In the High Priestess' weathered hands lay a stack of delicate thin sheets of cloth, *tela*, but they were no mere swatches of fabric. The power emanating from the textile collection was staggering. As the eight phases of the moon along the High Priestess' worn arms glowed brightly, Elowyn felt chills trickle down her spine. She felt the pure, divine magic that the High Priestess held as she stood before the crowd. Elowyn wondered if she herself could have held such unadulterated power within her own arms without trembling.

"The time has come to begin the ritual of the Favor of the Seven!" The High Priestess' voice rang clear and resonant in the den. "Gathered here are our newly marked divine fey and our Goddess-chosen candidates who will participate in this season's Trial. In this sacred ritual, we will ask the seven founding fey to grant their favor upon these new candidates in their quest for distinction."

Moving to the head of the two lines where the fourteen fey stood facing each other, she continued, "In my arms, I hold seven divine *tela* blessed by each of the seven original warlocks and sorceresses. These ancient relics of Neramyr have been used in the Favor of the Seven since the dawn of the New Age. Blessed innumerable times by wielders of divine magic, these *tela* have passed through the hands of countless candidates seeking divine judgment. Tonight, we continue this honorable tradition and seek favor from our seven divine ancestors who founded the feylands we cherish."

Now positioned at the front of the two lines of fey, the High Priestess stood between the newly divine fey on her left and the Goddess-chosen candidates on her right.

"As I call upon the original rulers of their sworn Houses, our newly marked fey shall accept and carry the *tela* of their kingdom. Let us begin!" With that, the High Priestess advanced between Finnor and Elyria, still clutching the collection of fabric in her arms.

"King Elmyr Fangwright of the kingdom of Eriden," her voice echoed.

Upon hearing the name of the founding fey, Finnor carefully withdrew the first *tela* from the High Priestess' possession and held it with reverence. "First king of Eriden, we seek your favor to grant upon these seven children of the moon in their upcoming Trial."

The *tela*, made of resplendent silk, rested in Finnor's palms. If Elowyn didn't know any better, she would've never suspected it existed millennia ago. The ivory strip, about six feet in length and twelve inches in width, appeared almost translucent in design; the gossamer sheets seemed so delicate that they would dissolve by his touch. Woven into the material were various ornamentations and embellishments of the seven realms and the phases of the moon. Finnor's palms then began to faintly glow in response to the newfound divine magic coursing through his veins.

"King Edhelm Blackbane of the kingdom of Erimead," the High Priestess intoned, moving down the line as each warlock or sorceress retrieved their kingdom's *tela*, pleading for favor from their first ruler.

"Queen Diantha Driftmoor of the kingdom of the Elune Isles," she continued.

A graceful sorceress with sun-kissed skin and turquoise hair stepped forward, claiming her kingdom's *tela*. "First queen of the Elune Isles, we seek your favor to grant upon these seven children of the moon in their upcoming Trial," she spoke with reverence.

As she spoke, Elowyn couldn't help but imagine that her hair resembled the color of the Swyn Sea.

This ritual repeated as Elowyn recalled the names of Neramyr's founding fey.

"Queen Theda Darkmaw of the kingdom of Orwyn," announced the High Priestess. A lively sorceress with short claret-red locks stepped forward to claim her kingdom's *tela*, speaking the venerated words.

"First queen of Orwyn, we seek your favor to grant upon these seven children of the moon in their upcoming Trial," the divine Darkmaw sorceress pleaded.

Draeden had said she was called Serafina. Her eyes darted through the participants of the ritual, searching for the face of the Darkmaw prince. After a moment of her eye's eager roaming, she found him.

There he was.

Elowyn's heart skipped three beats. Draeden looked absolutely devastating. He wore an auburn tunic with accents of rust and gold trimming the sleeves and collar. Clasped on his right shoulder was his golden *aureum*, flowing down his side as it paired with the radiant gold of his eyes. His skin was richly tan, and his cropped hair was meticulously arranged, not one claret-red strand out of place. It was as if the season of autumn were embodied in a striking warlock.

Faintly, Elowyn registered the High Priestess calling two more names. "Queen Aedda Skyborn of the kingdom of Prymont, King Oswin Mirthwood of the kingdom of Lochwald."

The voices and sounds in the den drowned into a distant drone as she locked eyes with Draeden. His intense gaze met hers, and he tilted his head, offering a slight smile that revealed his dimples. Elowyn felt herself nearly swoon at the sight. *Moons, he's distracting.* The stars in his eyes twinkled, hinting that he would seek her out after the ritual. Quickly tearing her gaze away before her own aura betrayed her shameless thoughts, she refocused on the ceremony.

"Queen Isadora Bloodweaver of the kingdom of the Iron Hollows," the High Priestess announced the final name, and Prince Thomys Bloodweaver stepped forward to retrieve his kingdom's *tela*.

"First queen of the Iron Hollows, we seek your favor to grant upon these seven children of the moon in their upcoming Trial," Prince Thomys intoned.

With the last *tela* removed from her possession, the High Priestess relaxed her arms and circled around the participants. After a brief examination of the seven newly marked fey, she turned to address the crowd again, a smile gracing her face.

"These seven divine fey will now tap into the reservoir of their newly claimed divine magic for the first time to channel the favor of the seven original founders of Neramyr. As they wield the divine magic of Caena for the first time, they must prove their ability to command such power, affirming their newfound status as divine warlocks and sorceresses."

Addressing the seven marked fey, she continued, "Shortly, you will attempt to wield the ancient, primordial magic of the Moon Goddess for the first time. From this moment on, you are no longer ordinary warlocks and sorceresses; you are divine, chosen by Caena herself, the highest magical ranking a fey can achieve in their lifetime."

The High Priestess resumed circling the fourteen fey standing on the stone platform.

"With these sacred *tela* you now carry, you will imbue your newfound divine magic within them. Just as your ancestors did, you will strengthen these *tela* anew. Once draped upon the shoulders of the chosen candidates, you will ask the seven founding fey to place favor upon them."

The High Priestess swiftly clasped her hands together and tilted her head skyward. Inhaling deeply, she filled her lungs and closed her eyes. The eight phases of the moon on her arms glowed brighter, illuminating the sacred markings only she could bear. Lowering her head, she reopened her eyes, their irises now clouded.

"I have invoked the Moon Goddess' attention. Our newly marked warlocks and sorceresses will now summon their divine magic to bless these ancient relics!"

A pulse of divine magic resonated throughout the Den of *Lunaris*, and the High Priestess stood motionless, signaling her role in the ritual was halted. It was now the responsibility of the newly marked fey to continue the ceremony.

Farthest from Elowyn, at the end of the line, Prince Thomys was the first to shift. He composed his features into a mask of concentration, tapping into his newly bestowed divine magic. His aura was absurdly potent, befitting his status as the heir of the Iron Hollows and the *primis*. Following his lead, the other six marked fey also began to channel their divine magic.

Prince Thomys remained still, seemingly calm, until his eyes widened in surprise. Elowyn's attention snapped to him as the first Bloodweaver prince's brow furrowed and then relaxed. The concentric reptilian markings on his body began to glow, starting from his chest and spreading outward. Despite the stretched effort, he maintained his focus, breathing steadily. The *tela* in his hands faintly glowed as he channeled his divine magic into it.

Meanwhile, the other six newly marked fey struggled to keep up. Each radiated with a moonlit glow from their divine markings. Elowyn watched as the Skyborn sorceress trembled, gripping the *tela* tightly while breathing raggedly. The Mirthwood warlock faced similar difficulties, sweat beading on his forehead as he struggled to wield the magic.

Finnor's expression was staunch, sweat gathering on his brow. Elowyn remembered his reluctance to tap into his divine magic yesterday. Yet, among the six, Finnor's aura resembled Thomys' the most—searing with resilience.

Thomys' *tela* was now shrouded with divine magic, the threads brilliantly aglow. The ornamentations woven into the silk shimmered with energy and vigor. As he beheld it, he released a breath, his tense posture relaxing as relief washed over him.

In the next heartbeat, Finnor's silk *tela* was imbued with a strength and energy parallel to Thomys'. One by one, the other fey channeled their magic into the fabric until all seven *tela* shimmered with divine energy, elegantly hanging from their grasp.

This signaled the seven candidates across from them to bend the knee and bow their heads. In unison, the seven divine warlocks and sorceresses draped the sacred *tela* upon the candidates' shoulders, the fabric falling down their arms and shrouding them in moonlight.

Elowyn observed some of the candidates wincing as the power settled upon their shoulders. Stepping back, the seven divine fey paused their part in the ritual, leaving the candidates to proceed.

Collectively, the seven candidates attempted to rise from the ground, carrying the weight of the divine magic upon their shoulders—many of the candidates were panting as they bore the burden. First, Sylas stood up steadily with only a grimace and Elyria ascended shortly after with a grit of her teeth, but nonetheless, they both remained standing.

As the Skyborn candidate, Iva, attempted to rise, she faltered abruptly and staggered back to one knee, her face flushing in humiliation. Despite her fault, she mustered on and anchored herself on two feet, still wobbling under the weight of the divine magic imbued within *tela*. Of the seven candidates, only Sylas and Elyria were standing firmly.

Once each candidate had risen, they turned their backs to the divine fey.

Suddenly, a powerful magic erupted from the stone platform beneath them. Moonlight surged through the stone, forming a pattern that traced seven spheres beneath the candidates' feet, resembling the sigils of the Divine Shallows. The moonlight continued to carve the sigils of the seven realms into the stone within the spheres. Once inscribed, a shimmering halo of moonlight enveloped each candidate.

The moonlight continued to flow like vines from the platform, suffusing the entire den. It radiated outward from the fourteen fey, reaching the seven royal families. Elowyn welcomed the moonlight's embrace as it beckoned her, feeling the crescents on her palms began to shimmer.

The moonlight traversed the moss-covered stones, ascending each level of the den. This phenomenon continued until the den's entirety was bathed in moonlight, and Elowyn swore she saw some individuals' eyes gleam with silver while others drew in breaths. The pull of the Moon Goddess felt extraordinary, like a halcyon of heaven and bliss.

The High Priestess clasped her hands together once more. "These fourteen individuals have successfully completed the ritual of the Favor of the Seven! Our founding ancestors have bestowed favor upon these seven candidates as they embark on their Trial of Caena!"

The Divine Shallows

The den erupted into deafening cheers as the High Priestess indicated the fourteen fey behind her. Slowly, the moonlight began to wane, and the glow from the sacred *tela* adorning the candidates' shoulders faded, marking the conclusion of the Favor of the Seven.

∼

"Elyria, you looked amazing down there!" Elowyn exclaimed happily, holding her sister's hands within her own as they stood in the Iron Kingdom's Great Hall.

"Thanks," Elyria smiled appreciatively. "The Moon Goddess' magic is incredible, but taxing. I think I'll head home to rest for the Third Day."

Elowyn's expression fell slightly. "Are you sure? I was hoping we could celebrate, but I understand if you're exhausted."

"I'm sure," Elyria reassured her, pulling her sister into a hug. "I'm lucky to have you."

"I'll see you tomorrow," Elowyn responded, returning the hug tightly.

As Elyria withdrew from the embrace, still holding Elowyn's hands, she smiled again. "I'll see you tomorrow."

Elyria motioned to Sylas to escort her to the outer walls of the kingdom in order to moongate back to Eriden. She offered a small wave as they disappeared through the crowd.

Elowyn let out a disappointed huff. She hadn't spent as much time with Elyria as she'd like before the Trial. She had five more days to say a proper goodbye. She'd just have to find the right time—no, she would make the time for it.

Scanning the Great Hall, Elowyn didn't recognize a soul. Lyra was nowhere to be found, probably moping somewhere. *Be nice*, she scolded herself. If she wanted to keep any friends, she'd have to start with having an understanding attitude instead of a judgmental one. *But over Theo, seriously?* Elowyn sighed. She had a lot of work ahead of herself if she was going to learn how to be supportive.

Interrupting her thoughts, a pinky finger linked around hers and a warm body pressed against her back. Someone leaned over her shoulder and whispered in her ear.

"Hello, Elowyn, I've been searching for you," Draeden's voice was warm on her neck.

Elowyn's face flushed at his closeness. Still linked with his pinky, she twirled around to face him.

"Hello, Draeden," she returned with a smile, her heart pounding.

"May I steal you away again tonight?" His golden eyes twinkled.

"You may," Elowyn laughed, feeling playful—she always felt like swooning around him.

Draeden guided her through the bustling crowd, the echoes of celebration drowning out their footsteps. Most revelers were lost in the merriment, oblivious to their passing. As they navigated the throng, Draeden's linked finger guided her into a secluded hallway, away from the clamor of the Great Hall. Their hushed tones and furtive movements felt like a recreation of the previous night and it sent a flutter through Elowyn's stomach.

After several turns, they arrived at an alcove nestled within the cavern wall. A cushioned bench, large enough for two, occupied the space, built for contemplation or quiet reading.

Draeden released her finger and settled onto the bench, casually draping his arm across the back. He flashed a charming grin. "What do you think?"

Elowyn surveyed the alcove, her gaze lingering on him before letting out a feigned sigh. "Not quite a balcony, but it'll do."

He laughed and so did she.

"Your laughter is beautiful," he said to her candidly. "In fact, everything about you is beautiful."

"Everything?" she teased, taking a seat beside him. As she nestled

The Divine Shallows

into the cushion, she was well aware of how close she was to him. "Do tell."

Draeden withdrew a snow-white strand from her shoulder, twirling it between his fingers with practiced ease. "Your pearl hair is beautiful. Your silver eyes are beautiful. Your lilac dress is beautiful. Your skin is beautiful. Your playful banter is beautiful. Your cleverness and charm are beautiful. And most importantly, your aura is beautiful." Each affirmation fell effortlessly from his lips. "You're enchanting and I find myself irresistibly drawn to you."

A shy smile blossomed on Elowyn's lips. "And do you say this to every princess you steal away in the night?"

"No, only to you," Draeden replied, his grin widening, dimples appearing. "Just to you."

"Good," she asserted, tilting her head towards him, enamored. "Keep it that way."

"I'll do anything you say," he shrugged, his arm slipping down to rest around her shoulders.

"Anything?" she raised her eyebrows, meeting his gaze.

"Anything," he turned to her. "Anything you want."

"Hmm..." she tapped her finger against her chin, extending her request. "Will you dance with me again?"

His eyes sparkled with delight at the invitation, and he grinned. "Always."

Draeden rose to his feet and with a flick of his wrist, summoned his magic. A moment later, a ballad of soft strings sounded as it floated in the small space around them, filling the air with a soothing song. He angled an arm behind his back and extended the other to her with an open palm, silently asking for her hand.

For a moment, she just admired his tanned skin and the moon-inked crescent moon that nestled within his calloused hand. She reached for him, and he pulled her on her feet towards him, his other hand resting at the small of her back. The music drifted around them in dreamy notes, filling their ears with a delightful melody. Draeden held her in his arms assuredly as he began to lead them into a reposeful sway. Their dance tonight was much more serene than the lively twirls from the day before. They spun sweetly in the alcove, their eyes speaking words louder than their voices could.

"I think you're beautiful, too," Elowyn whispered, studying his rich scarlet hair and striking golden eyes. His body, strong beneath his auburn tunic, brushed against hers, and his aura enveloped her in warmth and comfort. He was truly unforgettable; his essence was radiant with colors she rarely got to see.

Draeden's eyes twinkled in response, as though he could sense her thoughts. "You make me feel things I've never felt. There's something about you that's different... something indescribable. Being around you is enchanting and grounding all at once. You're all I want."

"You've only just met me, and already you're enraptured," Elowyn tutted.

"Well, if we're being sensible about it, I met you seven years ago... And I was charmed at first sight," Draeden smiled down at her. "But even if I hadn't met you then, would you blame me?"

Elowyn felt like she might collapse at any moment, her knees weak. She knew the Darkmaw prince had an irresistible hold on her. All she could think about was his magnetic presence. She was drawn to him in ways she couldn't explain. He was all she wanted too. Her aura must have given her away because Draeden gave a suggestive smile.

Guiding their swaying steps further into the alcove, Draeden slowed them to a stop. He looked at her, his golden eyes burning with need, and gently brushed a hand down her cheek, resting it at the bottom of her chin.

"May I kiss you?" he whispered.

Elowyn held his golden gaze and nodded.

Gently, Draeden tipped her chin up as he lowered his head to hers. His eyes sparkled with excitement and his lids fell halfway, his lashes luring her with longing. Elowyn welcomed his guiding hand and lifted her head to meet his. Their lips met tenderly, unhurriedly. He deepened their kiss, his mouth coaxing hers to answer to his demand. Elowyn complied, tangling her fingers in his hair, pulling him closer. Her desire for him intensified. She didn't want this moment to end.

A smile played on Draeden's lips as he pulled back from their kiss, brushing his thumb across her lips with care, admiring her delicate fangs, before dropping his hand from her chin.

"Why did you stop?" Elowyn asked breathlessly, her face flushed with heat from their embrace.

"Just one kiss for now," he said softly, reaching for her hand and clasping it. He intertwined their fingers as he placed a gentle kiss on their enfolded touch. "There'll be many more to come."

Leading her away from the corner, he wrapped his hands around her lower waist as she rested her arms around his neck. They swayed to the lilting strings once more, and Elowyn was utterly captivated by the warlock before her. Her eyes traced the angles of his jaw and the curves of his cheekbones. His allure was intoxicating.

But she knew this couldn't last. Reluctantly, she began to construct an invisible wall between them, piece by piece. After the week was over, she would return to Eriden and he to Orwyn. Both heirs of Neramyr, destined to rule over their own separate kingdoms.

He noticed the shift in her aura and pulled back, concern furrowing his brows. "Is everything all right?"

"Promise me that there will be more," she asked earnestly.

Elowyn didn't know what had come over her, but she didn't want to let this go. She pushed back against her mental safeguards, determined to keep whatever this was from being fleeting.

The only other fey Elowyn had ever kissed was a stone mason's son from Lochwald. He and his father had been commissioned to construct an addition to Eriden's royal castle, staying in the stewards' quarters for months until the structure was finished. Elowyn would meet with the son in the dark of night for stolen kisses and hurried caresses, but she always declined to acknowledge him in daylight for fear of her father finding out.

The night before he was to leave, Elowyn had proposed they meet in her bedroom, wanting to experience what it felt like to be thoroughly embraced by a lover's touch. But he never showed. Perhaps he came to his senses and realized he would be hanged if he were caught sleeping with the daughter of the Fanged King. Nonetheless, it was for the best; her father was in a fouler mood than she was that night. If they were caught, she believed her father would have tortured the fey until there was scarcely anything left of him, before having Bane dispose of his body in the pits of the Eriden mountains.

But this... Right now, she wanted Draeden wholeheartedly. Their kisses and embraces felt exhilarating, born from excitement rather than the adrenaline of fear and disobedience.

Draeden chuckled sweetly. "I promise."

"Now that's two promises you owe me. I'm keeping count," Elowyn teased, tracing idle circles on his shoulder.

"I haven't made up for my teasing yet?" he smirked, pulling her closer and gesturing around them. "A balcony. An alcove. Another dance. When will my debt be repaid?"

"One debt can be repaid with another kiss," Elowyn said.

Draeden let out a low sound and gripped her waist tightly as he claimed her lips again. Elowyn's knees threatened to buckle, but he held her firmly against him. Draeden's urgent kiss softened as he cupped her cheek and pulled back.

"You're perfect," he whispered, placing another brisk kiss on her lips before whisking her up in his arms.

Elowyn's eyes widened in surprise as he carried her back to the cushioned bench and settled in, cradling her in his lap. She sprawled her legs out and leaned into him, reveling in their closeness. He claimed a lock of her hair and began twirling it around his finger again.

The Divine Shallows

They sat there nestled together for a long span of time, sharing lingering laughter and secret smiles. They spoke about their past, their perspectives on the present, and their dreams for the future. Both of their hearts beat to the rhythm of the song still floating around them.

Elowyn's face ached from the heartfelt smile that remained on her lips. She thought to herself how wonderful it was to feel happiness like this.

13

Folded in Fourths

Emerging from the archway of a moongate, Elyria was enveloped in feylight. Just before it dissipated, she collided violently with the hard marble floor of her antechamber. She winced, her face contorting in pain from the impact of her fall. Elyria heaved raggedly, panting from the monumental effort it took to portal back to her bedchamber from the Iron Hollows.

Her arms throbbed as she cradled the one that braced her fall. Attempting to stand up, she quickly regretted her effort. A whimper escaped her lips. She forced herself upright while gritting her teeth, hauling her frame from the ground. She limped to the wall of her bookshelves and managed to reach the center of her recessed foyer just before her legs buckled, grasping desperately for the table to steady herself. The table shuddered under her abrupt grip, and the glass basin filled with violet and magenta-colored lilacs toppled to the floor, shattering into fragments.

Elyria's eyes turned dangerous as she seized control of her body with a ruthless mental grip of her own making. Clutching the tulle skirts of her gown, she forced her fatigued legs to carry her to the bookshelf on her right, rummaging through the stacks. Behind a tower of books, she extracted a small wooden chest nestled within a hidden space. With a click, she unlatched the chest and began sifting through its contents.

The wooden chest threatened to slip from her grip as she fought to steady herself. She took a deep breath to calm her nerves. Leaning against the walled bookshelf for support, she sank to the ground into a sitting position. Once stabilized, she delved into the chest's wooden walls, finding neatly organized scrolls, a collection of potion bottles, and various magical artifacts.

Fingering through the glass potion bottles, she selected one with a spherical bottom and a slender stem. With quivering fingers, she examined the contents—a colorless, viscous solution swirling inside. She withdrew two bottles, tucking one into her dress pocket while clutching the other in her palm. Her heart raced in a frenzy, and she felt slick with sweat. Hastily, she removed the stopper from the glass bottle.

She summoned her magic, lifting her fingers above the bottle's narrow opening. She called to the potion, beckoning the clear liquid out from the neck of the glass vessel. The thick, transparent fluid responded to her command, rising upward in a steady stream. Elyria adjusted her wrist, guiding the solution to gather around her bare palm and forming a fluid glove around her hand.

The colorless liquid faintly glowed a glacier blue. Without hesitation, Elyria pressed her glowing palm against her chest. As the magical solution seeped into her skin, she felt a sense of relief wash over her. Her shoulders relaxed and she released a sigh. Her breaths steadied into a rhythm, dispelling her panic with each passing moment. Gradually, the glacier glow faded, leaving no trace of the solution on her hand.

Leaning her head back against the wall of books, Elyria let out a sigh of exhaustion. When she felt steady enough to stand, she pushed herself up with a groan, still clutching the wooden chest. With effort, she turned and carefully replaced the chest among the stacks of books on the bottom shelf.

Though her panting had ceased, her body still protested with each painful step. Elyria made her way to the arched entryway leading to her bath chamber. She took only a few strides before she staggered toward the porcelain privy, holding back her braid as she retched into the bowl. Her chest heaved and her throat burned as bile rose. Finally, her stomach emptied, and she collapsed to the ground, spent.

Resting her cheekbones against the cool marble floor, Elyria felt exhaustion overwhelm her. *I'm so tired.* With weary ears, she listened to her surroundings carefully, ensuring she was truly alone before allowing herself to weep. Angry, clumsy tears streamed down her perfect cheeks and dripped onto the floor. One after the other, the tears shed in legions. She furled and unfurled her firsts in exasperation.

Elyria couldn't say how long she lay there, but eventually, her tears dried around her. With hollow eyes, she allowed herself to lament a moment longer before rising to her feet and making her way to the large porcelain tub in the center of the bath chamber. She turned on the faucet and watched steamy water fill the tub, veiling the room with mist. She plucked the other glass potion from her pocket and placed it on the bath's edge. She looked to the potion with reassurance, but then quickly, her eyes hardened with resentment.

She unclasped the golden *aureum* that hung off her back, followed by loosening the corset strings of her gown. She grimaced as she let the gown drape from her chest and let go, the layers of sage falling to the ground.

Elyria examined her shoulders and back in the mirror, her expression stiffening as she noticed reddened welts on her naked frame. Her aura shifted from one of distress to one of outrage. She harshly grabbed the glass potion and emptied it into the water. The water began to glow with the same glacier luminescence as before. Setting the empty bottle back on the bath's edge, Elyria winced at the throbbing pain from the wounds on her shoulders and back—the very places where the ancient *tela* rested in the Favor of the Seven. The surface of her shoulders were wrapped in a shawl of wounds.

Elyria approached the edge of the bath and turned off the faucet, then carefully stepped into the glowing waters, lifting one leg and then the other. As she sank into the warmth, she let out a small groan of relief. The tub was nearly filled to the top, stopping just below her neck. Surrendering her fury to the temperate tides, she allowed the glowing water into her body. It seeped into her skin, permeated her bones, and embedded itself into her very core. The luminescent waters worked their magic, washing away the wounds on her shoulders and fading them until her skin appeared anew.

As before, the incandescent waters began to dim and return to their former state. Elyria remained in the balmy bath for a while, until the water to cooled. Lifting her arms, she ran her fingers along the loose braid of her silken locks, carefully removing the wildflowers that were woven her hair until none remained. The three words echoed in her mind once again: *I'm so tired*. Cupping her hands, she collected the cool water within them and lifted it to her face, letting the droplets wash over her.

Elyria repeated this regimen thrice before finally lifting herself from the tub with a sigh. Wrapping herself in a towel, she mindlessly dried herself off and donned a simple silk robe. Once dressed, she made her way to the bedchamber.

Feeling somewhat better than before, Elyria headed towards the makeshift study nestled in the corner of her room. She settled into the cushioned chair at the desk, and traced her fingers along the underside of it until she found a hidden knob. After fiddling with the latch, a compartment door opened with a soft click. She retrieved a small iron chest from the compartment and placed it carefully on the table.

The iron chest, about the size of a tea saucer, had a dark coal exterior with smooth edges and curved bends. It looked like it might have originated from the New Age, but it held an air of primitive existence that hinted towards the Old Age. Depictions of the sky, moons, and stars were melded onto its surface. Among them were illustrations of the new moon, waning crescent, and full moon, all meticulously detailed in a manner befitting Neramyran craftsmanship.

Elyria summoned a tiny bead of magic to her palm and placed it on the iron latch, which produced a soft clink as it unlocked. Carefully lifting the lid, she rifled through the contents within, finding only a bundle of parchment. Among them, she extracted a worn and tattered sheet, its edges yellowed and frayed from age.

With spelled eyes, she scoured over the words written on the parchment, her mind consuming the information before her. Blinking, her silver irises returned, and she folded the parchment back into fourths, tucking it away in the iron chest once more. With a final closure, the lid latched shut with a magical clasp.

Elyria placed the iron chest back into its hidden compartment beneath the table's surface and she sat in contemplation, her hands interlaced beneath her chin. Peering through the swaying curtains at the midnight sky, her silver eyes displayed a moment of hesitation before settling into a resolute gaze.

Elyria strode to her closet and retrieved a set of plain trousers, a loose tunic, and sturdy brown leather boots. She dressed herself in the simple attire and secured her long ivory hair into a tight braid. From another armoire, she retrieved a thick, muted gray cloak, wrapping it snugly around her frame.

She returned to the antechamber and approached the concealed wooden chest from earlier, opening it to retrieve another glass bottle filled with viscous liquid. Tucking it into the pocket of her cloak, she frowned upon realizing it was the last in her inventory, mentally noting to replenish her supply later.

Pulling the heavy hood of her cloak over her head, she obscured her features, rendering herself unremarkable. With a final glance at the wooden chest, she tucked it back behind the stack of books before making her way to the cherry-stained door leading to the castle's hallway.

Elyria placed her ear against the embellished door to listen intently. She waited for a breath. With the Second Day of the Ceremony in full swing, the halls were unusually quiet. She summoned a pinch of her magic to the surface, just enough to cloak herself with a primary concealing spell—she needed to conserve the rest of her magic for later.

Carefully cracking the door, she slipped out soundlessly, pausing only to ensure the wards guarding her door were securely anchored before disappearing into the night.

14

Lore of Lunaris

A new dawn had arrived, casting streams of sunlight through the arched windows of Elowyn's bath chamber. Soft, pearly curtains swayed gently in the mountainside breeze, filling the room with a sense of calm. Elowyn sat in front of her vanity while Elyria combed her long strands with an ornately crafted brush.

"Your aura is so cheerful it's practically seeping from you," Elyria remarked as she continued brushing. "Anything you'd like to share?"

Elowyn's eyes lit up with excitement. "Actually, I do have something to confess," she began, clasping her hands together. "I kissed someone last night."

Pausing her brushing, Elyria arched an eyebrow curiously. "You kissed Draeden Darkmaw?"

Elowyn nodded enthusiastically. "Yes, and it was amazing," she confessed with a gleam in her eye. "Really amazing."

Elyria laughed. "I can tell. It's about time you had some fun with someone. It feels like ages since your last tryst with that noble boy, doesn't it?"

"Hey," Elowyn protested. "It wasn't that long ago... just a few months."

Changing the subject, Elowyn turned to Elyria with a knowing look. "What about you and Sylas Fenhart? You seem quite taken with him. 'Hopefully soon to be four'," she mocked.

Elyria's expression shifted, her gaze narrowing. "What about me and Sylas?" she replied evasively. "He's a strong candidate, that's all. It wouldn't be surprising if he returned with an *animus*."

"You *totally* like him. I can see it in your eyes," Elowyn goaded.

Elyria scoffed in denial, but then leaned in closer to Elowyn, her voice lowering to a whisper. "Okay, fine, *maybe* a little. But can you blame me? He has the most incredible sea-green eyes, and he's lavishly handsome, isn't he?"

"I knew it!" Elowyn gasped. "You two seemed awfully cozy when I spotted you together."

The two sisters continued to chatter and gossip about everything under the moon. Their conversation, at first gentle, soon bloomed into a series of unfeigned, deep, belly laughs. The two of them felt again their unconditional, unwavering bond that would never bend or break—a bond only sisters could share, and both were beyond thankful for that.

As the afternoon wore on, Elyria put the finishing touches on Elowyn's hair. With meticulous care, she wove pink lilacs into the braids in Elowyn's hair, adding a touch of whimsy to her ivory locks. Her hair was styled similarly to the day before, with half down and the other half braided.

For the Third Day, Elowyn wore a stunning, rose-tinted gown that complemented the lilacs in her hair. The dress featured a range of shades, from apricot pink to plum magenta, creating a gradient effect reminiscent of rose petals. Intricate gold thread-work lined the bodice and skirt.

The Divine Shallows

Her neckline was bare, save for the opal teardrop necklace that rested below the base of her neck. The dress' bodice was a tightly fitted corset that hugged her body. Tulle rose-shaped ribbons draped from her shoulders and drifted down her arms. And, of course, her golden *aureum* completed her look, clasped and flowing down from her shoulder blades.

Elyria skillfully painted a rosy, pink stain to Elowyn's lips and generously lined her eyes with kohl. With a brush of bronze pigment on her cheeks, Elowyn looked radiant, as graceful as a garden of blossoms in full bloom.

Next, Elyria attended to her own appearance, donning a gown equally as stunning. Her dress boasted a spectrum of rich yellows, vivid oranges, and glinting golds. Marigolds lined her crown of braids, framing her face as loose curls fell down her back.

Her lips were painted an orange-red and her eyelids were decorated with shimmering gold. The fabric was so lustrous, it nearly blended in with her skin. Her golden *aureum* was clasped at the crest of her shoulder blades' and it curved deeply, exposing her back. If there was a Goddess of the Sun that existed, Elyria looked like her.

Once both were ready, they both strode into Elowyn's antechamber and straightened their skirts.

"Ready to face Lochwald?" Elyria extended her hand.

"Ready," Elowyn took her sister's hand.

Calling to their magic, they were soon enveloped in a veil of feylight starbursts. Together, they entered through a moongate once more, ready to face whatever awaited them in Lochwald.

~

IN THE GREAT HALL OF MIRTHWOOD CASTLE, ATOP THE royal dais, rested two thrones unlike any other in Neramyr. These thrones appeared to be rooted in the dais, the base like the sprawling growth of a mighty tree. Crafted from ancient wood, they towered majestically, their legs and armrests twisting like the branches of a grand oak. The architecture of Lochwald mirrored the surrounding landscape of the Elberrin Forest, which stretched for thousands of miles beyond the castle's walls.

Claiming these thrones were King Dren and Queen Maeva Mirthwood, rulers of Lochwald. King Dren exuded a commanding presence, and he was the largest warlock Elowyn had ever seen.

His stature was imposing, his umber skin starkly contrasting the final Mark of Caena. Queen Maeva was equally admirable, her aura was as formidable as she was distinctly beautiful. Her chestnut-colored ringlets framed her face while a crown of gems rested upon her head. The king wore a surcoat the color of the pine with golden threads that coiled like vines.

Beside them stood their son, the prince of Lochwald, a younger reflection of his father but lacking the wisdom and foresight gained through ruling a kingdom for hundreds of years. Towering over Elowyn, he displayed an air of confidence, his emerald attire emphasizing his muscular physique. A golden *aureum* draped from his shoulder, completing his regal appearance.

At the prince's feet rested two remarkable creatures, the divine *animus* of Lochwald—grimwolves. Their leaden onyx fur and snarling snouts were menacing and their jaws were lined with wicked, whetted fangs. Muscular and sleek, they radiated a sense of power and ferocity. Elowyn couldn't help but be impressed—they were a testament to the strength and majesty of House Mirthwood.

"Welcome to the kingdom of Lochwald!" King Dren's booming voice filled the Great Hall of the Mirthwood castle. "Today we gather to celebrate the Third Day, the Lore of *Lunaris*."

Lochwald's Great Hall appeared as an extension of the Elberrin Forest, with crawling vines decorating the limestone floor and fountains bubbling softly like babbling brooks. Above, stained glass windows bathed the room in a warm, sunlit glow.

"On this sacred day, we join to unravel the legend of divine magic's origins in Neramyr and pay homage to our liberator, the Moon Goddess. Following tradition, our ceremony will commence at moonrise, at the sanctuary within the Elberrin Forest where the Shrine of Oswin rests. Please enjoy the glory and graciousness that the kingdom of Lochwald has to offer. Let the celebration begin!"

As a piano melody drifted through the air, the hall buzzed with chatter and servants circulated, offering glasses of honeyed *vinum*. Elowyn suppressed a sigh, already feeling weary from the week-long Ceremony, which had only just begun its third day. There was a limit to how much *vinum* she could drink and how much small talk she could endure.

Turning to Elyria beside her, she braced herself for what she dreaded most: saying a heartfelt goodbye. It wasn't a true farewell, but seven years was a long time.

"Hey, can we talk?" Elowyn asked. "Earlier, I saw a path from the courtyard leading into the Elberrin Forest. It's supposed to be gorgeous this season."

"Sure, anything to get away from this crowd," Elyria murmured, her gaze flickering uncomfortably around the bustling hall.

The two sisters slipped away to the Mirthwood castle's courtyard, where some guests were already enjoying the blooming gardens and mingling. The outdoor courtyard was enchanting, the flooring made of large limestone slabs, lined with balustrade railings draped in vines. Towering willow trees swayed gracefully in the breeze, casting dappled shadows in the warm sunlight. At the heart of the courtyard stood a grand three-tiered fountain, surrounded by inviting oak benches.

Elowyn and Elyria were about to descend the limestone steps leading into the Elberrin Forest when a group of female courtiers suddenly erupted into excited whispers.

"He's coming over here. Look, he's coming this way!" one of them exclaimed, her saffron hair bouncing as she spoke. The others gasped and clasped their hands, one even pressing a hand to her chest.

Elowyn turned just in time to see the prince of Mirthwood strolling casually into the courtyard with a charming smile. She would have rolled her eyes, but the sight of him made her halt. She understood why female courtiers' reactions. He conveyed a commanding aura of dominance and influence.

The Mirthwood prince took notice of Elowyn and Elyria, but first greeted his guests as he strolled through the courtyard. Noblefolk and court members welcomed him warmly, embracing him with hugs and friendly slaps on the back. He graciously bowed to the captivated ladies of the court and politely kissed the backs of their hands. Elowyn observed how everyone addressed him with high regard, as if his mere presence were praiseworthy.

Unlike the Fangwrights and Bloodweavers, the fey of Lochwald didn't seem intimidated by their ruling royalty. They appeared to have a friendly and familiar relationship with the Mirthwood royals, which struck Elowyn as peculiar. She wondered if the fey of Eriden would cower before her or embrace her when she became queen. Her father's presence often evoked the latter reaction.

Elowyn and Elyria remained by the limestone stairway, their soft smiles in place as Prince Caswin approached them, welcoming guests to his kingdom along the way.

As the prince neared them, Elowyn and Elyria smiled. When the prince finally reached them, he bowed deeply, his golden cloak swaying with his movement.

"Welcome to Lochwald, Princess Elyria and Princess Elowyn. It's a pleasure to host you as guests for the Third Day. Allow me to introduce myself formally—I am Caswin Mirthwood, the Crown Prince of Lochwald," he announced, his voice rich.

Elyria and Elowyn gracefully curtsied in response, returning his warm welcome.

"It's an honor, Prince Caswin. The kingdom of Lochwald is truly beautiful," Elyria replied.

"Yes, it's stunning," Elowyn added, tilting her head back slightly to fully direct her attention to him. "In fact, we were so drawn by the magnificence of the Elberrin Forest that we were hoping to indulge ourselves in a stroll through the woods."

"Of course, please enjoy yourselves. The Elberrin Forest is wonderful this time of year. Although, I will caution you that the forest is vast, and folk who are not as familiar with these lands have found themselves lost after straying from the path. I can arrange an escort to accompany you if you'd like," Caswin offered politely.

Elowyn noticed a subtle shift in his aura at the suggestion, a gentle and mild change.

"It's appreciated, Prince Caswin, but my sister and I will decline an escort. I don't believe we'll wander too far from the castle," Elowyn answered.

"Absolutely, I'll leave you both to carry on with your venture," he replied with a warm smile. "Feel free to call me Caswin, no need for formalities. It was a pleasure to meet both of you."

"Likewise, Caswin," Elyria chimed with an equally winsome smile.

Caswin dipped his head respectfully to them and gestured a small wave before turning to walk away. He headed in the direction where a few warlocks from his court were waiting in the courtyard. He led them down an indistinct path around the castle as the others trailed behind him, disappearing.

Elowyn couldn't help but notice the saffron-haired fey from earlier glaring at her and Elyria. Nearly all the females who had been present before were now projecting auras of envy.

Descending the limestone stairs, Elowyn whistled. "Sheesh, the prince sure is popular around here. The wellborn ladies of the court are eyeing us like vultures just because Caswin gave us an audience."

"I had no idea he was so adored. He held quite the influential air about him though," Elyria remarked.

"You noticed that too? It was like I felt compelled to turn my gaze to him for some reason," Elowyn said curiously. "There's also the fact that he's enormous. I swear he's bigger than half of these trees."

As they followed the natural path winding toward the start of the Elberrin Forest, Elowyn and Elyria crossed into the grassy tree line. Once fully into the forest, an entire ecosystem unfolded before them. Towering trees stretched hundreds of feet into the sky, with branches lining glorious green firs above them. Wildflowers dotted the mossy terrain, and patches of white-petaled flora that speckled the lands.

Chirping filled the air from every direction as birds fluttered through the brush of the trees. Ahead, Elowyn noticed a stream canopied by overhanging trees. Rich green vines lined the ground and the trunks, softening the sharp lines of the woodlands. The beauty of the forest embodied solitude, its untouched lands spanning for miles, the only division of Neramyr left completely natural and uninhabited by the fey.

Elowyn felt a blissful connection to the landscape around her, always sensing a mystical interrelatedness in the natural regions of Neramyr. From the majesty of the Eriden mountains, to the mineral caves of the Iron Hollows, and now to the wondrous wilds of the Elberrin Forest, each place held its own beauty.

"I wanted to talk to you," Elowyn began with a soft tone. "We haven't been spending much time together because of the Ceremony, which is understandable. But I just needed to tell you how much you mean to me before you begin your Trial. I'm going to miss you," she poured out, her feelings unraveling.

The skirts of Elowyn's rose-colored gown trailed the forest floor, but she didn't care if the pink trim dirtied. All she felt right now was a crushing gloom. She'd give anything for the ability to pause time or change fate.

"I'm going to miss you a *lot*. Seven years feels like a lifetime. There's rarely a day that goes by without talking to you," Elowyn expressed emotionally as she strolled aimlessly along the path. "I wanted to tell you thank you for being my sister. Thank you for always protecting me. I'm who I am today because of you," she admitted softly, her fingers idly tracing the folds of her skirts.

"You know, I've always looked up to you. And I'm really proud of you for what you've accomplished. You've fought for everything you deserved, and now you're a Goddess-chosen candidate. You'll become the *primis* because you earned it. And once those seven years in the Trials are over, you'll receive the final Mark. You'll return to Eriden with your own divine *animus*. You'll rewrite your story."

Elowyn parted her lips as if to speak more, but then closed them, restraining the words that fought to break free. She held back her fears of being alone, of facing their father without Elyria by her side. Those daunting thoughts remained locked behind sealed lips, understanding that Elyria didn't need to hear that right now.

With a heavy heart, Elowyn halted her wandering and turned to Elyria, her eyes filled with sorrow. "I'm just going to miss you a lot, Elyria."

Elyria's expression mirrored Elowyn's. Though her silver eyes revealed a sense of sadness, they also held an ocean of affection. "Come here."

Drawing her little sister into a tight embrace, Elyria held her close. "I love you, and I'm going to miss you just the same. You mean everything to me," she whispered. Releasing Elowyn slightly, she looked into her eyes. "I'm scared too—terrified even. I don't know what's going to happen in the Trial, but we'll be okay."

Elyria reached for the opal necklace resting on Elowyn's neck and gently cradled the gemstone in her fingers. "These charmed necklaces are two halves of a whole, remember? Always searching for a way back to each other."

The necklace around Elowyn thrummed warmly with joy, the magical gem rejoicing at the closeness of its counterpart.

"Now, no crying, or you'll ruin the makeup I spent all morning doing," Elyria teased, nudging Elowyn gently with her elbow. "Deal?"

Elowyn managed a smile through her tears and wiped her eyes. "Deal."

15

Grimwolf and Hellhound

THE TWO SISTERS WANDERED THROUGH THE SCENIC FOREST for another hour, taking pleasure in the calm away from the castle. Elowyn occasionally traced her fingers along the bark of the pine trees, admiring their rough, weather-beaten surfaces and wondered how long they had been standing. These towering wood pillars were once mere saplings, and now they stood mighty—a magnificent testament to Neramyr's origins.

As the sunlight filtering through the leafy canopy began to wane, casting shades of warm reds, soft pinks, and stunning oranges, Elyria let out a soft sigh. "It's almost time to return. We should start heading back."

"It's already nearing moonrise?" Elowyn remarked.

"At least today is just listening to the High Priestess recite tales of folklore and fables."

"Thank the Goddess for that." Elowyn nodded in agreement.

"We're supposed to gather at the Shrine of Oswin. Do you know the way?"

"I'm not certain, but I'm sure we'll find someone to guide us back towards the castle," Elyria suggested with a shrug.

"Good idea. Let's head back before it gets too dark," Elowyn said, lifting her rosy skirts and leading the way along the natural path they had taken earlier.

Both walked in silence for a while, mentally preparing themselves to rejoin the Third Day festivities.

Breaking the silence, Elyria voiced her thoughts. "Can you sense something different about this realm?"

"Yes." Elowyn nodded. "Lochwald feels different... It feels more alive. There's a mystical quality to it, but I can't quite grasp it."

"Right?" Elyria shook her head.

They quickened their pace, eager to reach the ritual on time. As they walked, Elowyn passed the brook she had admired earlier. They should be nearing the castle now.

"We've been walking for quite a while. How far do you think we've wandered from the castle?" Elowyn questioned, her expression confused.

"I'd say no more than two miles, given our pace. Let's just press on—we must be nearing it," Elyria replied.

Minutes passed by and their pace didn't slow. By this time, the sun had already departed, leaving dusk to bloom around them.

"This doesn't make any sense," Elowyn muttered, her brow furrowing as she scanned their surroundings. "We should have returned by now. This is the same direction we came from."

"It's getting dark, I can't tell anymore. I'm almost certain we're walking in the right direction," Elyria insisted.

"If we're late to the ritual, father will kill us." Elowyn said anxiously.

"Let's not panic just yet. We can just moongate," Elyria responded.

"Right, I should have thought of that," Elowyn scolded herself, shaking her head in frustration.

Calling to their magic, Elowyn and Elyria attempted to summon a moongate. Though it required more effort than expected, shimmering pillars eventually materialized. Stepping through the portal, they expected to find themselves back at the castle. However, as they entered, the portal disintegrated and left nothing but faint wisps of moonlight. They were left still standing amidst the darkness of the Elberrin Forest.

Elowyn frowned and turned to her sister. "They must have altered the wards in Lochwald after all the guests had already arrived."

Elyria nodded thoughtfully, remaining silent as she considered the situation.

"We're in trouble," Elowyn exclaimed, her distress evident. "You're a divine candidate, for Goddess' sake. You have to be at the ritual."

"It's okay, let's just figure this out," Elyria reassured. "I'm attempting to locate the castle with a spell, but there's something in the forest that's interfering with my magic. I can't seem to control it the way I need to. Can you try using yours?"

Elowyn attempted to call upon her magic, but confusion clouded her expression. "That's odd... I can't even sense my magic, let alone summon a location spell. This is getting creepy. What about a communication spell? Can you send someone a message?"

"I'm trying. It's like I can't do anything with my magic in this Goddess forsaken forest. My magic won't respond to me," Elyria replied, frustrated as she attempted to tap into her magical reserves once more.

They froze suddenly when something stirred from the darkness behind them—a branch snapped in the forest.

Whirling around, Elyria shoved Elowyn behind her body and crouched defensively. For a tense moment, they remained frozen in silence, their senses heightened as they strained to detect any further dangers from the darkness surrounding them. They were greeted with only silence, but Elyria did not surrender from her defensive stance.

Ahead of them, obscured by the thick trees, something stirred. Both sisters held their breath as they scanned the shadows with vigilant eyes. A large hidden silhouette emerged from the darkness, not just moving, but *prowling* towards them at a measured pace.

Elowyn's heart was pounding, her body was screaming at her to run. She couldn't discern her sister's aura through the panic that clouded her mind. She cursed the restrictive gown she wore, also regretting declining Caswin's offer of an escort. Elyria remained steadfast, but without their magic, they were defenseless.

Elowyn recalled her studies back home of creatures capable of stifling and muting magic, creatures she believed to be extinct. The only other explanation would be a dangerous sorceress or warlock with the ability to cast a magically oppressive hex on them. With no physical weapon available, Elowyn felt hopeless to defend herself.

Continuing to lurk from the shadows, the silhouette stalked closer to the sisters and revealed itself from the brush. Elowyn's heart stopped, eyes widened in fear. What she saw was like nothing she had ever encountered before. The creature that emerged from the veil of darkness resembled a beast of death incarnate.

Elyria's arm shot to her skirts, and she brandished a sleek dagger to arm herself, not faltering from her guarded stance. A surprised look came from Elowyn who had no idea where the dagger came from, but she thanked her older sister in her mind a thousand times over. Her gratitude was swiftly returned to terror at what stood before them.

The beast stood on four hideous legs. It possessed two massive hind legs and two slender forelegs. The creature looked like a breed mixed between a wolf and a hellhound. What was most petrifying about the creature was that it appeared like a rotting corpse, but it was alive, moving fluidly. Its form was thoroughly decomposed, as if an expired carcass were reanimated and controlled by another force. Clumps of its dark coat were ripped from its torso and underneath were decaying layers of rancid bone, souring flesh, and putrid organs.

The smell that festered from the open wounds was unbearable. The horrible beast was large enough to meet the height of their chests when standing fully upright. Elowyn shrunk further behind her sister, paralyzed with fear. The creature prowled closer, now ten feet away from them. Its lifeless eyes bore into them, their shade a muted gray, the color of nothingness. It began to crouch into an offensive position and bore its wicked fangs. Drool dripped from its malformed maw, and it snarled with outrage.

The snarl that erupted from its throat was not something of this world—it originated from the darkest pits of hell. Elowyn's knees trembled and her breathing turned wretched. Her eyes were fixed on the yellowing, corroding fangs of the beast that were lethal enough to gravely maim them both, perhaps even kill them.

Out of the shadows emerged two more creatures identical to the decaying beast before them, bringing their hunting party to three. The first positioned itself to attack, flanked by its two newly arrived companions assuming identical aggressive stances. Elowyn's resolve wavered as fear gripped her mind.

∞

"STAY BEHIND ME," ELYRIA WHISPERED. THE WORDS WERE barely audible, lost in the chaos of the moment.

Without warning, the first creature lunged towards them, eliciting a scream from Elowyn as it bore down on Elyria. In response, Elyria charged towards the creature, her dagger aimed for its jugular. With a swift motion, she slashed at its neck, but the beast evaded, only receiving a superficial wound. Snarling in pain, it directed its attention to Elyria.

Frozen by fear, Elowyn could only watch as Elyria faced the creature alone. Sensing her sister's distress, Elyria summoned her courage, determined to protect them both.

The other two beasts slinked around the sisters, surrounding them from all sides. The three canines began circling them, stalking the snow-haired sisters, their predatory instincts fully engaged.

Attempting to tap into her magic once more, Elyria found her reserves still trapped within an invisible cage, stifled by the oppressive atmosphere of the forest. Despite her fear, she refused to yield, summoning every ounce of her willpower to resist the unseen force constricting her abilities. With fierce determination, she launched a mental assault against the barrier confining her powers, desperate to break free.

As the three decaying canines lunged towards them, Elyria's panic surged into hysteria. She fought desperately to unleash her magic, driven by the singular thought of protecting her sister at all costs. With a final surge of defiance, she shattered the suppressive spell, raising her forearm to shield herself and Elowyn.

In an instant, a translucent barrier materialized before them, forming a protective sphere that shielded them completely. The three beasts, mere moments away from attacking, collided violently with the shield, their onslaught thwarted.

A surge of adrenaline coursed through Elyria as she sheathed her dagger and called upon her magic once more. While maintaining a portion of her power to sustain the protective shield, she directed the bulk of her focus towards the three snarling canines.

Raising her palm, Elyria summoned an inferno. She willed the flames to split into three fiery bolts and aimed each one of them to a respective rotting heart. But before she could release the fiery bolts, a strange pulse rippled through the air, stifling her magic once again. In the next moment, her flames were smothered. She willed her hand ablaze again, but failed to produce even a flicker.

Frustrated but not discouraged, Elyria hastily adjusted her strategy.

Thrusting her arms into the mossy land, she released a torrent of magic into the soil, channeling it into the ground. From her hands, luminescent tendrils seeped into the terrain and embedded themselves in the Elberrin Forest's network of roots and vines that sprawled beneath the forest floor. Elyria commanded the roots and vines to ensnare the beasts, binding and anchoring them to the ground.

The decaying canines gnashed at the vines trapping their limbs, but the coils remained secure as the beast's fangs attempted to shred them. With her labored breaths, Elyria grabbed Elowyn's hand and propelled her sister into motion, fleeing from the trapped beasts. As they ran, Elyria's mind raced for a solution, knowing that their makeshift restraints would soon falter, and the creatures would be hot on their heels once more.

Elyria cast a communication spell, projecting her plea for help as far as her magic could reach. *"Help! Somebody help!"* she cried telepathically, repeating her distress call like a blazing beacon in the ether. As they continued to run, she noticed Elowyn faltering, her complexion turning sickly, a stark contrast to her usual vibrant aura.

"Elowyn, we have to keep moving," Elyria urged. "They're gaining on us. We need to run faster, come on!" She pushed forward, pulling her sister along with her.

Behind them, the terrorizing snarls of the beasts grew louder, steadfast in their relentless pursuit. Despite the burning pain in her lungs and the exhaustion threatening to overwhelm her, Elyria pressed on, driven by sheer willpower.

Suddenly, her grip on Elowyn slipped, and Elyria skidded to a halt, her heart pounding in fear. Whirling around, she saw her sister sprawled on the forest floor slick with perspiration, her condition worsening by the moment. Unconscious, her breathing was shallow and her face was deathly pale, so divergent from warmth she always possessed.

Panic surged through Elyria as she realized the beasts were closing in.

"Get up, Elowyn!" Elyria pleaded, her voice choked with fear. As the creatures drew nearer, Elyria's resolve hardened. With no other option left, she turned to face the oncoming beasts, unsheathing her dagger, and summoning another protective barrier.

The rotting hounds charged at Elyria, battering against the protective barrier she had summoned. With each strike, Elyria felt desperation welling up inside her, knowing she couldn't ensure her and Elowyn's escape. The shield began to crack and fragment, slipping through her grasp despite her efforts to hold it together.

Just as Elyria feared her shield would shatter entirely, a bone-chilling, immobilizing voice reverberated through the forest,.

"*Oboedite mihi, messores mortis,*" the ancient voice rasped, commanding the decaying beasts to halt their attack. Instantly, the creatures obeyed—heeling, remaining at bay.

A hunched figure emerged from the shadows, causing Elyria's blood to run cold. Elyria's face blanched as it came into view and her grip on the dagger began to weaken. Though fey in appearance, there was something otherworldly about this being that set it apart from any creature of Neramyr—there was an evil rooted within this soul's very marrow.

Cloaked in black and shrouded in darkness, the figure had a wickedness that sent shivers down Elyria's spine. A hooded cloak wrapped around the figure, concealing its feeble frame. The figure's hooded face appeared female, thoroughly aged and decrepit.

Even the oldest fey in Neramyr did not bear the wasted, withered appearance that this hooded creature from another realm possessed.

"*Ave luna mala, filia vetus lunae. Magicam deae in perpetuum perisse putabam,*" the crone spoke in a foreign tongue, flashing a grotesque, disfigured smile at Elyria.

When Elyria remained petrified, the crone's wrinkled face frowned.

"Moon child, you do not speak the tongue of the Old Goddess?" she inquired in Neramyran, amusement dancing in her eyes. "How curious."

Elyria tensed her muscles, suppressing the tremors coursing through her body as she held the dagger firmly in her grasp, ready to strike.

"Do not step any further," Elyria managed to speak, the words clear and resonant. "I'll kill you."

The crone turned her nefarious flare towards Elyria, her eyes entirely black, bottomless pits. Her aura radiated wickedness, causing even the surrounding trees and vines to recoil.

"I cannot be killed, child. There are creatures within this forest that predate your kind's very existence. Beings your kind have never encountered, even after living thousands of lifetimes," the frail crone uttered as she slowly advanced towards Elyria, studying her intently. "But I sense a potent power within you, child. A rare magic, so infrequent, I have not encountered such in these lands since my youth."

"Stay away from us," Elyria warned again.

"I wonder what deeds you have performed to wield such incredible power," the crone mused with an eerie, chilling tone.

Before the crone could speak further, she was interrupted by the high-pitched whines emanating from the three decaying canines. A sinister hiss escaped her lips as she took two steps back from Elyria and the unconscious Elowyn. Her expression twisted into one of pure disgust, spitting another message in the unfamiliar tongue.

Her gaze bore into Elyria's soul while the next words fell from her lips. "*Ierum me videbis, filia deae veteris.*"

Elyria's legs weakened as she heard the dreadful, dark words directed towards her.

Next, the crone commanded the three canines. "*Ad ultimum spiritum oppugnabis!*"

With a final chilling glance at Elyria, the crone swiftly turned on her heel and vanished into the forest, swallowed by a mist of shadows.

The three decaying canines charged towards them, and Elyria cried out, shielding Elowyn with her own body, conjuring another protective barrier around them. However, to her astonishment, the beasts didn't attack. Instead, they rushed past them, their rabid howls piercing the air.

Elyria followed their gaze and was stunned to see a massive brindle-coated grimwolf leaping into action, pouncing on one of the decaying canines. The clash between the two creatures shook the forest floor as they fought fiercely. The grimwolf lunged for the decaying canine's throat, narrowly missing the beast. It retaliated with a vicious claw swipe, tearing through the grimwolf's fur.

From the shadows behind the grimwolf, four more of its kin emerged, rushing to its aid. Together, the pack of five grimwolves launched an assault on the three decaying canines, moving with coordinated precision. Elyria could only watch in awe as fur and fangs clashed in the brutal dance of combat. Yet, despite their efforts, the decaying canines fought back fiercely, each wound inflicted on them seeming to only be parried with a blow of their own.

The forest became a battleground, with savage beasts locked in a vicious struggle. Elyria remained paralyzed, cradling Elowyn in her lap, as she watched the savage spectacle unfold before her. Time seemed to blur as the battle raged on, the grimwolves tiring from their injuries while the decaying canines pressed on, their rotting forms deceptively strong.

The pack of grimwolves had split, the largest one engaging a rotten canine alone, while the remaining four adopted a two-on-one strategy. Snarls of fury and roars of rage filled the forest as the battle waged, each side fiercely vying for victory. The confrontation seemed evenly matched, with neither side gaining a clear advantage.

Suddenly, Elyria heard a soft moan escape Elowyn's lip, drawing her attention down. She gently brushed her hand along Elowyn's cheek, searching for any signs of pain. Elowyn's movements were fleeting, and she slipped back into unconsciousness. Elyria cursed under her breath, offering what little magic she had left to replenish Elowyn's energy. Her own strength was waning.

Ahead, a merciless presence swept through the forest, causing the ground to tremble beneath them. As Elyria's mind reeled with fear, she braced herself for what might emerge from the darkness.

In a flash of white, a sinister snarl echoed through the trees, causing both the grimwolves and the canines to pause their attacks. The brindled grimwolves fell back, leaving a wide berth for the approaching figure.

Father.

Elyria's heart pounded with dread as she recognized him. Even as she whispered his name in her mind, she dared not speak it aloud.

King Eamon bared his fangs, unleashing another deafening snarl that shattered the surrounding forest. The trees splintered, and the ground quaked beneath them. The rotten beasts turned their attention to the king, lunging towards him with vicious howls.

King Eamon seized the first rotten canine by the throat, his eyes brimming with venom. He swiftly slammed the decaying creature into the forest floor with lethal force, the impact vibrating with a thunderous crack. A guttural yelp escaped the canine's jaws as King Eamon crushed its windpipe with a sickening squelch, reducing its neck to a mangled mess.

As the second rotten canine lunged towards the king, another fierce figure intercepted it in a flash of snow. Elyria's face registered Finnor grappling with the creature. Finnor's demeanor was transformed, his usual timidity replaced by a murderous rage as he pummeled the festering creature with relentless fury. His barrage of strikes continued until the creature lay beneath him, reduced to an unrecognizable heap of fur and flesh.

The third canine rushed towards the king, but King Eamon was expectant. Again, with a bloodthirsty aura, he seized the creature by the throat, his grip unyielding. With a ferocious bellow, he tore the creature's head from its body, rotting tendons snapping as he ripped them apart. Despite the canine's desperate attempts to inflict damage, King

Eamon's fury knew no bounds. The creature's head was gruesomely torn from its body, leaving behind a trail of inky, black, rancid blood. He dropped the torso with a thud, the skull tumbling to the ground beside its dismembered body.

As the shield around Elyria began to fade, she watched in horror as the exchange between her father, Finnor, and the rotten beasts ended in mere seconds. With Elowyn in her arms, her sister's eyes fluttered with weariness, glazing her surroundings before she succumbing to senselessness once again.

King Eamon's furious aura mollified slightly as he turned his attention to his daughters. His gaze swept over them, unreadable yet discerning, before shifting to Finnor. With a clipped tone, he issued his orders.

"Commander, escort Elowyn back to Eriden and ensure she is seen by the royal mender," he commanded, his hands busy with cleaning themselves with a rag from his pocket.

"Elyria, you appear unharmed," he stated flatly, devoid of emotion. "Prince Caswin, you will accompany my daughter to the Shrine of Oswin to witness the Lore of *Lunaris*. However, I must speak with both of you momentarily."

From the group of grimwolves, the largest one emerged from the shadows, its form shrouded in mist before a snap echoed through the forest. Caswin Mirthwood materialized from the mist, a grimace of discomfort crossing his features while he adjusted his battered surcoat. He bowed respectfully to King Eamon before turning to acknowledge the other grimwolves.

"As you command, Your Majesty," Caswin responded, nodding to the other grimwolves.

The four remaining grimwolves stepped forward, enveloped in mist before another snap filled the air. Four young warlocks emerged from the mist, causing Elyria to look on in astonishment. Each warlock transformed into the males she had seen in the courtyard with Caswin earlier. They were not only warlocks but shapeshifters as well. The rumors of

Lochwald's formidable warriors were proven true—skilled in both magical and physical combat.

The warlocks under Caswin's command were battered and bruised. Some tended to their wounds, applying pressure to stop bleeding, or holding fractured ribs. With a nod from Caswin, they dispersed toward Mirthwood castle to seek further mending.

Finnor approached Elyria with a kind expression and offered her a look of sympathy. He leaned down and gently scooped Elowyn up within his arms. The moon-white scales inked on his skin began to glow as a moongate appeared and he stepped through, Elowyn in tow. Elyria reached out to Elowyn instinctively, but her arm felt numb, falling limply to her side.

Caswin, wearing a soft expression, approached Elyria and extended an arm. Gratefully, she accepted, uncertain if she could stand on her own.

The Fangwright king finished cleaning his hands, his expression grim as he turned to face Elyria and Caswin, "Tell me everything."

16

Soul of a Stranger

IN THE DARKNESS, ELOWYN STRUGGLED TO OPEN HER HEAVY eyelids, feeling as though iron chains weighed them down. Blinking against the blur, she gradually took in her surroundings. A familiar scent enveloped her, soothing and comforting. Beneath her, a soft mattress cradled her body, and layers of warm blankets cocooned her form.

A faint smile touched her lips as she recognized the setting of her four-poster bed, draped with a linen canopy. Her attention sharpened when she noticed movement near the entryway of her chamber. Two indistinct figures stood by the cracked door, engaged in conversation. One figure, slender, listened intently while the other, larger, and more robust, received a small, stoppered vial from the first.

As the slender figure slipped out the door, leaving it to swing softly shut, the larger one approached her bed with careful steps. Elowyn recognized his snowy hair, partially bound, and moon-inked scales— Finnor. Her eyes followed his movements as he placed the vial on her bedside table, seemingly unaware of her awakening. Silently, he settled into a chair beside her bed, rubbing his temples in an agitated manner.

Attempting to speak, Elowyn's voice emerged as a weak rasp. At the sound, Finnor's silver eyes snapped towards her, and he swiftly rose from his seat. With two long strides, he reached her side, guiding her back into a reclining position on the bed. Once she was stable, Finnor retrieved an empty goblet from the bedside table and filled it with water from a nearby pitcher.

"Water," he murmured softly, offering her the full goblet.

Elowyn's throat remained dry while attempting to thank him. Each word felt like sandpaper against her vocal cords, causing her to wince in discomfort. Frustrated by her inability to speak properly, she seized the goblet with trembling hands and drained it in one go. Finnor promptly refilled it and handed it back to her, repeating the process until she had consumed several cups. Gradually, she began to feel slightly better.

Handing her the glass vial he had placed on her bedside earlier, Finnor explained, "It's a healing potion from the royal mender. She instructed me to ensure you drank it."

Elowyn accepted the vial and removed the stopper, taking a swig and grimacing at the taste. She gestured for another goblet of water, which Finnor provided without hesitation.

"Why are you here?" Elowyn frowned as she struggled to piece together her memory. "The last thing I remember was…"

As pieces of the memory flooded back to her, Elowyn abruptly threw off the heavy blankets covering her and attempted to rise from the bed. However, dizziness overwhelmed her, and she nearly stumbled to the floor before Finnor caught her and guided her back to the bed.

"Princess, you must rest," Finnor pleaded, voice concerned.

"My sister," Elowyn gasped, panic seizing her. "I have to get to Elyria. She's in danger!"

"Princess Elyria is safe. Your father and I received her message and came as quickly as we could," Finnor reassured her, maintaining a calming timbre. "She's still in Lochwald witnessing the Lore of *Lunaris*."

A memory flickered in Elowyn's mind, recalling herself lying on the forest floor with her head resting in Elyria's lap. Vague images of her father's furious expression, Finnor drenched in blood, and a pack of five grimwolves flashed before her. She strained to recollect further details, but her memory abruptly ended there.

"We were being chased... How did we... How did we escape from the rotting hounds?" Elowyn asked, her expression filled with horror. "You were covered in blood..."

"Prince Caswin and his pack arrived first," Finnor replied somberly. "They held off the beasts until your father and I reached you."

"Caswin? The Mirthwood prince? What do you mean?" Elowyn's confusion deepened with each question.

Finnor appeared unscathed and immaculate, devoid of any traces of blood. Elowyn glanced down and realized she was no longer in her delicate rose-petaled gown but instead dressed in a nightgown, likely provided by the royal mender.

"Prince Caswin is a shapeshifter. Many fey sworn to House Lochwald possess the ability to shift between their fey and animal forms. For Caswin, a grimwolf. He and his pack fought off the rotting canines while we searched for you in the forest," Finnor explained.

Finnor's aura seemed fraught with a sense of remorse, as if he bore the weight of failing to protect the princesses of his kingdom at the first sign of danger. His responsibility as the Commander of the Feyguard in Eriden included safeguarding the royal family and all its subjects. Finnor scrunched his brow, as though a pounding headache was beginning to storm.

"Caswin can transform into a grimwolf? I had no idea," Elowyn remarked, slumping back, and resting her head against the bed frame. "Is that why there's such a commanding aura about him? Is he the pack leader of all the grimwolves in Lochwald?"

Finnor let out a soft chuckle. "Almost, but not exactly. King Dren serves as the male alpha, and Queen Maeva as the female alpha of Lochwald, jointly leading their pack. Prince Caswin holds the position of second in command, the beta grimwolf. As the heir of Mirthwood, once his father passes the title to him, he'll ascend as the male alpha. If he weds another fey capable of shifting into a grimwolf, she'll become the female alpha. It's quite rare for females to possess the grimwolf trait, making Queen Maeva exceptionally singular in her prowess."

"Do the fey of Lochwald have the ability to shift into anything else?" Elowyn inquired, her nerves easing under Finnor's reassuring tone.

"They do. There are warlocks and sorceresses who can assume various forms of animals native to the Elberrin Forest—stags, hares, hawks, foxes—typically creatures of the woodland. However, inheriting the ability to shift into a grimwolf requires highborn lineage, much like the Fangwrights and their fangs," Finnor explained, flashing a lopsided grin, his smooth, fangless teeth on display.

"Our fangs *are* quite exclusive," Elowyn teased, flashing a bright grin, her four canines peeking through her lips. "You can only possess these beauties if you're a direct descendant of King Elmyr himself. It's tough being this special."

Finnor adopted a playful tone. "Indeed, it's an honor to bask in your exalted presence, my princess."

A crooked smile formed on Elowyn's lips. "Was that a joke I just heard from the reserved Finnor Wynward?"

Finnor chuckled awkwardly, running a calloused hand through his hair. "I suppose so." His body seemed tense, uncertain of how to respond. He settled back in the chair, fidgeting with his fingers nervously.

"Thank you for coming to our aid," Elowyn said. "I was terrified. I felt paralyzed, unable to move or think. Once again, Elyria had to protect me."

The Divine Shallows

"I could teach you how to defend yourself," Finnor offered. "Especially now, as your father has assigned me as your personal guard."

"Why?" Elowyn's posture straightened, unease in her voice. "I've never had a guard before. I don't see why I need one now."

"Your father trusts no one else with your safety. Tonight has shown that there are threats awakening in Neramyr that could pose a danger to you, to your sister, and to the folk of Eriden," Finnor explained pragmatically.

"The Elberrin Forest spans for thousands of miles! There are regions that even the fey haven't ventured into. It's possible that those creatures were lurking within the forest for hundreds of years already. We're literally mountains away from Lochwald. I don't see why my freedom in Eriden needs to be stripped from me," Elowyn replied sharply.

"It's precisely because of these dangers that your father insists on your protection. He will not risk your safety," Finnor responded calmly.

"So, what now?" Elowyn's gaze bore into Finnor. "Are you going to watch over me while I sleep and follow me everywhere I go?"

Finnor blanched at her clipped tone.

"I'm sorry Princess, I must abide by King Eamon's orders. And I'm only here at the direction of the royal mender to ensure you're all right. If you're feeling better and desire me to leave, I'll be stationed outside your door if you need me."

Finnor, looking slightly flustered, began to rise, but Elowyn halted him with an outstretched hand.

"Wait, I'm sorry if I came across as rude," Elowyn said, her tone apologetic. "I know you're just following my father's orders. It's been a chaotic few hours, and I'm feeling a bit... on edge. And as a reminder, you can just call me Elowyn."

She offered him the friendliest smile she could muster, attempting to ease the tension, and Finnor settled back into his seat. Before she could speak further, her stomach growled loudly, and her face flushed in embarrassment.

"You must be hungry. I'll have the kitchen steward bring you something," Finnor insisted.

Finnor braced his arms on his knees and heaved up from his seat in a fluid motion as he strode out of the bedchamber to fetch a servant. Elowyn watched him leave the room before she hung her head and rested her face within her palms.

What in the seven hells just happened?

Just hours ago, she and her sister were being hunted in the Elberrin Forest by dreadful, decaying hounds. Now, Elyria was in Lochwald witnessing the Third Day while Elowyn found herself back in the safely in her room. A pang of shame pulsed through her as she recalled her own weakness and frailty in the face of peril—she had fainted for Goddess knows how long. Elyria was strong and noble-minded, self-sacrificing as always.

Elowyn shut her eyes tightly, allowing her insecurities to pummel her self-esteem. She had led a life of comfort and safety, facing little adversity beyond the scorn of her title. She was acutely aware of her limited talent as a sorceress, always paling behind Elyria in progress. She felt useless. How was she to protect and lead an entire kingdom if she couldn't even defend the one soul who mattered to her most?

Tears of frustration streaked down her cheeks as she grabbed a nearby pillow and buried her face in the plush. A muffled scream escaped her lips as she released her pent-up anguish into the fabric. Rising from the pillow, she pounded her fists into the sheets, groaning. Her earlier giddiness felt like a distant memory. Her thoughts briefly flashed to Draeden, wondering if he noticed her absence. Would he care for her if he truly discovered how weak her character was?

The door creaked open, and Finnor entered the room, carrying a tray of savory-smelling food. Elowyn's stomach betrayed her with a loud rumble; her face whitened in horror. Finnor paid it no mind, setting the tray on her dining table nearby and arranging the food for her.

"The kitchen was deserted, so I improvised," Finnor explained, his tone accommodating. "I found some smoked ham, cheese, bread, and apples. Hopefully it will suffice."

He pulled out a cushioned chair from the dining table and approached Elowyn, offering a steady hand. She found herself staring at the moon-inked dragon scales on his skin and the crescent moon in his palm. She winced as an image of him drenched in inky black blood briefly flashed through her mind.

He appeared so amenable, so dutiful and deferential before. She knew Finnor truly was an indomitable divine warlock. He was Eriden's Commander of the Feyguard for Goddess' sake. Nevertheless, he remained modest and respectful in his mannerisms. Elowyn wondered if it was his background as a blacksmith that influenced his humble demeanor.

Gratefully accepting his hand, Elowyn allowed him to guide her unsteady feet to the dining table and help her into the seat. She offered a thankful glance before eagerly digging into her food. Finnor simply nodded and headed towards the door.

As she finished a particularly unladylike bite, Elowyn blurted out, "Do you want some?"

"No, thank you," Finnor said politely. "I appreciate the offer, nonetheless."

"You can stay until I'm done if you want," Elowyn offered, gesturing to the chair beside her. "I imagine it must be rather dull standing outside my door."

"All right," Finnor agreed, though he seemed wary as he took the seat.

"Out with it," Elowyn prompted between a bite of her apple.

"Spare me your wrath when I tell you what else your father ordered me to do," Finnor said gravely.

Elowyn halted her chewing abruptly, fixing Finnor with a piercing glare. "What else did he command?"

Finnor swallowed hard, choosing his words carefully. "My new living quarters are to be on this floor, near your chambers. King Eamon wishes to ensure that I can swiftly aid you should any harm befall you or our kingdom."

He hesitated, his expression growing uneasy as he continued. "Additionally, he instructed me to place wards on your doors and windows. I am to be alerted if any being, fey or creature, enters or exits your chambers."

Elowyn's demeanor swelled with anger as she glowered at him, the room enveloped in a heavy silence. Her appetite vanished, replaced by outrage.

Finnor's eyes reflected the gravity of his next words as he spoke in a hushed tone. "Tomorrow, the king intends to bind your soul to mine with an Eternal Tethering spell, ensuring I can protect you if it be daylight or nightfall."

All at once, Elowyn stopped breathing.

This couldn't be real.

Numbness spread through Elowyn's body as she absorbed the weight of Finnor's words. The realization hit her like a tidal wave. The Eternal Tethering spell, a sacred bond sanctioned by the Moon Goddess herself, would bind her soul to Finnor's for eternity. If she faced danger or met her end, he would offer his life in exchange for hers.

Her fate, her very essence, would no longer be solely her own. Every decision, every thought, would be shared with Finnor. Once the spell was cast, there would be no turning back. Not even the Goddess could perform its undoing. If Elowyn's life hung in the balance, it would be Finnor who held the power to decide her fate.

The realization dawned on Elowyn that her father must have already petitioned the High Priestess for the Moon Goddess' blessing. But why? She wasn't yet of age or political status to receive a spell of such divine classification. Typically, it was bestowed upon monarchs at their coronation, a means to safeguard their kingdom's future.

In Neramyr, sacrificing oneself for another was seen as the highest form of nobility. As queen, Elowyn was expected to accept this honor with gratitude, to view it as a privilege—but not yet. Inside, she felt anything but honored. She felt trapped, her freedom and autonomy slipping away before her very eyes.

Moreover, the spell required only the Goddess' blessing and a willing fey to offer their life to be tethered. Finnor had already pledged his soul, and Elowyn couldn't prevent it even if she tried—her desires held no sway in this decision. Caena's blessing had sealed their fate, her judgment reigning supreme above all else.

Elowyn's chest tightened, her breaths coming in short gasps as if the air itself had turned to lead. Why her? Why would the Goddess take her agency, her right to her own existence away? Her father hadn't even considered relinquishing the throne yet! She had always believed her destiny would be determined in the stars, not dictated by a divine warlock sworn to obey her father's will.

"Get out," Elowyn commanded, her voice laced with hostility, and Finnor recoiled. "Now."

"Your father didn't want you to know, but I needed to tell you. The guilt on my conscience would be harrowing." Finnor's body stiffened, but he pressed on, "I cannot disobey my king. I am sworn to his court."

"You forget that I am to be your queen one day!" Elowyn's voice rose to a furious pitch as she slammed her hands against the table. "My soul is mine and mine alone! How dare you allow yourself to be tethered to me against my will with such an abhorrent spell before necessity calls for it!" She shook her head in disbelief. "This can't be... At nineteen, I am to be bound by force to another soul before I have yet to live? You may as well lock me behind iron and cede the key to the depths of the Swyn Sea!"

Finnor's face blanched, but his voice was hardened as he responded to her. "The moment I swore the blood oath to accept my position as Commander of the Feyguard to Eriden, I vowed my undying fealty to this kingdom. I am bound by blood to protect Eriden and its folk until my last breath and beyond. By my obligation to the Moon Goddess and to Neramyr, my soul is fated by the stars to protect you always," Finnor declared, his voice unwavering with credence as he held her gaze. "With or without the Eternal Tethering spell."

"Leave!" Elowyn spat, her words filled with venom. "Get out of my sight."

Finnor's expression remained unreadable as he silently rose from his seat and exited her bedchamber without a word.

Hours passed, and Elowyn remained seated in the cushioned chair, motionless as if carved from a slab of stone. Though her outward appearance was stoic, inwardly, her soul mourned the loss of her freedom. Her aura simmered with grief and her mind was plagued by turmoil.

Tomorrow, through the Goddess' divine blessing, her father would tether her soul to a stranger for as long as she walked the feylands of Neramyr.

As daylight filtered through her warded windows, Elowyn finally stirred from her immobile state, weeping silent tears of misery.

17

Eternal Tethering

Elowyn's face was gaunt as she stood within the calming waters of the Divine Shallows. She was dressed in a robe of all white, the linen billowing around her legs in the celestial shallows. At her waist, an alabaster cord was cinched around it in a knot and her hair was unbound, falling in soft waves around her hollow face. Her eyes held a vacant, empty gaze, devoid of emotion.

This morning, Ora entered woefully in her bedchamber to dress her for this ritual. The heaviness in her room was unbearable; it coated her throat and her lungs making it hard to breathe. Ora's face was unexpressive, but Elowyn knew her soul mourned with hers. A sorrowful understanding passed between them, knowing that Elowyn would lose something precious today.

Led into the Heart of the Temple by two male acolytes, Elowyn now stood at the center of the Divine Shallows, poised to fulfill the purpose her father had determined for her. She couldn't deny the bitter understanding that she was merely a pawn in his twisted game, destined to play out the roles he had assigned her: divine candidate, crown-princess, and now eternally-bound captive.

Clad in the same pale, unpigmented robes, her father was standing beside Elowyn to her left and the High Priestess was positioned to her right. However, Elowyn refused to look forward, for she knew Finnor would be there.

Her father had always been a reaper of ruin—now she considered Finnor one, too.

The four of them stood within the sacred Temple, arranged in four points, like a diamond. The mighty stone walls around them were so quiet that Elowyn felt the Temple of Caena was more haunted than hallowed. She thoroughly believed that the next time she found herself here would be to witness the Seventh Day, cheering Elyria on as she traversed the Bridge Between Worlds. Never did she expect she would enter these celestial waters so soon, shackled to a soul devoid of her will.

The High Priestess spoke first. "Now we shall commence the invocation for divine spellcasting."

Turning her ethereal, weathered face towards the two figures before her, the High Priestess extended her palms upward and the eight phases of the moon began to glow. Moonlight trickled and spread from her palms and snaked down from her hands into the celestial waters, causing the shallows to illuminate around them.

With authority in her voice, the High Priestess addressed the king. "King Eamon, sovereign of Eriden, declare your plea of divine spellcasting to the Moon Goddess, Caena."

Elowyn's father proclaimed to the heavens. "Blessed Caena, Goddess of the Moon, Savior of the Fey, Liberator of Neramyr, Mother of Worlds, I plead you to grant your blessing upon this divine spell of Eternal Tethering."

The High Priestess nodded and recited similarly, "Blessed Caena, Goddess of the Moon, Savior of the Fey, Liberator of Neramyr, Mother of Worlds, I plead you to grant your blessing to sanction this divine spell of Eternal Tethering at the hands of your child of the moon, Eamon Fangwright."

The sacred waters surrounding them began to swirl and churn as the reverberations of their words filled the Temple. Luminescence infused the water, pulsating with energy as the gateway to the Goddess' realm was opened by the High Priestess.

Elowyn flinched, feeling the intense power coursing through the waters around her.

Once more, the High Priestess spoke. "Finnor Wynward, son of Neramyr, declare your plea of divine spellcasting to the Moon Goddess, Caena."

Finnor announced his plea into the ether, "Blessed Caena, Goddess of the Moon, Savior of the Fey, Liberator of Neramyr, Mother of Worlds, I plead you to grant your blessing upon this divine spell of Eternal Tethering. I offer you my soul to tether in this realm, into the realm of death, and to all the realms beyond."

Elowyn's heart pounded in her chest, her breaths ragged like the turbulent waters below. Dread consumed her as she grappled with the nightmare unfolding before her. Her mind splintered and shattered with each passing second.

This can't be happening to me.

Desperately, she sought refuge within the High Priestess. "High Priestess, please do not let this happen yet," Elowyn whispered with panic. "I do not wish to have my soul tethered to a stranger against my will. Let my soul remain mine and mine alone."

The High Priestess responded with a leveled tone, "Moon child, the judgment of the Goddess has been passed. From this moment onward, your soul shall be tethered to another with her blessing."

Tears welled in Elowyn's eyes as she questioned the Moon Goddess. "Does Caena show no mercy?"

The High Priestess' tone softened slightly as she imparted divine wisdom. "Beloved child, the Goddess' judgment is absolute. She cherishes the fey of Neramyr as if we were born of her very kin. Caena has swayed fate to take this course and we must heed her direction."

The energy in the Divine Shallows surged with magic as the High Priestess prepared to enact the spell. She turned to Finnor and gestured to him with a moonlit hand to kneel in the sacred waters, offering his soul to be tethered by the Goddess.

"Finnor Wynward, kneel into these hallowed depths as you freely bare your soul for Caena to tether."

Finnor descended to one knee with deliberate care, a halo of feylight casting a shimmering aura around him. The waters of the Divine Shallows lapped gently at his waist as he lifted his gaze to meet Elowyn's eyes.

In that moment, she knew Finnor saw the anguish etched upon her features, the shock and disbelief unmistakable in her expression. She saw a flash of sympathy appear before he averted his gaze, steeling himself for what was to come. Elowyn could sense the voracity of his call to duty, the conviction that drove him to offer his life for the safety of his kingdom and his future queen.

"Finnor, there's still time. You don't have to do this—not yet," Elowyn pleaded with him, her voice barely above a whisper.

Yet, Finnor remained silent, his head bowed as he focused on the task at hand.

Elowyn turned to her father, her desperation palpable as she implored him to reconsider. "Father, please don't do this."

King Eamon ignored his daughter's pleas, his attention wholly devoted to channeling the immense power required for the Eternal Tethering spell. Moon-ink scales adorning his skin glowed with divine energy, the crescents on his palms emanating a brilliant light as he submerged his arms into the waters of the Divine Shallows.

As King Eamon invoked the incantation, the High Priestess joined in, her voice resonating with ancient power. The cave reverberated with the force of the spell, the waters pulsating with raw energy as Elowyn's surroundings became suffused with magic. Helpless, she clenched her fists as her Mark glowed, a futile attempt to stifle the radiance.

The High Priestess addressed Elowyn, "Beloved moon child, the time has come. The Goddess has spoken, and you shall now be claimed as you journey into her realm."

A halo of feylight began to coalesce beneath Elowyn, casting an ethereal glow around her. With a sense of dread, she shook her head in disbelief, retreating from the radiant portal that beckoned her. Her heart pounding with fear, she dashed away from the celestial waters, her agile legs propelling her against the relentless pull of the currents. Just as she reached the edge of the Divine Shallows, poised to escape the luminous cistern, the two male acolytes who had escorted her earlier seized her arms and shoulders.

"Let go of me!" Elowyn screamed as she thrashed against their forceful grips. Despite her effort, their hold on her was unbreakable. She fought with all her strength, her voice echoing with desperation. "Stop! I won't allow you to do this to me!"

Elowyn kicked and writhed wildly as the two acolytes hauled her back toward the High Priestess and the awaiting halo. Helplessly, Elowyn was dragged to the feylight portal and thrusted into the celestial waters. One of the acolytes gripped the base of her neck and shoved her downwards, forcing her onto her knees.

"Father, please, don't do this!" Elowyn cried to the king, who stood amidst the torrent of divine magic he was conjuring. Hopeless tears fell from her cheeks and dissipated into the waters below, as if they ceased to exist in the first place.

An otherworldly force tugged at her soul and Elowyn was submerged beneath the surface of the celestial waters, passing from Neramyr into the realm of the Goddess.

Beneath the sacred waters, Elowyn felt her body engulfed by their hallowed depths, the luminescent liquid filling her lungs. Panic initially seized her, but soon a tranquil calm washed over her as the water embraced her with a comforting warmth. Despite the instinctual urge to fear, her soul found solace in the water's embrace.

Elowyn's silver eyes surveyed her surroundings, her astonishment evident as her mouth fell agape. Before her stretched a celestial expanse, a vast cosmos adorned with countless twinkling stars. Drifting through this azure night sky, she remained clad in her alabaster robe, the fabric gently flowing around her as she awaited... something.

Time seemed to lose meaning. She lingered in this ethereal dimension, a faint smile gracing her lips as bliss and contentment permeated her being. In this moment, all was right with the world.

Joy and euphoria coursed through her, a sensation she had never experienced before. Bringing a hand to her mouth, she couldn't contain the gentle giggles that escaped her lips.

Yet, amidst this overwhelming bliss, a disquieting feeling began to tug at her. Swatting at the air, she resisted the intrusion, unwilling to let anything disrupt this moment of peace. But the sensation grew more insistent, evolving into a gnawing ache that throbbed at her temples.

Gasping aloud, Elowyn's euphoria shattered as a shock jolted through her. Eyes darting around the starlit expanse, she fought against the mirage. *This isn't what I want*, she realized, her mind clearing like a fog lifting. She began to oppose the otherworldly pull, yet as her own dispositions flowed back to her, she couldn't help but feel like this turn of fate was supposed to happen. Her desire to fight this divine spell dwindled as she relented to it—perhaps her life was never truly hers to control.

Suddenly, a tingling sensation spread through Elowyn's hands. With wide eyes, she observed two ethereal tendrils of moonlight dance across her palms, their incandescent glow mesmerizing. One thread graced her left hand, the other her right, gliding near the waning crescents etched into her skin.

In unison, the moonbeams arched, infusing divine energy into her palms, weaving across her skin. A delicate line of glowing ink emerged, tracing patterns around the crescent moons, forming an endless, seamless wreath—a symbol of no beginning and no end. The celestial mark symbolized eternity; its meaning etched into her very essence.

She sensed something within her core change immutably—something endless and absolute.

Elowyn felt the otherworldly pull at her soul once again as she emerged from the celestial waters, returning from the Goddess' realm. Still bent on one knee, Elowyn appeared again in the Temple of Caena, the divine waters dripping from her kneeled form. Across from her, Finnor mirrored her position, his gaze drawn to his own palms, now bearing the same sacred, wreathed mark.

"The Eternal Tethering spell is now complete," the High Priestess declared, her words drowned out by the thrum of celestial currents.

Elowyn couldn't hear her. She couldn't hear anything at all.

Elowyn merely stared at her own palms and began to construct a barricade within herself against the unfamiliar connection now woven into her soul.

18

Keeper's Aegis

THE KINGDOM OF PRYMONT UNFOLDED IN BREATHTAKING splendor, its ethereal castle perched high among clouds in a sky of blue. Elowyn gazed out from one of the castle's balconies, marveling at the city and towns nestled upon neighboring clouds, a metropolis of magnificent architecture and domiciles. What captivated her most were the fey of House Skyborn, gliding effortlessly between cloud communities on gossamer wings.

The Fourth Day of the Ceremony, the Keeper's Aegis, was hosted in Prymont this season. Elowyn's thoughts drifted to her childhood visits to the Skyborn castle, where she once befriended Syrilla Skyborn, daughter of King Nolas and Queen Emilyn Skyborn. However, their friendship waned as Elowyn's father kept her sheltered and shielded in Eriden.

Unable to bear the revelry and festivities with such a heavy heart, Elowyn sought solace on a secluded balcony, bringing her sister Elyria along.

In hushed tones, they shared whispers from the previous day in the Elberrin Forest, grappling with the events that unfolded in Lochwald. Elowyn tried to support Elyria through her distress, while Elyria comforted her sister when Elowyn revealed their father's actions. Elyria nearly erupted the sky as she told her, but Elowyn soothed her with reassurance before they parted ways for the Keeper's Aegis.

Nothing could change what had happened anyway.

As Elowyn watched the fey celebrate in the nearby floating factions, she couldn't help but envy their carefree existence, untouched by the weight of Caena's Trial. She longed to trade places with them, to be a mere bystander in the Ceremony, free from its burdens.

Elowyn's aura remained somber, still lingering from the morning's melancholy.

Unexpectedly, she felt a familiar finger entwine around her hand, gently whirling her around, meeting Draeden's golden gaze and his dimpled smile.

"I searched for you yesterday," he murmured, planting a soft kiss on her cheek. "I missed you."

His forthright affection tugged at Elowyn's heartstrings.

"What's troubling you?" Draeden inquired, sensing her disquiet. "Has something happened?"

Stepping back, he examined her closely, his caring eyes scanning for any hint of distress. It was then that he noticed her hands, reaching for one and cradling it gently, turning her palm to reveal the divine mark etched upon her skin. His aura shifted, a mix of disbelief and concern washing over him as he traced the intricate threads encircling her crescent moon.

"Who?" Draeden whispered, his voice heavy with emotion.

Elowyn attempted to speak the name, but her trembling lips betrayed her, and tears flowed anew down her cheeks. Draeden led her into a recessed corner of the quiet balcony. Tenderly, he enveloped her in his arms, holding her close as he rested his cheek against her head, his thumbs rubbing comforting circles on her back.

"I'm sorry, Elowyn," he murmured softly, his words a balm to her soul. "It will be all right. Maybe not now, but it will be."

Elowyn's tears flowed freely. "My father tethered my soul to Finnor Wynward."

"The Commander of Eriden?" Draeden's grip tightened momentarily at the name before easing. "Your soul is still perfect to me."

Elowyn gazed at Draeden through tear-filled eyes, gratitude overflowing within her. Wordlessly, she wrapped her arms around his neck, drawing him closer. She craved the solace and safety he always brought, seeking the warmth of his embrace. Tilting her head, she hovered her lips near his, and he leaned down, closing the gap between them.

Draeden leaned into her caress and his gentle grip fell to her waist. Their lips claimed each other with earnestness. Still engulfed in their fervid kiss, he brought one hand to her neck and cradled the base of it affectionately within his grasp. With that hand, he pulled her closer and deepened their kiss. She ran a burning hand through his claret-red hair and gripped his silken strands within her fist.

At her fevered touch, Draeden only grew more eager as he, too, seized a handful of Elowyn's snow-white locks. He pressed her body closer to him as if their connected bodies were still too distant. Elowyn was filled with a rapture as her mouth intertwined with Draeden's. Out of all the dalliances she had before, she hadn't felt an intoxicating euphoria like this. She wanted him, *needed* him. She was enraptured with security he offered her—a sanctuary all her own.

He would be the one she'd willingly give her soul to.

Draeden had showered her in a rainfall of kindness and compassion. He cared and tended to her emotions in a way she'd never received before. Stolen moments with him were seraphic; they were wildly enchanting, and she had no plans to abandon them. She could spend eternity in his arms, and it would still never be enough.

Draeden pulled away, his breath ragged, and reality came crashing back.

Elowyn creased her brow and yanked him back to her lips. He breathed a smile on her lips and kissed her tenderly, but firmly pulled away again.

"I need to take a step back." Draeden's eyes were dark and his breaths irregular. "Before I take you on this balcony floor."

"I'd like to see you try," Elowyn murmured.

A low noise escaped Draeden's throat as his eyes raked over her body. Before Elowyn could tempt him, he tore his eyes away from her.

"I will," Draeden vowed, his expression softening. "When the time is right."

Elowyn frowned at his decision. "Promise me then."

"I can offer more than just a promise," Draeden grinned devilishly. "I swear an oath to you."

"I've amassed two promises and an oath from you. I plan to collect on all three."

Draeden chuckled. "Consider one of them already fulfilled."

He clasped Elowyn's hand, her laughter music to his ears as he spun her around gently before leading her to a nearby bench. They settled down, and Elowyn nestled into his lap, finding comfort in the crook of his neck. Draeden's smile radiated warmth as he toyed with a strand of her white hair between his fingers.

"Tomorrow, you're off to Orwyn. I can't wait to show you around my home."

"What's your favorite part of Orwyn?"

"The city. I adore the folk of Orwyn. They're the heart of my kingdom."

"I've never been to a city. Not even back in Eriden. My father never allowed it."

Draeden turned to her, "Never been to any city? Ever?"

"Never."

"Well, we'll change that tomorrow. I'll show you all my favorite spots in the city. There's so much to see and do, especially with the Ceremony in full swing."

Elowyn's eyes sparkled with excitement. "Really?"

"Absolutely," Draeden murmured, planting a gentle kiss on her head. "We'll have to start at sunrise to make the most of it before the Fifth Day begins. And don't worry about the wards; I'll make sure we get through them."

Elowyn's expression faltered slightly. "I've never been to Orwyn, so I'm not sure if I could summon a moongate there on my own."

"I think you'd never forgive me if I made another portal joke. Since it's your first time visiting Orwyn, let's meet at the Temple, and I'll guide you from there."

"I'm excited to see your home," Elowyn said cheerfully as she sat up, turning to gaze into his golden eyes. "Thank you for wanting to show me."

"Always, anything for you."

"Do you have to rehearse being this charming?"

"It comes naturally."

"Your arrogance is bigger than the moon."

"What do you say? Have my ruses and wiles successfully courted you?"

"I'd say so."

Draeden chuckled and gently lifted her chin, tilting her head towards him as he leaned in to kiss her gingerly. He continued to cradle her, showering her with affection. Segments of Elowyn's sorrows from earlier began to unravel and unwind, waning at the hands of Draeden's admiration and intimacy. Her heart was beating to the rhythm of Draeden's, and she couldn't imagine another feeling more perfect.

"It brings us great pleasure to host the Keeper's Aegis in Prymont this divine season," Queen Emilyn Skyborn beamed. Seated upon her castle's dais, she occupied a heavenly throne hewn from stone. "On this Fourth Day, our candidates will choose a talisman to imbue with divine magic, creating an aegis to safeguard them during their Trial."

Beside her and King Nolas were the *animus* of Prymont, two feather-winged phoenixes. Elowyn observed Princess Syrilla standing beside the creatures, her flawless gossamer wings falling down her back.

Queen Emilyn's voice, sweet as honey, continued, "These aegis will serve as a connection, whether tangible or intangible, anchoring the divine candidates to Neramyr as they traverse the Bridge Between Worlds into Caena's realm. Whether they require strength, courage, perseverance, bravery, or hope, these aegis will remind them of their existence in Neramyr, reminding there is an end—a conclusion—to the trial."

Now it was King Nolas Skyborn who spoke from his throne. "The Keeper's Aegis will now commence as moonrise approaches. Our seven divine candidates have chosen their talismans to tether them to Neramyr. Under the guidance of the High Priestess, they will now initiate the connection of their chosen aegis to Neramyr."

The High Priestess emerged onto the dais from behind the two radiant thrones. Draped in an opulent robe of ivory silk adorned with threads of silver and pearls, she wore a tall headdress that veiled her face, reminiscent of the one she wore in the Iron Hollows.

"Fey of Neramyr, the time has come to begin the ritual of the Keeper's Aegis," she announced. "I shall summon each divine candidate to this dais. They will utter the sacred words before the Goddess as they present their talisman to Caena. The Goddess will imbue these aegis with her divine power, forging the tether that links the talisman to its keeper and to Neramyr."

Stepping forward, the High Priestess positioned herself before

Queen Emilyn and King Nolas at the center of the elevated platform. She then motioned toward her right, where the seven divine candidates awaited, and addressed them directly.

"Princess Elyria Fangwright of House Fangwright, please ascend to the dais and offer your chosen talisman to the Goddess of the Moon. Speak the sacred words to initiate the binding of your aegis to Neramyr."

Elowyn watched as her older sister ascended the stone staircase and approached the High Priestess.

"Blessed Caena, Goddess of the Moon, Savior of the Fey, Liberator of Neramyr, Mother of Worlds, please accept this aegis I offer unto you."

Carefully, Elyria lifted both arms to the back of her neck and delicately unfastened the opal teardrop necklace adorning it. Cradling the precious chain in her palm, she extended it to the High Priestess.

"Child of the moon, what have you presented to the Goddess?" the High Priestess inquired.

"I offer the Goddess a treasure invaluable to me. I offer Caena my most cherished possession," Elyria replied earnestly.

Elowyn's eyes shimmered with affection at her sister's choice. She instinctively reached for her own necklace and clasped it tightly in her hand. Her sister's chosen aegis stirred something within her, filling her with profound pride and unwavering love for Elyria.

The High Priestess inclined her head in acknowledgment to Elyria and gently cupped one of her weathered hands beneath Elyria's outstretched palm, while resting her other hand atop the aegis, enclosing it between her palms. As the High Priestess commenced a steady incantation, her aged palms began to emit a soft glow, casting ethereal light beneath the alabaster robe draped over her arms, all eight phases of the moon illuminated. A shimmering orb of feylight formed around the High Priestess' hands, enveloping Elyria's palm, and the aegis within its luminous embrace. Waves of divine energy pulsed within the feylight orb, saturating the room with otherworldly magic.

With a final surge of divine power, the High Priestess concluded her incantation, and the radiant feylight orb she had summoned began to dissipate into a hazy mist. Removing her hand from atop Elyria's palm, the High Priestess revealed the opal teardrop necklace, its silver chain bathed in luminescent moonlight. Turning to address the assembled crowd, she declared, "Your divine candidate has completed the ritual of the Keeper's Aegis! Princess Elyria Fangwright has forged the divine link and tethered her aegis to Neramyr!"

Though the crowd's applause was somewhat muted, Elowyn cheered enthusiastically for Elyria, her support resounding through the hall. Catching Elyria's grateful gaze from the crowd, Elowyn offered a nod of encouragement. She watched as Elyria descended from the dais and rejoined the assembly, standing beside Sylas.

The High Priestess then clapped her hands and continued, "Lynora Lionwind of House Blackbane, step forward and ascend the dais. Present your chosen talisman to the Goddess of the Moon and speak the sacred words to initiate the tethering of your aegis to Neramyr."

Following the same practice, the candidate from House Blackbane approached the dais and stood before the High Priestess.

"Blessed Caena, Goddess of the Moon, Savior of the Fey, Liberator of Neramyr, Mother of Worlds, please accept this aegis I offer unto you." Lynora held forth a golden ring in the palm of her hand.

Once more, the High Priestess inquired aloud, "Child of the moon, what have you presented to the Goddess?"

"I offer to the Goddess the heirloom of my birth mother, a family ring, to serve as my aegis," Lynora replied.

The High Priestess repeated this ritual for each of the seven realms in Neramyr. Elowyn pondered how these candidates decided what to offer to the Goddess as their aegis. All these possessions held significance to them, and she imagined it must have been challenging to select just one item to serve as their tether for the next seven years.

The Keeper's Aegis proceeded as the High Priestess called each divine candidate forward one by one. As the final candidate completed the ritual, Elowyn mentally recounted what each of them had offered to Caena as their aegis.

Her sister, Elyria, had chosen their shared opal necklace. Lynora Lionwind of House Blackbane had selected a family ring. Kerrick Graylon of House Driftmoor had opted for a sensation, the brine-filled scent of the Swyn Sea. Galen Wolfspire of House Darkmaw had offered a memory, the first time he witnessed a golden sunset gracing the badlands of Orwyn. Iva Rosefall of House Skyborn had chosen a silver amulet gifted to her by her father. Lillia Sagebrook of House Mirthwood had decided on a feeling, her devotion to her soul-bonded lover. Lastly, Sylas had chosen a sleek dagger that had been passed down in his family for generations; it had served as an aegis for many Fenharts in past Trials.

The conclusion of the Keeper's Aegis was met with thunderous applause, and a symphony of harps sounded to mark the ritual's conclusion and the beginning of the festivities. The hall was illuminated by floating orbs of feylight as courtiers and nobles cheered merrily and boldly, drinking deeply from their crystal goblets. Delicate clouds drifted around the tall ceilings while gossamer-winged performers glided gracefully in elegant arcs, twirling tulle ribbons in mesmerizing patterns like a stunning sunset sky come to life.

Elowyn navigated through the busy crowd until she reached Elyria, gathering her sister in a tight hug.

"I love you," Elowyn murmured, gesturing towards the teardrop necklace adorning Elyria's neck and then to her own. "This will be my choice in seven years, too."

Elyria smiled. "I love you more. Feeling any better?"

"Much better."

Before Elowyn could say more, she noticed Sylas and Lyra making their way towards them and offered them a small wave. Lyra floated over and wrapped her arms around Elowyn in a friendly embrace.

"Elowyn, I didn't see you in Lochwald yesterday!" Lyra exclaimed with a smile, her sea-green eyes sparkling. "I'm so glad I caught you today before you left."

Elyria glanced at Elowyn curiously but remained silent as she observed Lyra.

"Hi, Lyra," Elowyn greeted warmly. "You remember my sister, Elyria, right?"

"Of course. It's a pleasure to see you again, Princess Elyria," Lyra said with a curtsy and a smile. "You always carry yourself with such grace during the rituals. I wish Sylas could do the same."

Sylas colored at his sister's remark. "Hey! I'm doing just fine, Lyra."

"I think you're doing great," Elyria chimed in, her laughter as sweet as spun sugar. "I should know after all, I'm a candidate, too."

Sylas' face flushed even more as he rubbed the back of his neck, extending his hand towards Elyria. "Um, Elyria... Would you care to dance?"

Lyra's jaw dropped in surprise, her curiosity flaring.

"It would be my pleasure," Elyria replied with a smile, taking Sylas' hand as he led her to an open space where other courtiers were dancing.

Lyra turned to Elowyn, her jaw still agape, and grabbed her arm. "By the Goddess, did you see that?"

Elowyn was momentarily taken aback by Lyra's touch but relaxed, responding with a wry smirk. "Oh, yes. Sylas is clearly smitten with Elyria, and she seems equally enchanted."

"I've never seen Sylas show any interest in a female before," Lyra remarked, her hands clasped together, eyes alight with realization. "But soon, they'll be entering the Trial of Caena together. I've heard the soul-bonds formed between lovers in the Trials are unparalleled. Just imagine if they were to emerge from the Divine Shallows hand-in-hand?" Lyra sighed wistfully. "How romantic would that be?"

"Well, when it comes to the Trial, 'romantic' might not be the word I'd use," Elowyn replied, amused. "But you do seem to be in better spirits than the last time we spoke."

"I am!" Lyra beamed. "I'm taking your advice and sharing my happiness with those who nurture it. Yesterday, Prince Caswin looked stunning, but I ended up opting for this charming warlock from Driftmoor. And today, I already have my eye on a few divine warlocks here. That one over there in the ochre surcoat seems particularly intriguing."

"Oh," Elowyn began, momentarily caught off guard. "I'm not sure if that's exactly what I was trying to convey with my advice, but if it's making you happier, then I'm all for it."

"I know that look, Elowyn. Don't worry, a bit of physical touch is just what I need right now," Lyra teased. "After all, the bodies of the fey were crafted to be impressive and alluring for a reason. I'm just enjoying myself while exploring that reason."

Lyra winked at Elowyn, her smile dazzling. Elowyn couldn't help but smile back. Lyra was as gorgeous as she was enchanting. With her long, flowing mahogany locks and her mesmerizing green eyes, she held an irresistible charm. It was no wonder she could captivate anyone she met, leaving a lasting impression.

"If you ever decide you need a friend instead of a dreamy warlock, I'm here," Elowyn teased. "Though I must admit that warlock in the ochre surcoat *is* quite striking."

"Yes, he's quite something," Lyra sighed, then shifted her gaze to the left. "I have my eye on that one as well. Oh, Elowyn, help me decide."

"What's the determining factor?" Elowyn tilted her head, glancing.

"I'm not for certain... However, there's only one way to find out," Lyra whispered to Elowyn, leaning in close. "After I've had my fun with both of them, I'll be sure to let you know."

Lyra's laughter rang out like a chorus of bells as she squeezed

Elowyn's hand before floating off towards the male who had caught her eye. Elowyn smiled to herself, silently rooting for her new friend. Despite Lyra's heavy aura, there was a glimmer of light within her, surrounded by darkness. That flicker of healing and hope burned brighter than ever, even more so than in the Iron Hollows. It reassured Elowyn that Lyra would eventually find contentment someday.

Turning her gaze, Elowyn watched her older sister twirl with Sylas on the grand dance floor, a smile gracing her lips. What if Lyra was onto something about them entering the Trial of Caena together? Elyria deserved all the love and happiness in the world. Perhaps Sylas would be her perfect match for a soul-bond. Elowyn couldn't help but wonder if Elyria would even desire to soul-bond with another fey.

Elowyn was well aware of the rarity of soul-bonds in Neramyr. From a young age, she had been taught that only three types of soul-bonds existed in history: the soul-bond of Eternal Tethering, the bond between a fey and their *animus*, and the marriage soul-bond. While some believed these bonds were exclusive to the New Age, chroniclers argued that they also existed during the Old Age.

Elowyn knew of the eternal soul-bond that could form between two fey—her tether to Finnor still haunted her now. She was also familiar with the bond to a divine *animus*, as her father, mother, and uncle had all formed such bonds during their Trial of Caena. Without these bonds, Stryx, Bane, and Nerys would cease to exist in this realm.

The last type of soul-bond that could be formed was between two fey. This bond was born from devotion, passion, and love. It could be initiated by two fey speaking ancient, sacred words together, casting a spell that permanently bound their souls. This bond would endure as long as breaths fell from their lips and their hearts beat with ichor. It was an oath that lasted as long as their souls roamed the feylands, enduring not only in this realm but also in all realms beyond.

The marriage soul-bond among the fey could only be formed once, its binding eternal. However, not all soul-bonds among fey were created equal. Some could be more powerful and ideal than others, depending on the strength of the match. Many fey chose to forego this ritual, choosing to exist without the risk that their bond to another may not be as absolute as they believed—to ignore that maybe there was a soul-bond match out there that suited them or their chosen lover more.

Elowyn frowned as she considered this. With the burden of another tethered soul, would she ever find the perfect marriage soul-bond in her lifetime? Did her divine tethering to Finnor condemn her to a life of imperfect matches?

Since she was a feyling, Elowyn had always held onto the belief that she would find someone who would complement her completely, without reservation. She dreamed of finding her perfect match, a prince who would stand as her equal.

Her worries faded as she spotted Draeden across the hall, her heart skipping a beat at the sight of him. He held her within his golden gaze and waved, his dimples claiming her heart.

Elowyn moved towards Draeden, eager to bridge the gap, but her path was blocked as someone stepped in between them.

Elowyn came to an abrupt halt as she found herself face-to-face with princess of Prymont, Syrilla Skyborn.

Syrilla and Elowyn shared the same age. As dictated by the mysterious principle of the 'sacred seven' royal offspring, the heirs differed in age by no more than seven years.

The Skyborn princess was as beautiful as her mother, the queen of Prymont. Instead of the queen's honeyed locks, Syrilla's hair had hues of rose gold, a blend of blush pink, soft coral, and warm gold in her shoulder length strands. Her eyes, a mesmerizing smoky quartz, mirrored the color of slate thunderclouds. Sprouting from her delicate shoulder blades were sheer, gossamer wings. Describing Syrilla's wings as heavenly felt inadequate; they radiated an ethereal glow, reflecting the feylight in the room with an elegant glimmer.

"Elowyn?" Syrilla's expression was puzzled. "Moons, it's been nearly nine years since we last met."

Elowyn was caught unawares by the sudden encounter with the heir to the Skyborn throne. Memories of her flooded back, and she quickly gathered herself.

"Princess Syrilla," Elowyn replied awkwardly. "Indeed, it has been quite some time. It's wonderful to see you. You seem well."

"You can call me Syrilla," the princess smiled. "We were once good friends, you know."

Elowyn sensed the sincerity in Syrilla's words, stirring a wistful emotion within her.

"I remember. I'm glad we've crossed paths again," Elowyn admitted.

The two princesses of Neramyr stood in a moment of awkward silence, uncertain of what to say next. Syrilla absentmindedly twirled her thumbs in circles before breaking the silence.

"Would it be all right to ask why you stopped visiting me in Prymont?" Syrilla inquired candidly. "I sent letters. I even attempted to visit you in Eriden once, but my invitation to Fangwright castle was declined. I was informed that you no longer wished to see me."

Elowyn's expression shifted to one of confusion as she absorbed Syrilla's words. Elowyn couldn't recall precisely when their communication ceased, but she had always believed it was Syrilla who withdrew from their bond first.

"That's odd. I was told as a child that you declined my attempts to visit to Prymont."

A flash of frustration struck through Elowyn's emotions as guilt also riddled her conscience. She knew that it was her father who kept Syrilla's letters hidden, and it was he who spun the tale claiming that Syrilla refused her company each time Elowyn requested to visit Prymont.

Her father had always restricted her interactions with other feylands, even within her own kingdom. Yet, Elowyn failed to see the harm in maintaining her friendship with Syrilla. Her father wielded control over every aspect of her life. He would rather her suffer in loneliness than be influenced by entities out of his control—the only exception being her older sister. Perhaps their father feared that restricting Elowyn's presence in Elyria's life would prompt Elyria to sell her soul to the reaper of death to ensure he suffered eternally in this realm and all the realms beyond.

A sense of dread and unease settled deep within her as she came to a grim realization. Her father had succeeded in isolating her completely. The wreaths now branded on her hand were symbols of her lost freedom. In just three days, Elyria would embark on her seven-year journey, leaving Elowyn truly alone. Once the Ceremony of Caena concluded, she would have no legitimate reason to freely visit Draeden, Lyra, or Syrilla ever again. Despite her efforts to assert her independence, it seemed that her life would inevitably conform to her father's desires.

In that moment, Elowyn felt a surge of hopelessness engulfing her, a feeling that seemed impossible to overcome.

19

A Moment of Bliss

Despite the weight on her heart, Elowyn awoke to a fluttering sensation in her chest. Darkness still blanketed the world outside, with the moon casting its final shadows before sunrise. Excitement pulsed through her veins as she remembered Draeden's plan to meet her at the Temple at dawn, ready to guide her through a moongate into Orwyn. It would be her first time venturing beyond the walls of a castle, and her anticipation bubbled over.

Draeden had advised her to dress simply, in a modest dress and a hooded cloak, for their excursion into the city. As she contemplated the logistics of the upcoming Fifth Day, she wondered if there would be enough time to return to Eriden to prepare herself. At the very least, she needed to inform Elyria, perhaps even enlist her sister's help in procuring a change of attire. Elowyn couldn't help but smile at the thought of Elyria's inevitable curiosity, imagining her sister eagerly questioning her about the day's later adventures.

Elowyn rose from her bed and noticed a small parchment lying on her bedside table. Intrigued, she reached for it and unfolded the paper, smoothing out its creases. Honey and lilac greeted her as she read the neatly penned words, her sister's handwriting dancing across the surface of the page.

> *Dear Elowyn,*
>
> *I have an early engagement to attend to this morning. Regrettably, I won't be able to see you before the onset of the Fifth Day, which means you'll have to prepare without my expert hair braiding skills. Love you dearly. See you in Orwyn.*
>
> *Elyria*

Elowyn chuckled at the note and folded it neatly back into quarters. It seemed her plan to have Elyria bring her a change of clothes was no longer an option. She resolved to ensure she left Orwyn with enough time to return, dress, and arrive before the start of the Fifth Day.

Getting up from her bed, Elowyn began readying herself. She ran a brush through her ivory locks and fashioned them into a loose braid, though it lacked the precision of Elyria's work. She then selected a simple pale dress with a snug bodice and a flowing skirt to wear from her wardrobe. Lastly, she draped herself in a thick-spun cloak with a hood the color of roasted chestnuts.

Nearly ready to portal to the Temple, Elowyn's stomach grumbled loudly. She frowned, perhaps she'd sneak into the royal kitchen for a quick bite before departing. Surely the kitchen staff would still be asleep after the festivities of the Fourth Day.

Glancing out of one of the arched windows, Elowyn observed the faint hues of dawn, a dusky indigo that would soon give way to sunrise. Tucking a loose strand of her snowy hair behind her pointed ear, she ensured she had a small coin purse tucked into one of her cloak's pockets.

Stepping as quietly as she could, Elowyn approached the entrance to her bedchamber and pressed her ear delicately against the wooden door. She waited, her senses heightened, but heard nothing. Her stomach growled once more, and she cursed its refusal to be silenced. With utmost care, she eased the door open and peered into the long hallway beyond. Golden sconces adorned the marble walls, casting a soft glow that danced with the shadows. After a moment's observation, Elowyn slipped noiselessly out of her room.

Heading in the direction of the kitchens, she moved stealthily until a sound from behind caused her heart to sink.

"Where do you think you're going?" Finnor's gruff voice shattered the silence of the marble corridor, his tone more demanding than questioning.

Elowyn spun around to face him, her worry morphing into anger as she met his gaze. With clenched fists, her aura radiated with fury as she realized how Finnor discovered her presence.

"I do not answer to you." Her eyes were blazing like embers.

Finnor let out a weary sigh, running a hand through his tousled, snow-white hair. Moon-inked scales shimmered on his skin, catching the light of the sconces. He was dressed haphazardly in a loose tunic and leather pants, looking as if he had just rolled out of bed.

"Where are you going?" he repeated, his voice unchanged.

"The kitchens," Elowyn replied, truthful enough. "I was hungry."

"Then why are you wearing a common cloak?" Finnor countered.

"I've given you enough answers," Elowyn's lips tightened into a thin line.

"I'm not stopping you," Finnor replied truthfully. "I don't intend to control your life. I just need to know where you're headed so I can fulfill my duty as your feyguard."

"Was tethering my soul against my will not fulfilling your duty enough?" Elowyn struck back. "Just tap into the pits of your abominable soul and find me through the tether. At least that way you'll spare me the effort of speaking."

"I know you don't understand why I did it," Finnor muttered thickly. "I did it to protect you. Why can't you see that? It's not uncommon for Eternal Tethering spells to be bestowed on royalty. There's a reason it only requires the Goddess' blessing and a willing fey. Your bloodline and succession to the throne are crucial to the prosperity of Eriden. To Neramyr."

"Why don't you understand that I never wanted this?" Elowyn's voice rose. "The throne is Elyria's to inherit by birthright. It should've never been stripped away from her. You've served this kingdom for longer than I've drawn breath, yet you know nothing about it."

Finnor's expression hardened. "Regardless of how it happened, you're a Crown Princess of Neramyr, Elowyn. This is the fate dealt to you by the hands of the moon and stars. It's what's right and just."

"Have you no rationality of your own? You recite those words with such credence as if you intend to be a martyr for the moon. Will you shepherd a crusade against me if I suggest that the Moon Goddess was wrong for not marking Elyria as an infant? What if I told you that Eriden is a kingdom fueled by spite?"

Elowyn took a domineering step toward Finnor, causing his jaw to twitch with displeasure at her approach.

"Lest you forget, I am not the only daughter of Eriden. The folk of this kingdom treat their firstborn princess with bitterness, with acrimony and malevolence... Am I to believe that the foundation on which your beliefs lie are truly righteous? As your morals rest on their benevolent pedestal, where do they retreat to when the folk of Eriden scorn and maltreat their eldest princess?"

Finnor's expression remained indecipherable as he glared back at Elowyn. Silence sealed his lips, yet she did not relent from her verbal tirade against him.

"You are plagued with the belief that the stars and moon are faultless; you trust that there are no fates that are flawed, but you're wrong, Finnor. If you would've opened your mind and listened to me, instead of obeying the king's every whim, you might have understood that. What you did to me was detestable. You claim your duty is to protect me, but I will never forget how you stood there unshaken as I was withering away under my father's hand." Elowyn's words were laced with ire at each enunciation. "Under *your* hand."

Finnor's expression crumbled at her final words. He regarded her with culpable eyes, guilt stricken. Though he seemed prepared to speak, he ultimately remained silent, an allegory of unspoken regrets locked behind his lips.

Elowyn shifted her gaze to one of the arched windows, cursing softly as she noticed the sun beginning to rise.

"I'm leaving," Elowyn announced, turning on her heel. The encounter had left her appetite soured. "Don't follow me."

Finnor reclaimed his voice, his tone determined. "Tell me where you're going."

Ignoring his incessant inquiry, Elowyn summoned a portal. With purposeful strides, she crossed through the moonlit archway, her destination fixed in her mind as she disappeared into the feylight.

∾

THE TEMPLE OF CAENA BASKED IN THE GENTLE MORNING glow of the sun as Elowyn emerged from the fading feylight archway. She knew she was running late. With a quick scan of her surroundings, she found the temple deserted, devoid of any fey. Her heart raced as she hurried up the ancient stone staircase towards the antechamber. One question dominated her mind: was he there?

Pushing open the massive doors of the temple, usually left ajar, Elowyn entered hastily, her footsteps echoing on the marble floor.

Her eyes landed on a hooded male figure sitting on a bench with his head hung low, hunched over with his elbows resting on his knees. At her approach, the male lifted his head up and Elowyn recognized the locks of claret-red hair that remained untucked under the hood. Relief flooded her as her heart quickened at the sight of him.

"Elowyn," Draeden murmured her name on his lips as his golden irises lit up with relief. His handsome features fell into a dimpled smile.

"Draeden," she whispered back, a smile lighting up her features.

"I was worried you wouldn't come," he admitted, rising from the bench, and closing the distance between them in a few swift strides. With a gentle embrace, he brushed a kiss against her cheek.

Elowyn laughed softly, returning his affectionate gesture. Each moment with Draeden seemed more magical than the last.

"We need to hurry if we want to catch the best of the market," Draeden urged, intertwining their fingers. He summoned a moongate and with a gentle hold on Elowyn, he led them both through the moonlit pillars to Orwyn.

∼

DRAEDEN AND ELOWYN MATERIALIZED IN AN EMPTY cobblestone alleyway, emerging from the fading moongate. Draeden adjusted his hood, tucking his loose claret-red strands further into it. Turning to Elowyn, he gently brushed a loose lock of her ivory hair behind her ear, his bronzed hand lingering affectionately on her cheek. He then carefully tucked the rest of her silk braid into her thick chestnut-colored hood, satisfied with her disguised appearance, before offering her a warm smile.

"Welcome to Orwyn," Draeden announced. "Ready to explore the heart of the city?"

"Yes," Elowyn replied eagerly, excitement coursing through her body.

Draeden led her through the winding cobblestone alleyway, explaining that their masked appearances would allow them to move more freely through the city, especially on the bustling Fifth Day. Though he assured her of the good nature of Orwyn's inhabitants, he insisted on taking precautions to ensure her safety during her visit.

As they reached the alley's end, the sounds of the city became audible to Elowyn. Draeden reached into his cloak and retrieved a pair of slender gloves, handing them to her.

"An extra measure of caution," Draeden explained, gesturing to her moon-inked palms. He then retrieved another pair for himself, donning them swiftly.

"Thank you," Elowyn said, slipping her fingers into the soft fabric.

"I hope you're hungry," Draeden remarked with a grin, extending an open palm towards her. "Let me show you one of the best stalls in the market."

Elowyn clasped Draeden's hand tightly as he guided them out of the secluded alleyway. The narrow cobblestone passage unfolded into one of the most crowded streets Elowyn had ever laid eyes on. Her jaw dropped in awe as she took in the city's vibrant surroundings. The plaza was teeming with more fey than she had ever seen in one place. Almost everyone wore cloaks similar to her own, spanning from newborns to elders as venerable as the High Priestess herself.

Surveying the landscape of Orwyn, Elowyn couldn't help but release a slow breath of wonder. The city was nestled amidst majestic hills and bends, their russet-shaded rock formations flowing like hardened rivers. The sky above was a brilliant blue, contrasting beautifully with the rugged terrain. Everywhere she looked, the towering rust-colored hills encircled the entirety of Orwyn.

Amidst the public square, countless houses and living domiciles were scattered, their reddish walls crafted from sturdy clay. Elowyn's gaze wandered beyond the plaza, where she spotted a winding elevated path that encircled a towering hill. At its summit loomed the imposing

Darkmaw castle, its majestic walls also fashioned from smooth, reddish clay. From her vantage point, she could discern the arches and intricate carvings embellishing the fortress's formidable walls.

Returning her attention to the busy atmosphere of the plaza, Elowyn was swept up in the lively energy as the city folk prepared for the Fifth Day festivities. She watched with delight as groups of feylings chased each other playfully, their laughter filling the air. Females with bright smiles shuffled about, carrying baskets of ripe fruits and freshly harvested vegetables to various stalls for sale, their conversations filled with excitement.

Guiding Elowyn through the crowd, Draeden led her towards a stall already abuzz with activity, where a maroon-haired male was expertly kneading flour into fluffy pastry dough. Elowyn had to rise onto her tiptoes to catch a glimpse of the sought-after vendor. With practiced skill, he rolled the delicate pastry into small portions, filling them with stewed meat and vegetables seasoned with fragrant spices that set Elowyn's mouth watering. Nearby, another sheet of pastry was being filled with sweetened fruits infused with notes of cinnamon, vanilla, and clove, drifting delightful aromas towards her.

Suddenly, a stout female emerged from behind the male, carrying a large tray of freshly baked pastries. Wisps of steam still curled from the golden-brown, open-faced crusts, as if they had just been plucked from the oven moments ago. Setting the tray on the counter, she greeted the eager crowd with cheerful banter, exchanging parcels of pastries for coppers. Eventually, Draeden and Elowyn reached the front of the stall, where the fey gestured for them to approach.

"What can I get you folks?" she asked with a hearty voice. "Today we have puff pastries. For those with a sweet tooth, we have honeyed fig, apple, plum, or apricot; and for those who prefer savory, we've got braised pork with leek and mushroom."

Draeden arched a curious brow at Elowyn. "What do you think we should get?"

"Honestly, they all sound delicious," Elowyn replied, tapping her chin. "I can't choose, so I'll let you decide."

Draeden grinned and turned to the fey behind the counter. "We'll take one of each."

"Well, aren't you quite the chivalrous lad?" the stout fey chuckled, gathering five pastries, one of each flavor, into a small box and handing it to Draeden. "That'll be fifteen coppers."

Draeden pulled a silver coin from his cloak and handed it to her with a wink. "That's for making me look good in front of the lady. Blessings to you on this Fifth Day."

The fey cackled aloud, stashing the coin in her apron. "Many moon blessings to you, young lad." She turned to Elowyn. "Are you visiting from Eriden, darlin'?"

"Yes," Elowyn smiled. "I traveled here to witness the Fifth Day."

"I know a few folks from Eriden who moved out here for work," the fey continued. "Folks in Orwyn will pay a pretty coin for the protection of a warlock or sorceress from there, y'know? Merchants hire 'em when they export their goods through the bordering trading routes." She shook her head. "Blasted bandits and raiders looting from hardworking folk."

"I'm sorry to hear that," Elowyn remarked with a frown. "That's awful."

"Nothin' you need to be sorry for, dear. It's not you who's the miscreant," the fey said, turning back to Draeden. "Blessings, again. Now, I've got a long line of customers waitin' on me. Enjoy, and may the Goddess Mark you."

Draeden and Elowyn waved goodbye to the fey before veering off to a quieter section of the bustling streets. As they strolled, Elowyn pointed out the floral vendors they passed. The flowers of Orwyn differed from those she was accustomed to in the mountainous regions back home. Spindly wildflowers in shades of amber, violet, and cream were expertly arranged in beautiful bouquets. She admired bunches of five-petaled coneflowers in hues of sapphire, magenta, and blush, which Draeden identified as larkspur. But what truly caught her eye were the milky-petal blooms of the sand-lilies elegantly displayed on the stalls.

After passing several sweet shops and bakeries, they turned a corner near an alehouse and found an empty bench to sit together. Once seated, Draeden leaned forward and offered her the box of pastries, still warm after their walk. Elowyn peered inside to see the five flawless pastries nestled together. She reached for one but hesitated, withdrawing her hand. Furrowing her brow, she hovered her hand slightly above the pastries. With a subtle yet swift motion, she summoned a sliver of her magic and split each pastry perfectly in two.

"Now we can both try each flavor," Elowyn explained cheerfully as she grabbed one half of a plum pastry and took a bite.

The flaky crust melted in her mouth, releasing a burst of delightful flavor that danced along her tongue. She savored the sweetness of the plum, the soft hints of vanilla and honey, and the warmth of the clove. Before she knew it, she had finished her half. She wiped the crumbs from her fingers and found Draeden smirking at her with warmth in his eyes.

"What did you think?" Draeden asked, grinning. "Good?"

"So good," Elowyn replied, laughing as she reached for another pastry. "We have similar desserts in Eriden, but I've never tasted anything quite like this. You'd better hurry or I might eat yours too."

Draeden grabbed one half of his own pastry and popped it into his mouth, finishing it in two bites. Then he pointedly took a bite of the apricot pastry, teasing Elowyn. "I think you're the one who needs to hurry."

Elowyn laughed and rolled her eyes at him before reaching for the fig pastry and taking a nibble. "So, about what the vendor said back there... Are there many fey from Eriden living here? What about from other kingdoms?"

Draeden finished chewing before responding. "It varies. Some fey from other kingdoms are here on assignments or temporary stays. A few decide to settle in Orwyn permanently, but like in all kingdoms of Neramyr, it's hard to fully integrate outside of one's House."

"Come to think of it... Apart from the Ceremony of Caena, I don't recall seeing many fey outside of House Fangwright while living in Eriden," Elowyn remarked, furrowing her brow.

Draeden nodded thoughtfully. "Eriden's borders are notoriously difficult to breach. On the other hand, I can't think of a single kingdom that doesn't employ warlocks and sorceresses from Eriden. Your kingdom has a reputation for producing some of the most skilled magic-wielders in Neramyr."

"We *are* quite special," Elowyn added sarcastically as she reached for another pastry.

Draeden chuckled. "Indeed. Haven't I mentioned yet? I'm only drawn to you because of your illustrious magic-wielding capabilities. I've been trying to charm you into my employ."

Elowyn playfully thumped his arm. "I'll accept payment in pastries."

"Consider it done," Draeden said with a smirk. "I'll have the contract drawn by morning."

Elowyn laughed and rolled her eyes again, resting her hands on her stomach. "That was amazing. I'm completely full now."

As they conversed, they polished off the last crumbs of the delectable pastries. Draeden gathered the empty box with one hand and rose to his feet, extending his other hand to Elowyn. "Ready? There's still plenty more to explore."

Elowyn accepted his hand with a cheerful nod, and they strolled down the cobblestone street together, fingers intertwined. As they walked, Elowyn observed the modest buildings around them gradually giving way to grand and imposing structures. "Where are we headed next?"

"We're going to Orwyn's Art District," Draeden explained, his smile brightening. "It's a boulevard where enthusiasts of music, theater, painting, and literature can come together to celebrate their shared passions. I want to take you to one of my favorite music houses. I used to sneak out of the castle as a feyling and lose myself in the performances there for hours. I still do it now."

"That sounds incredible," Elowyn murmured, her curiosity piqued. With each step, she felt like she was unraveling mysteries she never thought she'd uncover. In Eriden, masterful musicians could be summoned to the castle at her whim, but this was different. Here, the artists performed for the joy of it all, not by the call of the crown.

"Here we are," Draeden announced, gesturing towards a large building with the same graceful arches Elowyn had spotted on the Darkmaw castle. A flight of limestone steps led to a pair of arched oak doors. Faint strains of music drifted from within, inviting Elowyn to step inside. A sign hanging from an iron beam swayed gently in the breeze, reading *Beauarde Tavern and Music House*. Elowyn felt a surge of anticipation and nerves coursing through her as she gazed at the welcoming doors.

She took a deep breath and realized that rather than feeling nervousness, it was actually excitement that filled her.

20

The Willow Spirit

Draeden guided her up the stairway, gently pulling open one of the heavy wooden doors. As they stepped inside, the enchanting atmosphere of the music hall enveloped Elowyn in a whirlwind of emotions. Waves of happiness, joy, and celebration flowed from the room, lifting her spirits. A radiant smile spread across her face, her eyes sparkling like stars against the night sky.

They made their way towards the small stage at the back of the hall, where a claret-haired lutist was strumming the final notes of a captivating melody. Elowyn and Draeden watched in rapt attention as the lutist concluded his performance with a flourish, eliciting cheers and applause from the crowd. Elowyn even found herself clapping enthusiastically at the music.

After the performance, the lutist bowed graciously to the audience and collected offerings from a chest at the edge of the stage. Draeden led them to a cozy table in the corner, assisting Elowyn to her seat before excusing himself to visit the bar.

As she waited for Draeden to return, Elowyn surveyed the crowded room, making sure to keep her hood secure. She observed the patrons chatting and laughing spiritedly, fascinated by their lively energy. Most had claret-red hair, indicating they were locals of Orwyn. Elowyn overheard lively debates about musical instruments and discussions about the evening's performances, immersing herself in the vibrant atmosphere of the music house.

At a nearby table, a male in a tawny cloak spoke hurriedly to his companions, "I heard Aunora is playing next." His companion turned to him, eyes widening slightly. "Aunora? I thought she was still touring with her troupe across Neramyr." The first male shook his head. "She returned for the Fifth Day. Queen Nikoletta requested her performance during the Ceremony of Caena." The second male exhaled sharply. "She's quite something, isn't she? To be both a divine-blessed sorceress and one of the most talented instrumentalists in Neramyr." The first male clicked his tongue. "The Goddess certainly favored her." The second male shook his head and took a sip from his mug. "That she did."

Draeden returned with two mugs and interrupted her eavesdropping. He handed one to her with a dimpled grin. "Gooseberry ale. You'll love it."

"Seems a bit early for a drink, doesn't it?" Elowyn raised an eyebrow, inspecting the amber liquid with foamy bubbles atop. "I've only ever had *vinum* before."

"It's the Fifth Day!" Draeden retorted cheerfully. "And you're here with me in Orwyn. Plenty of reasons to celebrate." He clinked his mug against hers and took a hearty swig.

"Fair point," Elowyn chuckled, reciprocating the gesture before taking a cautious sip. She raised her eyebrows in pleasant surprise as the cool liquid traveled down her throat, warming her stomach. With a sweet, fruity aroma and full-bodied flavor, the ale was a novelty from the *vinum* she was accustomed to. Setting down her mug, she nodded approvingly. "Definitely not the same as *vinum*, but I think I like it."

"I'll drink to that," Draeden chuckled, taking another sip from his mug. "The barkeep mentioned the next performance to me. Apparently, one of Orwyn's finest soloists has returned from their travels." His excitement bubbled over as he continued, "You're in for a treat. I still remember the first time I saw this performer... I was just a feyling, but it's one of my most treasured memories to this day."

"I believe you," Elowyn replied sincerely. "I overheard the table behind us discussing it too. Aunora, right?"

"Yes, her name is Aunora. She's not much older than us, maybe fifty years or so. She's gained quite a reputation in Orwyn. After she received her final Mark, she set out to travel with a troupe of musicians, performing all across Neramyr. And from what I've heard, she always performs as a soloist. Quite impressive, isn't it?"

"Absolutely. And she's a divine sorceress as well? Do you know when she completed her Trial of Caena?" Elowyn's admiration for the esteemed performer only grew as she learned more about her. She couldn't help but wonder if Aunora's troupe ever sought to perform in Eriden, though she doubted her father would have entertained such a request.

"She completed her Trial three seasons ago," Draeden confirmed. "Word spread like wildfire when she announced she'd be traveling with a troupe of performers across Neramyr. Usually, divine-blessed fey assume positions that employ their newfound magic or serve the realm in some way. But not Aunora; she chose music. By virtue of her Mark, she's still sworn to protect the realm's folk, but we're living in a time of peace now. There are other divine fey tasked with keeping danger at bay. I find her inspiring."

"I agree," Elowyn murmured, considering the extraordinary choice Aunora had made. She couldn't help but wonder what it would be like to have the freedom to choose her own path. If not for her title, would she have pursued a simpler life, perhaps as a florist like those she saw in the market? Would she have engrossed herself in scholarly pursuits in the library? Could she have even become a musician herself? "I think what she did was brave."

"Brave. I like the sound of that," Draeden said, reaching for Elowyn's hand and intertwining their fingers. "I'm grateful you're here, Elowyn. Being with you brings me more happiness than you realize."

Elowyn felt her cheeks warm at his sincerity. "You make me happy, too," she replied earnestly. Draeden had a way of making her feel complete, filling her with warmth and calmness with just a glance or a touch.

As the room fell silent, Elowyn noticed two large attendants from the music hall stepping onto the stage. They carefully brought forth a stunning instrument, one of the most beautiful harps Elowyn had ever seen. They positioned it on the stage, placing a cushioned stool beside it before stepping back and leaving the platform.

Elowyn's gaze traced the contours of the harp's neck, its wood coated in gold lacquer, appearing sleek and distinguished. Ivory-painted swirls embellished its surface, depicting images of the moon and stars against a backdrop of a golden night sky. The strings, like strands of opulent silk, lay within its body, promising rich and luxurious sounds.

The room fell into near silence, anticipation palpable in the air, as patrons awaited the next performance. Then, with a suddenness that caught Elowyn's breath, a slender sorceress emerged from behind the stage curtains. Her golden eyes met Elowyn's, and she felt a surge of awe at the sorceress's powerful yet graceful presence.

The Darkmaw sorceress possessed a heart-shaped face and deep claret-red locks, half of which were pinned up with golden hairpins, falling down her back. Draped in layers of flowing chiffon, she moved with a confidence and poise that captivated the room. Her bare arms and exposed skin revealed the intricate ivory markings of her divine Mark.

With ease, she settled onto the cushioned stool, the chiffon of her skirts spread around her like petals falling from a flower. In position, she prepared to weave her magic through the strings of the golden harp.

Whispers of awe and reverence filled the room as Aunora took the stage. Elowyn could hardly believe her luck at witnessing such a renowned performer. Every eye in the music house was fixed on Aunora while she gracefully lifted her arms, poised above the harp's strings. The room fell into hushed silence. Aunora released a breath and plucked the first flawless chord.

The harp's ethereal notes floated through the air, captivating Elowyn like a feathered seed of a dandelion caught in a gentle breeze. Each note Aunora strummed released an ethereal, airy tune that stole the breath from Elowyn's lungs. Aunora's fingers danced masterfully along the plane of strings, plucking and pulling in powerful controlled movements. She closed her eyes blissfully as her fingers danced along the threads with perfect precision, letting her artistry command the cords for her.

Aunora began to play a ballad for the room.

As she played, a story unfolded in Elowyn's ears, painted vividly by the haunting melody—it began as a seraphic song of a mother and child.

The harp's melody transported listeners to a morning many moons ago, when spring flourished, and a weeping willow swayed gracefully in the gentle sunlight. Beneath its verdant canopy, a mother sat, cradling her swollen belly with tender hands. A cry escaped the mother's lips, groaning as she welcomed her newborn daughter into the world under a full moon.

The mother was alone—still many miles away from home—only venturing forth to harvest the juniper berries that were bountiful this time of year. Her child was not yet due for weeks, but nonetheless, she thanked the Goddess her child came safely. Soon, exhaustion crept upon the mother, her eyelids weighing down like anchoring stones. "Just a short rest," the mother whispered to her daughter, pressing a kiss to her brow before falling into an inescapable slumber.

The harp continued to unfold the story in an illustrative aria; vivid notes began to thrum in powerful patterns, leaving Elowyn transfixed as each emotive clef drifted from Aunora's fingers.

Upon awakening, the mother found herself under a sky devoid of stars. She blinked, clearing the remnants of sleep from her eyes, her thoughts immediately turning to the bundle cradled in her arms. A radiant smile graced her lips as she uncovered the cloth to caress her newborn's face, her tender fingertips brushing gently across the soft skin. Yet, when she cupped the infant's face, a scream tore from her throat, disbelief and denial washing over her. The infant was cold to her touch, its chill piercing her like a steel blade. The mother's wails filled the air as she desperately called out to her newborn, but only deafening silence answered her plea.

Clutching the bundle tightly to her chest, the mother bellowed to the heavens, her sobs filled with grief.

She pleaded with the spirits of the feylands to spare her child, kneeling as she prayed to the stars for aid, yet the vacant sky offered no response. Begging the wind to breathe life into her newborn's lungs, she watched in despair as it waned and dwindled away. Turning to the soil, the mother implored the fertile feylands to lend vitality to her child's soul, only to be met with indifference. Forlorn, she sought strength from the rippling river, but it also paid her no heed.

She wept in anguish as each spirit disregarded her pleas and prayers. A final skyward cry for her lost child erupted from her throat, laden with desperation. At this, a spirit awakened from an endless slumber—the mighty willow beneath which she sat began to rouse.

The willow spirit considered the mother's plea, but only once first light dawned the horizon, did it break its silence. Gazing upon the mother, still as stone with vacant eyes, the willow called back the wind to whisper the terms of a bargain to her.

The Divine Shallows

The wind enveloped the mother, bearing the words of the mighty willow's bargain. Upon hearing the words, the mother's eyes widened, and with unwavering courage, she agreed to the tree spirit's terms. Accepting her answer, the mighty willow's branches lowered, tenderly cradling the silent bundle within its embrace. The mother knelt before the towering trunk of the willow, bowing deeply until her nose almost grazed the blades of grass below.

Observing the lifeless infant, the mighty willow sensed the absence of its soul in this realm. Harnessing the blazing energy of the rising sun, the willow illuminated the feylands in search of the child's wandering soul. Directing the wind's whispers, it instructed all it encountered to seek answers to a lost aura, adrift and unanchored. Commanding the river's currents, it tasked the waters to scour the seas and guide the child's soul back into this realm.

As hours stretched on, the mother's hope began to wane. "Patience," the willow reminded her, steadfast in its search for the lost soul of her child. With the sun sinking low on the horizon, despair gripped the mother once more, tears streaming down her cheeks. Moved by her sorrow, the willow warbled a lulling lullaby, soothing her troubled heart. Lost, the mother surrendered to the willow's gentle melody, finding comfort as her tears dried and a sense of ease washed over her.

She then gazed up at the midnight sky and drew in a sharp breath, beholding a scene of countless flickering stars. At the willow's bidding, the wind carried another message to her, and with joyous cries, she embraced the news.

The mighty willow revealed that her child's soul had returned to this realm, though it would take until morning to reunite with her newborn. Overflowing with gratitude, the mother thanked the willow profusely. The willow reminded the mother of their bargain and she nodded simply. Acknowledging her acceptance once more, the willow summoned an ancient, potent magic from its roots. As the land's vitality surged around her, the mother felt an arcane form of magic enveloping her, overwhelming her senses. Growing faint, the world dimmed around her, and she slipped into darkness.

The golden harp's strings continued to sing the bewitching ballad of the mother, child, and willow. Elowyn found herself forgetting to breathe, consumed by the heart-wrenching tale.

As morning broke, the mother stirred and opened her eyes, greeted by a sense of joy as the sun's warmth kissed her cheeks. Before her lay an unexpected sight: a cluster of ivory wildflowers cradling a bundle of cloth. With widening eyes, she beheld her daughter nestled within. Listening to the gentle rhythm of her child's breaths and the soft murmurs of her awakening, the mother marveled at the beauty of the moment. Attempting to reach for her child, she found herself immobilized, frustration bubbling within her.

Sensing her distress, the willow extended a comforting touch and spoke softly to her, reminding her of their bargain. Remembering their terms, the mother stilled, deliberating a question. "Will she remember me?" she asked the willow, who offered a sympathetic nod in response. "She will." Then came another question from the spirit, "Do you regret your decision?" The mother's answer was swift. "Never," she declared. "In this lifetime and all the lifetimes beyond, I would choose the same fate."

Aunora's fingers danced over the harp strings with fervent strokes, building towards an overwhelming crescendo that shattered Elowyn's composure, stirring something deep within her until the harp's melody softened into a soothing rhythm.

Many moons had come and gone since the mother struck her bargain with the mighty willow. Each day, she awoke by the willow's side, rooted to the spot where she had made her solemn vow years before. Seasons cycled like clockwork—wildflowers bloomed in patches, rain nourished the rivers, the sun bathed the land, and snow blanketed the feylands.

One spring morning, the mother rose by the willow's side, expecting the day to unfold like the countless ones before it. Yet, as she watched a passing fey gather juniper berries nearby, a glimmer flickered in her gaze.

The fey hummed a merry tune as she gathered the deep, black-purple berries into her basket. The mother watched in fascination, captivated by the graceful sway of the fey's movements. Memories stirred within her, reminding her of a time when she too moved with such ease—a time now long past. With her basket brimming with juniper berries, the fey let out a satisfied sigh, indulging in the sweetness of one berry before looking to the sun and settling in the shade of the willow.

The fey ran her fingers along the ivory wildflowers that grew around her as she plucked a stem to inhale its fragrance. She twirled the petals between her fingers before releasing them to the ground. Leaning against the trunk, the fey closed her eyes, feeling a mystical connection with the willow as she traced her hand along its smooth bark. A sense of lost familiarity washed over her, a smile gracing her lips as she surrendered to the comforting touch.

After a few moments of silence, the willow addressed the fey, though the willow knew her words would remain unheard. *"Daughter, you've come back to me at last."*

Aunora concluded her performance with a final, magnificent note, prompting tears to well up in Elowyn's eyes. Applause filled the music hall, and she turned to see Draeden's eyes shine with silver, mirroring her own emotions. Aunora gracefully rose from her seat, acknowledging the crowd with a smile and a bow before retreating from the stage.

"That was breathtaking," Elowyn confessed to Draeden, her voice filled with awe. "I don't think I've ever experienced anything more beautiful."

"I'm glad." Draeden smiled at her. "Now, this definitely takes the cake for one of my most treasured memories."

"I had no idea music could sound like that," Elowyn murmured.

"One day, I'll play something for you," Draeden promised. "Perhaps a piece on the piano, just for you."

"You'd really serenade me with the piano? Who knew you were such a romantic."

"How could you doubt it?" Draeden teased. "Haven't my heartfelt gestures proven enough? The more I offer, the more I find myself indebted to you."

"I suppose you're right. I stand corrected," Elowyn chuckled softly, shaking her head. "But rest assured, I intend to collect on those debts soon."

"I eagerly await it," Draeden affirmed. "But for now, we have other matters to attend to. I have another surprise in store for you."

"Today seems to be full of surprises," Elowyn remarked, a playful smirk tugging at her lips as she reached for his hand.

Draeden left a coin on the table before guiding them toward the exit of the music house. As they stepped out onto the charming cobblestone street of the Art District, they were greeted by the soft sun, indicating that the Ceremony was only a few hours away.

"Draeden?" A lilting voice floated from behind them.

Elowyn and Draeden spun around to find Aunora descending the limestone stairs, her elegant attire now replaced by a thick, brown hooded cloak.

Draeden's face lit up upon seeing the soloist. "Aunora!"

Aunora returned his smile, stepping down the stairs to embrace him warmly. "I thought it might be you in the crowd. By the Goddess, when did you become taller than me?"

"Likely because it's been years since you last saw me," Draeden chuckled. "I assume you're in town because of my mother's request?"

"Yes, that's true," Aunora answered. "Though, I've also been away from Orwyn for far too long. It was time to return home."

"How long will you be staying this time?"

"A few weeks... Maybe a month at most. I can't linger too long. My troupe will need me back on the road eventually. We'll be performing a few shows here in Orwyn, but we have plans to travel to the Elune Isles next."

"Ah, don't forget about us here while you're basking in the sun and swimming in the tides of the Swyn Sea," Draeden teased.

"Now that's an enticing thought..." Aunora laughed, then turned to Elowyn as if noticing her for the first time. "And who might your companion be?"

"Erm, please keep this between us, Aunora," Draeden interjected, placing a reassuring hand on Elowyn's back. "This is Princess Elowyn Fangwright."

Aunora's expression turned flustered, but she swiftly composed herself, offering a deferential nod towards Elowyn. With a quick motion, she pulled down her brown hood, revealing her face framed by deep, claret-red locks, and dipped into curtsy. "I apologize for my informality, Princess Elowyn."

"No need for apologies or formalities," Elowyn reassured her. "If anything, I should be commending you for your performance at the music house. Hearing you play was a wonder to experience."

"Thank you! All I've ever wanted to do is make others fall in love with music the way I have." Aunora's smiled. "Come to think of it, you may be among the first royalty from Eriden to hear me play."

"Really?" Aunora's words confirmed Elowyn's suspicion that the soloist's troupe had never been granted entry into Eriden's borders. "In that case, I feel even more honored to have experienced your music."

"I'm delighted to hear that!" Aunora beamed at Elowyn. "Well, I must take my leave to the royal castle and settle in before the start of the Fifth Day." She turned to Elowyn, embracing her warmly. "It's been a pleasure meeting you. Hopefully, we'll have the chance to meet again later tonight!" With a final hug for Draeden, she whispered something in his ear, to which he chuckled, before she departed in a different direction.

Draeden waved after Aunora, his laughter echoing through the air.

Elowyn arched an eyebrow. "Secrets aren't any fun."

"What she whispered isn't exactly a secret," he grinned. "Aunora warned me to not to act like a fool and mess this up."

"Oh," Elowyn murmured, her cheeks flushing. "I think you should definitely follow her advice—I quite like her perspective."

"I was already planning on it," he grinned.

They strolled across the cobblestone street and soon found themselves back in the bustling square they had visited nearly an hour ago. Elowyn's eyes widened in wonder as she beheld the transformation that had taken place. The cobblestones now gleamed with a midnight black hue, illuminated by twinkling feylights that danced beneath the feet of passersby like stars in the night sky.

Looking up, Elowyn marveled at the sight of glowing moons and stars hovering above the market square, conjured by the magic of the fey of Orwyn. Each ethereal projection depicted a different phase of the moon or a radiant star, casting a spellbinding aura over the square. Elowyn gazed skyward, her heart swelling with delight at the display.

Since the dawn of the New Age, during the Fifth Day, the folk of Neramyr take part in the Offering. This ritual is one of the most favored days of the week-long affair, namely because it celebrates the magic that runs freely in the veins of fey. What sets this ritual apart is that any fey who can wield magic is welcome to participate, regardless of their social standing.

On this day, the fey offer a portion of their own magic to the heavens to honor Caena.

Each magical offering manifests as a celestial formation, appearing as a phase of the moon or a star. The appearance of these projections varies based on the strength of the magic wielder. Those with stronger abilities conjure phases of the moon, while those with lesser magical abilities contribute smaller stars. These ethereal manifestations linger in the sky leading up to the ritual. When the High Priestess utters the sacred words of the Offering, the fey of Neramyr relinquish their hold on the magic, allowing it to ascend to Caena's realm.

Legend said that this ritual recurs every seven years to replenish the magic within the feylands. Some believe that the magic offered transforms into the very stars seen in the night sky, others say the magic nurtures the land. Some claim that the Goddess herself accepts the magic to preserve the divine link to the Bridge Between Worlds—the path between Neramyr and her divine realm.

The sight before her stirred a wave of nostalgia within Elowyn; she reminisced about watching the Fifth Day festivities from her bedchamber window as a young feyling. In the last Ceremony, at the age of twelve, she had summoned a crescent moon in her palm to offer to the Goddess. She could still vividly recall the joyous squeals she shared with Ora in that moment. Later, she discovered that Elyria had conjured one of the most radiant full moons witnessed in centuries, earning praise even from the High Priestess herself.

Elowyn found the collective release of magic by the city folk of Eriden to be nothing short of magical, like witnessing millions of shooting stars ascend into the night sky.

"I'll never tire of the Fifth Day," Elowyn remarked.

"Neither will I," Draeden agreed, giving her hand a gentle squeeze.

Together, they strolled across the cobblestone streets painted with fey-created constellations, leaving a trail of twinkling stars in their wake. Amidst the busy marketplace, they maneuvered through the stalls until they reached the serene alleyway where their journey had begun. Draeden summoned a moongate portal with a flourish and extended his hand to Elowyn once more.

"I know I promised to show you more of the city, but I couldn't let you leave Orwyn without experiencing this as well," Draeden said, his smile bright.

Elowyn returned his smile as she took his hand, ready to follow him wherever their adventure led, disappearing behind the veil of feylight.

21

Offering

Emerging from the moongate with Draeden, Elowyn found herself standing atop one of Orwyn's magnificent burnt-orange rocky hilltops. It was a location far removed from their previous surroundings; even from this summit, she couldn't spot the familiar landmarks of the market square or the grand arches of Darkmaw castle.

"Where are we?" Elowyn asked.

"I wanted to show you one of Orwyn's hidden oases," Draeden replied as he ran a hand through his hair. "I stumbled upon this place while riding Orix across the badlands."

"Orix?" Elowyn's head tilted.

Draeden brought his thumb and index finger to his lips and let out a sharp whistle. In response, a piercing screech echoed from below the rocky hilltop, and soon a majestic feather-winged gryphon emerged into view. The chestnut-hued creature soared gracefully before landing a short distance away from them.

"Orix, I want you to meet someone. This is Elowyn," Draeden

addressed the gryphon, reaching out to pat its massive beak. He then motioned for Elowyn to approach. "Elowyn, meet Orix. He's my father's divine *animus*. Orix is quite gentle and sweet-tempered."

Elowyn took a tentative step forward and extended her hand for Orix to inspect. Her words carried a mixture of nervousness and wonder as she addressed the divine creature. "Hello, Orix. You're quite the handsome gryphon."

Orix took a deliberate step towards Elowyn and sniffed her outstretched palm. Chittering, he nudged her hand playfully, eliciting laughter from Elowyn as she stroked his sleek feathers. The texture was remarkably soft, smoother than silk to her touch. Orix squawked with delight, standing on his lion-like hind legs to flap his wings cheerfully. Their powerful beats created gusts strong enough to require Elowyn to ground herself firmly, so as not to be swept away by the wind.

"It seems Orix has taken a liking to you," Draeden remarked happily. "That makes things much easier." With another whistle, Orix turned to Draeden, approaching him obediently and lowering himself to offer his back. Draeden effortlessly swung his leg over Orix's spine, mounting him with practiced ease. Extending a hand towards Elowyn, he offered her an encouraging smile. "Now comes the best part."

Elowyn's eyes sparkled with excitement as she accepted Draeden's hand and mounted Orix with his assistance. Positioned in front of Draeden, she felt his strong arms securing her from both sides, a warmth spreading through her as she resisted the urge to lean back into him. Sensing her reaction, Draeden leaned forward, which caused her cheeks to flush even more. He whispered something playful in her ear, rousing laughter from her in response.

Straightening his posture, Draeden let out a low whistle, signaling Orix to take flight. With a triumphant screech, Orix propelled himself into the air with powerful beats of his wings. Soon, Draeden and Elowyn were airborne, soaring through the sunset sky. Elowyn couldn't help but notice how different flying on Orix felt compared to riding

Bane or Stryx. While the firedrakes' flights were rugged and vigorous, flying on Orix felt graceful, effortlessly fluid.

Elowyn lifted both hands to the sky as she let her fingers dance in the wind. Laughter bubbled from her lips like a playful melody as Orix glided across the orange hilltops.

"Just a few more hills and we'll reach our spot!" Draeden shouted, joining her in laughter.

Orix continued to glide smoothly over the badlands until he reached a grassy hill covered in verdant greenery. Tucking in his wings, he descended towards a niche in the burnt-orange landscape, aiming for a smooth stretch of ground just above it. With precise movements, Orix landed, his talons and paws finding purchase on the solid ground. He lowered himself, inviting Draeden and Elowyn to dismount.

Draeden hopped from Orix's back first, landing on the grassy terrain. Extending his arm, he assisted Elowyn as she slid from the gryphon's back, murmuring her thanks, and affectionately brushing her fingers across Orix's feathers. Draeden then rewarded Orix with a piece of jerky from his cloak pocket, which the gryphon eagerly devoured before letting out a contented chitter. Draeden chuckled and gave Orix a final pat before the majestic creature took off, soaring into the sky.

"Where's he off to?" Elowyn said, watching the gryphon take flight.

"He's hunting. There's plenty of small game in the recesses of the rock formations. He's always thrilled to be out here," Draeden explained. "Now, close your eyes. I'll guide us to the oasis."

"I have to close my eyes?" Elowyn asked skeptically, but she complied, as she took hold of his hand.

"I won't let you fall." Draeden guided her carefully down the grassy hilltop and into an open clearing. He positioned her into a specific direction before covering her eyes with both hands, his fingers closed. "Are you ready?"

"Yes," Elowyn replied eagerly, a laugh escaping her lips. "The suspense is driving me mad."

Draeden removed his shielded hands and dropped them to his side. "You can open your eyes now."

Elowyn's delicate eyelids fluttered open, and she gasped in awe at the scene before her. It was a hidden paradise, a glistening oasis nestled within the cavity of the rocks. Tall palm trees surrounded the serene waters, their fronds creating a canopy of shade. To the right, a blanket was spread out with a cloth-lined wicker basket.

"Did you set this up?" Elowyn asked, astonished. "This is one of the most thoughtful things anyone has ever done for me."

"Surprise," Draeden chuckled nervously, rubbing the back of his neck. "I wanted to show you one of the hidden gems in Orwyn. It may not be as grand as your mountain castle or as ethereal as a kingdom in the clouds, but there's a serene beauty here, too."

"It's perfect," Elowyn turned to him with appreciation shining in her eyes. "This is something I'll remember forever."

"That was the idea," Draeden grinned. "Now, let's enjoy lunch."

Draeden led her to the plush blanket and helped her settle onto one of the cushions placed atop it. Taking his own seat, he began unpacking the contents of the wicker basket. Setting out a place setting for each of them, he poured a sweetened fruit drink into two glasses, handing one to Elowyn. She accepted it gratefully, relishing the taste. Draeden continued to arrange sandwiches, fruits, and sweets on a tray, then raised his glass in a toast to her.

"Here's to your first time in Orwyn," Draeden smiled warmly, clinking his glass with hers. "And cheers to your first time riding on a gryphon."

"Here's to more firsts with you." Elowyn lifted her glass to him. She couldn't deny the happiness she felt with him. Perhaps she had more in common with Lyra than she realized.

As the day passed, Elowyn's fondness only grew. She studied the contours of Draeden's face, committing every detail to memory. His golden eyes held her gaze, more precious to her than any treasure. The claret-red strands of hair framing his face were both charming and alluring all at once. Her eyes wandered over his body, no longer cloaked, clad in a simple loose tunic and pants. She admired the cord of his muscles, visible with his animated explanations. She found herself lost in the sound of his voice, unable to focus on anything else.

"I have one more surprise for you," Draeden said, his tone nervous yet eager. "I know how much you love dancing and music. So, before you came, I crafted an enchanted bell for you." He produced a small silver bell, no larger than a button, and extended it to Elowyn. "It's charmed to capture any sound and replay it indefinitely. However, it can only capture a sound once—I recorded the song we heard in the music house together. Simply ring the bell, and the notes will play for you."

Elowyn opened her mouth, but no sound emerged. She struggled to find her voice, her heart pounding with overwhelming emotions. With trembling hands, she reached for the silver bell, holding it delicately in her palm. The air seemed to still, holding its breath in anticipation.

Elowyn closed her eyes and rang the bell.

The ethereal notes of Aunora's song filled the air, wrapping Elowyn in a cocoon of emotions. She listened intently, every note resonating within her soul, stirring memories and feelings she couldn't quite articulate. Tears threatened to spill from her silver eyes as she savored the bittersweet melody until it faded into silence.

"I wanted to give you something special to remember your first time in Orwyn," Draeden began, but his words were abruptly cut off.

"Swim with me," Elowyn interjected suddenly, surprising Draeden.

He stumbled over his response, taken aback by her unexpected question. "I... I didn't bring a change of clothes."

"It's all right, we won't need them," Elowyn said hoping to sound nonchalant, already making her way towards the tranquil oasis.

Throughout, Elowyn struggled to contain her emotions, but her heart swelled with gratitude. Never had she experienced such genuine care and affection from a lover before. Each step she took was accompanied by the pounding of her heart, overwhelmed by the need to express her appreciation for his kindness. With trembling hands, she began to undress. Her thick cloak lay discarded nearby, leaving her only in a simple dress. Casting it aside, she stood in her undergarments, hesitating briefly before discarding them as well, too apprehensive to glance back and see if Draeden was watching.

Yet, she felt the weight of his gaze upon her, piercing through her like golden arrows. Banishing the thought from her mind, she stepped cautiously into the oasis. The water enveloped her calves in its comforting warmth. As seconds passed in silence, Elowyn summoned the courage to glance back, finding Draeden's gaze on her.

He remained in his loose tunic and pants, yet his attention was solely fixed upon her. She observed his unmoving figure, uncertain if he even drew breath. Doubts gnawed at her, questioning if this was a mistake, but then she felt the intensity of his gaze upon her bare form. His golden eyes traced a path from her flushed cheeks to the curves of her body, igniting a fire within her. Elowyn held his gaze as his breaths quickened, his hunger evident in its golden depths. Then, in a sudden surge of desire, Draeden shed his own garments and closed the distance between them.

His hands found her face, capturing her lips in a fervent kiss. Elowyn melted at his touch, her fingers greedily exploring the contours of his muscled back. Draeden's kiss grew more demanding as he tightened his grip on her, his touch igniting a passionate response within her. A soft moan escaped her lips as she surrendered to his embrace, kissing him with equal fervor. With a gentle yet possessive touch, he cupped her breast, sending waves of desire coursing through her veins. The sensation of his touch elicited a primal longing within her, a hunger for more.

Draeden's palm fell from her breast and brushed down her waist until it hovered below, to a part of her that was aching for his touch. His other hand gripped Elowyn's waist tightly as he continued to kiss her. Elowyn moaned, nearly hysterical from the teasing. Draeden smirked at her pining and gave into her desire. He brushed a finger along her heat and began rubbing it in slow, sensual circles. A gasp escaped from Elowyn's lips as a wave of pleasure struck through her from the all-consuming, slow-burning spark that Draeden was kindling within her.

Her mind cherished this moment, savoring a choice that was finally wholly her own.

Elowyn's breaths began to hasten as Draeden pulled his lips from hers and began trailing sultry kisses along her neck, quickening his circular movements, his bronzed fingers now slick with her. Draeden began vigorously rubbing her heat, adding fuel to her fire, letting Elowyn's moans command his pace. The flames within Elowyn grew wildly, seconds away from bursting aflame. He could sense her nearing her peak. Elowyn felt something inside her rupture from inconceivable pleasure and she finally collapsed in Draeden's arms.

Draeden's smile widened as he pressed a tender kiss to her forehead before cradling her entire body in his arms. There, Elowyn allowed the soothing warmth of the water to calm her senses, her body still tingling from the waves of pleasure that had coursed through her. Nestling into his embrace, she traced gentle circles on his chest, and basked in the tranquility of the moment.

"You have no idea how beautiful you are," Draeden whispered.

"You should definitely do that again," Elowyn murmured, eyes twinkling with affection.

"You're quite insatiable." Draeden teased. "Have you always been this difficult to satisfy?"

"I might need seconds or thirds," she said, leaning into his touch. "But in truth, you're the first fey with whom I've felt this way with."

Draeden's playful demeanor softened, and he gently spun her around to face him, her waist submerged in the warm water. Catching the serious tone in her voice, he regarded her with a considerate expression.

"Are you serious?" he asked.

Elowyn nodded, her gaze dropping to her fingers as if suddenly captivated by them. Draeden reached out, cupping her chin tenderly and lifting her gaze to meet his own. His golden irises shimmered with warmth and affection.

"Thank you for trusting me," he said softly. "And if there's ever anything that makes you uneasy, I want you to let me know. I care about you."

"I will," Elowyn reassured him with a soft smile. "Every time you say something lovely, I feel like I'm melting. You've completely enamored me, you know?"

"I hope you've realized that I've been enamored by you from the beginning. I'm just glad you're finally catching up," Draeden chuckled, closing the distance between them once more. "Have I mentioned that you're the most beautiful fey I've ever seen?"

"Once or twice, maybe," Elowyn laughed. She ran her fingers through her ivory braid, unraveling it, anything to distract herself from the heat rising in her cheeks. "But I must say, you're incredibly handsome. It's hardly fair."

"Is that so?" Draeden leaned forward to place a soft kiss on her lips. "Tell me more."

Elowyn felt that burning heat start to bloom within her again. "I find everything about you arousing. From your golden gaze that makes my knees weak, to your skin that makes me want to touch and taste you everywhere."

Draeden's eyes scoured over Elowyn as he seized her waist after she spoke. He lifted her up from the oasis' shallows and held her firmly against him and kissed her deeply, as if he could never have enough of her. Elowyn wrapped her legs around Draeden's torso and slid her arms around his neck, her unbound snow-white hair falling to her waist in waves. Draeden gripped her backside coarsely, supporting her as he carried her out of the shallow waters. Elowyn felt the hardness of his length pressing against her and it made her breaths jagged. Draeden's sure-fire steps carried them back to the plush blanket as he continued to kiss her passionately, tossing the earlier contents off the fabric.

He bent down to rest Elowyn's head on one of the cushioned pillows, setting her body down carefully. He was crouched over her, both of his hands resting on her thighs as he stared at her unclothed form. His golden eyes tore into her as she bared herself before him. Draeden planted an arm next to her head and leaned forward to kiss her again. With his free hand, he licked two of his fingers as he led them down the plane of her waist and found her heat again. He rubbed it sensually, reveling in the moaning aches coming from her. Elowyn arched her back as the feeling of pleasure began to build at her core in towering heights.

Draeden bent down to taste her, licking the pebbled peaks of her breasts with seductive strokes of his tongue. Elowyn's pleasure intensified and Draeden's eyes turned wild. He plunged a finger into her and relished in her wetness for him. Elowyn lifted her hips at his touch, letting him know that she savored his new endeavor. He added another and continued to stroke his fingers. Elowyn gripped the blanket's fabric and focused on nothing but the incomprehensible gratification she was feeling. She became unbound and a ripple of satisfaction carried her to her climax.

When she quieted, Draeden moved to rest beside her on the blanket. Both laying on their backs, their lungs rose and fell with hurried breaths. Turning her head, Elowyn looked at him, still reeling from her fading climax.

"I want all of you," Elowyn said sincerely. "I trust you."

Propped on his elbow, Draeden turned to her. "Are you sure?"

"Yes," Elowyn affirmed.

Draeden hovered himself above her and Elowyn reached for his neck, lowering him into a soft kiss. She ran her fingers through his claret-red locks, savoring the warmth from his closeness. Elowyn's heart unfolded, yielding to a newfound emotion in her. She didn't believe this was love just yet, but it was looming that line. A sense of bliss unfurled inside her, spreading through every fiber of her being. It felt undeniable, precious, and unmistakable. In this moment, she knew without a doubt that this was everything she wanted.

They shared a deep kiss, bodies intertwined. Elowyn felt his hardness press against her, slick with desire. Draeden's hips worked in rhythmic movements and his kisses became more urgent. Elowyn beckoned him to her entrance and Draeden became undone as he gripped her breast and thrust himself inside her. Elowyn gasped sharply, feeling his hardness inside her pulling and pushing tenderly. He began trailing his lips along her neck and to the side of her face.

"Are you okay?" Draeden whispered, nipping her ear.

"Yes," Elowyn breathed, pulling his face into a kiss.

Draeden returned her embrace, gripping both his hands around her hips, burrowing deeper in her. Her body demanded him, tightening around his length and he sensed her climax approaching. The thought of it sent him increasing his pace to match her need until pleasure overwhelmed them both, careening them over the edge.

He slumped beside Elowyn, reaching for her body and pulling her close to him as he wrapped his arms around her. The two of them nestled into each other, delighting in each other's company and the intimate moment. Draeden gently toyed with a strand of Elowyn's snow-white hair, twirling it between his fingers as he spoke softly.

"Dusk is approaching," he murmured. "The sunsets in Orwyn are breathtaking. I'd love for you to watch it with me, but I worry you'll be late returning to Eriden before the Fifth Day begins."

Elowyn lifted her gaze to the sky, watching as the clouds transformed into a palette of rich amber, luminous gold, burnt orange, and crimson red. This moment held such significance for her that she couldn't help but smile.

"Let's stay here, together, for the Fifth Day," she declared, her eyes filled with affection. "We can make our offerings to Caena from this oasis. We can participate in the Offering from anywhere."

Draeden hesitated for a moment. "What about your kingdom? Would they mind your absence from the Fifth Day?"

"There will be more Fifth Days. Right now, I don't care. I just want be with you."

Eventually, he nodded and replied, "All right, let's do it."

Elowyn's eyes sparkled with delight as she showered Draeden with kisses, expressing her gratitude. She playfully pushed him onto his back and straddled him, feeling nothing but affection for him. Their passion ignited once more, and they made love under the setting sun, then again in the shallow oasis.

As moonrise approached, they summoned their magic, each projecting their own celestial creation from their palms. Draeden conjured a waning gibbous moon, brilliant and luminous, while Elowyn crafted a perfect crescent moon, radiant and breathtaking. Together, they released their magical projections into the sky, watching as their moons ascended, leaving behind trails of shimmering feylight.

Observing the celestial display, Elowyn marveled at the thousands of magical offerings floating above Orwyn, each one a tribute to the Fifth Day. She wondered if Ora, Bane, Stryx, and Nerys were witnessing the phenomenon in Eriden as well. In that moment, she felt a profound connection with every fey in Neramyr—each soul cherishing the sky above with wonder.

They gazed upwards, their eyes brimming with wonder. The celestial display above symbolized the conclusion of the Offering, magic newly replenished in the feylands once again. With contentment, Elowyn nestled into Draeden's arms, watching the glimmering skies.

In that moment, her heart overflowed with bliss, knowing that this memory would be etched in her soul for the rest of her life.

22

Beginnings of Betrayal

THE WHITE SANDS OF THE ELUNE ISLES' SEASCAPE LOOKED like something plucked from Elyria's wildest imagination. The oceanside caressed her features in a temperate embrace as she wiggled her toes in the lush shore, letting the luxurious beach mold her footprints in the sand. Casting her gaze upon the Swyn Sea, she marveled at its majestic beauty. Its waters shimmered with shades of cerulean blue, glistening aquamarine, and hues of emerald as it lapped the seashore.

Elyria breathed in the brine-filled air, hoping to still her racing heart. Today marked the Sixth Day, the *Vitus*. Weariness lingered beneath her composed facade, burdened by the weight of her responsibilities. Sleep eluded her once again, leaving her with only her troubled thoughts for company. The absence of her sister, who had spent the day before in Orwyn, added to her unease. Feeling the opal necklace around her neck, memories of yesterday's worries resurfaced.

The events of the Fifth Day had unfolded slowly, dragging on until moonrise, prompting Elyria to question her sister's whereabouts at nightfall. Though tempted to scry her location, she instead sought answers from Finnor during the Offering, suspecting Elowyn was entangled with the Darkmaw prince. Her suspicions were confirmed when Elowyn later slipped into her room, giggling like a lovestruck maiden as she recounted every detail of her passionate tryst in the oasis.

Elyria couldn't suppress a smile at her sister's happiness. Elowyn deserved joy and contentment in her life—even as her own eluded her. Elyria had stopped seeking happiness long ago, finding comfort only in her sister's presence amid the shadows that surrounded her. Her entire existence seemed to be a quest for answers that remained a mystery. Why had the Goddess left her unmarked as an infant? Why had her name been spoken seven years ago? Was the Moon Goddess so cruel as to subject her to a childhood of ridicule, only to offer her a chance to prove herself worthy now?

She pushed away these thoughts before they could consume her with anger, reminding herself that questioning her fate would never alter it. She had trained herself to feel so little that she wondered what remained of her beyond emptiness. Her heart thudded loudly in her chest, drowning out all other sound. *Just breathe. Calm down.* She repeated the mantra to herself, as if they could rescue her.

"Elyria?" A familiar voice sliced through her disquiet like a steel through skin.

She turned to see Sylas smiling at her, and she felt grateful that her demeanor remained composed despite the unrest within her. "Hello, Sylas."

"Are you enjoying the sea?" he inquired politely, his bare feet shuffling into the sand.

Though Sylas had been seeking her favor in recent days, Elyria remained wary of his intentions. Despite his seemingly genuine nature, she hadn't yet let down her guard. Offering him a soft smile, as she had done each day before, she replied, "Very much so. I've beheld the Swyn Sea thrice now, and its magnificence never fails to captivate me."

The Divine Shallows

"I can relate to that sentiment," Sylas replied openly to Elyria. There was a raw sincerity in his gaze, and a part of her sensed that he wasn't merely referring to the sea.

"Are you prepared for tonight?" Elyria asked, avoiding his gaze as her silver eyes remained fixed on the deep blue depths of the sea.

"I am," Sylas affirmed, sensing her unease in the silence. He drew closer to her until his bronzed, moon-inked hand hovered just inches from hers, offering silent comfort. "Yet, I find myself unable to fully relax."

Turning to face him, Elyria met his sea-green eyes, mirroring the beauty of the waters surrounding them. "I find that the impending Seventh Day unsettles my nerves even more. Tomorrow, we'll be crossing the Bridge Between Worlds."

Sylas fell silent, his hands finding the pockets of his trousers, his mahogany waves dancing in the breeze. "I know," he finally murmured.

With a shared nod of understanding, Elyria and Sylas stood together on the soft shores of the Swyn Sea, awaiting the arrival of sunset, when the *Vitus* would begin.

∽

THE MAJESTIC DRIFTMOOR CASTLE RESTED UPON ONE OF THE seven islands of the Elune Isles, appearing as if sculpted from radiant pearls and carved from alabaster-hued coral. Its walls housed intricate channels and waterways, paying homage to the Swyn Sea that surrounded it. Each kingdom of Neramyr possessed its own captivating allure: the mountains of Eriden, the forests of Mirthwood, and now, the singular beauty of the Elune Isles. Each were a sacred realm within the feylands.

Elyria, now dressed in a stunning floor-length gown, had exchanged her earlier chiffon shift dress for the occasion. The monarchs of the Elune Isles always encouraged their guests to treasure the sea and sands, appreciating those who didn't shy from their wading waters. Hence, when formally invited to the Elune Isles, many from Neramyr would stroll barefoot along the shoreline of the Swyn Sea to pay tribute to its magnificence. If fortunate enough, a fey might catch sight of the two guardians of the Elune Isles gliding through the crystal depths: the *animus* of Queen Aletta and King Tydred, loch hydras—dual-headed serpents of the Swyn Sea.

Elyria's attention was drawn to a figure passing by, her eyes settling upon her Uncle Edwyn. He entered the Great Hall of Driftmoor in attire befitting the customs of the Elune Isles. His surcoat, a brilliant teal, was embellished with golden threads weaving powerful patterns across his torso and sleeves. Draped on his arm was a sorceress sworn to House Driftmoor; she possessed deeply tanned skin, iridescent abalone eyes, and hair cascading in waves of lapis lazuli. Clad in a dress of turquoise chiffon that left little to the imagination, she radiated a striking beauty, accentuated by the golden *aureum* draping down her back and her divine Mark decorating nearly every inch of her body.

As they passed by, Elyria acknowledged her uncle and his guest with a kind nod of her head. Her knowledge was limited around him; however, she was well aware that secrets within the Fangwright family were as abundant as the grains of sand along this island's shore. The lapis-haired sorceress met Elyria's gaze, offering a demure smile as she leaned into Uncle Edwyn's side to whisper something. Edwyn nodded in response to her murmurs, his hand resting gently upon hers as they made their way to her.

Despite her Uncle Edwyn's pleasant smile, hidden beneath her composure, Elyria couldn't shake the shudder that ran through her at his resemblance to her father. "Dear niece," he began, his voice warm, "I'd like you to meet Princess Cleora Driftmoor, sister of Queen Aletta Driftmoor, and princess of the Elune Isles."

With poise, Elyria dipped into an elegant curtsy, her gaze meeting that of the Driftmoor princess. "It's an honor to be welcomed as a guest

The Divine Shallows

of House Driftmoor, Princess Cleora. The kingdom of the Elune Isles is beautiful."

"Please call me Cleora," the princess replied, inclining her head towards Elyria. "The pleasure is all ours. I wish you luck in the *Vitus* today." Her voice was melodic, eloquent, and refined.

"Thank you, Cleora," Elyria responded, offering a grateful smile to the Driftmoor princess, captivated by the prismatic, iridescent irises that mirrored her own. "I hope to leave a lasting impression on those who are watching."

If Elyria had to estimate, Cleora must have been two centuries old. In Neramyr, it was notoriously difficult to gauge age based on appearance once individuals reached their late twenties or early thirties—a truer indicator of age was one's aura. Cleora possessed an exceptionally compelling aura, weighty and prominent.

"And you shall certainly impress, Elyria," Edwyn declared with confidence.

Before Elyria could discern the source, she felt a wave of displeasure wash over her. Queen Eddra materialized into view, her arms resting at her waist, her vulpine eyes revealing her disdain. A palpable aura of antipathy clouded the elegant planes of her face as she regarded Princess Cleora, who was draped upon Edwyn's arm.

Queen Eddra wore a gown of sapphire, her snow-white hair bound beneath an opal crown. As formidable as Cleora's aura was, her mother's aura was a behemoth in comparison. Edwyn stiffened at Eddra's arrival, but quickly masked his reaction with indifference as he nodded respectfully to her. Princess Cleora's irises flickered between the two Fangwright royals, narrowing imperceptibly. Tactfully, she dipped her head to Queen Eddra and offered a bright smile.

"Welcome to the Elune Isles, Queen Eddra. It is an honor for our kingdom to host this season's Sixth Day. The tales of your power and influence have not gone unnoticed among the fey of the Swyn Sea. Prince Edwyn and I were just expressing our anticipation for your daughter's performance tonight," Cleora remarked, turning her attention to Elyria, and placing a supportive hand on her arm.

Queen Eddra's gaze followed the Driftmoor princess's touch before returning to her face. "Princess Elyria is a formidable sorceress. Perhaps my judgment is influenced by a mother's pride, but I have no doubt she will emerge as the *primis* of this season's cohort."

Elyria held in a heavy exhale, feeling the tension thickening between the three royal fey. Anxiety gnawed at her bones as she contemplated the *Vitus*. The Sixth Day held immense significance for a divine candidate. During this ritual, the High Priestess would call upon the Moon Goddess to witness the abilities displayed by the seven selected candidates. Each candidate would perform their skills in their chosen manner, with the success of their performance greatly influencing their chances of being named the *primis*.

Becoming the *primis* is highly coveted, it meant crossing the Bridge Between Worlds first and returning to Neramyr after completion of the Trial first—meaning the *primis* will also receive the final Mark first.

To be declared the divine *primis* is to be differentiated as a god among gods where magic is the governing constant.

In ages past, the Sixth Day, the *Vitus*, had been a formal exhibition of power and prowess, a demonstration of one's worthiness to the Moon Goddess as a divine candidate. But in recent times, the *Vitus* had transformed into a fierce competition among the seven candidates. Elyria felt reduced to nothing more than a racehorse to be gambled on by the coin lining the pockets of the fey. She despised the feeling of being trapped, her autonomy and agency lost.

"Thank you for your words, mother. I will strive to make you proud," Elyria replied, her voice steady despite her discomfort. "And thank you for your support, Princess Cleora."

"The honor is truly mine, Princess Elyria," Cleora responded, her iridescent eyes shimmering as she turned to Edwyn. "Now, my dear, we must depart and join my older sister and brother-in-law. We have preparations to attend to before tonight's announcement." With that, she guided Edwyn in a different direction, offering Queen Eddra a parting smile. "Please excuse us, Your Majesty."

As Cleora and Edwyn left, Queen Eddra's intense gaze followed them, her displeasure obvious. Elyria knew all too well the simmering animosity between her mother and her uncle, yet rarely did her mother's composed facade crack in public. It was a testament to the tension that brewed beneath the surface. Elyria remained silent as her mother's thoughts churned, her silver eyes staring into the hall with a vacant gaze.

Where was her father in all of this? She was relieved to be spared his presence, but she knew he lurked in the shadows somewhere. The Fangwright monarchs rarely attended such gatherings together, preferring to maintain their distance from each other.

Her mother regained her calculated poise, her eyes returning to the present. Her arms remained in their regal position above her waist, elbows gracefully tucked to her torso. Without a word, she placed a hand on Elyria's arm before silently disappearing into the crowded hall. Elyria stared at the spot where her mother had touched her, feeling conflicted. She had never quite understood her mother. While her father openly displayed wickedness and ruthlessness towards her, her mother seemed to oscillate between contempt and care. Elyria would have preferred her mother to express her disdain outright rather than engaging in this indistinct game of mother and child.

A bright aura appeared behind her, and she spun around to find Elowyn beaming at her, with the Darkmaw prince in tow.

"Elyria!" Elowyn exclaimed cheerfully, pulling the tall, claret-haired prince closer. "This is Draeden Darkmaw, the prince of Orwyn." She turned to the prince. "Draeden, meet my older sister, Elyria. She's amazing, she's everything I've told you about and more."

Draeden bowed deeply and offered a charming smile. "It's an honor to meet you, Princess Elyria. Your sister speaks as highly of you as she does fondly. I've heard so much about you, thanks to this one here." He nudged Elowyn playfully, and she shrugged in response.

"How could I not talk about my most favorite sister to have ever walked the feylands?" Elowyn remarked.

"Hello, Draeden," Elyria greeted, dismissing the formalities of their titles with a wave of her hand. "I don't think a single day has passed this week without Elowyn mentioning the handsome prince who's been sweeping her off her feet."

Draeden's grin widened, his dimples appearing. "Is that so?"

Elowyn rolled her eyes. "Oh, great. See what you've done, Elyria? Now his head is bigger than the moon."

Watching the two amidst playful banter, Elyria saw her sister laugh with such delight that it made her heart ache. It ached in a bittersweet manner—overjoyed that her little sister appeared so happy, but crestfallen that she would be torn away from her for seven years tomorrow. She hoped that Draeden could offer her comfort and companionship in her absence. As much as she wished this happiness would last, she also feared how fickle love could be. Would Elowyn experience heartbreak? And who would be there to soothe her tears then? While seven years apart seemed measurable in Neramyr, within the Trial, time was fluid and uncertain.

Worry bubbled within her and suddenly she felt she needed a moment alone before the ritual began.

"I'm glad you two found each other," Elyria said sincerely. "You both seem genuinely happy." She tried to maintain her composure as she addressed them. "I can see why my sister is fond of you, Draeden. She's the most important thing in my life, so please do treat her with care." Elyria's anxiety began to take root. "And Elowyn, I'll come find you after the *Vitus*, all right?"

Elowyn looked to her sister with a hint of concern, noticing the sudden shift in her aura. She reached for Elyria's hand. "Hey, you're going to do amazing. We'll be rooting for you every step of the way."

"I'll be fine, don't worry about me," Elyria reassured with her best smile. "Trust me, I've been preparing for this moment for a long time. And speaking of preparation, I should get going." With a reassuring squeeze of her sister's arm and a parting wave to Draeden, she stepped away from them.

Her hurried steps led her to a quiet hallway in the castle, away from the Elune Isles's Great Hall. She continued down the corridor until she reached a pair of wooden double doors. Pressing her ear against the wood, she listened for any signs of movement or occupants. Hearing nothing, she opened the doors and entered an empty lounge. The decor and furnishings were vibrant and lively, influenced by the beauty of the sea kingdom.

As she wandered around the unoccupied lounge, she felt the tension within her begin to ease. Since childhood, she had taught herself to find peace in insolation. Her thoughts quieted as she focused on her breathing, her fingers trailing along the plush chaise styled after textured beds of coral. Above, a chandelier crafted from cream-colored shells cast a pearlescent glow, reflecting the light in dazzling shades. Spotting a wine decanter on a side table, she poured herself a glass of the *vinum*, hoping the hosts wouldn't mind—she was a guest after all. With a shrug to herself, she took a generous sip, relishing the warmth as it traveled down her throat.

Moving to the window overlooking the Swyn Sea, she watched the rhythmic waves and wandering currents course around the castle.

As a child, Ora had regaled her with legends of the fey of the Swyn Sea, claiming they could breathe underwater as effortlessly as they did on land. Ora had also shared a folktale with her, one that spoke of a time long before the Driftmoor castle stood, when the fey of the Elune Isles once dwelled beneath the waves in an undersea kingdom. It was said that Queen Diantha Driftmoor, the first queen of the Elune Isles, had claimed the shores of the Swyn Sea to establish her kingdom following the fall of the Old Age and the dawn of the New Age.

Through her divine magic, the Moon Goddess had rid the Swyn Sea of its cold-hearted kelpies and wicked water spirits, leaving its once troubled blue waters free of foul creatures. In her absence, Caena entrusted Queen Diantha to be the keeper of its peace in her stead.

The new sovereign of the sea had only her sister and a handful of survivors by her side after the Goddess' liberation of the feylands. Diantha named the feylands upon which she governed the Elune Isles, a collection of seven seemingly uninhabited islands. However, beneath the surface, an entire community existed that had been suppressed by the beasts who lurked in the Old Age.

Queen Diantha soon discovered the existence of merfolk dwelling in the depths of her kingdom. As a compassionate and benevolent ruler, she reached out to the merfolk's leader, sharing tales of the Moon Goddess' might and her role in freeing of the feylands. She spoke of the divine magic now coursing through her veins as evidenced by the moonlit markings on her hands and body. Sworn by oath to protect the sea and its waters, she extended her hand in coalition with the merfolk, promising to reign with compassion and understanding.

The merfolk expressed profound gratitude, celebrating their newfound freedom from the oppressive Old Age during which their undersea community had suffered greatly, causing it to splinter and dwindle over the years. Yet, as time passed, the bond between Queen Diantha, the merfolk, and their leader only grew stronger, forging a trusting relationship between the surface dwellers and those beneath the waves. Their alliance solidified into an unbreakable bond.

One day, the merfolk leader humbly requested an audience with the queen above, seeking her hand in marriage. Queen Diantha joyfully accepted his proposal, and their love was celebrated throughout the land and sea, sung for centuries. The sea queen cherished her fey and merfolk kin with unwavering devotion, willing to safeguard their well-being with her life in this realm and in the realms beyond.

For a time, the fey and merfolk existed in a blissful age of harmony and gaiety. However, one fateful day, the king of the Elune Isles fell gravely ill. Queen Diantha, being fey, outlived her merfolk husband, and was powerless to extend his life. Devastated by his passing, she mourned deeply, her heart heavy with grief. Unable to bear the reminders of all she lost, Diantha refused to drift below the depths of the Swyn Sea, never to return.

From their union, Queen Diantha bore a child of fey and merfolk heritage, capable of existing effortlessly on both land and in the sea. Many inhabitants of the Elune Isles shared this dual inheritance, their lineage tracing back to both fey and merfolk ancestors. Over millennia, this trait continued to be passed down through generations, though this kingdom beneath the waves became lost to lore, known only through retellings of the oldest fey. Merfolk living in the Swyn Sea were now few and far between, the divide between the fey and merfolk widening—time being the faultless reason.

Elyria was unsure of what truths lay in the folklore she had been told. In her youth, she had showered Ora with countless questions about Neramyr's history, sometimes wondering if her handmaiden concocted stories simply to satisfy her curiosity. Now she sat finishing the last of her wine and returned the goblet. With steady breaths, she welcomed the fresh air wafting in through the window. Straightening her gown, she prepared to rejoin the gathering when she heard hurried footsteps and murmured voices outside the doors.

Panicking, Elyria ducked behind a nearby bookshelf, veiling her aura and cloaking herself with an invisibility spell. The wooden doors swung open, and she strained to hear the low voices that filled the room. Peering cautiously from her hiding spot, she recognized Sylas and another male warlock engaged in a secretive conversation.

Cursing inwardly, Elyria scolded herself for concealing her presence. After all, she was a guest of the Elune Isles, a royal candidate participating in the Ceremony for moon's sake. She had every right to seek privacy in an empty chamber to prepare for the *Vitus*. Now, if the two warlocks were to discover her deception, it would cast suspicion on her motives.

The two warlocks continued their conversation in hushed tones, making it difficult for Elyria to discern their words with clarity as they stood with their backs turned to her.

Suddenly, Sylas straightened his posture, running a hand through his hair in a display of unease before releasing an exasperated sigh. "My answer remains the same as it has always been, Kerrick."

Elyria froze at Sylas' words, edging slightly closer to the end of her hiding spot to get a better view of the warlock he was addressing. Recognition dawned on her as she realized it was the Driftmoor candidate, Kerrick Graylon, whose name had been spoken by the Goddess seven years ago. However, his face remained obscured behind Sylas' figure.

"Don't be foolish, Fenhart," Kerrick retorted. "One of us deserves to be named *primis* after the *Vitus*. You know it as well as I do."

"I want the title of *primis* just as much as the rest of you, but the decision is not mine, or any of yours for that matter," Sylas answered, his hand now rubbing the back of his neck in irritation. "It's the Goddess' choice alone."

"The *Vitus* should be a showcase of our full potential. How can the Goddess assess our ability to protect the feylands if we're merely performing parlor tricks on stage? Securing the title of *primis* is crucial for establishing our reputation as divine warlocks or sorceresses," Kerrick asserted, crossing his arms over his chest. "While only one of us can claim the title, *primis*, we can still ensure that the rest of us cross the Bridge Between Worlds before her. Consider this, upon our return, we'll receive the final Mark before she does. The sooner we return, the more divine magic will be at our disposal."

"For the last time, my answer is no," Sylas said with irritation. "For the love of the Goddess, will you quit your attempts to persuade me otherwise?"

"What's causing these reservations?" Kerrick scoffed. "What has changed your stance? We've been planning this since the moment we were chosen as divine candidates. You've been following her all week, yet you've provided us with nothing significant."

"I'm working on it," Sylas sighed. "But it's irrelevant now. The *Vitus* is hours away."

"There's still time." Kerrick grew more agitated. "We've discussed this every week since our training in the Spires. Are you truly willing to abandon this opportunity? When we're on the brink of success?"

"I just need some time to think," Sylas grumbled. "She's different than I anticipated. She's not as easily manipulated as we had assumed. I can't get any information from her. I have a bad feeling about this."

"You were the one who proposed this plan to all of us seven years ago. Among the non-royal candidates, you're the most likely to become the *primis* of our cohort. What has changed? You possess the strongest magical abilities among us. You've been preparing to claim the title of *primis* since the beginning of our candidacy," Kerrick pressed.

"It's useless. She's a royal candidate," Sylas responded sharply. "It's tradition. The *primis* will always come from royal blood if they're selected as a divine candidate."

"To hell with tradition," Kerrick shot back. "You're too stubborn to acknowledge that times are changing, Sylas. You want to speak so highly of tradition? Well, consider this: the Moon Goddess left her unmarked as a member of the royal family. That's unprecedented in fey history. The eldest Fangwright princess serves no purpose, then and now. Even the king of Eriden can't conceal his embarrassment. If the Goddess truly cared about tradition, she would've blessed her with the Mark upon her birth."

Sylas countered with an edged voice, "The Moon Goddess still declared her candidacy regardless of that. It's not something we can overlook."

"Look, we still have a chance to claim the title of the divine *primis*, even with a royal candidate in our cohort," Kerrick persisted. "Think about the Clever Queen. Before she became queen consort, she was announced as the Fangwright candidate in her season by the High Priestess, despite everyone expecting the prince of Eriden to be chosen. Prince Edwyn has royal blood and is the brother of King Eamon, yet lowborn Eddra Sunhaven was selected. Nothing is impossible."

Silence hung in the air as Sylas absorbed Kerrick's arguments, his fists clenched in frustration.

"Listen, everything I'm saying just reinforces the idea that we shouldn't see the Fangwright princess as a threat. It's no secret that there's something off about that family. Especially with their unfortunate history with the Moon Goddess. They're cursed, and we both know it. I highly doubt she'll even make it through the Trial," Kerrick added.

"Do you ever know when to stop talking?" Sylas' tone grew tense. "My stance hasn't changed, Kerrick."

Kerrick met his irritation head-on. "Is it because you're interested in her?" He chuckled dryly. "If I knew your standards were that low, I'd suggest you try your luck with some of the creatures lurking in the Swyn Sea."

Sylas spun to face him. "Watch yourself, Kerrick. I've let you express your thoughts, but my patience is wearing thin."

"She's pleasing to the eye, I'll admit," Kerrick countered. "But remember, you're a divine candidate for Goddess' sake. There are plenty of females from all seven kingdoms here. Just find someone else to occupy your time and focus on what really matters."

"This conversation is over. I don't have time for this," Sylas answered.

Kerrick clicked his tongue in disappointment and sighed, approaching Sylas with a sense of camaraderie. "You know I see you as a brother after everything we've been through. Lillia, Lynora, Iva, Galen... we all do. We can't do this without you." He gave Sylas a meaningful look, briefly patting his shoulder before exiting the lounge.

The Divine Shallows

Alone now, Sylas sank onto the chaise, his head dropping into his hands as he sighed in frustration. After a moment, he lifted his head and glanced around the room, noticing the wine decanter on the side table. With a sense of resignation, he pushed himself up, bracing his knees as he approached the table. Pouring himself a goblet of wine, he raised it to his lips and drained it in one gulp. Replacing the goblet, he took a steadying breath and shook his head as if trying to clear his thoughts.

Elyria held her breath as she watched Sylas begin to pace the room. She remained still, not daring to make a sound as he moved about in the confined space.

Sylas muttered quietly to himself, his gaze darting back and forth aimlessly as he paced. Running a hand through his hair, he eventually came to a stop. With a determined air, he adjusted his surcoat and pushed open the doors, leaving the lounge behind.

Elyria waited until the doors had closed completely, and then she waited a few minutes more. Her heart continued to beat wildly as she replayed the conversation between Sylas and Kerrick in her mind.

A flood of emotions swelled within her—anger, betrayal, and disappointment. She chastised herself for ever believing that Sylas was any different from the others. How foolish. Her entire life she had been born into a world where everyone discarded her. The Cursed Princess, the Unblessed Daughter of the Moon, the Unmarked Candidate. Why would anything change now? She was destined for a life of isolation and rejection. She loathed herself for entertaining the idea of finding friendship in him.

Releasing her hold on the invisibility spell, Elyria emerged from behind the bookcase. Her eyes narrowed as her breathing steadied. This revelation changed nothing. She would face this alone.

Everything was still as she planned.

23

Vitus

THE ONSET OF THE *VITUS* WAS SWIFTLY APPROACHING AS the sun dipped below the horizon, casting its final light over the waves, signaling the impending start of the ritual. This season, the *Vitus* was hosted on a smaller islet north of the main island where Driftmoor Castle resided. The gathering was a grand affair, with countless highborn fey from the seven realms in attendance; the number of guests and spectators tonight far exceeded those of previous nights.

Now attired in leather pants, a snug tunic, and sturdy boots, Elyria stood within the confines of a gridded arena. Large wooden crates scattered across the arena floor contained various items. Overhead, feylight orbs floated, casting their gentle glow upon Elyria and the six other candidates down below. Positioned atop a raised platform, Elyria stood at the center of her house sigil—a firedrake. The platform for the divine candidates resembled the Divine Shallows, with seven spheres arranged in a circle, each representing a House of Neramyr. In the center stood a flat tile depicting a stone-art crescent moon, symbolizing the Goddess of the feylands.

The High Priestess stood atop the stone crescent, clad in her customary ceremonial gown of alabaster. Elyria harbored a deep-rooted dislike towards the High Priestess, though she couldn't pinpoint its exact source.

Perhaps it stemmed from the High Priestess' declaration of Elyria as unblessed before the assembled monarchs of Neramyr, sealing her fate with a curse that would shadow her throughout her life. Moreover, the High Priestess served as the ambassador and emissary of the Moon Goddess, further intertwining her with the forces that had brought Elyria such sorrow. Whenever Elyria found herself in the presence of the divine Priestess, a sense of unease and caution enveloped her.

Surveying the six other candidates on the platform, Elyria mentally recited their names in order from her position. To her left stood Sylas on the sigil of House Bloodweaver, followed by Lillia Sagebrook of House Mirthwood, Galen Wolfspire representing House Darkmaw, and Lynora Lionwind from House Blackbane. Elyria's apprehension peaked when her gaze landed on Kerrick Graylon, positioned on House Driftmoor's sigil. Completing the circle to her right was Iva Rosefall, the candidate from House Skyborn.

Despite their shared status as candidates, Elyria felt a sense of alienation from her fellow warlocks and sorceresses.

Indeed, earlier in the lounge, she had overheard Kerrick sharing how the other candidates had formed strong bonds with each other. She closed her eyes, mentally distancing herself from their favoritism towards each other. Her father's refusal to allow her training at the Seven Spires only served to deepen her isolation from the cohort.

However, she suspected that the prejudice against her would have persisted regardless of whether she had spent the last seven years training alongside them at the Spires.

It would make no difference to their opinions of her.

Nothing would.

Opening her eyes once more, Elyria sought out Elowyn in the crowd. High above, she scanned the area where the royalty from the seven realms were seated. Spotting Elowyn beside their parents and the newly appointed Commander, Elyria felt a wave of comfort wash over her. Elowyn raised a reassuring hand towards her, her smile encouraging. Amidst the sea of snow-haired fey behind her, Elyria only saw her little sister's face. Returning Elowyn's smile, Elyria turned her attention back to the arena.

As her gaze returned to the High Priestess, she locked eyes with Sylas, who stood ten feet away. He offered her a gentle smile and a supportive nod. Suppressing the bitter retorts bubbling in her throat, Elyria refrained from revealing that she had overheard his private conversation. Instead, she masked her distrust and returned his smile. His lips moved silently, forming the words 'good luck' to her. Suppressing an eye roll at his pretense, she redirected her focus, digging her fingernails into her palm to distract herself from his feigned camaraderie.

"Today marks the Sixth Day in the Ceremony of Caena!" The High Priestess' voice resonated across the arena, commanding the attention of the thousands of fey gathered. As her powerful voice filled the stadium, the audience fell silent. "Today, we are gathered here to witness the sacred ritual of the *Vitus*. On this day, we come together to witness the talent of the seven chosen divine candidates. Soon, I will invoke Caena's judgment to determine which candidate is worthy of the title of *primis*."

The High Priestess continued, "Tonight, the chosen candidates will showcase their mastery of magic under the watchful gaze of the Moon Goddess, vying for her favor to claim this illustrious title. The *primis* will be unveiled tomorrow on the Seventh Day, during the Crossing of Kin. Let us rejoice as we usher a new generation of divine magic wielders to protect the fey of Neramyr and uphold the peace of the New Age!"

The crowd erupted into applause and enthusiastic cheers, their excitement unmistakable throughout the arena. Spirited shouts echoed from every corner, confirming the crowd's eager anticipation for the *Vitus*. As the dynamic ovation enveloped her, Elyria felt her heart rate quicken under the weight of thousands of stares fixed upon her.

From the High Priestess' weathered palms, the inked crescent moons began to glow, casting an otherworldly light. Beneath the sleeves of her alabaster robe, the eight phases of the moon inked along her arms also illuminated. Motionless, the High Priestess blinked, her eyes turning a translucent white as she spoke, "The connection to Caena's realm holds firm. Tonight, the Moon Goddess will bear witness to this sacred Ceremony." The air in the arena crackled with ethereal magic, and Elyria felt a tingling sensation as if the moonlight itself had intensified. The High Priestess declared, "Following tradition, we will grant the honor of the first performance to the candidate representing the hosting kingdom."

The crowd sworn to House Driftmoor burst forth in proud cheers and admiration for their candidate. With a graceful gesture, the High Priestess extended a slender palm towards Kerrick Graylon.

"I humbly accept this honor, High Priestess," Kerrick bowed deeply towards her, his smile taking on a subtle twist. "However, for this season's *Vitus*, our cohort has decided on a unique approach—a collective performance, showcasing our talents simultaneously for the Goddess."

The High Priestess' demeanor stilled as she responded coolly, "Such an aberration from tradition is unusual, Kerrick."

Kerrick cleared his throat, his tone smoothing over with practiced diplomacy. "Indeed, High Priestess. Nevertheless, we defer to your judgment."

There was a brief silence before the High Priestess spoke again. "Very well." With a single nod of acknowledgment, she stepped into a moongate that materialized before her, joining the other monarchs of the seven realms in the stands above, leaving the divine candidates below in the arena.

Elyria's gaze lingered on Kerrick, her expression guarded. As if sensing her scrutiny, he met her eyes, his grin widening slightly.

The High Priestess' voice echoed across the arena, "Let the *Vitus* begin!"

The explosion of cheers from the crowd was thunderous, filling the air with tangible excitement. The entire arena was pulsating with suspense.

A translucent ward began enveloping the seated monarchs and royalty of Neramyr. It expanded rapidly, spreading over the seated spectators surrounding the stage below. This magical barrier cloaked the audience in the stadium, acting as an invisible shield to protect them in case any demonstration from the candidates extended beyond the arena's high walls.

Kerrick strode away from his House sigil, greeted by the enthusiastic cheers of the Driftmoor crowd as he made his way to the center of the arena. He possessed the archetypal appearance of a Driftmoor-born fey, with long, lapis-colored waves cascading down to his tanned chest. A few stray strands framed his cheekbones, escaping the knot that bound half of his hair. Casting a brief glance towards Sylas, he then turned his cerulean gaze skyward.

Raising his palms and lifting his arms slightly, Kerrick saturated the air with a thrum of magical energy. Elyria observed as the clouds in the twilight sky thickened and began to churn, ebbing and rippling into a brewing storm. It was predictable, almost mundanely so. She nearly muttered her observation under her breath, knowing full well Kerrick's proclivity for elemental magic.

Each fey born into a House of Neramyr harbored a natural affinity for a specific class of magic tied to their kingdom's lineage. While some could master all seven classes, most excelled in only one or two, typically aligned with their House's inherent nature.

The denizens of the Elune Isles, including the Driftmoor fey, were particularly adept in elemental magic. Elementals could manipulate various natural elements to their will, encompassing light, darkness, weather, flora, metals, minerals, and so forth. Similar to all magic-users, the extent of their gift and strength varied. Judging by Kerrick's divine candidate status, Elyria had to suspect he was unquestionably gifted to be chosen by the Goddess.

Lost in her thoughts and entranced by the swirling clouds above, Elyria scarcely noticed the subtle transformation unfolding around her. It wasn't until she felt the ground beneath her feet sinking—or was it rising?—that she snapped back to attention. Glancing down, she realized her boots were partially submerged in brine-filled water. Casting a quick glance towards the stands, she witnessed sleek currents flowing over the barriers and into the arena. Kerrick, it seemed, was summoning the very waters of the Swyn Sea to flood the arena.

In an instant, the gentle currents morphed into violent torrents, surging forth and inundating the arena. The water level escalated rapidly, creeping up her shins with alarming speed. To her right, Elyria observed Iva unfurling her alabaster wings from beneath her lavender locks. With a graceful flap, Iva ascended a few feet above the water, her lithe form soaring like a phoenix into the skies. On her left, Sylas navigated towards one of the large wooden crates scattered across the arena.

As she surveyed the arena, Elyria noticed the other five candidates also gravitating towards the crates. Lacking specific abilities to maneuver the waters like Iva, with her wings, or Kerrick, with his merfolk heritage, they began dismantling the crates and swiftly constructing makeshift rafts. With practiced efficiency, they stacked the wooden walls atop each other, interweaving rope to secure them together. In a matter of moments, they had fashioned sturdy rafts capable of supporting their weight.

Elyria couldn't discern any change in the aura of the other candidates. It was as though they were unaffected by Kerrick's manipulation of the arena terrain. What could they be plotting? She pondered this question as she hurriedly made her way to an unclaimed wooden crate, swiftly assembling her own raft. Tying the final knot of rope, she scrutinized her makeshift creation. It was rough and hastily crafted, but it would suffice for the moment.

Elyria noted the water level rising at an alarming pace, exacerbated by the relentless downpour summoned by Kerrick. The rain hammered down mercilessly, the drops striking the surface of Elyria's skin harshly. Shielding her eyes with her hand, she attempted to peer through the deluge, but the sheets of rain remained obscuring her vision. With the water now reaching her waist, the raft she had fashioned began to float. Pressing down to test its stability, she confirmed it could support her weight. With a heave, she hoisted herself onto the wooden surface, finding her balance on the raft that extended no more than four feet around her.

Was this Kerrick's performance? Summoning torrential rain and flooding the arena? His control over the elements was impressive; Elyria had no doubt he could unleash even deadlier, more destructive manifestations if he so chose. There wasn't even so much as a flicker of fatigue from the Driftmoor warlock's aura. Was this the standard for all the divine candidates? It was becoming clear just how formidable an elemental Kerrick truly was. Could he escalate this rainstorm into a full-blown monsoon? How much devastation did he plan to unleash?

These questions swirled in Elyria's mind as the arena transformed into an extension of the Swyn Sea enraged in the midst of a tempest.

Anxiety coated her emotions as she grappled with the uncertainty ahead. She had little insight into the capabilities of these fey, knowing next to nothing about them. *Fool,* Elyria cursed herself for not delving deeper. Even if she couldn't train at the Spires, she could have at least familiarized herself with her rivals' abilities.

Balancing on her makeshift raft amidst Kerrick's intensifying rainstorm, Elyria battled the wild, tumultuous waves threatening to engulf her. Beneath the deluge, she struggled to discern the other six candidates. How long could Kerrick sustain this tempest? As she scanned the area, she counted: *one... two... three... four... five... Wait, five? There should be six. Who am I missing? Oh, right—Kerrick.* His absence from the surface signaled his likely presence beneath the water's depths. Elyria reminded herself to remain vigilant with the Driftmoor candidate lurking below.

A torrent of magic rippled through the arena, triggering Elyria's attention. *Who was that?* A tall, sinewy, dark-haired figure caught her eye—Lynora. Elyria observed as she channeled an impressive amount of magic, her aura pulsating with energy. Lynora began rapid incantations that caused Elyria to tense. *Is she really going through with this?*

Elyria narrowed her eyes, watching as Lynora summoned something substantial—but what?

Her thoughts raced to recall information about the Blackbane sorceress. Fey from Erimead specialized in evocation magic, capable of amplifying existing phenomena, emotions, actions, and so on. They could even augment another warlock or sorceress' magic. The strongest among them could even summon spirits or banish creatures to other planes. Was Lynora truly powerful enough to evoke such a significant force as she felt now?

In response to her question, a gateway materialized above the arena, causing Elyria's skepticism to morph into caution. Positioned approximately twenty feet in the air, the gateway expelled a colossal silhouette that plummeted with a deafening shriek into the arena's dark abyss. The impact of the creature crashing into the water was so forceful that Elyria was catapulted from her raft, her body plunging into the water's embrace and engulfed beneath its waves.

As she collided with the water's surface, a surge of shock rippled through Elyria. This was nothing for which she had prepared. The unfolding reality shattered her preconceived notions of the ritual. What was transpiring was completely unorthodox for the *Vitus*. The ritual was meant to be an orderly showcase of individual talents, meticulously honed over months for the Moon Goddess' observation.

But this was different. This wasn't a mere demonstration. It was really combat.

This is what they wanted? Elyria's temper swelled at their crass strategy. *Fine by me.* She felt her body being tossed in all directions underneath the waves. Darkness surrounded her as she fought to orient herself underwater. She spotted a faint glow of feylight from above and propelled herself in that direction. The faster she swam, the more likely she could avoid whatever Lynora summoned into the arena. With each powerful stroke, she ascended, breaking the surface with a gasp of relief as air filled her lungs. Her snow-white hair clung to the sides of her face as she swiveled around in the water, scanning for one of the rafts. It appeared that she wasn't the only one who was disoriented by the chaos that now engulfed the flooded arena.

"Elyria! Over here!" Sylas' voice pierced through the relentless rain.

She turned towards the sound of his muffled voice, spotting him on a nearby wooden raft with his arm extended towards her. Despite the raging storm, he skillfully guided the raft in her direction. Her reservations about Sylas lingered, but being on the raft was far preferable to being in the water. With some effort, Sylas maneuvered the raft close enough for her to grasp his arm, hauling her up onto the unsteady wooden surface.

"What in the seven hells did Lynora summon?" Elyria shouted over the pounding rain, struggling to maintain her balance on the choppy waves.

Sylas offered a steady hand for Elyria to hold onto. "She's summoned a blood-eyed eel!" He yelled back, his voice barely audible over the downpour. "It was Kerrick's idea to summon something we could use our magic on instead of just showcasing our abilities!" He cursed under his breath. "I knew this would be too dangerous. I tried to convince them not to!"

A massive shadow emerged from the dark depths, accompanied by wild cheers from the spectators. Elyria tensed as she beheld the sight before her. The monstrous blood-eyed eel breached the surface, its head thrashing wildly as its fierce jaws snapped with fury. Its sleek body shimmered with shades of tawny browns and burnt oranges, blending in a sinister pattern. Towering over them, the blood-eyed eel possessed vicious spiked fins along its spine, its build nearly twice the size of a firedrake.

Elyria couldn't halt her mind from analyzing the recent events. The summoning of such a massive entity by Lynora must have depleted a significant portion of her magical reserves, if not nearly all of it. Elyria found herself woefully unprepared for the plans the other candidates had devised. She clenched her teeth. *It's no matter.* She'd have to adjust to the reality of the situation; she was no stranger to adaptation—she'd done it all her life.

From an indistinct direction, Elyria swore she heard Kerrick's maniacal laughter. Suddenly, his lapis-blue hair flashed into view, and he materialized before her. She observed the contours of his body, now covered in translucent, prismatic scales. The sleek armor-like plates enveloping Kerrick's form seemed almost invisible, like a thin layer of glass armor. Though she recognized these protective scales as common for those of merfolk heritage, she was intrigued by them. Her gaze shifted to Kerrick's outstretched arm, hovering above the water while a surge of magic emanated from his downturned palm.

Elyria watched as something took shape in his grasp, gradually elongating until a jagged spear materialized in his grip. Understanding dawned on her. Kerrick manipulated the sand carried in by the flooding seawater, fashioning a weapon from countless grains of eroded rocks and minerals.

With heedless abandon, Kerrick propelled himself forward with astonishing speed, aiming for the undulating head of the blood-eyed eel. His strike found its mark at the creature's unsuspecting neck, coating the tip of his spear in blood and drawing a harrowing screech from the ambushed beast. Swiftly, Kerrick retreated beneath the murky depths, leaving the blood-eyed eel to writhe and thrash in search of its blue-haired assailant.

The spectators in the audience began chanting and hollering Kerrick's name. Elyria observed the spectators thrusting their fists into the air, some pressing eagerly against the magical barrier as if it could grant them a closer view.

Her eyes darkened at the sight of their ecstasy. *Barbaric.*

Her focus snapped back to Kerrick as he emerged from the waves once more, brandishing his forged spear and driving its jagged tip into the neck of the monstrous eel. The spear tore through the creature's sheeny hide, extracting another agonizing screech. Before Kerrick could retract his weapon and seek refuge, the blood-eyed eel expelled a noxious, coppery substance from its throat, spraying it in his direction.

The foul substance struck Kerrick's upper torso and outstretched arm, clinging to him and sizzling as it made contact with his skin. The stench of burnt flesh filled the air as Kerrick cried out in agony, clutching his injured body as he tumbled back into the water.

"Kerrick!" Iva's scream pierced the arena as she called his name from above. The lavender-haired sorceress plummeted from the skies, diving headfirst into the waters after him.

Moments later, Iva resurfaced, dragging Kerrick's limp form above the waves. He groaned in misery as she pulled him to safety, seeking refuge on Lillia's nearby raft. Together, they hoisted Kerrick onto the raft. Elyria winced at the sight of his injuries. The acid spray from the blood-eyed eel had ravaged his flesh, leaving his upper chest and shoulder marred by scorched wounds. Large chunks of muscle had been eaten away, exposing bone, fat, and tendon.

Iva's urgent yell caught Lillia's attention, and she nodded in understanding. While Iva remained crouched over Kerrick, Lillia swiftly turned to face the monstrous eel.

Despite the violent rocking of her raft, Lillia's aura was steadfast as she tucked her tight brown ringlets behind her ear and focused her attention on the beast, raising both of her umber arms above herself and her comrades. Though Elyria could not see it, she could sense it immediately. Lillia conjured an ironclad barrier around herself and the other candidates to shield them from the looming danger. Lillia was an abjurist sorceress by nature, sworn to House Mirthwood, she possessed the unique ability to create and dismantle powerful magical wards and barriers—some potent enough to prove lethal if breached.

With the shield firmly in place, Lillia turned her gaze toward the blood-eyed eel. The creature, relentless in its pursuit of Kerrick, screeched and lunged at the trio. Its mangled jaw collided with the shield, but upon contact, a pulse from the magical ward sent the beast hurtling backward, flung ten feet into the waves as it released an enraged shriek.

After a few fleeting seconds, the blood-eyed eel recovered and began slithering through the choppy waves toward Lillia's shield. While its massive body rotated, menacing tail poised to attack, Lillia registered what the blood-eyed eel intended to do. Lillia braced her arm just moments before the eel swung its monstrous tail with a brutal strike. The tail careened with explosive force, striking the three candidates with brutal precision. A deafening crack reverberated through the air as their raft was sent hurtling backward, crashing into the arena wall with a thunderous blow that caused the structure to shudder and send rubble tumbling down.

The air reverberated with the impact, and Elyria instinctively shielded her eyes from the flying debris. As the dust settled, she discerned a massive fissure in the fractured arena wall.

Upon witnessing the destruction, Elyria shook her head in disbelief. Surely, they could not have survived such a violent collision.

Yet, to her astonishment, Elyria observed their raft bobbing forcefully on the water's surface, Lillia's protective ward still intact, and the three candidates unharmed. The resilience of the Mirthwood sorceress's barrier was remarkable; most would have shattered under the sheer force of the impact, bringing certain doom. With a furrowed brow, Elyria pondered the possible explanations. It could either be that Lillia had reinforced her ward right before impact, or that she had revoked the amount of physical damage inflicted by the blood-eyed eel. Given abjurists's capability to nullify or dampen both magical and physical abilities, it was plausible that Lillia had employed both techniques.

Meanwhile, the blood-eyed eel, frustrated by its failed attack, regrouped, and launched another assault on the three warded candidates. Unleashing a torrent of coppery acid, the creature flung it at the protective barrier, causing Lillia to strain as she channeled more power into bolster the ward's integrity—now sizzling from the searing assault.

Elyria was so engrossed in observing the unfolding scene that she scarcely noticed Galen, the claret-haired Darkmaw candidate, nearing the blood-eyed eel on his raft. However, the raft was no longer the crude structure it once was; it had transformed into a sleek catamaran, effortlessly gliding through the waves. In Galen's hand, he wielded a vast coil of rope, collected in a remarkably short span of time—an impressive feat given its length, likely spanning hundreds of yards.

As Galen neared the engaged blood-eyed eel, he hunched over his catamaran and heaved a contraption forward. Elyria sucked in a breath as she saw him stabilize a spear catapult on the forward cockpit of his catamaran. *How had he managed to construct such a device amidst the chaos?* Loading an iron spear into the sling, he aimed it expertly at the creature's spine. The iron spear gleamed with a flawless polish, starkly contrasting Kerrick's rough sand-forged weapon. It seemed as though Galen had sourced it from an expert blacksmith. With a calculated haul backward, the Darkmaw warlock released his grip on the catapult, letting his iron spear fly.

As the heavy iron javelin soared through the night sky, it struck the blood-eyed eel with a sickening thud. The creature let out a pained wail before crashing beneath the dark waves. Galen leaped up with a triumphant whoop, met by thunderous applause from the spectators. His celebration was short-lived as he began gathering the rope at his feet, coiling it around his shoulder and forearm quickly.

Observing this, Elyria could only wonder how he acquired all his arsenal. Then it dawned on her... Galen was an artificer—a warlock crafter, a magicsmith. The realization struck her as the pieces fell into place.

With the threat of the beast no longer on them, Iva directed Lillia to stabilize Kerrick's torso. Iva was still hunched over Kerrick; her membranous alabaster wings were spread open protectively. Her delicate hands hovered over Kerrick's marred and mangled upper body. The Skyborn candidate's eyes were closed as concentration contorted her face. Tendrils of moonlight began creeping down her arms and slithered to her delicate hands. The wisps of moonlight then drifted towards Kerrick's destroyed shoulder and seeped into the wound. Kerrick recoiled and cried in pain as the moonlight saturated the surface of his tattered flesh. Slowly, the ravaged flesh began to regenerate as Iva siphoned more of her magic into Kerrick's wound.

The charred flesh gradually began to reconstruct itself, with cords of muscle intertwining back into their former state. Kerrick's cauterized arteries, charred bones, and blistered ligaments were reborn, returning to their original form. Such a level of restoration magic was truly remarkable. Typically, this kind of magic was only performed by the most powerful fey in the Healer's Keep in Prymont.

Iva continued to channel her magic into Kerrick until his bones were fully mended, his skin unscathed and unbroken. It was only when Kerrick's complexion regained its color, and his fading aura was restored that Iva slouched with relief.

Witnessing Iva's extraordinary powers, Elyria could not help but recognize her potential as a sought-after divine sorceress. Having a healer of this caliber in one's arsenal would be considered a great asset by all seven realms. She knew that restoration magic was indisputably one of the most coveted classes of magic, with the ability to heal physical and magical ailments, recover what was once lost or destroyed, and regenerate nearly anything—the only limitation beyond a restorator's magic was death.

Through extensive training, Skyborn warlocks and sorceresses could even concoct potions that pushed the boundaries of what was naturally possible, bordering on the metaphysical. While they may have lacked physical strength, they more than compensated with their intellect and magical prowess. In terms of fey biology, the scholars of House Skyborn were unparalleled, able to even exploit their opponents' bodies in combat. A restorator's magic had the potential to stifle another's airway, stagger the body's ability to clot off a wound, weaken bones until they snapped, or exhaust muscles to the point where they could no longer contract. Elyria understood that only a fool would underestimate Iva's strength because of her slender frame. However, it seemed that Iva had chosen not to showcase this aspect of restoration magic to the spectators thus far.

Despite her disdain for Kerrick, Elyria could not help but envy how quickly his ally came to his aid. But envy had no station here as the wounded blood-eyed eel erupted from the depths, bellowing belligerently.

Elyria whipped her attention towards the ominous beast and saw that Galen had already positioned himself nearby. The monstrous eel's beady crimson eyes locked onto the claret-haired Darkmaw candidate and his catapult, recognizing him as the one who launched the spear—all its fury now directed towards Galen. Galen was prepared for this, maneuvering his catamaran behind the beast with the spool of rope in tow.

With the rope primed in his grip, Galen flung the cords like a lasso around the eel's head with deadly precision. His aim was true as the rope snared the blood-eyed eel's neck, and Galen quickly pulled it taut, securing and fastening the lasso while the beast thrashed violently. In a matter of seconds, Galen had subdued the eel, though it continued to rage and thrash, its fury aimed towards Galen and his unprotected figure atop the catamaran.

The blood-eyed eel unleashed a vicious shower of acid towards the Darkmaw candidate. Elyria's spine tensed as she witnessed the copper sludge hurtling straight towards Galen. The volume of acid was considerably larger than what Kerrick had faced. If Galen suffered a more severe injury, would Iva still have the reserves to heal him? Could she mend that extent of damage?

The coppery substance coated Galen in a sickening layer, but to Elyria's surprise, he remained unharmed and unfazed. *How? Was he immune to the acid?* Through the rain, Elyria squinted and noticed a faint glow emanating from the rope slung around the blood-eyed eel's neck. *So that's how.* Galen had enchanted the rope. One of the ropes must have been imbued with magic to neutralize the eel's acid.

A smirk blossomed on the Darkmaw candidate's lips, but his hubris was short-lived as the blood-eyed eel screeched and whipped around, aiming its monstrous tail straight at Galen's catamaran. Panic flashed across Galen's face as the beast's tail poised to strike directly in his path. Making a split-second decision, Galen released his enchanted rope and hurled himself into the dark waves to avoid the impact. He narrowly evaded the eel's tail, which came crashing down seconds later, shattering his catamaran into pieces.

Immediately, Elyria noticed that the faint glow enveloping the rope around the blood-eyed eel's neck had disappeared. It seemed that the Darkmaw warlock's enchanted rope only functioned while he was channeling magic into it; now it was just an ordinary rope.

Galen's claret-red head popped through the water's surface as he clambered for a piece of the catamaran that drifted near him and seized it.

The blood-eyed eel spotted Galen and lunged. Elyria watched Sylas' face pale.

Galen lifted the fragment of the catamaran above his head and his magic coated the surface. It transformed into a thick wooden shield just in time as another thrash of the eel's tail slammed down. Galen's makeshift shield shattered at the blow and the impact sent him flying in another direction. He landed with a crash into the depths again as the beast lunged towards him once more.

This time, the blood-eyed eel maneuvered so quickly Elyria barely registered it. The creature closed in on Galen, shooting forward and capturing him within its jaws. The eel clamped down Galen's torso and he let out a hysteric scream as the fangs of the eel pierced his flesh. The Darkmaw warlock was bleeding from his abdomen profusely, and his blood began dripping down the throat of the blood-eyed eel. Pain rippled across Galen's face as he yelled again while the sea creature tossed him in the air and caught him by the leg.

Dangling from the eel's jaw, Galen struggled as the creature clamped down on his lower limb—a sickening splintering sounded in the air and Galen's leg shattered from the jaws of the blood-eyed eel. The claret-haired warlock cried out in agony, desperately attempting to free himself from the beast's grasp.

In the next instant, Sylas released his grip on Elyria, leaving her to steady herself on the turbulent waves. His face contorted in panic as he thrust his arms forward, unleashing a torrent of magic so potent that Elyria dropped to her knees from the sheer force. Her body plummeted downward, and she barely managed to catch herself with her arms. Fighting through the fog in her mind caused by the proximity to Sylas' magic, Elyria shook her head to clear it and lifted her gaze upward. Confusion etched across her features as she beheld the scene before her.

Beside her, Sylas still stood with his hands thrust forward, but sweat dripped from his entire body as he trembled. She followed his line of sight, mystified.

Galen remained unscathed on his catamaran, preparing to launch himself into the air and seek refuge beneath the waves. The blood-eyed eel's tail hovered ominously above, mere moments from striking his vessel. But how?

Wait. Elyria blinked. *This already happened.*

"Run!" Sylas bellowed towards the Darkmaw candidate. "Run, Galen!"

Beneath Galen's feet, the waves glowed softly, swirling, and pulsating with magic. In the blink of an eye, Galen landed on the water's surface with a thud, remaining upright with his hands braced against it. It should have been impossible. Elyria's eyes widened in confusion. The waves appeared unchanged, still rippling and churning, yet Galen knelt upon their surface. She watched as the Darkmaw candidate pushed himself upright and dashed in her direction. With an exasperated grunt, Sylas continued channeling his magic, creating a solid pathway upon the waves for Galen to find refuge on their raft.

This was the magnitude of Sylas' abilities as an alterist. He manipulated the laws of reality by reversing time and solidifying liquid. Elyria weighed the actuality of it—this was the scope of power Bloodweaver warlocks and sorceresses possessed.

Galen continued his frantic escape across the waves, evading the blood-eyed eel, which shrieked in frustration at his unexpected getaway. Above the arena, the storm in the skies ceased—undoubtedly Kerrick's doing to provide Galen with a chance to find better footing. The blood-eyed eel pursued the Darkmaw candidate, snapping at his heels. Yet, Galen traversed the waves at an astonishing speed. He was only a few feet away when Sylas dropped to his knees in exhaustion, releasing his power, unable to sustain it any longer.

Galen managed to fling himself onto their raft, landing heavily in front of Elyria. His feet wavered as he attempted to regain balance, but he stumbled into her, causing her to lose her footing and tumble off the raft without warning.

Elyria heard Sylas calling out her name just before she plunged into the dark waves. The rush of water filled her ears as she was submerged again. With powerful strokes of her arms, she fought against the current and surfaced. Elyria pushed her slick strands of snow-white hair away from her face and scanned the arena. Sylas and Galen had drifted several feet away, too far to reach immediately, considering the blood-eyed eel lurking nearby. Keeping herself afloat with her arms, she searched for safety in the swirling waters. Fortunately, she spotted an unoccupied raft a couple of meters away.

Elyria extended her hand toward it, weaving a thread of her magic to coax the wooden raft toward her. Responding to her call, it began drifting slowly in her direction. Soon, the wooden raft was just inches away from her grasp. She reached out, finally making contact, and held it in place to pull herself atop it.

Just as she was about to hoist herself onto the solid wooden surface, something seized her leg.

Startled, Elyria jerked her leg firmly, but whatever had captured her foot refused to let go. Irritated, she turned around to identify the source. Elyria found herself face-to-face with Kerrick's sapphire gaze as one of his scaled hands clamped around her ankle, his serpentine smile sending chills down her spine. Furious, Elyria's hand shot out toward him, readying a spell attack, but it was too late.

"Gotcha." Kerrick grinned wickedly before yanking her down into the depths.

Elyria was dragged beneath the waves once more, vowing to herself that this would be the last time. Kerrick pulled her deeper and deeper, the pressure from the water's depth compressing her body uncomfortably. She kicked at him in a futile attempt to loosen his grip, but it was in vain. Kerrick glided through the water as effortlessly as a siren, and Elyria found herself at the mercy of his mischief as they descended further. Before long, her head began to thunder, and her chest heaved as air bubbles escaped from her mouth. Elyria suppressed the involuntary reaction to breathe and forced herself to focus on breaking free.

Bitterness began to alight within her, and she nurtured it like a flame, stoking the emotion until it ignited. Elyria fought against the relentless current that dragged her, clawing her way toward Kerrick, using her own limbs to inch closer to him. Fortunately, Kerrick remained oblivious to her approach, his lapis hair trailing behind him as his hand remained firmly clasped around her ankle. He was too bold, too careless. Elyria found herself mere inches away from him, folded in half at the hip.

That's when she lunged for him.

Elyria's right hand shot forward, seizing a fistful of Kerrick's lapis locks, and she jerked his head backward until their faces were inches apart. Kerrick's cerulean eyes widened with surprise as he attempted to push her away, but Elyria had already gripped both sides of his temples.

Summoning her native magic forward, Elyria felt a surge of power coursing through her arms, erupting from her palms as it flooded into Kerrick's mind. She commanded one word, a single utterance that reverberated in his psyche: pain. Instantly, Kerrick's face contorted in agony, his body going limp as he released her immediately, trembling in silence. The tables had turned, and now it was Elyria who wore the look of satisfaction. Though fatigue began to creep over her like a silent shadow, she lingered in this moment of retribution, watching him closely.

But soon, her lungs screamed for air. Suppressing her self-indulgence, Elyria pushed Kerrick's form away from her and propelled herself toward the surface. As she breached the water's surface, she gasped for air, filling her lungs with precious oxygen. Treading water, she quickly spotted the abandoned raft again and swam toward it. Gripping the wooden raft, she hoisted herself atop it, kneeling on the surface to catch her breath for a moment. In front of her, the chaos continued to unfold in the arena as Lynora and Lillia battled against the blood-eyed eel.

Elyria watched them work together in a coordinated assault, operating like twin blades forged from the same sword.

Sylas remained on the wooden raft from which she had been thrown just a short distance away. Iva circled the skies with vigilant eyes, ready to use her restorative powers if needed. Galen had crafted another catamaran and was launching attacks from another contraption he concocted. The crowd's enthusiastic vigor was impossible to ignore. It seemed the five other candidates had dealt quite a bit of damage while she was being dragged beneath the surface by Kerrick. How much time had passed? It couldn't have been more than ten minutes since the ritual began.

From the corner of her vision, Elyria noticed Kerrick's head emerge from the inky depths. Her gaze bore into him, refusing to back down or lose her edge. The stunt she pulled before was meant to unsettle him. However, she hadn't intended to inflict any irreparable harm; she just wanted to let him know she could. What she didn't expect was the smile that spread across Kerrick's face as their gazes met.

That's when she felt the creeping throb gnawing at her abdomen. Elyria slowly lifted a hand to press against her stomach, wincing. As she removed her hand, she looked down and saw her fingers slick with red ichor. Beneath her tattered tunic, she discovered a deep laceration across her waist. Stunned, a sharp pain began to register in her mind as her adrenaline no longer masked her injury.

Elyria's breathing soon became sluggish and laborious. Her mind started to fog and turn muddled. She blinked hard, shaking her head to clear it, but the feeling persisted. *What's happening?* She commanded herself to concentrate as she attempted to slow the bleeding from the wound. She was no Prymont healer, but she could try to staunch the flow. Managing to clot off the wound, she turned her attention back to Kerrick. Now, her breaths were strained, and her muscles began to stiffen. *What's happening to me?* Even as her body began to shut down, her eyes remained alert.

Kerrick's smirk remained vindictive as he lifted a spear out of the water to show her. It was different from the one crafted from sand he fashioned earlier to impale the blood-eyed eel. This one was made of a brilliant ochre-colored coral with hardened polyps. *Serithium.* Elyria looked at the shaft and saw the spear tip smeared with her blood. She recognized the unique pattern of the poisonous coral and cursed. Serithium coral was noteworthy for its paralytic properties and notorious for its slow metabolism from the body. Depending on the amount of serithium her body absorbed through her wound, Elyria could be paralyzed for hours. The effects were just beginning now, but as time progressed, she would be unable to move. Just as she prepared to unleash a torrent of obscenities towards Kerrick, he looked past her and thrust the ochre spear through the air, letting it fly.

With a powerful arc, the weapon soared over her and headed straight for Sylas. Elyria's eyes trailed the spear and watched Sylas catch it effortlessly with one hand above his head. She turned to face him, and his sea-green eyes collided with hers. His body went taut for a second, but he tore his eyes away from her and brought the tip of the colorful spear to his eye level. He turned his attention to the weapon instead. Sylas raised a hesitant hand and ran it across the tip of the spear, messily smearing her stained blood on his hand. Elyria saw that his aura was lashing chaotically, as if in conflict with itself. A look of confusion spread across her face at his strange action, but then her eyes widened as she made the connection.

The poison was overpowering her nervous system, dispersing like a disease. Yet, she summoned the strength to laugh sourly. Her aura flared with fury, and she pointed an accusatory finger at Sylas.

"You're a *fucking* legacy, aren't you?" Elyria's voice surged across the arena.

Sylas' sea-green eyes locked with hers briefly, then lowered as they retreated. His deafening silence was the only answer she needed.

Elyria clicked her tongue and shook her head. *Spineless coward.* "Of course you are."

Very rarely, magical warlocks or sorceresses of Neramyr were born as legacies. These exceptional fey possessed an innate ability beyond their natural magical talents, a gift passed down from the ancient rulers of their House—this solitary ability, or feat, could not be learned or gained otherwise. While typically reserved for descendants of royal bloodlines, occasionally, a legacy emerged from other lineages.

If Sylas Fenhart was a Bloodweaver legacy, the blood that he had in his possession, *her blood*, was going to be her downfall.

Legacies were extraordinary. Legacies were invaluable. Legacies were powerful. Legacies were dangerous. Legacies were to be feared.

"I'm sorry," Sylas' voice was distant as he answered her. "This was the only way we'd stand a chance."

Elyria tried to muster a counterattack, but the serithium coursing through her veins left her too weak to cast. With each passing moment, she felt her control slipping away, her body growing increasingly unresponsive.

Sylas summoned his feat before he could hesitate further and the hand that was coated in Elyria's blood flared a moonlight ivory. The smeared streaks of red started to dissipate in a delicate plume of pale smoke that trailed to the skies. Elyria felt thousands of magical strings fabricated from Sylas' spell bind themselves to her while she was too immobilized to resist the effects of it. Elyria rallied any remnants of her magic to combat it, but her attempt was futile.

Sylas remained impassive as he commanded his spell to ensnare her. With a powerful motion, he outstretched his hand toward Elyria, fingers curling methodically. She sensed the invisible cables tighten around her as Sylas secured his hold on her. At his command, Elyria's posture straightened despite the paralyzing effects of the serithium, her expression becoming vacant.

As Sylas lowered his arm, Elyria's body mirrored his movements.

Her limber legs bent at the knee, lowering her into a kneeled position upon the wooden raft. The unseen threads continued to direct her until she was seated with folded legs, her arms slackening. With a final flick of Sylas' wrist, Elyria's head bowed in resignation, her silver gaze dropping to her lap.

Sharp as a blade, humiliation and shame cut through Elyria as she sat in submission before the entire arena. Her body was no longer her own; every movement was controlled by Sylas, her limbs and life's core at his command. As a Bloodweaver legacy, Sylas possessed the ability to manipulate her body through the blood he had spelled. This unique power was inherited from the first queen of the Iron Hollows, Isadora Bloodweaver. The spell functioned by tethering itself to the victim's blood, granting the caster increasing control with each drop spilled.

In this instance, Sylas had used only a scant portion of her blood to bind her to the spell. Elyria knew if he had elected to use more, he had the capability to transform her into a vacant marionette at his disposal. At least he had allowed her the clarity of mind while under his control. Through her studies, she had learned of lesser fey having been magically manipulated by this feat, and those fey had performed unspeakable acts beyond their control at the hands of a Bloodweaver legacy.

As a legacy herself, she understood the gravity of another legacy's power. When it came to House Bloodweaver, their inherited ability was especially sinister.

Elyria's body remained yielding to the magical spell, obediently kneeling at Sylas' command while the battle unfolded around her. Though immobilized, Elyria watched as Sylas joined the other five other candidates in their cavalier combat against the blood-eyed eel. From her periphery, she saw the six of them assail the creature with incredible skill and magical deftness. Even in her captive state, she couldn't deny the extraordinary skill and magical ability displayed by each of them. They were all remarkable—any one of them deserving of the title *primis*.

Then it dawned on her.

The Divine Shallows

So that was their scheme. The serithium. The Bloodweaver feat. Her powerless position as they left her discarded on the wooden raft. They intended for her to be overlooked and dismissed by the fey of Neramyr —they aimed to have the Moon Goddess desert her once again.

All this effort on their behalf was to render her unsuitable as a divine candidate.

And here she was, unwittingly playing her part in their strategy, a chess piece falling into place.

24

A Legacy is Born

IF ELYRIA COULD MUSTER A CHUCKLE, SHE WOULD HAVE. She realized that the other divine candidates had succeeded with every maneuver they made since the very beginning of the ritual.

The six other candidates had already showcased an impressive array of their talents, skills, and abilities for the Moon Goddess to witness. Each had demonstrated their prowess to the fey of Neramyr in their respective class of magic. They all had shown courage, persistence, and solidarity not only as a cohort, but also individually as warlocks and sorceresses.

Throughout the *Vitus* thus far, Elyria had been nothing more than a spectator, merely watching along with the audience—her calculating nature gained no victories tonight.

She had done nothing, accomplished nothing.

Right from the start, it was evident she was unaware of the other candidates' strategy. She had been tossed and flung into the depths of the arena more times than she cared to admit. She appeared as a damsel in distress when she took refuge on Sylas' raft and held onto him for stability. She seemed incapable and helpless as Kerrick dragged her below the waves. Her lone magical counterspell had gone unnoticed, concealed beneath the waters, only for her to emerge as a double-crossed fool who had been poisoned and exploited to the benefit of the Bloodweaver legacy. And now, she found herself kneeling in familiar disgrace, awaiting to be overshadowed once again.

Shame loomed over Elyria like a dark blight waiting to smother her, causing her composure to wither with each passing moment. Had she mistaken kindness for cruelty when Sylas' spell granted her mind clarity? Elyria's mind flashed back to seven years ago when her name was announced by the High Priestess as it echoed in the Heart of the Temple. She recalled the crushing silence right before the whispers of bewilderment and denial began, those whispers which then turned into outright rejection and refusal.

The memory of what she endured threatened to shatter her credence in herself. *No.* She could not do this again—she would not do this again.

There were more fey in Neramyr than stars in the sky that believed she was unfit to be a divine candidate. Why go through the lengths to suppress and contain her like this? Were the others truly so afraid of her potential to be chosen by the Goddess over them?

If so, their fear was poorly placed—it should be directed at *her*.

Elyria was no longer in control of her movements, but she was still the master of her own mind. Her aura hardened as she drowned out the atmosphere around her. Elyria detached her sense of smell, taste, touch, sound, and sight from the surrounding arena and channeled that focus entirely on herself. She felt the steady rise and fall on her own chest. She heard the calming whir of air filling her lungs and the lulling whoosh as she exhaled. Elyria listened to the steadfast thumping of her heart and committed its beating melody to her memory. She worked to dispel the serithium from her bloodstream, expunging the toxin. She looked

The Divine Shallows

inwards and saw the whorls and swirls of her aura, reaching out to its comforting glow. Her aura stirred at the familiarity of her touch. It pained Elyria to see all that she had become, all that she had achieved, now shackled, and bound beneath a spell.

This was not how the *Vitus* would end.

In her lifetime, she had been robbed of so much and settled for far too little—but the title of *primis* was *hers* to claim.

Reaching out to her aura, her life essence, Elyria called to it. At the request, her aura roused to her command, and something awakened within herself. Her mind swept over her body, scouring, and searching for the foreign magic that bound itself to her, ensuring no stone was left unturned.

Before long, Elyria identified each link in the chain of magical bindings that shackled her. She was Elyria Fangwright, a trueborn princess of Neramyr and the blood of the first king of Eriden flowed through her veins. She refused to exist as a prisoner in her own body.

Elyria's mind seized the magical binds one by one, rooting them out until the very last one was within her mental grasp. She knew her next action had to be performed with precision, aware that she had only one chance—just one opportunity to make it count. She couldn't be certain how long it would be before Sylas become aware of her efforts.

In the back of her mind, the rhythmic thump of her heart sounded, and she replayed the beat over and over like an unwavering anthem. Elyria recalled the oath she made to herself seven years ago—a promise she intended to uphold until her dying breath. This reminder spurred her into action.

With newfound energy and strength, Elyria called upon her native magic once more, commanding it to break free from the confines of Sylas' spell. She felt the tendrils of power within her stir, laboring to overcome the enchantment that bound her. Gradually, her magic returned to her, fragment by unfaltering fragment. The sensation was unparalleled, as if everything had been restored to its rightful place.

Elyria hadn't realized the void that had consumed her from the absence of control over her own magic. Throughout her life, her native magic had been an extension of herself, a loyal counterpart. She knew, just as it had always been and always would be—her magic would not falter her now.

With her magic fully under her reign once more, Elyria directed a violent torrent of power at the magical confines that imprisoned her. Elyria's magic erupted throughout her body, splintering the spelled links one by one in rapid succession as she snapped her head upwards.

Instantly, Sylas spun around, his face overtaken by shock. He abandoned his coordinated assault with Kerrick against the blood-eyed eel and hastily redirected all his magic, channeling into the legacy spell, but it was too late.

Elyria had emerged from her prison of submission, donning a look of venom—wearing it as if it were made of the finest silk.

"How?" Sylas exclaimed in disbelief, his eyes wide with alarm. "That's impossible."

Kerrick, noticing Sylas' sudden distraction, turned to follow his gaze, only to be met with the sight of Elyria standing tall and free from the grip of the Bloodweaver feat. At once, his confidence faltered at the sight of her.

What she did defied all logic—Sylas was correct about that. Yet, there stood Elyria, liberated from the grasp of a legacy spell. Legacy spells were among the most potent and powerful classes of spells, being nearly impregnable, but there were always exceptions—and Elyria was an exceptionally powerful sorceress.

Whether it was that she descended from a royal bloodline, or that she possessed a legacy status herself, or that she sacrificed her soul towards strengthening her magic, all that was certain was that Elyria gave rise to her prevailing outcome, defying the odds.

If Sylas had taken more of her blood to imprison her mind in his legacy spell, perhaps Elyria would still be shackled under his influence.

But while the exact reason for her liberation would remain unknown, it was no matter now.

Standing tall on her raft, Elyria thrusted her arms and unleashed a torrent of magic towards the other six candidates. She felt her magic wrap around their minds like iron chains, instantly overwhelming Lynora, Lillia, Iva, Galen, and Kerrick. Elyria had expected most of her competitors to succumb easily, but what intrigued her was Sylas' strong resistance against her mental manipulation.

Turning her attention to Sylas, Elyria confronted the last mind she needed to bend to her will. His sea-green eyes met hers with unwavering intensity, revealing a psyche admittedly much stronger than the others. If Elyria had remained under Sylas' legacy spell, he might have been chosen by the Moon Goddess as the cohort's *primis*. Almost certainly.

"You've been quite busy, Sylas," Elyria remarked bluntly. "Colluding with the others to bring about my downfall long before I even knew who you were."

Sylas remained silent, his aura telling of his discomfort. But before he could respond, Elyria continued.

"I overheard your conversation with Kerrick in the Driftmoor castle's lounge," Elyria pressed on. "In truth, I was deeply disappointed. I believed you cared for me, but it seems I was merely reminded of the cruelty deep-rooted in the fey of Neramyr. And you, Sylas, are no exception."

Sylas shook his head before responding. "My actions were driven by one goal, and that goal alone: to be named *primis*. I do care for you, Elyria, but this is not personal. You, of all fey, should understand the sacrifices required to prove oneself worthy in the eyes of the Moon Goddess."

Her anger pitched as she hurled her words at him.

"No, Sylas," Elyria's eyes flashed with intensity. "You know *nothing* of what it means to prove yourself worthy to the Moon Goddess—you know nothing of the cost. Pray tell, what have you endured at the judgment of the Moon Goddess? What do you know of the price paid for being seen as unworthy in Caena's eyes? As you pursued your hunt for divine greatness these past seven years, I have labored my entire life for mine."

Elyria took an eerie step closer. Her next words echoed in Sylas' mind and his mind alone.

"Do not equate the cost of your aspiration to what I've sacrificed for my salvation."

Sylas blanched at her voice in his head, an exchange for only him to hear.

"I didn't mean to—" His sentence was abruptly cut off by a brusque wave from Elyria, sending a sharp pulse of magic through the air.

Elyria refused to indulge Sylas any longer. With a flicker of her magic, she shattered his psyche, his body stiffening with a vacant expression as she dominated his mind. Then, she directed her attention to the other six candidates, who now stood in a trance-like state under her mental control. An ember of anger ignited within her as she watched them, blank and biddable on their rafts. How could she let herself so easily perform within their playwright? Elyria's resentment threatened to cloud her judgment, but she refrained.

Now was not the time for rash decisions; the *Vitus* was far from over.

Her next move demanded more precision and concentration. With all six competitors under her mental sway, she swiftly cast the next spell. Turning her palms upward, she channeled her magic towards them, weaving into their minds, threading through their thoughts until they gave way to her mental siege. With one final maneuver, she managed to completely overwhelm their psyches, gaining total cognitive control.

With her magical grip firmly established, Elyria commanded them with a single thought.

Kneel.

The Divine Shallows

In unison, the six candidates stiffly dropped to their knees on their rafts.

Bow.

Obediently, all six of their heads dropped to their chests, submitting to Elyria.

With what Sylas could only achieve through a rare Bloodweaver feat and a conduit, Elyria had accomplished a similar effect with her own psionic abilities. Yet, there was no victory in her expression. Even through the lens of retribution, Elyria's expression remained frustrated. Her psionic magic was not enough to garner the Moon Goddess' attention.

This outcome was not part of her meticulously laid plan—months of training seemed wasted in this moment of doubt and uncertainty. Elyria's aura churned as she struggled to quell her inner turmoil. What had driven her to turn her magic against her supposed comrades? Would the Goddess perceive it as cowardice, or worse, as a petty act of retaliation? Caena, all-seeing and all-knowing, would surely sense Elyria's wavering confidence.

Shutting her eyes tight, Elyria tried to silence her spiraling thoughts.

She cursed herself for not staying the course of her own plan, but she conceded it was far too late for that. At this stage in the *Vitus*, she needed to act now.

It was amidst her contemplation when she belatedly realized the waves within the arena had grown eerily still. Her eyes flung open, hastily scanning the surroundings, yet she found no trace of the blood-eyed eel. When had it vanished? How much time had elapsed during its absence? Elyria cursed her oversight. Undoubtedly, the creature was using this lull to recuperate itself.

Surveying the motionless depths, she clamped her fists in frustration.

The *Vitus* could end at any moment; there was no definitive duration for how long the ritual would last. As all things were, the timespan was determined by the Moon Goddess. The ritual would end when Caena deemed she had seen enough to render her judgment.

In previous seasons, its length had varied greatly. The most recent *Vitus* lasted a mere five minutes, concluding immediately after Prince Thomys Bloodweaver's performance. Within that fleeting timespan, the Goddess severed her connection to the High Priestess, signifying her selection of a victor. In contrast, the *Vitus* prior to that had stretched on for nearly three hours.

That meant Elyria understood one thing for certain—the Moon Goddess was still observing the ritual. Her decision for a victor had not yet been reached.

There was still an opportunity to execute her original plan. An air of readiness emanated from Elyria as she surveyed the surrounding waters. If the blood-eyed eel was withdrawing from the fight, she would draw it to resurface. Inhaling deeply through her nose and exhaling slowly through her mouth, she turned her gaze to the stars, meeting the radiance of the full moon. A shadow of a smile tugged at Elyria's lips as she anchored her feet on her raft. Elyria lifted both of her tanned arms with her inkless palms upturned and she invoked the moon's power.

Suddenly, a crackling surge of magic thundered across the arena. From Elyria's upturned palms, two fierce columns of flames the color of winter frost erupted. These ivory infernos swelled, illuminating the starlit sky over the arena. As the plumes of flames grew, they began to take shape, morphing into blazing silhouettes of monstrous firedrakes beating their mighty wings in the moonlit sky.

Collective gasps streamed from the crowd as the whispers of one word were repeated in waves—*moonfire*.

The two blazing firedrakes circled the sky under Elyria's command as a blistering cold cloaked the air, causing gooseflesh to ripple across Elyria's skin, yet she continued to guide the glacial firedrakes to the corners of the arena. A sweat broke across her brow, but she siphoned more of her magic into the phantom firedrakes, both apparitions breathing brutal beams of moonfire into the lulling waves below. Where the moonfire struck, the waves froze and crystallized. Spotting the blood-eyed eel retreating, Elyria directed the twin beams towards the creature, gradually encircling it until it was trapped within a narrow opening of water.

Elyria was mindful to construct the open cavity away from the other candidates, confining the blood-eyed eel to the southern barrier of the arena. Above them, her phantom firedrakes hovered the skies in waiting. Elyria bided her time for the moment the eel would emerge from the depths; however, it never came. Uncertainty fell upon her shoulders, but she pushed it aside and concentrated on her goal. Breathing hard, she amplified the power that wielded her arctic dragons, commanding them to unleash a magnified inferno, piercing the frozen waves to lower the water to subfreezing temperatures, coaxing the eel to the surface.

To her satisfaction, her plan succeeded—it was now warmer at the surface of the arena than the depths below.

Suddenly, the eel's shadow darted from beneath the ice and burst out of the cavity with a frantic shriek. At once, Elyria directed another moonfire beam to seal the opening, leaving the blood-eyed eel with no means to escape. The beast slithered and floundered on the icy surface as it attempted to right itself. It began to spray metallic acid aimlessly and the droplets sizzled on the chilled surface of the arena. Elyria's aura cringed, finding no joy in the creature's distress. With a swift maneuver, she released her legacy spell, causing the moonfire dragons to dissipate into silvery plumes of smoke, returning the arena to the dim glow of feylight.

As a Fangwright legacy by birthright, Elyria possessed the unique feat to wield moonfire, a gift inherited from the first king of Eriden. Even among legacies, very few Fangwright warlocks and sorceresses have truly mastered the ability to tame it. Moonfire could only be effectively harnessed at night when the moon's temperature reached a freezing point. The wielder channeled the rays emitted from the moon, controlling and dictating its powerful energy. Moonfire subsisted at a numbing temperature, piercing enough to suspend the tides of the Swyn Sea ten times over.

Moonfire was as dangerous to the wielder as it was destructive to the target. The wreckage and devastation moonfire could cause was unpredictable—only those with great stewardship over their magical abilities could channel the gift.

Nonetheless, Elyria had conquered this demanding feat, and tonight she was determined to ensure that the Moon Goddess and the fey of Neramyr acknowledged this.

With deliberate steps, Elyria strode from her raft onto the frozen battle ground and stalked towards the monstrous creature. It continued to shriek and flail as Elyria closed the distance between them. Only once she stood mere paces away from the creature did she pause, facing it with certitude. Closing her eyes, she called upon the full moon once more, feeling its incandescent rays caressing the surface of her face.

Harnessing its power, she thrust both arms towards the blood-eyed eel.

A torrent of destructive moonfire erupted from Elyria's palms, striking the sea creature with unbridled force. The eel staggered backward, engulfed in ivory flames, it's cries stilled as swiftly as they sounded.

Elyria released her legacy spell, allowing the moonfire to dissipate, leaving shimmering silver plumes swirling in the night sky. Before her, the eel remained frozen in place and where it stood. A groan began to sound beneath it, growing louder as the eel's body began to slant. It gained momentum until it toppled over, shattering into countless fragments that scattered across the arena.

Elyria released her mind manipulation on the other six candidates, but they remained unmoving even in their liberation. The entire arena fell into a heavy silence as mere seconds stretched into an eternity.

From above, the High Priestess' voice resounded throughout the arena.

"The Goddess has severed the divine tether between our realms, signaling the conclusion of the ritual of the Sixth Day," she declared. "The Moon Goddess has cast her judgment upon these seven divine candidates, and her ruling will be announced tomorrow during the Crossing of Kin. Let us commend our candidates for their completion of the *Vitus*!"

Elyria's heart was pounding fiercely as she turned to the crowds, her gaze roaming the stands. Finally, her eyes locked with her father's, the king of Eriden, and she met his steeled expression with one of her own. The arena fell silent around her, save for the sound of her own ragged breaths, but she refused to let the exhaustion unfold upon her face.

This time, Elyria did not cower in the face of their silence.

This time, in the face of Neramyr's disbelief, Elyria bowed before them with conviction.

25

Born to Wield

"Oh no," Elowyn whispered, her body tense, fists clenched as she peered over the stands. Her silver gaze remained fixed on her sister's kneeling form. Though only moments had passed since the Bloodweaver candidate cast his legacy feat upon her, Elyria remained unmoving and her aura was muted, now quieted beneath the spell. "Come on, Elyria," Elowyn murmured in desperation.

This *Vitus* unfolded unlike anything Elowyn had anticipated. The scene before her was entirely unusual, diverging from the customary practices of the ritual. She, along with the entire arena, was taken aback when the Bloodweaver candidate revealed himself as a legacy. By disclosing his status, Sylas established his potential to alter the outcome of the *Vitus* entirely.

In Neramyr, legacies were revered as much as they were rare. Elowyn knew it had been decades since a fey born outside of the royal bloodline possessed a legacy status. Not even her mother, the queen of Eriden, inherited this distinction.

The realization unsettled Elowyn's aura.

At the onset of the *Vitus*, she had held an unwavering confidence in her sister. But with the emergence of another legacy in the ritual, there was no telling what the Moon Goddess would make of it.

Elowyn couldn't recall if two legacies had ever competed in the same *Vitus* before. Nonetheless, an irking voice in her mind reminded her that when her turn came to participate, she would face six legacies—six royal candidates. She shook her head, attempting to banish the thought, and redirected her attention to the arena as she released a flustered breath. Arms drawn tightly to her chest, she watched as the other divine competitors battled the foul creature summoned by the Blackbane candidate.

Elowyn's gaze anxiously shifted to Elyria, still ensnared under the Bloodweaver feat, kneeling on a raft with her head bowed low. She bit her lip nervously. *If anyone can overcome a legacy feat, it's you, Elyria.* Elowyn's attention then darted to the Driftmoor candidate as he and Sylas orchestrated a calculated assault on the sea creature. A small gasp escaped Elowyn's lips as she observed the sapphire-haired warlock from House Driftmoor summon a towering wave with a sweep of his forearm and hurl it towards the sea creature.

The summoned wave crashed into the creature, engulfing it completely just as Sylas cast another spell upon it. The waters surrounding the blood-eyed eel began to churn, thickening with viscosity. The creature's frantic movements slowed as it thrashed against the treacherous tide, now formed semi-solid. Sylas' arms extended powerfully, his fingers laced in a cage-like fist. The beast writhed within Sylas' grasp and Elowyn sensed the unmistakable sensation of a great deal of magic being channeled.

Elowyn speculated on the source, initially fixating on Sylas, but quickly realized her assumption was incorrect. Her eyes snapped to Elyria's form, and Elowyn released the breath hitched in her lungs. Before anyone else in the audience could comprehend what was unfolding,

Elowyn witnessed her sister's vacant expression morph into one of malevolence. *Elyria did it.* In awe, Elowyn watched as Elyria overcame the Bloodweaver feat and counter spelled each of the other candidates. Though there was a cryptic exchange between Elyria and Sylas, she effortlessly asserted control over all six of their minds. Elyria compelled them to kneel in submission before her, assuming the position from which she had just freed herself.

Beside Elowyn, Finnor released a low whistle at the sight, impressed by Elyria's actions and the message they conveyed.

Next, Elowyn sensed conflicting auras rippling across the audience. She worked to stifle the pleased expression that was blooming across her face, but her sense of satisfaction halted when she observed Elyria pause. She recognized that look. Her sister was grappling with something within herself. *You've got this, Elyria.* Almost as if hearing Elowyn's silent encouragement, Elyria finally raised her gaze to the midnight sky. With focused intent, her moonless palms turned upward as she began summoning a powerful sum of magic that rattled the arena.

Breathtaking pillars of ivory flames erupted from Elyria's upturned palms, and Elowyn's mouth fell agape. She had witnessed those ominous white flames only once before. A blend of fear and awe enveloped her. *Moonfire.* Elowyn couldn't discern if the word escaped her own lips or was murmured by another member of the audience, but the word began to ripple across the arena with the force of a raging river. Elowyn watched as the flames springing from her sister's hands began to morph, taking on the form of magnificent, winged silhouettes—moonfire firedrakes.

"By the Goddess," Finnor whispered under his breath, reclining back in his seat. "That's incredible."

Elowyn knew he was right. To wield moonfire was a formidable feat in itself; to manipulate moonfire to this extent was unimaginable.

As the white flames danced before Elowyn's eyes in the arena, an unfamiliar memory ensnared her.

Suddenly, she found herself transported back home, standing in her father's study. The king of Eriden stood before the crackling flames of the hearth, while Elowyn lingered behind him silently, hesitant to speak unless spoken to.

"Elowyn, you are destined to be the future queen of our realm. Do you understand the weight of this responsibility?"

Elowyn blinked and shook her head. Her father sighed. "Come, stand beside me." He gestured for Elowyn to join him, and as she moved closer, he knelt to her level. "At this moment, you have celebrated five namedays. You are still a feyling, but soon you will be called before Caena. The Moon Goddess has chosen to Mark you at birth, and when you reach candidacy age, she will demand you to prove yourself worthy of this blessing."

Elowyn winced at the thought.

King Eamon chuckled softly and placed both of his hands gently on her shoulders. "Worry not, Elowyn. As my daughter, you are destined for greatness. You are the sole blood-heir to the Fanged Throne. As the heir, you have inherited the gift bestowed upon House Fangwright by King Elmyr. Do you know what this gift is?"

Elowyn shook her head once again.

"Many moons ago, during the dawn of the New Age, the Moon Goddess granted each of the founding monarchs of Neramyr a unique gift—a legacy to be passed down to the future guardians of the feylands. These seven gifts are exalted, meant to be wielded by only those with noble intent and just cause."

Elowyn's eyes grew curious as her father continued. "The first king of Eriden was granted the gift of wielding a special form of magic from the Moon Goddess: moonfire. Moonfire is one of the primary forms of magic the Moon Goddess used to vanquish the creatures of the Old Age."

King Eamon guided Elowyn to an arched window in the study and together they gazed at the night sky. He closed his eyes and drew a measured breath. "Close your eyes, Elowyn. Can you feel the moonlight touching your skin? Do you sense its divine essence?" Elowyn furrowed her brows for a moment, concentrating, before nodding in affirmation. He continued, "Mastering the ability to harness moonfire fully is said to take years, but I managed it in mere months. And just as I did, you too will master moonfire swiftly. Would you like to give it a try?"

At the proposition, Elowyn paled. King Eamon chuckled once more. "It's quite all right if you're afraid, Elowyn. Such power should never be underestimated; understanding the gravity of the magic you wield will make you a finer sorceress than most."

He turned back to her. "Watch my hand."

Elowyn studied her father's upturned palm, noticing the intricate moon inked dragon scales adorning his fingers, hand, and exposed forearm. Soon, she felt the pull of potent magic as it gathered in her father's palm. At the center, a small flame flickered to life, its glow as white as snow. Elowyn gasped, taken aback by the sensation. She instinctively wrapped her arms around herself, feeling a chill. "Father, the fire—it's white! And so cold."

A hint of amusement graced King Eamon's expression. "This is moonfire, Elowyn. The white flames are born of the moon's energy at its coldest point. This magic can only be wielded when the moon surfaces the night sky; the fuller the moon, the more potent the moonfire. During my reign, only two living fey have demonstrated the ability to harness moonfire. It is indeed a rare gift to inherit."

Elowyn furrowed her brows once more as she looked up at her father. "Is it you and mother?"

King Eamon shook his head. "It is me and your Uncle Edwyn. Soon, a third moonfire wielder in this kingdom will emerge. My true-born daughter, you shall carry on the Fangwright legacy." He tenderly pressed a finger against Elowyn's heart.

Elowyn glanced down at her father's candid touch. "What about Elyria? Does that mean she gets to wield moonfire, too?"

At her inquiry, her father's expression darkened, and his jaw tightened. "No, never."

Elowyn clamped her mouth shut, instantly regretting her words. Quickly, her father's darkened demeanor dissipated, and he cleared his throat. "Mastering moonfire is incredibly challenging, but once you have mastered wielding it, the moonfire will respond to your touch. Moonfire is lethal, but in the hands of a skilled warlock or sorceress, it becomes merely another form of magic."

King Eamon curved his wrist, and the moonfire within his palm swelled, morphing into a miniature firedrake. The tiny flame dragon rested comfortably in his hand. Elowyn's eyes brightened at the sight. "It looks like Stryx!"

Her father then slightly curled his fingers, and the moonfire dragon spread its wings, lifting itself into the air. With a gentle bend of King Eamon's wrist, the moonfire dragon soared upward and gracefully arced back down, descending until it landed in the center of his palm. Upon contact, the moonfire dragon dissipated, leaving behind only a passive ember in its stead. "I am going to pass this flame to you, Elowyn. Though you may not yet have the capability to summon moonfire on your own, you were born with the capacity to wield it."

The king extended his palm to her slowly. "When you receive this flame, Elowyn, you must be cautious. The sensation of moonfire may be overwhelming. It is the most potent magic you have encountered thus far—you must not let it overwhelm you. You are both the vessel and the conductor of the moonfire. Allow it to flow through you freely. Do not be intimidated by its power; instead, guide the white flames to your will. For now, do not concern yourself with shaping the moonfire. Simply hold it within your grasp and let it burn gently." Her father nudged his palm toward her once more.

The chilling touch of the moonfire made Elowyn shiver, but she dared not disobey her father.

As Elowyn's hesitant hands reached for the white flame, her father's warning echoed in her ears. "Be careful, Elowyn. Take control of it slowly, and never let it overpower you. Even if it becomes too much, do not succumb to it." King Eamon brought the tranquil flame to Elowyn's waiting palms, meeting her gaze with seriousness. "Are you prepared?"

Elowyn's heart urged her to refuse, but a feeble "yes" escaped her lips. Her father nodded and carefully transferred the white flame into her cupped hands.

The instant the moonfire made contact with her skin, Elowyn screamed.

The flame erupted into a violent pillar within her grasp. Elowyn collapsed to her knees, tears streaming from her silver eyes in a frenzied stream. She struggled to draw breath, to speak, to do anything beyond endure the unbearable agony of the consuming white flames as they swallowed her whole. She feared they would devour her entirely, leaving nothing of her behind. The raw, icy burn of the moonfire surpassed any pain she had ever known.

"Elowyn, listen to me! You must control the moonfire! You must contain its power before it overwhelms you. Focus on guiding its path, don't resist the flames, direct them! Command the moonfire to dwindle and wane!" Elowyn remained frozen, save for her trembling hands clasping the searing white flames. Bent over in agony, she tried to speak, but her lips formed no words.

"Elowyn, extinguish the flames! You've let the moonfire run rampant through you, drawing on your native magic." King Eamon swiftly gathered her trembling form, pulling her away from the moonlit window. With urgency, he clasped her hands in his, dispelling the moonfire. "I can halt the flame, but I can't halt the flood of moonfire already coursing within you. You must sever it from your magic before it's too late." Holding Elowyn's tear-stained face in his hands, he implored her to focus. Though terror filled her eyes, she managed to meet his gaze. "Concentrate, Elowyn!" But she could only shake her head, silent sobs choking her throat. Her father cursed under his breath, his eyes reflecting his anguish.

For a moment, disquiet washed over him before he closed his eyes, calling upon his divine magic.

Gently cradling Elowyn's hunched figure, he whispered into her snow-white hair, "Goddess, forgive me."

A forceful rise of magic erupted from the king, ancient and powerful, wrapping Elowyn in a shimmering cocoon. Like vines, the magic entwined around her aura, binding it in place. He had severed her connection to her own native magic, extinguishing the moonfire within her bones. As her magical aura stilled, Elowyn's body slackened, her eyelids drooping shut.

With trembling hands, the king laid Elowyn by the hearth, her head resting on his lap as he surveyed the damage. His touch grazed her mangled, contracted fingers, now a deep plum hue. Her once soft lips were cracked and chapped, her sun-kissed skin drained of color, replaced by pallor and ash. He held out his palms, tendrils of moonlight coiled around them, casting a soft glow.

As he reached for Elowyn's marred hands, the door to his study burst open and the queen of Eriden appeared like a windstorm, wild and full of fury.

As Eddra's gaze fell upon Elowyn, she let out a horrified scream, her voice trembling with hysteria. "Eamon, what have you done?" The queen rushed to her daughter's side, her hands hovering uncertainly, torn between the urge to heal and the fear of causing more harm.

Meanwhile, the king, his palms still illuminated with restorative magic, muttered mutedly, "I've stilled her native magic, but not before the frost of the moonfire settled within her. I am capable of correcting this."

Turning to her husband with a mix of disbelief and wrath, the queen exclaimed, "Have you lost your senses, Eamon? Allowing her to wield moonfire at such a young age?" She forcefully pushed his hand away from Elowyn. "Don't you dare touch her." Her voice carried a dangerous edge. "You will do no such thing. You know as well as I do that the damage extends far beyond her hands. You've already done enough."

Ora's stout figure appeared in the partially open doorway, alerted by the screams. "Your Majesties! What's happened?" Her eyes widened in shock as they landed on Elowyn, her hand instinctively covering her mouth to stifle a gasp.

With a grave expression, the queen's voice quivered as she issued commands. "Ora, fetch the royal healers immediately. Bring only those trained exclusively at the Healer's Keep. Quickly, now!" She emphasized the urgency with a firm nod. "Go!"

∼

ELOWYN SNAPPED BACK TO REALITY, TO THE ARENA, AS confusion clouded her thoughts while she tried to piece together the fragments of the memory. Despite her efforts, she couldn't grasp the full scope of what happened. The sight of moonfire had reignited a forgotten memory, but there were gaps in her recollection, leaving her bewildered by the newfound revelations. She remembered her father showing her moonfire for the first time, yet the details of what followed remained elusive, shrouded in mystery.

She glanced down at her hands, flexing and extending her fingers. How had she forgotten the pain of healing from the frost burn? It must have been agonizing, even with the aid of Prymont's finest healers. Perhaps the ordeal had been so unbearable during her youth that she had subconsciously blocked out the memory.

Elowyn could have pondered this further, but the arena fell into a deathly silence, punctuated only by the sharp echo of creaking. She turned her gaze towards the frozen arena, where the blood-eyed eel was now unmistakably encased in jagged shards of ice. The creature teetered, its slanted form inching closer to the frozen ground. Then, with a deafening crash, it finally succumbed, shattering into thousands of icy fragments upon impact.

Beside her, Elowyn heard the High Priestess' voice ringing out, carrying across the entire arena. "The Goddess has severed the divine tether between our realms, signaling the conclusion of the ritual of the Sixth Day. The Moon Goddess has cast her judgment upon these seven divine candidates, and her ruling will be announced tomorrow during the Crossing of Kin. Let us commend our candidates for their completion of the *Vitus*!"

The arena fell into a hushed silence following the High Priestess' proclamation of the *Vitus'* conclusion. Amidst this quietude, Elyria's gaze rose, seemingly directed towards Elowyn.

Or so Elowyn initially thought.

However, tracing the trajectory of Elyria's stare, Elowyn realized that her older sister's true target was their father.

Elowyn observed her father's unbreakable composure. His face was devoid of emotion, giving nothing away. Yet, where his hands rested upon the seat's armrest, a hairline fissure had appeared in the stone that was not there before. Elowyn only felt the darkness of his aura as he leveled Elyria's stare with one of his own.

Her eyes then widened as she watched Elyria bow boldly before their father, her older sister's contemptuous glare just as unrelenting as his.

Elowyn looked between her father and Elyria with unease.

In the moment where Elowyn believed she would be cheering for her older sister, she instead feared for her.

26

Remembrance

Elowyn found the atmosphere at the Driftmoor castle's post-ritual celebration to be lacking in genuine celebration. Despite the exchange of pleasantries and banter among the fey, the oddity of Elyria's performance in comparison to her unblessed status couldn't be ignored. Dismissive compliments were mingled with thinly veiled criticism as Elowyn navigated through the crowd, her golden *aureum* trailing lightly behind her. Though she attempted to block out the snide remarks, a few still pierced through the noise.

As she passed by a raven-haired fey from Erimead, likely of noble lineage, Elowyn couldn't help but overhear her disparaging tone as she conversed eagerly with a sorceress from Lochwald. Fragments of their conversation still reached her ears.

"What an impressive display of magical prowess from the unblessed Fangwright!"

"Especially for someone deemed unworthy by the Goddess! It's a shame she wasn't blessed as a child. Even if she returns from the Bridge Between Worlds, she'll never attain the first Mark."

"Exactly! She might receive the final Mark after the Trial, but she'll always be lacking the crescent markings on her palms, forever limited in her divine potential. How unfortunate!"

A flicker of irritation crossed Elowyn's features as she seized a glass of honeyed *vinum* from a passing servant more forcefully than intended, taking a sip from the crystal goblet. With a composed exhale, she turned gracefully towards the two women.

"Good evening. I couldn't help but catch snippets of your riveting conversation," Elowyn remarked, raising her glass in a subtle gesture. "I'm curious to learn your names."

The sudden interruption from Elowyn caused the two fey to pale and shrink under her scrutiny. Their gazes flitted nervously from Elowyn's golden *aureum*, to her ivory locks, finally settling on her fanged smile. Recognizing her identity, they exchanged a flustered glance before both offering innocent smiles and performing quick curtsies.

The Lochwald sorceress swallowed audibly before speaking, "Princess Elowyn Fangwright, it is truly an honor! I am Brynna Crowe of House Blackbane. And this is Olessa Pend of House Mirthwood."

Elowyn maintained her passive smile, inwardly knowing she would forget their names as soon as the encounter ended but seeing no need to reveal that. She took a moment to articulate their names slowly, as though committing them to memory. "It's a pleasure to meet you both, Brynna Crowe of House Blackbane and Olessa Pend of House Mirthwood. I'll be sure to relay your flattering comments about our kingdom to my father, King Eamon. He would be delighted to know the names of those who hold his realm in such high regard."

The two females appeared as if all blood had drained from their faces.

Finishing her drink, Elowyn clapped her hands together with mock enthusiasm. "How fortunate! Just before our encounter, I was searching

The Divine Shallows

for my father's whereabouts. Now I can inform him of our exchange." She pretended to scan the crowd. "Oh moons, I must take my leave before I forget your names to share with him." With an elegant curtsy befitting a princess, she flashed another charming smile before gracefully departing.

Upon turning away, Elowyn couldn't help but roll her eyes as she exchanged her empty glass of *vinum* for a full one from a nearby tray.

Since the conclusion of the *Vitus*, her mood had soured, a blend of various factors contributing to it. Foremost among them was the looming final day of the Ceremony, with Elyria set to embark on her Trial across the Bridge Between Worlds, leaving Elowyn to face Neramyr alone. The thought of Elyria's departure stung, though Elowyn quickly dismissed it. After all, it wasn't Elyria leaving her; if anything, the blame lay at the feet of the Moon Goddess for these fated turn of events.

Elyria and their father were nowhere in sight. Elowyn would have willingly offered her soul to the eight moons if it ensured her sister was met with civility in the face of the seven realms. As she drained the contents of her current glass of *vinum*, she reached for another.

At the crux of it all was her father's inability to treat Elyria with anything but contempt. A child born of his own flesh and blood meant nothing to him; only power and status held significance in his eyes.

Elowyn supposed she held little power and had inherited a false status, making her equally insignificant in his eyes.

Elowyn's troubled mood knew no bounds. She had inquired about Elyria's plans for the *Vitus*, only to be met with secrecy. Yet what transpired in the ritual today was certainly not what her sister had suggested. It shocked Elowyn to learn that Elyria had taught herself to summon and wield moonfire on her own—it was yet another skill Elyria possessed that Elowyn lacked.

The countless glasses of *vinum* failed to distract Elowyn from her incessant comparisons with her older sister's abilities.

Where could Elyria be? And Draeden? Even Lyra seemed absent.

Elowyn gripped the teardrop necklace hanging at her neckline. The gem emitted a soft hum, though too faint to discern whether her sister was nearby. With a resigned sigh, Elowyn helped herself to another glass and resumed her quest for a familiar presence.

∽

"Fey of Neramyr," Queen Aletta Driftmoor announced, her cutlery gently tapping against a crystal goblet for attention. "What a remarkable conclusion to the Sixth Day of the Ceremony! Our divine candidates have successfully completed the *Vitus* under the watchful gaze of our beloved Goddess. May the blessings of the many moons shower upon them tonight!"

With her lapis hair pinned back, Queen Aletta's complexion, richly tanned by the sun, nearly copper, offered a striking contrast to the moonlit hues adorning her skin. The final Mark, unique to those pledged to House Driftmoor, depicted drifting waves and coastal mist.

"Tonight, we have yet another reason to rejoice!" The queen's smile radiated warmth. "My sister, Princess Cleora, has accepted a long-awaited betrothal to Prince Edwyn Fangwright." She lifted her glass in a toast toward Cleora and Edwyn, positioned to her left on their thrones. "It has been many reigns since such a harmonious union between two royal houses has been witnessed! Prince Edwyn has captured the heart of my sister, and it fills me with joy to witness such profound devotion. It is a love that even Queen Diantha herself would bless with great enthusiasm. Under the light of the next full moon, the royal couple intends to exchange the soul-bond, uniting them not only in this realm, but all realms beyond. Please join us in celebrating their betrothal and extend your heartfelt wishes for their happiness!"

Perched atop the courtyard's highest balustrade, Elyria observed Queen Aletta's announcement from the shadows. Leaning against the stone column railing, she surveyed the bustling crowd below, preferring the cloak of the night sky. Hidden from view, she felt a sense of solace, away from the festivities that she dared not partake in. The mere thought of joining them was overwhelming, and encountering Sylas would only stoke her anger further. Elyria had noticed Elowyn's search for her since the celebration began, but she deliberately suppressed the magical connection between their necklaces, knowing her younger sister would only attempt to console her about the *Vitus*.

Concern pricked at her as she observed Elowyn indulging in her sixth glass of fey wine. Elyria pondered whether her overprotectiveness over the years had done more harm than good. The notion stung, but she recognized that Elowyn needed to learn to stand on her own once she was gone.

Pushing aside the guilt, Elyria redirected her focus to the gathering below. Her gaze fixed on her mother, Queen Eddra, who clapped politely alongside the other fey, wearing a pleasant smile. Yet, despite her outward disposition, Elyria sensed the underlying fury in her mother's aura. She had learned to decipher her mother's concealed emotions over the years. Whenever Queen Eddra appeared too perfect, too content, it signaled that she was hiding something. The Clever Queen harbored numerous secrets, and despite Elyria's efforts, she had only uncovered a fraction of them in her twenty-six years.

Initially, Elyria found hiding to be frightening—detesting being alone and cloaked by darkness—but gradually, she grew to appreciate the hidden nooks and corners of the castle and the safety they provided.

She quickly discerned that fey behaved differently when they believed they weren't being observed. And similarly, their behavior shifted when they were aware of being watched.

Her discoveries held their weight in gold, hence Elyria's choice to remain concealed in the darkness, surveying the mingling crowd below.

In the calm expanse of the Eriden mountains, the pre-dawn sky hung heavy with darkness, the first light of morning still hours away. No more than thirty minutes after their return from the Elune Isles, Queen Eddra received a sealed missive, delivered by hand from a Neramyran informant. The message contained the same cryptic contents as the six missives before it, all arriving on consecutive days since the start of the Ceremony.

Queen Eddra recognized it was no mere coincidence that these messages began on the first day of the Ceremony. In Neramyr, coincidences were regarded with skepticism—often, they were calculated rather than merely coincidental.

Atop one of the mountain peaks, Eddra tenderly ran her fingers over the smooth, ivory scales decorating Stryx's hide. Her gaze drifted to the starlit sky as she murmured, "She remembers, Edwyn."

Edwyn stood nearby, his sapphire firedrake poised behind him, his expression inscrutable. "I know," he replied with a grave look. "They both remember."

Meeting his gaze with a composed expression, Eddra nodded in understanding. Turning her attention skyward, she crumpled the scroll tightly in her fist. At once, the parchment ignited into flame and disintegrated into ash, leaving only a faint trail of smoke in its wake.

With a formidable stride, Eddra mounted Stryx in a single fluid motion. United with his rider, the chalk-firedrake emitted a piercing cry before launching himself into the sky, his powerful wings propelling him upward. Stryx disappeared into the darkness, vanishing among the shroud of gray clouds.

Meanwhile, the prince exhaled deeply as he surveyed the darkness, his gaze shifting to his *animus*. With a gentle touch, he patted the blue dragon's hide, a silent communication passing between them. Afterward, Edwyn mounted Nerys effortlessly, and the dragon charged toward the edge of the summit. With a powerful leap, Nerys soared into the air, her membranous wings beating against the night.

With cryptic eyes, the Clever Queen and the Fanged Prince embarked on their journey through the obsidian skies, hastening toward the Elberrin Forest.

27

The Cherry-Stained Door

In the quiet of dawn, Draeden cradled Elowyn's sleeping form in his arms, admiring her peaceful features. He observed the gentle rhythm of her breathing, a comforting sight after the strife she endured. Last night had been unexpected; Elowyn had sought him out, her eyes filled with tears and her heart heavy with weariness. Knowing the burdens she carried, Draeden couldn't fault her for feeling overwhelmed. Just days before, she had been forced by her father to forge an Eternal Tethering bond with the newly appointed feyguard of Eriden—a decision that still ignited a throe of anger within him.

Within Neramyr's royalty, the Eternal Tethering bond was not unheard of; his own father, King Kyrus Darkmaw, possessed three Eternal Tethering bonds himself. Yet, typically, the bond was entered into willingly, a formal commitment freely offered by one fey to another to forsake their life to the bond if it necessitated it. The Eternal Tethering bond was sanctioned and blessed by the Goddess and fulfilled through the High Priestess in this realm.

If the Moon Goddess did not endorse the bond, the bond would not take.

Draeden was curious as to why the Moon Goddess accepted Elowyn and Finnor's bond when it was presented before her. Most heirs did not take the bond before their coronation. In legend, it was warned that taking the Eternal Tethering bond before coronation condemned the reigning ruler to a felled fate—it was ill-fortune to tempt the throne with the longevity of another monarch.

Though he dismissed this as mere folklore, Draeden couldn't discern any honorable motive for Elowyn to accept the bond at her age.

As Elowyn stirred slightly in his embrace, Draeden froze, careful not to disturb her. When she settled back into sleep, he gently brushed a stray strand of white hair from her face, his brow furrowing as he remembered her distress from the night before. In her anguish, she had implored him to take her somewhere safe, away from the burdens of her world. And so, he had brought her to the oasis in Orwyn—the only place he believed could offer her respite, while still ensuring the Eriden feyguard could locate her if needed.

A flush of warmth spread across Draeden's cheeks as memories of their recent embrace flooded his mind. His heart raced as he recalled each kiss, every touch exchanged and shared beneath the stars. She was the first fey to ignite such intense emotions within him. Perhaps it was the ethereal connection he felt when they first met in the Temple of Caena, or the way she observed the world with the same keen eye as he did. It could have been the moments he caught her stealing glances at him, or the thrill he felt when their eyes met across the room. Whatever the reason, he was utterly captivated. Draeden had always understood the depth of fey emotions, but now he grasped why kingdoms had fallen and wars had been waged in the name of love.

He would do anything for her. He felt it with his soul.

As if sensing his profound affection, Elowyn's eyes fluttered open, a soft smile gracing her lips. It was his undoing. Leaning in, he pressed a tender kiss to her lips, his hand gently tilting her chin upward. Elowyn responded in kind, her fingers tangling in his crimson locks. Their kisses deepened, fueled by desire and longing as the dawn began to break on the horizon. In the soft light, Draeden admired Elowyn's graceful form, feeling a surge of desire course through him.

With a groan, he surrendered to the overwhelming passion, his actions guided by tenderness and care. He traced kisses along her skin, savoring the curves of her body until their lips met once more. Their bodies joined, and only when Elowyn found release did Draeden allow himself the same, his movements urgent as he held her close. As they lay intertwined, bathed in the glow of morning light, Draeden cradled Elowyn in his arms, cherishing the intimacy they shared.

"How are you feeling?" Draeden's gaze was earnest as he spoke.

"Better now that I'm with you." Elowyn played with a strand of her hair. "Thank you for being there for me last night. I know I wasn't at my best. But... I'm still trying to wrap my head around what happened during the *Vitus*. I can't believe how the ritual was performed. Why did the High Priestess allow it?"

Draeden wore a pensive expression. "To be honest, I'm still puzzled myself. The ritual has always been a solitary performance for each candidate, unchanged for millennia. For it to suddenly deviate... I can only wonder if the Goddess desired it to be this way."

Elowyn sat up, turning to him. "Are you suggesting that this is how the *Vitus* will be conducted from now on? That we'll be using our abilities on each other when it's our turn to compete?"

He shrugged. "Possibly, if the Goddess wills it. We might not have much say in the matter."

Draeden's words left a sinking feeling in Elowyn's stomach. She knew he was right. If the Moon Goddess allowed this change, Neramyran tradition was being redefined at her behest.

Changing the subject, Elowyn asked, "Did you know that Sylas is a legacy?"

"No, not at all. I was just as surprised as everyone else in the arena," he replied. "The Bloodweaver feat is unnerving, to say the least. For your sister to break free of that legacy spell suggests she's far more powerful than anyone ever imagined. As a feyling, I learned about the seven feats, and I distinctly remember my scholars emphasizing how dangerous moonfire can be. For your sister to wield it to such a degree is beyond comprehension. Despite what the fey of Neramyr may think, I believe she'll be named *primis* tonight."

"She will. I'm certain of it," Elowyn affirmed, twirling another strand of her hair. "I still haven't fully mastered my legacy feat... have you?"

"Not quite," Draeden chuckled. "But we have time. We have seven years until our Trial."

"As always, you're right," Elowyn conceded, then nudged him teasingly. "I have an idea. How about you make me another enchanted bell and record your words of wisdom for me to listen to whenever I want?"

Draeden's tone turned serious. "Elowyn, I would never subject an artifact to such misuse. As a magicsmith of integrity, it goes against everything I believe in. Besides, knowing you, the bell would be ragged from overuse within two days!"

"Hey!" Elowyn jabbed him in the ribs this time. "You're insufferable!"

They both cackled with bright smiles and full laughs that reached their bellies. Draeden hoped that in those moments, Elowyn felt a sense of ease and relief. He saw a beauty in her that could never be captured, even if he spent his whole life crafting an artifact to encompass it.

They lingered in the oasis, savoring each other's company, letting the worries of the future slip away, if only for a little while. They knew that come the next dawn, their lives would be irrevocably altered, but for now, they found happiness in this moment.

EMERGING FROM A MOONGATE, FINNOR MOVED SILENTLY through the walls of Eriden's castle. His expression remained impassive as he followed a path toward one of the council chambers. Soon, he stopped before an iron door and raised a hand to rap against its hard surface.

"Enter," came a low voice.

Finnor slipped through the entrance, closing it behind him, and then bowed. "My king."

"Finnor," the king responded. "What news of the tether?"

Approaching him, the commander replied, "Her mind still resists the Tethering."

The king intertwined his fingers, resting his elbows on the armrests of his seat. "Continue to nurture the link; she will accede."

"Of course."

"What about her absence last night?"

"The tether revealed her location in Orwyn. I followed, as instructed."

The king's brow arched. "Orwyn?"

"Yes. The princess has developed a kinship with a warlock from her cohort."

"Whom?"

"Draeden Darkmaw."

King Eamon said curiously, "Kyrus' successor?"

"Yes, Your Majesty."

"I see." The king's expression remained unreadable. "And where is she now?"

"The princess has returned to Eriden. I tracked her arrival moments ago."

King Eamon's gaze turned thoughtful. "Can you discern her intentions with the Darkmaw warlock through the bond?"

"From what I can gather, she seems sincere."

"She will begin her training at the Spires soon. The Darkmaw warlock may prove useful yet." The king dipped a feathered pen into an inkwell. "Keep me informed of their actions."

"As you command."

King Eamon began writing on a parchment, pausing briefly. "Be prepared to influence her judgment through the tether if I deem it necessary to intervene."

Finnor's mind flickered with uncertainty, but his sense of duty quelled his unease. "As you wish, my king."

∽

ELOWYN STOOD BEFORE THE CHERRY-STAINED DOORS OF HER sister's chambers, her fingers wrapped around the teardrop-shaped gem that hung from her neck. Its magical hum was gentle, yet powerful, awaiting its other half just beyond the wooden entrance. Elowyn hadn't spoken to her sister since before the *Vitus*, knowing that Elyria sought solace in silence.

Still, she couldn't resist the urge to seek her out.

She raised her fist and rapped on the door, the sharp sound echoing through the empty corridors of the castle.

"Elyria? It's me. Can I come in?" Silence greeted her, stretching uncomfortably as Elowyn shifted nervously on her feet. "I understand if you're not up for visitors, but I wanted to check on you before the Seventh Day. I just want to make sure you're all right."

Attempting to open the door, she found it firmly sealed, protected by various wards. Despite her efforts, it remained closed, impervious to her touch—no one could enter unless Elyria willed it.

"What if we just lay together and do nothing? I promise not to leave any crumbs on your silk sheets," she added, attempting to lighten the mood with a joke. But the silence that followed felt heavier than before, weighing down on her with a sense of defeat.

With a resigned sigh, Elowyn turned away, the distant echo of her footsteps mingling with the silence of the castle halls.

As she retreated from her sister's chambers, the opal gem nestled beneath her collarbone protested, silently urging her to go back. Elowyn tightened her grip on the gem as if it would comfort the stone. The necklace had always served as a constant connection to her sister, but it would soon become a marker for her absence.

Elowyn did her best to suppress her gloomy aura.

Tonight was the night where her sister entered the Trial of Caena, and it felt too soon.

28

Crossing of Kin

THE SEVENTH DAY UNFOLDED IN ERIMEAD, THE FINAL OF THE seven kingdoms to host the Ceremony. Situated adjacent to Eriden, Erimead was only separated by a large channel of water that divided the mountainous territories. Despite being neighboring kingdoms, Elowyn had ventured to Erimead only a handful of times during the years.

King Balt and Queen Nyra Blackbane ruled this realm, blessed with twin sons near Elowyn's age: Prince Lox and Prince Llyr Blackbane. They both possessed hair of silken onyx, but the one defining feature that separated their otherwise mirrored appearance was their eyes. Lox had a pair of sapphire blue eyes while Llyr had one eye of sapphire-blue and the other of emerald-green.

Eyes of which Lyra would not stop droning on and on about.

"Llyr is simply *divine*. Just imagine how perfect the names Llyr and Lyra would be together? It feels like fate," Lyra gushed, her hands clasped beneath her chin. "And yet, Lox carries this heavenly-yet-mysterious allure that sets him apart. Don't you agree?"

"They're twins, Lyra," Elowyn remarked matter-of-factly, meeting her friend's gaze squarely. "They're practically identical."

"Well, aren't you a bore now that you've already found your prince. Let me indulge in my fantasies then," Lyra shot back.

"By all means, daydream away! I wouldn't dare to disrupt your desires," Elowyn grinned. Softening her tone, she added, "Either of the princes of Erimead would be fortunate to have you, Lyra."

Lyra straightened her posture, arms crossed over her chest. "At least you've come to your senses at last." Then, a spark ignited in her eyes as she continued, "Oh! I'm not usually one for gossip, but have you heard about the chatter brewing among the fey of Erimead? It appears they're quite divided over which heir will be chosen as the Blackbane candidate by the High Priestess tonight. Only one can be selected, isn't that dreadful?"

Elowyn found herself puzzled by Lyra's remark, as she had never given it much consideration, but there was truth in her table talk. Only one of the Blackbane twins could be named as a divine candidate for the upcoming Trial. It was a gut-wrenching circumstance, particularly if the brothers shared the close bond they appeared to have. She wondered if it caused any strain between them.

"Right, only one can…" Elowyn's voice trailed off, her thoughts lingering on the weight of the situation.

As twins, the Blackbane princes had been compared to each other since birth. However, once one of them was chosen as a divine candidate over the other, an undeniable shift in their status would occur. The first of them to receive the final Mark will cleave the divide between the two; a permanent reminder to the other that the difference between them no longer lied in the color of their eyes.

Lyra continued in a hushed tone. "And there's speculation that the son chosen as the divine candidate tonight will also be declared the Crown Prince of Erimead. How awful for the other prince! To lose a throne for a reason beyond their control seems unjust."

"A fate decided by the Moon Goddess is rarely fair," Elowyn expressed crossly.

Lyra's hand flew to her mouth in horror. "Oh, Elowyn. I didn't mean to bring up anything untoward. Please forgive me. Moons, sometimes I speak without thinking and end up making a fool of myself."

"Lyra, you have nothing to apologize for," Elowyn reassured her friend, reaching out to place a comforting hand on her arm. Then, with a playful smirk, she added, "Now, if you're interested, I can introduce you to Lox and Llyr. Since you mentioned it, I must admit that the names Llyr and Lyra do seem to complement each other quite nicely."

Lyra responded with a symphony of laughter and a warm embrace. The two of them made their way toward the courtyard, where the two young princes were engaged in conversation with fey from various kingdoms. Lox noticed Elowyn's approach first and waved to her in greeting.

"Elowyn!" Lox greeted her with open arms and a smile that stretched from ear to ear. "It feels like ages since we last spoke! Seems like the only time I catch sight of you is when you're soaring through the skies on your father's massive firedrake. Speaking of which, how's the fiery beast?"

Elowyn bristled at the comment. "That's hardly a respectful way to refer to the king of Eriden."

Lox rolled his eyes in good-naturedly. "Oh, moons. You haven't changed a bit."

"Oh, right. You meant Bane... Well, he's broody and taciturn as always." Elowyn chuckled at her own quip. Recalling the name of the winged ophis favored by Lox, she asked, "Aeras is doing well?"

"She's still as fierce as the day I first met her." He grinned, speaking of Queen Nyra's *animus* with admiration.

Peeking over his brother's shoulder, Llyr joined the conversation. "On the contrary, Liros remains the sweet-tempered and kind-hearted soaring serpent he's always been."

"You know what they say about sacred *animus*; they're drawn to those who reflect their essence most similarly. In Liros's case, it seems he's drawn to Llyr's gentle and meek spirit," Lox joked, giving his brother a playful pat on the back.

Llyr gave his brother an unbothered glance and shrugged. "Well, brother, there's nothing wrong with being reserved and refined. You should give it a try sometime. Anyway, it's good to see you again, Elowyn. It feels like it's been ages since you last visited Erimead. We never did get the chance to race each other around the mountains like we planned when we were feylings, did we?"

"I doubt I would've been able to ride Bane back then. If we had gone flying, I probably would've plummeted to my death, so I'm grateful we never tried," Elowyn chuckled, deflecting the question in the hopes that Llyr wouldn't pry further about her isolation from the other kingdoms. Fortunately, it seemed to work.

Llyr merely chuckled in response and redirected his attention to Lyra. "And who do we have the pleasure of meeting here?"

Before Elowyn could introduce Lyra, her friend spoke up for herself.

Lyra, as charming as ever, spoke in a voice as smooth as honey. "I'm Lyra Fenhart of House Bloodweaver," she introduced herself, extending a poised hand toward the two princes.

Llyr arched an eyebrow unexpectedly, while Lox greeted her gesture with a wide grin. Taking her hand in his, Lox pressed his lips softly against her skin. "A pleasure to meet you, Lyra Fenhart of House Bloodweaver. By any chance, are you related to Sylas Fenhart?"

Lyra's lips curved slightly at his charm. "As a matter of fact, he's my brother."

"Brilliant! Who knows, perhaps one day you'll surprise the seven realms and reveal yourself as a legacy as well."

Elowyn noticed a subtle change in Lyra's demeanor after the comment, but she maintained her composed and self-assured demeanor. Her eyes sparkled as she said, "You flatter me, Prince Lox. I might just do that. I'm full of surprises, you know."

Lox chuckled. "I look forward to you revealing your cards when the time comes." He then motioned toward his brother. "As much as we'd love to continue this conversation, Llyr and I have a few other guests to greet before we head to the Temple for the Crossing of Kin."

"We'll catch up with you both there," Llyr added with a wave before the princes disappeared into the crowd.

The fey in the courtyard began to disperse, with some already making their way to the Temple. The Seventh Day would commence once the moon fully ascended, and Elowyn still hadn't seen or heard from Elyria since the Sixth Day. She pushed aside the unsettling feelings that bubbled to the surface and focused on something else.

Once the Blackbane twins were out of sight, Elowyn turned to Lyra and casually touched her arm. "Is everything all right? I don't want to assume, but I sensed that something might be bothering you."

Lyra appeared anxious for the first time that evening. "Oh, it's nothing."

Elowyn's concern deepened, but she chose not to press further. "All right. Just know that I'm always here for you if you need me."

Lyra adjusted her gown and cleared her throat nervously. "It's something I usually avoid discussing, but with everything happening, I know I'll have to confront it soon."

"Only if you're comfortable," Elowyn said sincerely.

"Right. Here it goes…" Lyra glanced down at her clasped hands. "I adore my brother more than anything. I've admired him all my life. Sylas is truly remarkable, but it's easy to feel overshadowed by him." She began to shift on her feet. "Our parents were ecstatic when he was chosen as the Bloodweaver candidate for this season. As you know, being selected by the Moon Goddess and accomplishing divine greatness is the highest honor one can achieve." Lyra straightened her dress skirts. "Sylas captured Caena's attention, but I fear I never will." She sighed heavily. "Moons, what am I even saying? The truth is, I know I never will."

Lyra met Elowyn's gaze with seriousness. "Sylas told me he's felt the Goddess' presence his entire life… He said he's sensed her divine power countless times. It's understandable, given that he's a legacy. He was blessed with that gift from Isadora at birth." Lyra glanced back at her feet. "He'll be the next Fenhart in what seems like generations to become a divine warlock. But me? I've never felt the Goddess' presence. I've never been acknowledged by the Iron Queen."

The mention of Isadora Bloodweaver, the first queen of the Iron Hollows, triggered a memory of the Second Day when Elowyn was escorted through the Iron Kingdom's wards and barriers. After she had rather impulsively punched Theo in the face for insulting her sister, Theo had mentioned at one point that Isadora had taken notice of her. Elowyn remembered the ivory ink crescent moons on her palms glowing in the dimly lit cave and the profound connection she felt to Neramyr. It had been an extraordinary sensation.

In truth, it felt otherworldly.

"My native magic is barely a trickle compared to Sylas' torrent. Since the day I could harness magic, I have trained tirelessly, until my eyes grew heavy and my limbs weary. Yet, despite how hard I tried, I fell leagues behind Sylas. Each day served as a stark reminder that our abilities were no longer paces apart, but worlds apart. His selection as a divine candidate during the last Crossing of Kin was hardly unexpected," Lyra confessed, her shoulders sagging. "I'm not destined to be chosen as a divine candidate, nor will I ever bear the final Mark."

Lyra shook her head. "How can I believe that the Goddess will choose me in the years to come, Elowyn? Seven years will pass, time and time again, and I will be coveting a fate that was never mine to have. Tonight, at the Temple, Caena will select the seven kin of Neramyr's monarchs for her Trial. The truth is that those destined for divinity are kings and queens, princes and princesses, and the few chosen children of the moon." Lyra let out an unsteady breath. "This I know to the very marrow of my bones, I am not among one of them—I am not one of you."

Elowyn's emotions stirred from Lyra's outspokenness. Despite her own doubts and insecurities, she understood the undeniable reality of her lineage. As the daughter of a king and as a descendant of one of the founders of Neramyr, her candidacy was unquestioned. Elowyn knew, without a doubt, that she would ascend as a divine sorceress and eventually rule Eriden as its next queen.

Only seven divine warlocks and sorceresses were chosen every seventh year. Lyra, despite being the daughter of a noble, was just that and nothing more. The improbability of Sylas being chosen as a divine candidate from among the thousands of warlocks in the Iron Hollows was already staggering. If Lyra's judgement of herself held true, the likelihood of her becoming a divine sorceress was slim to none.

"I suppose greatness wasn't written in the stars for me. Unlike you, or Theo, or even Sylas," Lyra admitted. "No matter how hard I try to push it aside, everything I've known is about to change. Sylas will return home after seven years as a divine warlock, and knowing him, he'll have embarked on some noble quest for the good of Neramyr," she mused with a soft chuckle. "And tonight, you'll be named the Fangwright candidate. Soon, you'll be whisked away to train at the Seven Spires alongside Theo. It seems like everyone I hold dear is destined for so much more," she sighed, furrowing her brow. "As for me? I have nothing to offer but a pretty face."

Her next words were sorrowful. "There's a separation between the divine and the native fey. The intricate marks that decorate your skin set you apart in immeasurable ways, by nature—like calls to like—and I am certainly not like you." Lyra smiled sadly. "It may not be fitting to ask this of a princess, but there is no such thing as pride in friendship. Promise me this, when greatness claims you—I beg of you not to forget about me."

Elowyn reached for her friend's hands. It dawned on her then, the depth of Lyra's wounds. It all made sense now—the profound sadness stemming from her friend's aura when they first met. Lyra had mentioned how she dreamed of what life would be like if she had been born a princess of Neramyr, of what she may not have lost.

Elowyn was keenly aware of the stark division between the divine fey, the native fey, and those without magic at all. It was this division that prompted Draeden to take such precautions during her visit to Orwyn—covering her moon-inked palms with gloves, draping her in a cloak, and guiding her through hidden alleyways. As Lyra had expressed, Elowyn's markings set her apart from the masses, and nearly everyone Elowyn knew was considered one of the privileged.

Being divine meant Elowyn was seen differently, spoken to differently, and treated differently.

Despite the divide that separated them, Elowyn gathered her friend in a tight embrace. "I promise," she vowed softly.

THE TEMPLE'S FOYER GREETED ELOWYN AND LYRA WITH ITS familiar polished stone. With a sense of urgency, Elowyn guided them towards the Heart of the Temple, their footsteps echoing against the elaborate marble entryway. Each time she passed through the enchanted archway, Elowyn couldn't help but marvel at its rich history. Etched into the ancient marble trim were the names of Neramyr's original fey rulers. Beyond the threshold lay the sacred entrance to the Heart of the Temple, veiled by a protective ward that resembled a slice of midnight sky. This illusion was a vista of dusky azure, adorned with countless twinkling stars, an enchanted homage to the most sacred place in Neramyr.

Beside her, Lyra stepped forward, her fingers delicately tracing the carved marble surface until they reached the name of the first Iron Queen, Isadora Bloodweaver. With a reverent whisper, Lyra invoked the name of her kingdom's founder, then closed her eyes and took a deep breath. Pressing her thumb to her lips, she gently bit down, drawing forth a bead of crimson. With devotion, Lyra offered her blood to Isadora's name, watching as the drop glowed before disappearing into the stone, accepting her tribute. With a graceful sweep of her dress, Lyra passed through the midnight sky mirage, crossing the threshold into the Heart of the Temple.

Following in her footsteps, Elowyn repeated the sacred ritual, offering her own drop of blood in homage to her kingdom's founder and the countless fey who had come before. Her offering was accepted by the ancient ward, and Elowyn stepped through the gateway, feeling the gentle caress of a starlit breeze against her skin as the Heart of the Temple unfolded.

Stepping into the sacred expanse, Elowyn found the lofty chamber teeming with hundreds of attendees, the crowd swelling with each passing moment. Yet amidst the throng of fey, her gaze was drawn precisely to the one figure she had searched for since the previous day. Even with Elyria's back turned, her silhouette was unmistakable to Elowyn. Seeing her older sister, Elowyn couldn't help but release a sigh, the tension that had gripped her for hours finally easing, though the ache in her heart persisted.

Elyria stood in silence near the Divine Shallows, a statue of composure before the stone sigil of House Fangwright submerged beneath the sacred waters. Clad in a tunic as dark as midnight, a stark contrast to her snow-white hair bound in a tightly woven braid, Elyria radiated a commanding aura. Despite her outward calm, Elowyn could sense that her sister's true emotions were shielded behind a shroud of rehearsed control. Elyria refused to be preyed upon, neither her aura nor her mind.

Intently, Elowyn gathered the folds of her ruby gown and navigated through the crowd, her path leading her closer to her sister.

As she pushed through the thickening mass of bodies, Elowyn's frustration mounted, and she soon realized the reason for the congestion. A path was being cleared through the crowd for the High Priestess, who was making her way toward the Divine Shallows. *The ritual is beginning already?* Elowyn redoubled her efforts, forcing her way through the throng, drawing irritated glances that tempered upon noticing her golden *aureum*. Though still some distance from her sister, Elowyn watched as the High Priestess, draped in long robes of alabaster, glided toward the shallows with each graceful step.

Elowyn let out a frustrated groan as she maneuvered through the crowd, desperately seeking a path that would lead her to Elyria before the ritual commenced. Even if it meant just a few fleeting moments together, she had to make the attempt. There were still so many things she wanted to say.

With the High Priestess nearing the Divine Shallows, time was running out.

Standing on her tiptoes, Elowyn stretched toward her older sister, her voice rising above the chatter of the crowd as she called out, "Elyria!" and waved her hand frantically. Determined to reach her, Elowyn pushed forward, finally emerging at the front of the crowd, only a few feet behind her sister.

"Elyria," Elowyn uttered once more, her voice filled with urgency. Though she saw a flicker of recognition in her sister's aura at the sound, it vanished beneath her shield of composure. Elowyn knew then that Elyria had heard her, but her sister remained unwaveringly turned away.

Now it was too late.

The High Priestess had reached the celestial shallows, raising the hem of her robe as she prepared to step into the waters. With each stride, the silken fabric billowed behind her until she stood at the center of the Divine Shallows, atop the large tile sphere bearing the image of a crescent moon.

Anger surged within Elowyn as she stared at her sister's back. *Why won't you speak to me? This is our last chance to speak to each other for the next seven years, and you can't even acknowledge me?* Elowyn hurled her thoughts toward her sister through her magic, hoping they would breach Elyria's defenses. Yet, she knew deep down that her words would never reach their mark, as Elyria's mind remained sealed behind an impenetrable barrier.

In the presence of the High Priestess, the Heart of the Temple fell into a hushed stillness. With upturned palms, she addressed the gathered crowd, her voice carrying with authority, "Welcome to the Heart of the Temple. Tonight, we are gathered here to witness the Crossing of Kin. On this auspicious day, the Goddess will reveal which one of her children shall tread the Bridge Between Worlds first and embark upon her divine Trial."

An intense excitement charged the atmosphere within the Temple, anticipation buzzing among the fey. In fact, the Seventh Day stood as one of Neramyr's most momentous occasions, with each iteration being retold over generations of fey. To witness the emergence of the greatest warlocks and sorceresses within the feylands held great significance. These divine fey would assume roles as guardians and protectors of Neramyr, upholding the order of the New Age. Even long after their passing, those bearing the final Mark would be celebrated through lore and legend.

Once more, the voice of the High Priestess echoed through the chamber. "Rulers of Neramyr, approach your House sigil."

At her directive, the fourteen monarchs of the seven realms advanced toward the Divine Shallows, halting before their respective symbols. With a tilt of her head, the High Priestess closed her eyes, her irises now veiled with a translucent sheen upon reopening. An ethereal magic suffused the Temple as the sacred markings along her arms began to glow faintly, depicting the eight phases of the moon. The tranquil waters at her feet responded to her divine power, transforming into rhythmic ripples.

Then came the declaration from the High Priestess, "Let us begin."

In unison, the fourteen rulers of the seven realms stepped closer to the edges of the Divine Shallows, their upturned palms mirroring each other's as they encircled the celestial waters. Together, they invoked their divine magic, drawing upon the ancient power bestowed by their Goddess. The moon-inked markings on their bodies began to glow, each pattern unique, from dragon scales to whorls of waves and thunder. As the magical moonlight flowed through their varied markings, a mystical veil enveloped their fourteen silhouettes.

In tandem, the monarchs of Neramyr and the High Priestess directed their divine energy into the waters. Elowyn understood the significance of this moment—such potency of divine magic at once occurred only twice every seven years. Once, on the First Day, to open the gates to Caena's realm for the returning children of the moon, and now, on the Seventh Day, to usher in the next cohort of divine candidates through the Bridge Between Worlds. The amount of divine energy pulsating within the Temple was extraordinary, yet it paled in comparison to the boundless power of the Moon Goddess possessed.

The High Priestess intoned ancient incantations in the old tongue, the hallowed waters responding to her summons with stirring ripples, as if awakening from a seven-year slumber. Reunited, the sacred shallows embraced the mother tongue of the first fey, a spoken word that became adrift through time—only remembered now through fleeting phrases and short-lived songs. The potent magic woven in the Temple filled the air with a thick, heady presence.

With a thunderous pitch, the High Priestess proclaimed, "The Moon Goddess has answered our plea and has opened the gates to her realm. Now, the seven chosen children of the moon must step forward into the Divine Shallows and face divine judgment before our Goddess!"

In a single, synchronized movement, Elyria and the six other candidates entered the Divine Shallows, each claiming their position upon their House's sigil with deliberate steps.

The Divine Shallows

The stone-art sigils glowed in response to their presence, except for one glaring exception.

Elowyn continued to wish for her sister to turn around, but Elyria's gaze remained fixed upon the stone-tile firedrake beneath her feet. Elowyn understood the reason all too well. As the moon-inked markings on the palms of the other candidates began to radiate with brilliance in harmony with the hallowed waters, Elyria's hands remained bare, her sigil devoid of moonlight.

"Candidates, the Moon Goddess has chosen you to undergo her Trial and face her judgment, and now the moment has arrived for the *primis* to be revealed!" declared the High Priestess, addressing the gathered crowd. "May the blessings of a thousand moons guide them as they traverse the Bridge Between Worlds!"

The Temple walls shuddered with applause, and eager glances emerged from the candidates and the fey alike as their hungry eyes searched the waters for a gateway to Caena's realm to appear—an answer to whom the waters would claim as this season's *primis*. While the gazes of six divine candidates flitted back and forth, brimming with ambition and desire, one figure stood unmoved amidst the fervor.

This figure was Elyria.

Elyria remained impassive, her appearance almost meditative. It struck Elowyn as strange to see the desperation emanating from the other six candidates, filling the Temple with intensity, while her sister remained indifferent. With a heavy breath, Elyria reached for the necklace adorning her throat, clasping the teardrop stone within her palms, gripping it tightly as if it would sprout wings and take flight.

In that instant, Elowyn startled, Elyria's voice flooding within her mind. It sounded pained, brimming with sincerity.

"I've run out of time in this realm, Elowyn. And for that, I deeply regret. Please, heed these words carefully. One day, the truth of Neramyr will unfurl and you will face the crossroads of fates. When that time comes, I only hope that you possess the strength needed to traverse the paths

presented before you. What you will face will feel impossible to overcome, so promise me this... Promise me that you will remember, Elowyn. Remember it for how it was, for how it is, and for how it will be. Remember everything."

Finally, Elyria looked back, turning only to face Elowyn. Tears shimmered in Elyria's eyes, revealed to the entire Temple, but only meant for Elowyn to see.

"I remember, Elowyn. I remember everything. But now, I've run out of time."

Breaking their locked gaze with a series of furious blinks, Elyria redirected her attention to the Divine Shallows. The waters stirred at her feet, and she drew a measured breath, her grip tightening on the opal stone that sat on her neck, clutching onto it as if it were a lifeline.

Without looking back, Elyria spoke to Elowyn's mind one final time.

"I hope to see you again, Elowyn. If the moons are merciful, I will. However, the moon's spurn has never spared me in this lifetime. So, if this is goodbye, I love you—I love you more than life itself."

With those parting words lingering in the air, Elyria faced the Divine Shallows once more. The waters before her grew fierce as a shimmering halo appeared at her feet. Her figure illuminated in an ethereal light as she stepped forward into the celestial waters. In an instant, she vanished from the Temple, leaving no trace behind.

Elowyn stumbled forward, her hand reaching out instinctively towards the spot where Elyria had stood, as if she could hold onto her for a moment longer. *"Wait, Elyria! What do you mean? What does any of that mean?"* A forceful ache tore through Elowyn's heart as her sister's presence faded away, each glimmer of her aura dimming until it faded entirely.

Overwhelmed, Elowyn battled against the tears threatening to stream down her cheeks.

With her next exhale, Elowyn came to terms with the reality that her sister was no longer in this realm.

29

Crossroads of Fate

Elowyn's eyes were wild with fright, her heart pounding with the thunder of drums as she struggled to make sense of her sister's cryptic message. *What did you mean, Elyria?* Confusion etched itself across Elowyn's features as she replayed Elyria's words in her mind. In mere moments, her world was shaken by words she couldn't decipher. *"One day I'll discover the truth about Neramyr? I'll face the crossroads of fates?" What does any of that mean?*

Amidst the stunned silence of the Temple, Elowyn faintly heard the High Priestess' proclamation. "It is my honor to reveal your *primis* for this season's Trial of Caena! Let us praise Princess Elyria Fangwright of House Fangwright!"

Incredulity and dismay painted the faces of the other candidates, their hopes dashed in an instant. Whispers and murmurs swirled around the courtiers, but Elowyn was oblivious to them. She didn't notice Sylas crossing into Caena's realm second, nor Kerrick as the third candidate.

The disappearance of the remaining candidates from Neramyr's realm went unnoticed by her.

All Elowyn felt was the leaden weight of the silver chain dangling around her neck.

The opal necklace around Elowyn's neck was mourning, its melancholy deeper than it had ever experienced in all the years she possessed it. The iridescent opal grieved at the sudden separation of its counterpart; the magical bond between the two stones severed by the unknown of another deity's realm. The opal ached fiercely, for it had always been two halves of a whole—inseparable, kind of like sisters.

As each candidate crossed the Bridge Between Worlds, the gateway to Caena's realm closed.

With the gateway sealed, the High Priestess turned to address the assembled fey, her arms raised with palms upturned. A powerful hum of magic radiated from the High Priestess as the crescent moons nestled in her hands began to emit a soft glow. The rays of moonlight streamed upwards, creeping along her arms like vines as they illuminated the eight phases of the moon etched upon her skin. The threads continued to coil up her arms and trailed around her throat, encircling it, rising until it ceased right before her lips.

The High Priestess began, "As the Seventh Day draws to a close, the Moon Goddess has made her selection. It is now time for me to announce her chosen seven candidates worthy of participating in the next season's divine Trial."

Slowly, she parted her lips, and streams of moonlight poured forth, flowing down her body in rivulets. The currents continued their descent until they mingled with the waters of the Divine Shallows, forming luminous clouds around her feet.

Elowyn felt a compelling force tug her attention back to the High Priestess, guiding her gaze towards the center of the Divine Shallows where she awaited what was to come. Her eyes noted the open mouth of the High Priestess, but beyond that, she also sensed the presence of an otherworldly being, its voice resonating powerfully within her mind. As it always had been, the primordial voice was neither male nor female, unable to be placed.

In unison, the voices of the High Priestess and the primordial being filled Elowyn's mind, speaking in the ancient tongue of the fey.

"Since the dawn of the New Age, every seventh year, seven candidates have been chosen to face Caena's judgment in her divine Trial. The Moon Goddess has made her choice, designating one candidate from each kingdom. It is time to reveal her selection."

The eager anticipation that had filled the Temple moments ago dissipated, replaced by a candid realization. Elowyn understood, as did everyone in the congregation of the Temple. There were no kings clenching their fists, no queens holding their breath, no hopeful aspirants yearning for greatness.

This Seventh Day held no speculation about who would be chosen by the Goddess.

Once again, the rich voice enveloped the minds of the assembly, its gentle caress embracing their auras.

"Let us now begin the unveiling of the seven candidates who will partake in the forthcoming Trial of Caena."

Elowyn bowed her head, focusing on the rhythmic ebb and flow of the currents before her. She remained fixed on the ground, undistracted even as she sensed movement across the room. The faint shimmer of moonlight amidst the Temple's shadows was unmistakable—another fey's palms were alight with a sacred glow.

Silently, Elowyn tallied the candidates from each of the seven realms. She held an unshakeable certainty as to which names would be announced, she was as certain as how the moon rises with each night and falls with each dawn.

The hallowed voices in Elowyn's mind declared, "Princess Syrilla Skyborn of House Skyborn, step forth into the Divine Shallows and claim your candidacy."

One. Promise me that you will remember, Elowyn.

Whispers of the 'sacred seven' rippled through the room. Yet, Elowyn remained steadfast, her gaze fixed downward.

"Prince Draeden Darkmaw of House Darkmaw, step forth into the Divine Shallows and claim your candidacy."

Two. Remember it for how it was.

"Princess Nynerra Driftmoor of House Driftmoor, step forth into the Divine Shallows and claim your candidacy."

Three. Remember it for how it is.

"Prince Caswin Mirthwood of House Mirthwood, step forth into the Divine Shallows and claim your candidacy."

Four. Remember it for how it will be.

"Prince Llyr Blackbane of House Blackbane, step forth into the Divine Shallows and claim your candidacy."

Five. Remember everything.

"Prince Theoden Bloodweaver of House Bloodweaver, step forth into the Divine Shallows and claim your candidacy."

Six. Because I do, I remember.

At this moment, Elowyn lifted her gaze as the primordial voice unveiled the last chosen candidate.

"Princess Elowyn Fangwright of House Fangwright, step forth into the Divine Shallows and claim your candidacy."

Seven. And I've run out of time.

Elowyn sensed a primordial tug in her chest, an inexplicable sensation that flooded her being with wonder, akin to the moment her soul intertwined with the Eternal Tethering bond. Just like her counterparts, the ivory inked crescent moons on Elowyn's palms began to radiate with the gentle light of the moon. Yielding to the divine summons of the Goddess, she moved instinctively, her feet carrying her forward as if guided by forces beyond her grasp.

Her glowing palms seemed detached from her own will as they gathered the fabric of her ruby red skirts, moving her towards the edge of the hallowed waters. With a hesitant breath, she stepped into the inviting waters, feeling an ethereal warmth she knew only the Goddess could devise. As she waded towards the stone-tile firedrake, memories of Elyria's sudden disappearance flooded her mind, leaving behind a void she couldn't fill.

Mustering her courage, she agreed to the sacred stone's blind bargain, as one reluctant foot settled upon the tile firedrake. A surge of divine magic engulfed her as it coursed through her body, seeping into her flesh and bone. With determination, she placed her other foot within the stone ring, standing firmly at the heart of House Fangwright's sigil, her presence acknowledged by the brilliant glow beneath her.

The primordial voice resonated in her mind for one last time, marking the end of the Ceremony of Caena. Yet, unlike before, there were no jubilant cheers or applause echoing through the Temple.

Instead, the fey of Neramyr wore masks of reverence and veneration as they beheld the princes and princesses chosen to embark on the upcoming divine Trial.

Amidst the adulation, a noble fey of high lineage stepped forward. Blessed with only the first Mark, he bowed in deference to the 'sacred seven'. This action ignited a flame, spreading like wildfire that swept through the gathered crowd. Throughout the Temple, heads inclined, knees bent, and bodies lowered in respect for the candidates chosen by their Moon Goddess.

Elowyn caught sight of Lox amidst the crowd and his face was one born of storms. His aura, painted with somber shades of gray and blue, revealed the inner conflict he harbored, yet he too bowed in deference to his brother—his future king.

It seemed she was not alone in suffering over a sibling this night.

Elyria's haunting words ricocheted in Elowyn's mind, each repetition deepening the sense of foreboding that gripped her soul. The finality and heartache in her sister's voice reverberated within her, unsettling her to the core.

In that moment, a fearfulness seized Elowyn, a nagging sense that her sister's words were referring to something far beyond the Trial of Caena.

~

That night, sleep eluded Elowyn. Instead, she found herself drawn to the familiar cherry-stained door of Elyria's chamber, seeking the comfort of the wood-carved mountains and winding rivers. As her hand reached for the gold-worn latch, the once-enchanted door now felt ordinary—the magic it once held had faded.

With a gentle push, the door yielded, swinging open easily. Stepping into the room, Elowyn was surprised to find that the barrier her sister had once summoned was no longer intact, but instead replaced with another, one that allowed her entry. Elowyn remained cautious about the newfound enchantment; however, she had no doubt that it was the spell work of Elyria's.

The antechamber lay cloaked in shadows and darkness, yet Elowyn paid no mind as Elyria's familiar aroma of lilac and honey enveloped her. Drawing in a deep breath, she let the scent linger for a moment before navigating towards the bedchamber in the darkness. With meticulous care, she avoided disturbing anything as she entered the room. The familiar sight of the four-poster bed greeted her, its organza drapes fluttering gently in the breeze from the nearby arched window. Sliding off her slippers, Elowyn sank into the plush white mattress, pulling the linen covers snugly around her chin.

In the sanctuary of Elyria's bed, Elowyn managed to finally escape into slumber at last.

As Elowyn drifted into her dreams, a vision unfurled, shrouding her mind in an arcane mist that thickened with each passing moment.

Within this haze, she became a mere spectator as a scene materialized before her, drawn into its mysterious depths.

∼

In the dead of night, the Temple of Caena lay shrouded in an unsettling stillness, its hallowed halls devoid of occupants save for two solitary souls. One of these souls belonged to a fey, with eyes of silver and hair pure as newly fallen snow. Though still appearing in the bloom of youth, she bore the weight of countless lifetimes upon her slender shoulders.

The fey was searching for something—an entity that could not be gained through copper or coin, but with blood and oath.

Before the Divine Shallows, the fey sank to her knees, draping herself along the smooth edges of stone that contained the sacred waters and waited. Time stretched on, seasons flowing like currents in a river. With each passing year, hope blossomed anew in spring, desire simmered in the heat of summer, and longing mingled with the cool winds of autumn, only to be tempered by the harsh chill of winter.

Yet still, after countless years, the fey waited in silence, her everlasting patience a fascinating riddle, intriguing an ancient soul that dwelled within the temple's depths.

Finally, an ominous voice arose from the Divine Shallows. "What is it that you seek, fey?"

"You." The fey shifted her gaze, boring into the celestial waters, reciting a timeworn verse:

> *In shallows deep, where silence weeps,*
> *Desires stir, as patience sleeps.*
> *A dark power prowls, its presence dire,*
> *Blood and oath it demands, to feed divine fire.*

A low, sinister laugh echoed in answer.

"You've lingered at my realm's edge for eons," the darkness murmured. "Are you prepared to bargain with me? I will claim something of yours: past, present, and what is yet to be."

"A small price for all that's gained," the fey replied.

"Is that so?" The words echoed around the fey indistinctly. "I have lived countless lifetimes and dwelled through realms where time bleeds through ages like ink takes to paper. Your lips speak falsehoods as easily as steel cuts flesh, but your aura betrays truth."

"What you crave lies within me," the fey countered. "So, claim it."

The ancient soul merely grinned.

Abruptly, ethereal talons ensnared the fey within a malevolent grasp, sinking into flesh and drawing forth crimson droplets of blood. The fey was dragged into the divine currents, as whispered words from nameless realms of unclaimed worlds were spoken—awakening an ancient spell, the fey forever bound by an eternal oath.

∼

Elowyn was torn from the vision, gasping, and jolting upright in bed.

A searing pain coursed through the opal pendant on her neck, shattering something deep within her aura. Elowyn gasped, clawing desperately at her throat, tearing the chain away in terror. Dread gripped her as she beheld the opal stone now cradled in her trembling palms—it was lifeless, once full of warmth had now turned cold as ice.

In a panic, Elowyn flung aside her covers and dashed out of bed, tossing the necklace onto the mattress as she recoiled from it. Back pressed against the wall, she steadied herself, eyes squeezed shut as she struggled to make sense of the ordeal, drawing deep breaths to calm her pacing heart.

She knew all too well the weight dreams carried in Neramyr—they always held dire implications.

As Elowyn's mind raced, she sensed a pulse emanating from beyond the bedchamber. Nervously, she turned towards it, her feet hesitant as she approached the entryway. Peering cautiously around the corner, she found the living chambers deserted. Stepping out of the bedchamber, she entered the book-lined living space, scanning every corner for any sign of intrusion, yet everything appeared undisturbed.

Moments later, Elowyn pivoted to leave, but halted suddenly as a peculiar sensation seized her attention. A faint aura emanated from a nearby bookshelf, its essence foreign, nearly otherworldly. Overcoming her dread, Elowyn cautiously approached the source, her gaze narrowing as she delved into the stacks. Behind a cluster of books, the faint energy pulsed, prompting Elowyn to investigate further by shifting the volumes aside.

Nestled within the concealed alcove behind the stack of books, Elowyn, puzzled, discovered a small wooden chest. Carefully, she retrieved the chest and examined it closely, only to find its latch firmly locked. Despite her efforts to open it, the latch remained stubbornly shut, suggesting the chest had been warded against unwanted access.

With a nervous exhale, Elowyn summoned her native magic, feeling it swell to her fingertips as a shimmer coated them. Hovering her hand above the closed lid, she sought out the magical links that bound the chest. Detecting multiple wards, she hesitated, but found one she felt narrowly confident she could break. She began channeling, though abjuration had never been her strong suit. To her surprise, as soon as she attempted to break the ward, it dispelled, along with all the other wards protecting the chest.

Elowyn's face revealed both shock and confusion as the lid of the chest swung open effortlessly. Inside, she found neatly arranged scrolls, some empty potion bottles, and several unfamiliar objects. Despite not recognizing any of the items, she examined them carefully. She unrolled one of the scrolls, finding it blank, while another contained a list of common books. It appeared that all the scrolls were either devoid of content or filled with inconsequential writing.

Elowyn's curiosity piqued further as she shifted her focus to the bottles nestled within the chest. They, too, appeared devoid of contents, their glass surfaces reflecting the dim light of the room. Tentatively, she reached for one of the bottles, feeling the cool smoothness of the glass beneath her fingertips. With caution, she uncorked it and lifted it to her nose, expecting the faint aroma of a potion or elixir. However, to her surprise, there was nothing—no scent wafted from within.

Perplexed, she furrowed her brow, her mind grappling with the puzzle before her. Had these vessels ever held any substance, or were they merely ornamental? The absence of scent suggested the latter, yet the presence of the chest in her chambers and the lingering magical energy hinted at a deeper mystery.

Finally, Elowyn turned her attention to the assortment of objects scattered within the chest. She first examined a metallic item that vaguely resembled a key, although its irregular shape and jagged edges made it seem more like a crude rod. Its weight felt ordinary, similar to holding a piece of plain silver or iron. She then picked up a thin, curved disc with a dark, coal-like hue and a surface riddled with pits. Despite her attempts to discern its purpose, the nature of the object eluded her. With a bewildered shake of her head, she returned the disc to the chest and reached for the final item.

The final item resembled a brooch. Elowyn turned it over in her hand, scrutinizing its intricate details. Crafted from gold and no larger than a copper coin, it featured a colorless stone at its center, gleaming even in the dim light. Tilting the brooch, she squinted at the circle of text engraved on its surface, finding it filled with more symbols and unfamiliar characters than recognizable words. Perplexed, Elowyn returned the brooch to the chest with a frustrated sigh, closing the lid. Far from clarity, she found herself even more mystified than before.

After carefully returning the small wooden chest to its hiding place, Elowyn stepped back, pondering why it had been concealed at all. Its contents seemed entirely ordinary and unimportant. Perhaps they held sentimental value to her older sister, Elowyn speculated. After all, she herself possessed cherished items, like the charmed bell Draeden had gifted her.

With her baffled thoughts somewhat assuaged, Elowyn retreated to the bedchamber. She knew sleep would escape her tonight. Her gaze fell upon the opal necklace still nestled in the folds of the plush linens where she had cast it.

With a resigned sigh, she approached and picked it up. As the opal stone lay in her hand, Elowyn's heart sank.

More than anything, she hoped what had happened was merely an illusion or a trick played by her mind, but it seemed too real. The necklace cradled in her palm felt utterly lifeless, devoid of the magical energy it once possessed. Determined not to succumb to haunting thoughts, Elowyn chose to overlook the opal stone's absence of warmth. "There's no need to worry," she whispered to herself, seeking reassurance. "Elyria is fine."

Elowyn straightened her posture, standing taller as she firmly held the opal necklace and moved to her sister's study table. With a flick of her fingers, she summoned a flame to light the wick. The candle's gentle glow pierced the darkness of the chamber, casting dancing shadows across the room. Elowyn glanced at the necklace briefly before attempting to fasten it around her neck. However, her fingers fumbled, and the opal necklace slipped from her grasp, tumbling to the floor.

Elowyn grumbled in frustration as she pushed the chair back and hunched to the floor to retrieve the necklace. She gathered the opal stone in her palm, ready to rise, but an odd shadow beneath the desk grasped her attention. Intrigued, Elowyn knelt down and crawled beneath the table, candle in hand. A shiver ran down her spine as she sensed a familiar energy, her fingers tracing the underside until they found a concealed knob. With a determined effort, she manipulated the latch until it clicked softly. A hidden compartment revealed itself, unveiling a small iron chest pulsating with the same magic as the one before.

The chest was forged from metal and its size was no bigger than Elowyn's splayed hand. Surprisingly light, she lifted it onto the study table's surface. Despite its outdated appearance, the chest remained well-preserved, its sides covered with intricate symbols depicting stars and lunar phases. However, when she attempted to open it, the lid resisted her efforts. With a frustrated sigh, Elowyn called upon her magic once more to dispel the ward.

Just as before, the ward encasing the metal chest dissolved effortlessly. Elowyn sensed that the situation was becoming increasingly cryptic. Nevertheless, she proceeded to open the lid and reveal its contents. Within lay a bundle of parchment, which she carefully extracted and inspected. Among them were sheets that seemed aged and weathered, while others appeared freshly added. Elowyn's disappointment grew as she realized that these parchments were similar to the scrolls discovered in the previous chest.

As Elowyn unfolded each page, they were just as unremarkable as the those from earlier. The parchments contained lists of ingredients for basic potions, excerpts on moonfire, botanical descriptions of various flora, and even some with aimless doodles and scribbles. It puzzled Elowyn as to why her sister would go to such lengths to conceal such ordinary items.

In truth, Elyria wouldn't resort to such elaborate measures to conceal something insignificant.

Considering this, Elowyn remembered how Elyria's heavily warded door had opened effortlessly for her, and how the hidden chests within her chambers seemed to beckon with their pulsing energy—as if eager to be discovered. She pondered over the spells and wards that safeguarded the chests; they were spells that would challenge even seasoned warlocks or sorceresses. It became clear to Elowyn that Elyria must have orchestrated it all, manipulating the wards to respond to her magic. Yet, the reason behind Elyria's intentions remained a mystery to her.

Elowyn examined the stack of parchment with heightened inspection. After turning the parchment over in various angles and entertaining the thought of her own sanity, Elowyn eventually discerned something—a unique concealment spell, barely perceptible to the untrained eye, yet undoubtedly created by Elyria herself. It was a spell that Elyria had created and compelled Elowyn to learn until she had mastered it.

Elowyn's heart drummed within her chest, a symphony of apprehension and curiosity, as she cradled the bundle of parchment. Trusting her instincts regarding Elyria's intentions, she summoned a flicker of her magic and channeled it into one of the pages she extracted from the stack. With bated breath, she watched as the text detailing *Scael's Secrets to Scrying* began to stir and shift upon the parchment. Letters and symbols danced and rearranged themselves, weaving a new narrative.

Bewildered, Elowyn read the true contents of the parchment. When she lifted her gaze from the paper, her eyes fixed vacantly on the wall ahead. The emotions swirling within her remained indecipherable. With a trembling hand, she set down the enchanted note and reached for another. As she released it, the script once again reshuffled, concealing its true message behind the guise of *Scael's Secrets to Scrying*. Methodically, Elowyn repeated the process, each time discovering a hidden truth only to watch it dissolve back into deception.

As the night dwindled and the first light of dawn crept in, Elowyn continued unraveling the secrets concealed within each note. At one point in her pursuit, she retrieved the chest hidden behind the books and delved into its contents. What were once ordinary lists of book titles now displayed unfamiliar titles—some written in a language entirely foreign to her. The idle doodles had metamorphosed into detailed maps depicting uncharted regions of Neramyr. Each revelation added another layer to the unknown.

The weight of her discoveries left Elowyn dizzy and nauseous, her head swimming in a sea of uncertainty. She sat motionless at the study desk, surrounded by the aftermath of her frantic search: parchment strewn haphazardly, scrolls scattered in disarray, and a spent candle leaving behind only a puddle of wax.

In Elowyn's hand, she held one parchment in particular—the scent of it lingering with lilac and honey. She had read over it again until her eyes grew weary, clutched it coarsely enough that the paper grew worn and tattered.

Now, bathed in the soft morning light, Elowyn read the letter once more to herself.

> Elowyn,
>
> There are wicked truths to feykind that have been buried and hidden from us. Truths that have been encased in silent tombs of an evil that you cannot fathom. This evil is not embodied in vicious claws and vile fangs; it hides behind benevolent smiles and lurks beneath the guise of good nature.
>
> I tried to shield you from these truths, to keep you safe. I thought I could uncover the secrets of those who possess such nefarious ploys, of those who wrongfully hold such power. I wanted to spare you from this fate, but I was a fool to believe I could. Now I know in the marrow of my bones that it can only be you.
>
> All the knowledge I have discovered is hidden within

these parchments. I was too reckless, and I ran out of time. I can only hope that what I have learned will lend you more. Promise me that you'll remember, Elowyn. Remember it for how it was, for how it is, and for how it will be.

Remember everything, for your life depends on it.

All my love,
Elyria

THANK YOU

As this part of our journey together into the realms of Neramyr draws to a close, I would be forever grateful if you could take a moment to share your thoughts with others by leaving a review. Your feedback and opinion not only allows me to learn and to grow as an independent author, but also helps other readers discover this book.

Thank you, always.

All my love,
Alexandra M. Tran

GLOSSARY
NAMES AND TERMS

Bloodlines

DRIFTMOOR Bloodline of Diantha Driftmoor
FANGWRIGHT Bloodline of Elmyr Fangwright
BLACKBANE Bloodline of Edhelm Blackbane
BLOODWEAVER Bloodline of Isadora Bloodweaver
MIRTHWOOD Bloodline of Oswin Mirthwood
DARKMAW Bloodline of Theda Darkmaw
SKYBORN Bloodline of Aedda Skyborn

Seven Realms of Neramyr

ELUNE ISLES Kingdom of House Driftmoor
ERIDEN Kingdom of House Fangwright
ERIMEAD Kingdom of House Blackbane
IRON HOLLOWS Kingdom of House Bloodweaver
LOCHWALD Kingdom of House Mirthwood

Glossary

ORWYN Kingdom of House Darkmaw
PRYMONT Kingdom of House Skyborn

Ceremony of Caena

FIRST DAY The Banquet of the Blessed
SECOND DAY The Favor of the Seven
THIRD DAY The Lore of *Lunaris*
FOURTH DAY The Keeper's Aegis
FIFTH DAY The Offering
SIXTH DAY The *Vitus*
SEVENTH DAY The Crossing of Kin

Magic Classifications

ABJURATION a class of magic typically associated with protection, defense, and warding off harmful influences
ALTERATION a class of magic that involves changing or modifying the properties of objects, creatures, or the environment
ARTIFICE a class of magic that revolves around the creation, manipulation, and enchantment of objects, devices, and constructs
ELEMENTAL a class of magic that harnesses and manipulates the power of classical elements: earth, air, fire, and water, as well as other elements
EVOCATION a class of magic that focuses on the direct manipulation and control of energy to produce specific effects. It involves the conjuring and shaping of forces to create various phenomena
PSIONIC a class of magic that deals with the manipulation of mental energy, psychic abilities, and the power of the mind. It draws upon the innate mental abilities of individuals to produce effects
RESTORATION a class of magic centered around the mending of

Glossary

wounds, ailments, and afflictions. It encompasses a variety of spells, rituals, and techniques aimed at restoring health and vitality. In addition, restoration magic can be used to influence or manipulate the body

Terminology

AEGIS a talisman imbued with divine magic that serves as a tether to Neramyr during the Trial
ANIMUS a soul-bonded creature procured in the divine Trial
AURA an indicator of a fey's magical prowess or dominance
AUREUM a golden cloak, customary attire for royalty
BASILISK a mythical serpent
DIVINE MAGIC magic that is gifted to a fey upon completion of the divine Trial
DIVINE SHALLOWS a cistern of sacred water from which the Moon Goddess emerged to liberate the first fey
ETERNAL TETHERING a soul-bond that allows a fey to offer their life in exchange for another through the divine tether
FEY otherworldly beings closely associated with nature, magic, and mystical realms
FEYLING young fey
FIREDRAKE fire dragon
FOLK population of fey
GRIMWOLF a creature combining traits of a wolf with otherworldly characteristics such as enhanced strength, speed, and agility
GRYPHON a creature with the body of a lion and the head and wings of an eagle
LEGACY a fey possessing one of the seven magical abilities, or feats, that is passed down from the founding rulers of Neramyr. This magical gift cannot be learned or gained otherwise
LOCH HYDRA a dual-headed sea serpent

Glossary

NAMEDAY birthday

NATIVE MAGIC magic a fey is born with

OPHIS winged serpent

PHOENIX an otherworldly bird with brilliant plumage, usually in shades of red, orange, and gold

PRIMIS a divine candidate who is selected by the Moon Goddess as the most worthy of their cohort

SCRYING a practice of magic that involves staring into a reflective surface, such as a mirror, stone, or water, to see images and visions

SERITHIUM an ochre colored coral noteworthy for its paralytic properties

SORCERESS a female fey capable of wielding magic

TELA ancient relics made of sheer, ivory silk about six feet in length and about twelve inches in width

VINUM fey wine

VITUS a divine ritual where candidates display a performance of magic, power, and skill

WARLOCK a male fey capable of wielding magic

ACKNOWLEDGMENTS

Of all the people that I owe my thanks to, I will first start with my husband, Austin. Thank you for being my own sun, an endless source of warmth that brightens my whole world. Without you, this book would not be standing here so tall. Your love, support, and faith in me inspired me to create the realms of Neramyr. You've supported me in every endeavor, cheering me on even when I couldn't do the same for myself. You are the love of my life, my soulmate, and my best friend.

Next, I would like to give thanks to the readers and supporters of my early drafts. To Emily Tran, my sister and my other half, the world is a brighter, funnier, and happier place because of you—I love you to the moon and to Saturn. To Claire Lavender, my cousin and the first person I drafted a book with—Tonight I'm going to dance for all that we've been through. To Sophie Kero, our friendship and shared love for fantasy is something I will cherish as long as I live—I've had the time of my life fighting dragons with you. To Tuyet Pham, my aunt—Thank you for showing me that you can do anything you dream, like writing a book. To Cassie Nguyen, thank you for being who you are, I am forever changed because you came into my life—I'd float forever in a hot air balloon with you. To Allie Larson, our friendship bloomed at a time when I needed it most and I will forever be grateful to you—may we always share our love for the same books and clothes. To Macy Green, my first true beta reader—thank you for taking a chance on this novel. Thank you to my mom and dad, I hope I make you proud.

Lastly, thank you to my readers. Thank you for being a part of my debut novel, *The Divine Shallows*. Your support means everything to me. I began this manuscript during a time where I felt lost, and by the end of it, I was able to find myself. I am a nurse who dreamt of becoming an author, and now years of hard work are coming to fruition. As I watch the progress of my dream unfold, I couldn't be more happy to have finally found this passion. With my stories, I hope to keep the magic of reading flourishing and the wonder of books blooming.

ABOUT THE AUTHOR

Alexandra M. Tran is an emerging Vietnamese-American author of epic fantasy romance. Her debut novel, The Divine Shallows, is the first installment in a series of seven spellbinding novels yet to unfold. In addition to writing, Alexandra is a registered nurse from Nebraska. She enjoys spending time with her husband and two cuddly cats. You can find her daydreaming about what to write next or catch her captivated by a fantasy book beside a sunlit window.